Plumb Twisted

A Fortuna, Texas Novel
Book 2

Rochelle Bradley

Visit my website at: RochelleBradley.com

Library of Congress Catalog Number: 2018958059

ISBN-13 978-947561-02-1

DEDICATION

To those been manipulated, stalked, and battered under the guise of love. You are worthy of love, and your happily ever after is out there. Never give up.

ACKNOWLEDGMENTS

For my writing buddy Chris... Thanks for Cody inspiring Loren Order. Someday Cody will get his own series. Keep writing!

Carol and Linda: your friendship is inspirational. Thank you for suggesting the wedding toast and inadvertently providing one of Fortuna's crazy names.

To my beta readers Lynn, Sally and Dawn: thank you for investing your time and giving me your insight. Your attention to detail helped polish Plumb Twisted into a jewel. You are awesome.

Dawn your constant words of encouragement and love have helped me persevere through a tough time.
Thanks for being my friend.

.

CHAPTER 1

Cole

A BLUR DASHED ACROSS THE road; Cole Dart jerked the wheel and slammed the brakes. The pickup fishtailed, careened to the left, and then lurched to a halt in knee-high prairie grass. His heart in his throat, he pried his fingers off the wheel and blew out a long breath. "That could have been a whole hell of a lot worse," he grumbled, squeezing his eyes shut.

He'd been distracted. What the hell had he been thinking? A low chuckle escaped his lips as he scrubbed his face. Cancer hadn't killed him and he'd be damned if a deer would.

Cole glanced in the rearview mirror. *No muffler in the road. The baling wire must have held.*

A clear morning dawned as the truck bumped over the primitive road toward the Big Deal's homestead cabin. Today, he would get paid to taxi a new employee around town. It was something that wouldn't make him smell like sweat, dirt and cattle.

At the cabin the previous morning, Cole had approached the owner of the Big Deal longhorn ranch, Brad Davidson. Brad and the foreman, Curly Moe, had welcomed a willowy blonde to Texas. Cole had removed his hat and waited for the conversation to end.

Driving a woman around town had sounded easy enough, but why was he so nervous?

Because Piper McCracken was cute. That, and the way she'd gasped when he'd asked "Do you like romance?" Boy, had that come across wrong.

1

No wonder she'd turned bright red. Her wide eyes had scanned him from hat to boots, making it hard to breathe.

Thank God Curly stepped in, saying, "Cole means books. What kind of novels do you read?"

She'd frowned and tilted her head to stare at him again, but the pretty blush remained. "I don't do romance. I like action-adventure, thrillers, and mysteries. My favorite is *Leviathan,* book one of the Loren Order series."

Curly laughed, elbowing Brad. "She doesn't do romance."

"We'll see how long that lasts," Brad muttered.

Cole shifted as Brad explained the small cabin's history and other useful information, like the landline and indoor plumbing. Since Cole had stood there looking useless, Curly had volunteered him to chauffeur Piper to Fortuna to buy a car.

White knuckled, Cole clutched the steering wheel while searching for other kamikaze deer. The gravel crunched under the tires of his small pickup and his stomach churned.

Happy with his life, he didn't need the complication of a relationship right now. Or ever.

Slowing, he approached the wood framed building. The front door stood open, spilling light out onto the porch floor. Piper sat in a rocker with her feet folded under her.

Cole admired Piper for having the gumption to pack up and leave everything behind. He wasn't brave enough to leave his family or home. Not that he wouldn't mind a change, but his life was like a perfect-fitting pair of boots. He was comfortable.

He arrived earlier than the expected time. Cole had wanted a chance to collect his thoughts, but that wasn't going to happen. Piper held a white mug to her lips, frozen, her eyes wide. A weight settled in his gut. He turned off the truck.

He swallowed, meeting her gaze. The neckline of Piper's yellow sundress dipped down, exposing creamy skin. Heat washed over him, the air suddenly oppressive. The floral print reminded him of wildflowers and he hoped she smelled like sunshine on the prairie.

No.

He willed his mind away from such thoughts. He couldn't have a woman in his life. It wouldn't be fair to her. He would never be the man she'd need. It was best not to start anything.

Her red tipped toes peeked out from under the dress. Cole took a deep breath and pushed open the truck door. He slowly ambled toward Piper, stopping before her. "Morning."

Piper

"Good morning," Piper replied, unable to move. The most-gorgeous-cowboy-ever appeared at her cabin an hour early. Maybe this was Texan for on time.

When she'd met the cowboy, he'd worn a snug-fitting T-shirt over muscled arms, shoulders and chest. He was tall, lean around the hips, and his full lips had worn a crooked half-smirk. As she had gazed at him, she'd been hit by pure animal attraction. And when he'd mentioned romance her panties could have ignited.

Cole had worn jeans, boots and a hat, but today he'd opted for a polo shirt. The pale blue shirt matched his sultry eyes.

She couldn't stare at his face all day, could she?

Piper swallowed. If the man picked her up, carried her to the bed and ravished her completely she'd be powerless to stop him. A sip of the cooling coffee snapped the spell, and she remembered her manners.

"Can I offer you a cup of coffee?" Piper shifted her feet to the dusty wood floor. His gaze followed her toes. "It's just instant and not very good, but it has caffeine."

Cole cleared his throat. "I know a place," he paused, following her into the cabin. "It has the best coffee in town."

"Place?" Several images scrolled through her mind. Barns, dives and pool halls. Maybe the VFW had the best coffee.

"Restaurant," he clarified. He removed his black hat and fingering the brim, held it in front of him. A navy bandanna covered the top of his head, hiding his hair, but his lashes and eyebrows were dark.

She refrained from jumping for joy as she dumped the ashtray tasting liquid down the drain. "Care to show me?" Good thing she'd faced away from him. Had she always been so bold? Not until recently, when she moved to Texas without a second thought.

Her father's death led to her bravery. She missed him every day. He'd have supported her decision to try something new. Her mother had hastily remarried her father's best friend. The newlyweds' bliss further prompted her decision. And then there was her stalker.

"I planned on it, that is, if you want to go?" Cole shuffled his feet.

He can't be aware how cute he is.

"Sure." She scanned the room for her bag, pausing on the sixth book of the Loren Order series open on her bed. The one-room cabin was the equivalent of a studio apartment. Searching consisted of turning her head until she found the purse on the dinette's chair. "What's good there?"

"Besides the coffee, they have the best hotcakes this side of Dallas."

Piper chuckled, not sure about the accolade, but was game to find out.

Cole

When Cole and Piper arrived at the truck stop, Cole flagged down the owner, Norma Stitts. She waved them in. He took Piper's elbow and led her to a booth.

Piper inspected the bookshelf by the door, then gazed around the room, taking it all in. Cole tried not to stare, but it proved hard not to watch her first encounter with a Texas truck stop.

"There are three men reading romance novels," she said in awe. Packed with men, but also a few women and children, Stitts' was hopping.

"I'm surprised it's not more," Cole said, rubbing his chin.

"Really?" Piper's eyes widened.

"See that bookshelf? It's a major exchange center for the book trade."

"Book trade?"

"You'll have to ask Miss Jessie about how it started," Cole explained.

"Mrs. Barnes, my boss?"

"Yes. Sorry, I've called her Miss Jessie for years."

A man entered the restaurant, placed two books on the shelf, then ran his finger down the spines in the line and pulled out another. He paused, reading the back.

"Do you see that man?" Cole asked, and she nodded. "He's a farmer. Owns a couple hundred acres, a modest spread, and he loves romances."

The farmer pocketed the book. He picked out two more before leaving.

"Ah, romance books. This is what you meant yesterday?" Her cheeks pinked.

"Yes." He cleared his throat, which had suddenly gone dry. "It started with a personal challenge to one man, a dare. He didn't back down. He liked the books and dared others. Then it spread like wildfire on dry prairie grass."

They ordered and sipped the rich dark coffee. "This is good." Inhaling deeply, she gripped the ceramic mug as if it held ambrosia.

He leaned back and relaxed. Warmth spread through his body, happy to have pleased her.

"So who dared you?" she asked.

He nearly spit coffee.

"I mean, why do you read them?"

"I like the stories."

"You mean you like the sex." She tilted her head and grinned.

Sure, he liked the steamy scenes, but that wasn't the whole reason he read them. "I like happy endings," he offered with a shrug. She raised a skeptical eyebrow. "Okay, I like the hot scenes, but only because of the love." He swallowed.

"Love?"

The waitress placed food on the table, saving him. They ate in silence except for an occasional comment about the flavor of the food. After Piper pushed an empty plate away, she asked, "Are all cowboys like you?"

Uh oh. "Like, how?"

"You know, crunchy on the outside, gooey on the inside?"

Cole laughed. "Most likely," he answered, as another man took more books.

"I don't like romance stories," she admitted in a quiet voice. Before he could ask, she explained, "The heroines are too soft. I don't like to read about weak women. Plus, those men always have movie star looks, amazing careers and are billionaires. You can't find your soulmate in a romance book."

"But you might find personality traits you like," he offered. She shrugged, not buying it. "I don't see the women as weak—only flawed, with obstacles to overcome."

"I suppose everyone has flaws."

"What's yours?" he asked with a smirk.

"Liking the wrong type of men," she muttered.

His stomach clenched. "That's a cop-out answer." He'd unfairly asked, so he offered his shortcoming. "I'm self-conscious about my looks."

She inspected him critically and sweat broke out across his forehead. "Most people are."

He leaned close and whispered, "It keeps me from talking and interacting with people. I get nervous and won't go places if there's a crowd." It had been years since the operation and it still affected him.

"You're fine, Cole. You're more than fine." Piper shifted in her seat and leaned forward. "Look, you're out talking to me and I'm a stranger and a woman."

He nodded. "Normally, I'd be a basket case of nerves."

"Looks are all personal taste. Someone might think you're ugly or someone might think you're the sexiest man alive. The thing you have to ask yourself is: does their opinion matter to me?" She smiled sweetly over the rim of her mug.

"What's your opinion?" he blurted, needing to know.

"Does it matter to you what I think?"

"Yes. It matters greatly." It was true, but he didn't want to ask himself why. The smile that lit her face made his heart hitch. She set her coffee down.

"Well, Cole, I like the crunchy-gooey combo. It's very appealing." She blushed, long eyelashes hiding her eyes as she looked at the table. "I find you..." she paused, drumming her fingers against the side of her mug.

"Pretty, right?" A short, old woman said as she slid into the booth next to Cole and pinched his cheek. "This one's a hot tamale."

"Hello, Ms. Hardmann." Cole's face felt like the temperature of the sun. He rubbed his cheek. "This is Piper McCracken. Piper this is Desire Hardmann."

"Hello, young lady." Desire took Piper's hand and squeezed. With a wink, she yelled over her shoulder to a man in a white apron, "Hey, Hugh Stitts! Come over here and meet Cole's Russian mail-order bride."

CHAPTER 2

Piper

A LARGE, STEEL BARN WITH an anime caricature of a woman caught Piper's attention. The painting had abnormally round eyes and an exaggerated bust. The ranch logo of two capital Ds back to back were the bikini top cups.

"That's odd, but appropriate on so many levels," Piper muttered to Cole.

He parked near the front of the Barnes' ranch house. Piper didn't automatically get out, but was mesmerized by a strange sight. Cole opened her door and offered a hand. She didn't need help, but the temptation to touch his tanned skin won out.

She pointed to the shrubbery in the front lawn. An orange blur flashed between bushes.

"Oh, that's Tippy," Cole said.

"What's a Tippy?"

He smirked, expounding, "She's a three-legged tabby cat."

"Tippy, the three-legged cat?" Piper laughed. "Good thing they didn't name her Lucky."

They stepped onto a wide covered porch with a swing. Piper contemplated the unusual feline while Cole knocked on the door.

A moment later, Jessie Barnes swung the door open wide. "Welcome to the Double D," she greeted with a toothy grin. "Come on in. Let me give you the tour. It's so good to meet you." The petite woman gave Piper a

7

quick hug. They'd Facetimed several times to discuss the business and local area.

Piper loved the stone fireplace with the rough-hewn mantel, the focal point of the living room. They roamed the first floor. Down the hall was an office with a large desk and a filing cabinet. The open walk-in closet revealed a mess of dress forms, fabric bolts and boxes in need of a professional organizer.

"I guess, this will be where you'll work," Jessie said waving her hand.

"You guess?" Cole teased, echoing Piper's thought.

"She can take the cordless phone anywhere she wants in the house, or even sit outside on the front porch," Jessie smiled.

"Wait, you're saying I can work outside on that big porch swing?" Piper grinned, amazed.

Jessie tucked a strand of auburn hair behind her ear. "Well, I could set up my grandfather's old office in the barn, but it would get dusty and loud in there."

"Matt would welcome a pretty girl in the barn," Cole said, crossing his arms.

"Who's Matt?" Piper asked, conjuring the image of a legless dog.

"He's my husband's younger brother."

"He's fresh out of high school but a good hand," Cole admitted.

The tour continued upstairs. Piper followed Jessie up to the sewing room while Cole disappeared into the kitchen. Diagrams of bras, nightgowns and panties were pinned to one wall. Yellowed paper featuring vintage pencil sketches of women wearing skimpy clothing intrigued her. In the corner stood several bust forms. The wood floor was littered with bits of thread and lace. A small table, with piles of cut fabrics, was wedged between two sewing machines.

The other half of the room astounded Piper. Paperback novels stacked floor to ceiling. "Whoa."

"I know, right?" Jessie blew hair out of her face. "This is what's left of my grandma's obsession. The whole room used to be filled."

"Whoa," Piper repeated.

"Yeah. I found one old sewing machine, the patterns and my grandma's diaries hidden in the center of the mess. Grandma was a stripper. What an eye opener. It took a while to swallow that pill. My grandpa Don loved Grandma, despite her past. They met, fell in love and eloped like characters in one of those novels," Jessie laughed softly.

The massive collection had given birth to a business and a marriage. "Thanks, Grandma," Piper said, or she wouldn't have a job in Texas.

The women found Cole sitting at the kitchen table reading the romance novel he'd plucked from the shelf at the truck stop. Engrossed in the story, he didn't notice them enter the room. He stretched and crossed his long legs.

He glanced up when Jessie said, "You can use the refrigerator for your lunch. Make yourself at home. Piper, I know that old shack doesn't have a washer or dryer so you're welcome to use mine. They're in here."

Piper followed Jessie into a large utility room with a slop sink in the corner. There was a large hanging bar over a folding table. Piper hadn't noticed a laundromat while in town. "Thanks, I appreciate it."

Cole

Jessie poured Cole and Piper lemonades. He listened as Jessie expounded on her business ideas, giving Piper an earful. Uncomfortable with the topic, Cole tugged on his collar. He liked lingerie, but thought it should be kept between a man and his woman. Categorizing it as a business could take the romance out of it. Then again, Piper now worked in that line of work. He absently wondered about her phone voice. A hint of a smile graced his lips before frustration made him push all thoughts of Piper away.

The sound of a vehicle pulling up the drive caught Piper's attention. She hopped up and glanced through the side window. It wasn't her car. While Piper had signed papers, Cole suggested Parker Ford drop the small compact at the Big Deal Ranch, not the Double D. She was stuck with Cole all day. He smiled.

"That's a large trailer," Piper said.

Jessie jumped up and glanced out. "Yes, we got a good deal. We're going to get horses soon. There haven't been horses on the Double D since before Grandpa died."

"Who are they?" Piper asked pointing out the window.

"Josiah and Matthew, the Barnes brothers."

"Are all cowboys sexy?" Piper whispered, as if it was one of life's greatest mysteries.

Cole and Jessie exchanged a look behind her back. Jessie winked at Cole. He felt heat to the tips of his ears.

"Mine is," Jessie said with pride.

The men unloading the trailer were similar in size and coloring and wore the same color shirts. "Are they twins?" Piper asked.

"No. They're six years apart in age." Jessie said. "Josiah is older."

"Wow."

"Come on, I'll show you the barn and introduce you to my family." Jessie moved to the door but Cole stood ready to open it.

Tippy zipped into the open barn aisle, causing a ruckus. The cowboys cursed and yelled and the orange tabby scurried back outside.

The women rounded the corner leading into the barn. A large burlap bag lay on the ground torn and small pellets were scattered all over. A royal mess. A man's hindquarters leaned over into a stall. He spoke with his brother and didn't realize the others approached behind him.

Jessie raised a hand to smack the man's tush. "I wouldn't do that," Piper warned.

Matt Barnes turned around with a start and straightened. He smirked when he noticed the tall blonde. Jessie seemed perplexed. She must have mistaken Matt as her husband. It riled Cole that Piper could distinguish between the men's rear ends.

"Well, *hel*-lo sunshine," Matt said to Piper with confidence Cole could only wish for.

Josiah came out of the closet-like stall with a push broom. He smiled at the group and set the broom aside to hug his wife.

"This is Piper. She's working for the Double D now," Jessie introduced.

Piper shook both men's hands. Matt held Piper's hand longer than usual. He was young, but Piper might be snared by his brash persona. Cole stuck his hands in his front pockets, trying to keep his expression neutral.

"Would you like me to show you around town, say, tonight?" Matt asked Piper.

"I don't know. You'd have to ask my husband," Piper said with an alluring smile.

Jessie squeaked and Josiah and Matt exchanged a look. Cole cleared his throat, and they glanced at him. His face heated. "We saw a friend of yours this morning." Cole looked at Jessie.

"Who would that be?" she asked.

"The little old lady who looks like Spock," Piper said with a wry grin.

"Oh no," Josiah muttered, tossing a glance to Jessie. "Tell me she didn't do something funny."

"I wouldn't consider it funny per se," Piper mused.

"Ms. Hardmann loudly introduced Piper as my Russian mail-order bride to the entire morning crew at Stitts'." Cole still wasn't sure how he felt about it. At the time, it embarrassed the dickens out of him. The whole community would think he and Piper had married. He should be angry. Piper wasn't upset. After the shock wore off, she had laughed.

"No freaking way," Matt said slapping his knee. "That lady is hilarious."

"It's horrible," Jessie said, looking at Josiah helplessly. "That rumor will run wild through town." She placed a hand on Piper's arm. "I'm really sorry."

"It's no biggie. Honest. It's a small town and I'm new and a novelty. People will be curious about me until they get to know me or someone else new comes along." She smiled at the Barnes crew. "Seriously, it can't be any worse than a small office."

"It didn't help that you spoke Russian," Cole declared, rolling back on his booted heals.

"Piper, you didn't!" Jessie squealed.

The men laughed. Matt elbowed his brother. "Maybe Ms. Hardmann has met her match."

"It was only 'da' and 'n'et', yes and no." Piper shrugged.

"Don't forget 'dasvidaniya'," Cole reminded.

"And goodbye. That's all the Russian I know. I probably pronounced it wrong." Piper crossed her arms as a slight blush tinged her cheeks.

"Who'd know?" Matt asked.

"Well, that Spock lady knows the truth and so does Hugh. When I went to wash my hands, he welcomed me to America, and I set him straight. The only time I've been out of the country is when I visited Canada." Piper smiled again. "Anyway, it's Cole's reputation that will suffer the most from this."

Cole wanted to disagree. If people believed he'd married a beautiful woman, it might be a good thing. "You might lose dates," he countered.

She laughed and touched his arm, the warmth sent shivers down his spine. "I just got here. I'm not ready for any of that. In a town full of romance-seeking men that will work in my favor."

"She won't have to break any cowboys' hearts," Jessie agreed.

"They're gooey on the inside," Piper said softly. She glanced down the barn aisle starry-eyed and walked toward an ATV. Matt followed her. They discussed the machine while Cole watched, frowning.

"Do I want to ride a cowboy?" Piper exclaimed loudly, her face bright red. She backed away from Matt and glanced at Cole with wide unblinking eyes. He couldn't help the crooked smile that formed. Her mouth fell open, and she blinked twice. Damn. He'd done it again. His face flashed hot, but he pointed to the vehicle.

"The ATV's name is Cowboy," Matt howled. "Would you like to go for a ride?"

Piper's brow furrowed. Tempted. She thought about it, but decided against it. Cole blew out a long breath. He didn't want to witness Piper having a ball while holding onto Barnes' waist.

CHAPTER 3

Piper

PIPER'S FIRST DAY WORKLOAD WAS light, but she found the people interesting. She sorted Jessie's email, snail mail, and boxed orders. Cole had stayed at the Barnes residence while she worked. Josiah must have worked him because Cole was dusty when he offered her a ride back to the Big Deal ranch.

Her used compact car awaited her, parked next to Brad Davidson's large SUV. The car salesmen had assured her of the car's sound condition. What astounded her was his declaration to take it back if she didn't like its performance on the primitive road to her cabin.

She slowly drove the little car down the gravel drive. Besides being dusty, the car handled the trip well. The cabin was dark and unwelcoming. The bag of groceries she'd bought at the quickie mart would have to tide her over until she found the Wertz grocery store.

Cole visited on horseback twice that first week, both times in the morning before she left for work.

As one week turned into two, Piper fell into a pattern at the Double D. Answering the phone grew easier. She spoke with two important Austin boutique owners and took orders. She also helped Jessie to focus on the sewing, carrying pieces of fabric or offering an opinion when asked.

Jessie introduced a few of her friends to Piper. She hit it off with one girl in particular, Kelly Greene. The unmarried woman warned her about local cowboys. Kelly was involved in a frustrating on-again off-again relationship. She vowed to take Piper to the neighboring town of Nockerville to go dancing. Piper welcomed the friendship. While she enjoyed Jessie, her husband and the ranch hands, Piper missed the closeness of girlfriends. So far, Cole had been the only friend she'd made, and he was a shy, but hot, guy. She saw him as less of a bed ornament and more of a bestie.

A small stack of romance novels blocked the cabin doorway one evening. *Cole.* He'd shared some of his favorites. She flipped through the books, recognizing the bottom one as something of a Fortuna treasure. Carefully, she opened the battered paper cover. On the inside, every inch contained initials of previous readers. Jessie's grandmother, Undine Love Davidson, marked each book she read, and the tradition carried over to the townsfolk. Most of the initials belonged to men, which she had learned from Jessie.

The Visitation featured a romantic romp about a man in love with his neighbor. He wore angel wings and visited her during the night, invading her dreams and, eventually, her heart.

Men acted out the part of the main-character, sometimes in public which led to arrests. It saved a marriage, too. Even Jessie had bought Josiah a pair of angel wings for his birthday, a little detail Piper wished she hadn't learned.

She set the books on the table. After dinner, she sat on the front porch reading *The Visitation* until it was too dark to see the pages.

Piper sat in her car in the crowded parking lot, reluctant to venture into Hammered, a local bar and restaurant, because it was the Barnes' hangout. It felt odd to invade their space.

A memory resurfaced and teased a smile out of her. "You're not the only turd in the toilet. You get flushed and then you're surrounded by shit," Bob McCracken used to say. Sometimes he changed it to: poop in the pot. Whatever fecal vernacular her father had used, it meant she was never truly alone.

Piper sucked in a deep breath and pushed the car door open.

She hesitated in the tavern's entry, wondering if she should seat herself or wait. A few men read books while they ate. She grinned and stepped inside, following one man with a stack of books. The handsome romance lover had dark hair and eyes. He winked at her. Piper didn't know most people, but everyone knew the new girl when they spotted her. There was no hiding in public.

Josiah sat on the stool at the end of the bar. He sucked on a longneck bottle. Next to him, Jessie smiled, leaned close and rubbed his arm. Josiah responded by hugging his wife and placing a kiss on her forehead. Josiah wasn't the most talkative fellow, but he'd do anything for Jessie. Someday Piper hoped to find a love like that, but her man would not step out of a romance novel.

The man she'd followed in set the paperbacks on the bar, and the chubby bartender greeted him. The bartender motioned to a shelf in the corner full of novels. They exchanged a few words then the book borrower selected more. Paperback romance novel loving men were an oddity.

Piper slipped into a booth and perused the menu. A heavyset woman in her fifties greeted her. "Hiya hon, you're new here." The woman's name badge read "Sharon."

"Yes, I've been here less than a month. I work for the Double D."

"I knew you weren't Russian," Sharon chuckled.

"That was Ms. Hardmann's doing," Piper admitted with a shrug.

"What a welcome!" Sharon slid in the booth across from her. "My husband, Holden, and I own this place. I'm Sharon Dix and my daughter is over there waiting tables. Her name is Piccadilly, but everyone calls her Pixie."

"I'm Piper McCracken. I'm from Chicago, not Moscow. My dad was a plumber, not KGB. I live in the homestead cabin on the Big Deal ranch but work for Jessie."

Sharon offered a few entrée suggestions, took Piper's order, then disappeared into the kitchen.

Sometime during the meal the Barnes spied her. After she'd finished eating, Jessie took her by the elbow and introduced her to everyone in the tavern. The man playing pool with Josiah was Kelly's love interest, Sawyer Hickey.

"I've heard about you," Sawyer said to Piper.

"I've heard about you too," she volleyed.

He grinned. "It's nice to know my reputation as Hammered's best pool player remains intact."

"Oh no. That's not what I heard," Piper said. From Kelly she understood he would flirt and act as if his ego filled the room. She messed with his shot. He missed the hole.

"Well, darlin', did you hear what a romantic I am?" Smiling, he leaned into her personal space.

Piper laughed. "Don't be silly. I heard you were a smart-ass."

Josiah and Jessie laughed. "She heard correctly," Jessie agreed.

"She has your number," Josiah said.

"You." Sawyer pointed to Josiah, who shook his head while laughing.

"Me," Kelly offered from behind him.

Sawyer whirled around and studied Kelly. "I'm doomed if the ladies gang up on me."

"Sorry I'm late," Kelly said. She waved her hand. "I had a parent meeting that ran long."

Sharon brought Kelly a drink in a carryout cup with a lid. "Are you out of glasses?" she asked.

"Yes, I'm sorry, but the dang dishwasher is acting up again," Sharon huffed.

"What's wrong with it?" Piper asked. "Did it blow a breaker?"

"No. The thing won't drain, then the bottom fills and it floods. It's a big mess." The older woman appeared on the verge of tears. "No one can come out until tomorrow."

"I can look at it, if you like?" Piper offered, setting her drink down.

"What can you do?" Sawyer asked, raising a brow.

"Her dad owned a plumbing business," Jessie said. "She's fixed our slop sink."

"It can't hurt," Sharon said and motioned to Piper. "Follow me."

Piles of dirty dishes cluttered the counter next to the deep double basin sink. The commercial-grade dishwasher's door gaped open, exposing a pool of cloudy gray water. Humidity hung in the air.

One man worked the grill and fryer while another prepared the plates, bread, tomatoes and other condiments. A young woman scrubbed dishes.

Sharon handed Piper a pair of rubber gloves, then picked up a cotton dishtowel. "Move over, Lucy. It's your turn to dry," Sharon said, handing Lucy the towel.

"Thank you. My fingers look like prunes." Lucy rolled her shoulders and picked up a plate.

Piper donned the yellow gloves and prayed they didn't have a hole. She knelt down, reached inside and searched the bottom for the drain. The dirty standing water made it difficult. The strainer was clear. That could mean two things; either the dishwasher was broke, or a clog resided elsewhere.

"Was the dishwasher working earlier?" Piper asked.

"Yes," Sharon replied. "The drain's been sluggish for a few days but hasn't backed up before."

Similar to a home under-the-counter model, the dishwasher was a space saver. Any large containers or bowls needed to be washed in the stainless sink.

"Mrs. Dix, can I pull it out?" Piper asked.

"Land sakes, child, call me Sharon and, yes, do what you need to do." Sharon wiped her face with the back of her hand before thrusting both hands into the soapy water.

Piper rolled the heavy appliance forward until there was a crack. She peeked behind and noted the intact pliable drain hose. She rattled off a list of things she needed. They turned off the water and power supply to the machine. Piper tugged the washer away from the wall so she could maneuver behind it. She unhooked the hose from the washer and the wall line. She emptied the tube of residual liquid. When she held it to the light, it was empty. The clog was in the trap or wall. She shimmied into the small space, grateful she'd worn jeans instead of a sundress. She used the adjustable wrench to loosen the nut and dumped the waste water into an empty green five-gallon pickle bucket.

Success. She found the clog and pushed the goop out with a screwdriver. Wedged between the unit and the wall, she worked methodically until the trap was clean. Inspecting the wall pipe, she found it coated with slime.

She replaced the PVC trap, taking care to make it tight. Next, the drain hose. In the small crevice, she refastened the clamp. A nostalgic feeling hit and she sucked in a breath. As a child, she used to help her father. She'd hand him tools, or sometimes just keep him company. The sudden heaviness in her heart caused her eyes to water. She blinked the tears away.

Three pairs of legs waited, one wearing a pair of cowboy boots. The black boots led to jeans and Cole's long legs. He leaned down and his blue eyes glimmered mischievously. Piper bolted upright, smacking her head on the underside of the counter. She let out a chorus of unladylike expletives.

"That's not Russian," Holden said, then chuckled.

"It's not French either," Piper grumbled, rubbing the spot where a bump formed.

Cole offered Piper a hand and pulled her to her feet. Holden pushed the unit back into place. He adjusted the dial and turned it on.

Sharon put ice in a bag and handed it to Cole, who gingerly touched the knot forming on Piper's head.

"I came to see if you needed any help," Cole said with a sheepish smile. "How's your head?"

"I'm okay. Maybe it knocked some sense into me." She hissed when he touched the bump.

Holden opened the dishwasher's door. There was less water than before. "You're a miracle worker, my dear," he said with a smile. His chubby cheeks exposed a dimple. "Thank you."

"I'm glad I could help. You should probably clean out the drain cover," she suggested.

"I will." He turned to his wife who was taking an order out. "Get Piper a beer or whatever she wants." Sharon nodded and left the kitchen. She reappeared a moment later.

Holden scratched his chin. "We haven't had this much excitement since somebody stole my balls."

Mortified, Piper glanced at Cole, but that was a mistake. He shook his head; his eyes crinkled with mirth. Piper covered her mouth to hide a smile.

Sharon patted Holden's arm, then reassured Piper with a wink. "It's a good thing we had extras in storage. The town prankster made sure we got them back."

Holden placed his hands on his hips. "But not before they were exhibited all over town!"

CHAPTER 4

Piper

"BEER IS MY KRYPTONITE," PIPER wheezed. Thunder rumbled in her head.

Cole kept quiet as he drove to the Big Deal ranch. She'd arranged with the Barnes to take her car to their home and Cole volunteered to ferry Piper to work in the morning.

"I mean, I only had three beers and one was while I ate. You'd think it wouldn't 'fect me but it does. I'm talkative, right? That happens. At least, that's what Justin says." Her head flopped back on the headrest.

"Who's Justin?" Cole asked.

"My fiancé." Piper took a deep breath and jabbing a finger into the air, turned to him. "Correction. Justin Saine is my crazy-stalker *EX*-fiancé. He's a jerk."

"Crazy-stalker?"

"You know, followed me to work, followed me home, followed me shopping. Everywhere I went, there he was. Kinda like God but in an ominous creeper way. He called me constantly, too. I got a new phone number and moved to my brother Fletcher's house to escape." She rubbed her forehead with her palm. "I should've shot him."

Cole chuckled. "Yeah, maybe you should have."

They rode in silence, but the thundering continued. The windshield wipers screeched against the glass. "Does my head look heavy? It feels heavy. Why does it feel heavy?" She groaned.

"It's fine. You're fine. It's the kryptonite."

"Beer, ugh." She snorted. "Just be glad I didn't talk in Russian again or run around stripping off my clothes. Or both. That would've made the town talk." She giggled and her head bobbed forward again.

"You wouldn't have done either." He turned the wheel and started up the Big Deal's long drive.

"Kryptonite. It makes you do things."

"You wouldn't have done those things. Not in public, anyway."

She remained quiet. Her forehead crinkled as she gazed at him. "I could have."

"I wouldn't have let you," he said with a shake of the head.

"Why?"

In a low voice Cole said, "If you talked Russian, then you'd be my mail-order bride, and my wife would only run around naked in private." A slow smile spread on his lips.

Heat pooled in her chest. She squinted, watching his profile until the grin slipped off his face. Cole swallowed and glowered. Thunder boomed. She rubbed her temples again. They bounced along and she clutched the handle.

Cole

Lightning flashed like paparazzi cameras. The wind picked up, and the temperature dropped, promising to be one heck of a storm. Cole walked Piper inside the tiny cabin. She lowered herself to the twin bed and bent over, her head in her hands.

A grin stole over Cole's lips. She'd stacked the romance novels he'd given her on the table, one splayed open upside-down. So the non-romance girl was getting her romance on.

"Are you enjoying *The Visitation*?" he asked. The angel talked to the heroine while she was sleeping, planting seeds of love into her subconscious mind. It was hokey, but endearing.

"I'm not finished yet," she mumbled.

"His flaws are like mine," Cole admitted.

"He's cute and sweet, but shy." Piper cringed when it thundered. The door blew shut. She jumped to her feet, chest heaving.

"Do you want to know my crippling fear? I doubt you'll find it in any book," she said, turning toward him. Her face shone ashen even in the dim light. The thunder rolled again as if prompted. Her eyes widened. She held out her trembling hands.

Cole took her hands in his and steadied them. "It's a natural fear."

"It paralyzes me. I freeze if there's even a mention of a tornado," she whispered. "What will I do if a tornado touches down? There isn't a basement or shelter of any kind."

Fortuna got twisters sometimes, and spring was tornado season. The bathroom had a standalone shower, so no protection. Under a mattress offered minimal shelter from debris, but not if the roof or house and everything in it blew away.

"Sit down a minute, Piper."

She took a seat at the table, watching him as he checked his cell phone. Nil reception. "Can I make a call?" He pointed to the house phone. She nodded, then he dialed. "Hey, it's me. Can you do me a favor? Good. Check the radar for the storm that's coming." He paused, listening. "How long will it last?" Again he waited. "There's no shelter at the homestead."

Piper opened a book, but didn't look down at the pages. She focused out the window.

"Piper?" She met his gaze. "This storm cell will last for hours. There will be high winds, and conditions are right for tornadoes."

A groan gurgled out of her open mouth.

"If you want to pack an overnight bag, you can come with me. There's a storm shelter if we need it."

She nodded and stood, scraping the chair on the floor. Tears welled in her eyes. He couldn't help but pull her into his arms. For a moment she rested. When she sighed, his heart warmed because they fit together. His blood raced, and he cleared his throat. "Do you have a bag we can use?"

She broke free of his embrace, pointing to the cabinet under the sink. He opened it, finding paper grocery bags. It wasn't exactly the kind of bag he had in mind, but it would work. He held it open while she plopped clothes into it. Lightening flashed and Piper jumped, freezing like a statue when the thunder came. The wind whipped around the rustic structure, causing eerie whistles and howls. They needed to hurry if they were to keep ahead of the storm.

He prompted her. "Toiletries? Makeup?"

She grabbed toothpaste and brush then they headed to the truck. The whole time he drove, she stared out the back window as if Satan himself chased them.

"Piper, tell me why you fear storms?" he asked, casting a sideways glance.

With one hand clamped on his forearm, in a monotone she whispered, "I was four. My grandmother, mom, brother and I were traveling home from a family reunion in Iowa. It was a long boring trip until the storm hit. There was hail and torrential rain. My brother and I wanted to crawl into Mom's lap, but she was driving. I'm sure it didn't help my mom's nerves each time it thundered that we would whimper or yell."

Cole passed A Hole in One donut shop. The employees, known as A-holes, stared out the drive-thru window.

"Mom stayed on the highway and floored it. We broke free of the rain and that's when she cursed. My mom never cusses." She took a deep breath before continuing droning on. "All I could see in the rearview mirror were her frightened eyes. Out the window, a patch of trees bent in half. Not saplings, but trees with thick trunks. Together, Fletcher and I looked out the back window. All I could do was stare. The tornado was dark gray and moving so fast it blurred. The noise was horrific. I thought it would run us over."

Cole pulled onto a lane and started a twisted ascent into a wooded yard. Lightning flashed. Thunder boomed, making Piper squeak. Large windows covered the front of a wood A-frame house, and the front door light lit the path to the door. Cole took the paper bag full of Piper's belongings and ushered her to the house. He twisted the knob, and the wind caught the door. It slammed against the wall, sending the framed art askew.

Piper

Briefly illuminated by lightning, Piper noticed a kitchen toward the right and a living room on the left. A sofa lined the window wall. Rain pelted the house, sending rivulets down the glass. Piper watched the storm out the large two-story windows like it was on a big screen. Cole closed the front door. The bag he held crinkled when he sat it on the kitchen counter. She took a step toward him but hesitated in the dark.

Cole pulled the refrigerator door open and reached inside. Light blinded her. She blinked, listening for Cole. Something tugged on her hand. Looking down, a pale face stared at her. She shrieked and so did the kid. Thunder joined the party, and they both jumped.

"Are you scared of the storm too?" the little boy asked. His eyes were blue and shaped like Cole's.

Piper nodded dumbly. She hadn't considered Cole might have children, a girlfriend, or a wife.

"It's okay, lady." The boy grinned and tightened his grip on her hand. "You don't have to be afraid. You're not alone."

That's right. She wasn't the only turd in the toilet. Others floated with her in the sewer of life. She returned the squeeze and smiled. "Thanks, buddy."

Cole flipped the light switch, and the storm receded from the house. "Piper, this is Beau and my mother, Florence." He handed her a bottle of water.

An older woman rose from a lounge chair. Chunky and wearing a friendly smile, Florence extended a hand.

"So here's my new daughter-in-law," Florence teased. Her smile exposed dimples.

Piper froze, unable to form words. "I," she started.

"I went to get my hair done at the Tease Me Salon. Desire Hardmann owns it. She told me about the breakfast you and Cole had."

"Actually, there were four of us, if you count Desire and her mouth," Cole stated.

Piper noted the woman's fuzzy, pink pajamas. Similarly attired in Star Wars pajamas, Beau yawned. It was late, but the storm was loud.

"I'm sorry, Mrs. Dart. I would never—" Piper tried.

"Honey, I know Desire. You couldn't have done a thing to stop her." Florence patted Piper's hand. "Call me Flo. Mrs. Dart was my mother-in-law, and I don't like to be reminded I'm old enough to have a twenty-eight-year-old son."

"Nana, is Piper gonna marry Cole?" The boy had been paying attention to the adults. Piper and Cole shared a look. Her face heated and his turned red.

"Not tonight," Flo said.

"Is she going to sleep with us in your bed?" Beau asked.

"Why would she do that?" Flo asked.

"She's afraid of thunder too." He glanced at Piper. "She'll feel safe if she's with you, Nana."

"I think Piper will be all right."

Beau tipped his head and studied Piper. "Then she'll sleep with Cole and he'll keep her safe."

"Goodnight, Beau," Cole said as the boy hugged him tight. "You can ask Piper all the questions you want in the morning."

"Okay." He nodded with a gap-toothed grin. "G'night."

Piper sat on the sofa and watched Flo lead Beau up the stairs to the second story. The open banister led to the balcony. They disappeared down a hallway and the light clicked off. The vaulted ceiling peaked overhead with a wooden beam. Charming. Even though there was limited floor space, the two-story openness made it seem large.

"That's the kitchen," Cole said with a wave of his hand. "Here's the family room. If you walk back here, there's a bathroom, a utility room and an office." he said, pulling her up and down a short hall. "Upstairs are two bedrooms. Mom and Beau share the master and I have the other. Unfortunately, there are only two beds. A king, with a lady who snores and a kid who kicks, and mine."

Piper wondered what Ms. Hardmann would say about his bed. The rain pounded the roof harder, and the lights flickered.

"Of course, there's the sofa," he said with a smirk.

No way. She wouldn't get a wink of sleep with a quarter inch of glass separating her from the storm. "If you really want to sleep on the sofa, you can," she teased back, crossing her arms.

Cole picked up the paper bag again and led the way to the stairs. She followed him. With each step, her stomach weighed more. The hallway had two doors. He ignored the closed one and entered the other. The queen bed had a navy quilt, and was flanked by oak nightstands. He lit a candle on a nightstand, and the light scent of vanilla filled the room. He turned down the bed while she used the bathroom.

The bedrooms shared the toilet and tub but had their own vanity. She washed her face and brushed her teeth. Shifting items around in the paper sack, she realized she'd forgotten yoga pants for sleeping. Clutching the bag to her chest, she returned to the bedroom, but stopped dead in her tracks. In nothing but his boxer briefs, Cole tugged the blind cord. She swallowed. His chest appeared to be chiseled tan marble. She closed her eyes, inhaling deeply. Thunder boomed. She jumped, dropping the bag.

"What's wrong?" he asked.

"I didn't pack anything to sleep in." Her face heated, and she stooped to pick up the spilled contents.

"That's not a problem," Cole grinned wolfishly.

"Cole," she growled, covering her face with her hand. Like she wanted to be romantic when frightened out of her skin. Jerking and squeaking each time the thunder cracked would make for fond memories. Intimacy would not happen. Not tonight.

"Settle down, Piper. I've got you covered." Cole pulled open a dresser and plucked out a bundle. "Will this work?" He handed her a striped gray T-shirt.

"Yes. Thank you." She brought it to her nose and inhaled. It smelled like Cole. She lifted her eyes and devoured his sculpted body once more. *This was a bad idea.* She pivoted, fleeing back into the bathroom.

Cole

Cole turned off the table lamp. The candlelight danced but provided enough light to see the bed. He made sure the blinds and drapes blocked as much light as possible, but he couldn't do a thing about sound waves or the skylight.

He glimpsed the silhouette of her long legs before she flicked off the bathroom light. Piper exited the bathroom wearing his shirt. He tried not to consider what she might or might not have on under it. The bed shook as she sat on the edge.

"Thanks for doing this for me, Cole."

He wanted to laugh. Safety was his primary goal, but hell, there were some good benefits. It'd been a long time since a woman graced his bed. "Anytime," he replied, meaning it.

"I might take you up on that," she said slyly. Did he detect flirting? Her fingertips brushed his upper arm, making his skin tingle. She found his left hand.

On the other side of the bed, he fisted the sheet and tried to ignore the rising temperature. He stared out the skylight with the image of her shapely thighs seared in his mind. Then she did the unthinkable: pulling his hand to her lips, she kissed his knuckles.

Words stalled in his throat. The icy shield around his heart began to thaw. Smiling into the darkness, he squeezed her hand.

Thunder boomed shaking the house. Piper gasped, trembling. Cole reached out and pulled her against him. She rested her face against his chest and when her breathing calmed, he whispered soothing things into her ear.

CHAPTER 5

Piper

"PIPER, PIPER, PIPER!"

Heart hammering, she woke with a start.

"Get up, get up, get up!" Beau pleaded. He jumped up and down on the bed next to her.

"I'm awake," she said, sitting and pulling the covers up to her chest. Glancing to Cole's empty side of the bed, her heart ached.

"Beau, leave Piper alone." Framed in the bathroom doorway, Cole stood with a towel wrapped around his waist. His damp body glistened, but oddly he already wore the bandanna.

"Ah, Cole. It's time to get up, or she's gonna miss Nana's pancakes." With a pout, the boy slid off the bed.

"Piper is our guest. Nana won't let her starve." He shooed the boy out of the room.

"I know. But you better hurry before I eat 'em all. They're the best pancakes in the world."

Cole closed the door. "Sorry. He's a little enthusiastic about breakfast."

"I can tell." Piper smiled as her gaze raked the long-legged man. She fantasized about touching the corded muscles of his arms, chest and...

Cole cleared his throat and shifted his weight, remaining by the door. One of his big hands clutched the edge of his towel and the other rubbed the back of his head.

"Oh," she said sliding her feet to the floor. "I guess I should get ready so you can get dressed." She picked up her bag of stuff and started toward the bathroom.

"Piper," Cole said. He relaxed his stance. "There's a towel set out for you."

"Thanks. Is it pretty pink like yours?" she teased. With a grin, she closed the door, not waiting to see if his cheeks matched the color of his towel. She showered and dressed in record time.

Together they descended to the kitchen table. A heavenly scent filled the room, reminding her of childhood Sunday mornings. Beau sat on his knees and squeezed half the bottle of syrup onto his plate.

"I heard these are the best pancakes in the world," Piper mentioned, taking the seat Flo indicated.

"Mmhmm," Beau agreed around a mouthful.

"In our little world maybe," Flo said with a chuckle.

Quiet settled while they ate although Beau kept asking about Chicago and Piper's childhood. When they'd finished, Cole helped his mother clean up the kitchen and Beau pulled Piper to the sofa, all the while talking her ear off.

"Cole kept you safe, didn't he? He's strong and gives good piggyback rides. Cole takes me to the rodeo when it comes to town. Have you ever been? You should come with us."

Geez, did the kid breathe?

"Hey, can we take Piper to the rodeo?" Beau called out.

"Sure, kid," Cole said, placing a plate in the dishwasher.

"See? Cole's a great guy." Beau grinned.

Piper leaned closer to the boy, inspecting his freckles. He was a cute kid and like a rubber ball bouncing up and down. "Why do you call him Cole?" *Why not Dad?*

With a crinkled brow, Beau quirked his head like a puppy. "That's his name."

"No, I mean, he's an adult. Most adults have another name in a family. Like your Nana. Her name is Florence, but you don't call her that." If Fletcher or Piper would have called their parents by the first names, their patooties would have been blistered.

"Oh." He nodded. "Guess I could call him Uncle Cole, but..." He shrugged.

Uncle. Of course. Beau looked so much like his uncle, Piper assumed he was Cole's.

27

A pang of longing hit. Her heart warmed to the little gap-toothed smile as it reminded her of her niece and nephew. Piper had become the favorite aunt while staying with Fletcher and his family. The kids had served as a distraction from her stalker.

"Piper?" Beau placed his small hand on her knee. His round face wore a worried look.

She blinked tears away. "What's that?" she asked pointing to a dark corner. A neck of a guitar popped up above a short shelving unit that held a crap load of paperback novels. *Were they Flo's or Cole's?*

"It's a get-tar." He ran to the stringed instrument and picked it up. He waddled careful to avoid the furniture. "See?" The instrument was almost as long as Beau. She gently took the six string acoustic from him and sat it on her lap. "Can you play?" Beau asked, sitting next to her on the sofa. He bounced up and down on the cushion.

Play was a matter of opinion. She strummed the strings and grimaced. "It sounds like a dying cat." Immediately, she started tuning it string by string. She might not play well, but she had a great ear. It was a gift she had used in high school theater and choral productions. She'd never sung a solo, yet she always kept her group on pitch. She preferred being behind the scenes and never wanted to be center stage.

Strumming the strings again, she smiled. "That's better."

Beau stopped fidgeting and watched her fine tune a last string. Piper tried an E cord then shifted to another, but it didn't sound right. She plucked with long fingernails. She hummed with the cord but couldn't put two together fast enough to start a song.

"You sound like an angel," Beau whispered.

"Thanks, kiddo." She smiled at him and stopped plucking. "Is this your guitar? Do you want to play?"

The boy's eyes widened, and he shook his head. "That's my Papa's. I'm not allowed to touch it."

But he'd brought it over for her to examine. Piper stared at the polished wood and her stomach churned. She glanced over to the adults who would have a say in the matter, but Cole had moved to stand next to her. She hadn't heard him approach. He reached for the instrument and she released it.

Cole sat across from them and strummed it. Beau and Piper exchanged a look.

His long fingers worked the strings like a pro. He tilted his head, closed his eyes and played with tangible emotion. The sound waves swirled, caressing her soul like a lover's touch. It wasn't country music or rock-n-roll; he played a classical piece.

"It sounds good, Pipes," Cole said.

The combination of music and the nickname her father gave her caused tears to well. *Pipes.* Bob McCracken had been the only one allowed to call her that, but hearing Cole utter it made her insides warm. Coupled with the passion in which he played, her heart shifted a little more in his direction. *What if the man loved like that?*

The room had gone quiet. Piper snapped her eyes open, not realizing she'd closed them. She swiped the tears off her cheek.

CHAPTER 6

Cole

COLE SLAMMED THE GATE SHUT on the truck and carried the chainsaw over to Curly. He greeted the regulars gathered around the foreman.

"Now that Cole's here we can get this show on the road," Curly announced.

"I see why he was late," Gimme Malone teased, as he watched Piper head to the porch. Gimme, the youngest on the Big Deal at twenty-two, was wiry and topped out at five foot eight inches. He was a good hand and would do what was needed to get the job done. Cole never minded having the kid around, but that might change if Gimme continued to ride him about Piper.

Arlon Topp whistled. "I'd be late too." The crusty cowboy elbowed Slim Pickens, who grinned but was smart enough to hold his tongue. "Ah, lighten up Cole," Arlon said. The older man's face was a road map of wrinkled, leathery skin. His bright eyes recognized Cole's unease, but Arlon's years earned him the right to poke fun.

Cole's good mood bubble popped the moment he'd pulled up to the barn and the men saw Piper. He turned to his boss, ignoring the others.

Curly inspected him. "Is there going to be an issue?"

"No. I just need my space," Cole mumbled.

"You'll have plenty of time to nurse your thoughts when you're picking up debris or running the chainsaw. Just watch yourself." Curly gave instructions to the men. It seemed several trees came down during the high winds. One blocked a main road on the property and others leaned over trails. "Brad, Josiah and a few others are already out there."

Gimme hopped into the back of Curly's pickup. He slung an arm around an orange water cooler. Slim climbed up and leaned against the cab. In his thirties, his nickname had nothing to do with size. He rolled and lit a cigarette. Curly sat behind the wheel, Arlon took the middle bench, and, as Cole took the passenger seat, he threw a look back at the ranch house.

Piper talked to Jessie on the large porch. She glanced up and held his gaze long enough to make his cheeks blaze red. He couldn't help but return her smile.

"Yep, I'd be late too," Arlon said with a chuckle.

Curly drove through the property. The grass seemed greener and the sky bluer than the day before. Once they neared the wooded acreage, the wind damage became apparent as limbs littered the ground. Snapped branches hung from trees. Across the road lay a fallen live oak. Josiah wore goggles as he sawed, and Brad pulled the limbs away from the trunk. Sawyer, Josiah, and his brother Matt cut the smaller branches and tossed them onto a pile.

The truck stopped and the work paused. The men gathered around the cooler. Curly and Slim were to stay with Josiah. Arlon, Gimme, and Cole would go with Brad to the bridle path.

Vegetation created a tunnel over the trail. Not once while riding through on horseback had Cole considered the trees overhead. Brad handed him a spray can of neon orange paint. "Cole, walk ahead and mark the trees for us. We'll get started here and follow you through."

Cole nodded and shook the can. He marked one with an X. It would knock a rider out of the saddle. As he worked, his thoughts turned to Piper and their drive over. When her phone rang, she hadn't recognized the number and let it go to voicemail. The caller had tried again. "If it's important enough, they can leave a message," she said matter-of-factly. The third, fourth, and fifth times she sent it directly to voicemail.

He'll never forget the look on her face when she said, "It's him." Her face turned a sickly white, even her lips. Wide, unblinking eyes watched the road and the mirrors searching for the boogieman. She clenched and unclenched her hand on the phone all while the phone kept ringing.

"Him who?" Cole asked.

"Justin." Piper tilted her head back and groaned. "He found me. What am I going to do?"

"Turn the damned thing off." Cole gripped the wheel hard. He'd like a minute or two with this Justin character. He grinned a tight-lipped smile.

Piper had turned the phone off and tossed it into his truck once they reached the house. She didn't want access to it and he couldn't blame her. *That Justin guy is ridiculous. Get a clue. No means no. Move on and let go.*

Now Cole was worried about her, dammit. She was bold and strong, but anxiety and anger eroded her nerves. After the initial shock wore off, she deduced someone had given out her number. He stopped her from sending an angry text by reminding her she'd have to switch on the phone and might accidentally answer it. Piper had slumped into the seat, stared out the window, and not uttered a word the remainder of the drive.

Cole tagged another trunk with twisted bark. He envisioned the face of Justin and sprayed the X. A chainsaw to the guy's neck was one way to solve the problem. For someone not wanting a relationship, he sure was investing time. *Hypocrite.* It was strictly friendship, and he didn't want to see his friend hurting, especially by a stalker.

Well, he knew one way to help with the phone. He could offer to record the outgoing message, making it voice *male.*

Piper

Piper threw the mobile phone on the twin bed and walked to the dresser. She was tired, and it wasn't from any physical activity. She pulled on a pair of comfy sweats and flopped onto the bed. Picking up the dreaded device, she pushed the power button. It took a minute for the thing to boot, but once on and connected to the Wi-Fi it started chiming and vibrating like crazy. The voice mailbox was full. Was that possible in the digital age? She retrieved the first message. It was Justin. He missed and loved her. He was a lonely, miserable man. Being wanted felt good, but the moment passed as the next messaged played.

"This is your fault. You ruined me. I can never love anyone like I loved you. Didn't it mean anything when you pulled me inside you—" she cut it off. All the disgusting ranting wouldn't change her mind.

She flipped over onto her back and sent a nasty message to her brother and mother. One of them was responsible. She pressed her eyelids closed and gritted her teeth. Tears escaped. Justin shouldn't be affecting her like this. She beat the bed with her fists.

"What did that bed ever do to you?" Cole asked from the doorway. His tone was light but his eyes held concern.

Piper sat up and wiped her face. Cole had a reason for showing up unannounced—in one hand he held her bag from their overnight. Her face heated as she remembered Cole's glistening abs. Then a wicked grin spread over her face: What if Justin knew?

"Why did you leave the dinner party? You didn't even say goodbye to Arlon. I think you might've hurt the old fool's feelings." He pulled out a ladder-back chair and sat.

"He shouldn't have pinched my butt," she said, crossing her arms.

The tease left Cole's voice. "Did he now? I'll have a talk with him."

"It's not necessary, Cole. He's harmless." Piper stood and pulled open the refrigerator, offering him a beer. She twisted off the lid to a water bottle and sat across from him. "You should have seen the playfulness on his face. I think he wanted me to think it was you, but I knew it wasn't. You wouldn't do that."

"Wouldn't I?" He quirked a brow.

"Not today after what happened, and not there." There was no way in hell Cole would embarrass her in front of his boss, and hers too. Brad and Jessie offered dinner to anyone who'd helped to clean up after the storm. Brad grilled steaks and corn while the hands all used the showers in the bunkhouse. Jessie conducted dinner preparation like a symphonic masterpiece. The girls chopped large quantities of fruit for salad and set the table. Piper hadn't been to such a large gathering since a Christmas office party. She did more observing than talking. The only person to notice the dark cloud over her, besides Cole, had been Jessie. When Jessie hugged her, Piper almost broke down. She held the tears at bay, but decided to leave the party.

"I guess you know me pretty well," Cole admitted.

Piper shrugged. "There's a time and place for everything, and that was not the time or place for anything."

They locked gazes as seconds ticked away. Her phone startled them. Piper shrank into the seat. Cole stood, scraping the chair against the wood floor. He strode over and picked up the offensive device. He glanced at the screen before answering, "Hello, Fletcher."

Cole's gaze sought Piper. Knowing it was her brother, she relaxed and let out a shaky pent up breath.

"Yes, sir. She's here, but I'd like a few words if you don't mind. That's right, I'm Cole. It's a pleasure. What do you know about this Justin character harassing your sister?"

Piper watched as Cole and Fletcher talked, planned and worried about her. As Cole paced the small room, she imagined Fletcher was doing the same in his home office.

She found a piece of paper and penned out a message then passed it to Cole. "Oh, your sister is asking you to mail her package." He paused listening. "Which one, Piper?"

"The silver one," she said, then leaned in so her brother could hear. "Goodnight, Fletcher." She got ready for bed and crawled under the blanket. She watched Cole until her eyes were too heavy to stay open. His presence offered safety, and that safety wrapped around and hugged her like insulation on a pipe that keeps it from freezing.

CHAPTER 7

Piper

"KELLY SAT ON THE SOFA, waiting for Piper to finish taking the order. She grinned like a kid who'd won a dare. Piper speculated it had something to do with Sawyer. Another call came in. She put the first one on hold to answer it.

"Piper, there's a man answering your phone. What happened? Was it stolen?" Her mother's anxiety slipped out of the earpiece. Piper hadn't wanted to worry her, but she was still miffed about Justin. Someone blabbed how to get hold of her. Fletcher begged off, and that left Mom.

"This is the business line, Mother," she said curtly. "My phone is my phone and my number hasn't changed, only the voicemail message."

"But why, dear? You scared me."

"Because Justin has it."

"No. How?" she squeaked out the question.

"Someone gave him my number—that's how." Piper remembered the client on the other line. "I need to get back to work."

She finished up the order and blew out a long breath. Kelly waited, drumming her fingers on the arm of the chair.

"What?" Piper asked.

Kelly grinned. "I have an idea. Let's go down to Nockerville and go dancing. There's this cute place with karaoke. Under the Table has awesome wings, and it's always a great time."

"You want to sing?" Piper quirked an eyebrow.

"Heck no, but it sure is fun to watch the drunk people try." Kelly giggled.

"Okay, I'm in. Next question. Girls' night or dates?"

"Girls' night. I'm about done with men." A sad look passed, but a smile broke out a second later.

"Sounds great." Piper hadn't visited the neighboring town yet, plus she'd help Kelly forget Sawyer.

In front of her, Kelly pushed open the door to Under the Table, a waft of stale beer and fried food meeting her nose. Flat screen TVs and beer paraphernalia hung on the brick walls. Piper found an empty booth along one side, and the dark green vinyl seat squeaked as she slid over it. They ordered an appetizer and beer. As Piper sipped, she glanced around the sports bar. A woman, surrounded by her goofy friends doing backup motions, sung her heart out. Too bad she was off key.

"The karaoke stage doubles as a dance floor," Kelly said, pointing to the rear wall. "They'll give our ears a break soon and turn on music so people can dance. Do you like to dance?"

"Sure," Piper said with a smile. She used to love to go clubbing.

When the karaoke intermission came, the singer reluctantly returned to her table and dancers started two stepping around the dance floor. Kelly accepted an offer to dance. She and her partner knew how to move.

Piper watched in amazement. She could sway to the beat, but remembering steps was another thing, and so was playing follow the leader. She sighed, closed her eyes and tapped her feet to the music. Piper drained her glass and ordered another. Twice cowboys asked her to dance, but she begged off. They moved on to other women eager for a man's hand. Couples bumped and moved together during slow songs.

Piper studied the pub. A group of women celebrating a birthday took up three tables. They laughed and drank like fish. There were two groups of men doing the same although they hung out near the pool tables and dartboards. Basketball played on all eight of the flat screens. Cheers erupted when a team did well.

Stools ran the length of the horseshoe-shaped bar. Tall tables surrounded it, allowing people to stand. Men sat alone nursing drinks at the bar. A tubby man downed glass after glass of a clear liquid. Another sat with a longneck bottle and observed, like her. With his straight shoulders and short hair, Piper guessed he was military. He was guy-next-door cute with sandy brown hair and light eyes. His gaze flicked from televised game, to pretty girls, to a group of loudmouthed guys. The group must have brought him some amusement because his lips quirked into a smile.

Pulled to the dance floor again, Kelly grinned. She'd wanted to forget Sawyer and dance her blues away. "Sawyer won't commit," she'd said, while looking down at her hands. "We've been dating for months. You'd think he'd know by now." She looked up at Piper. "No sense wasting time on a dead-end."

Piper understood dead-ends. She had her own to contend with. Like an alley in a horror movie with high walls and a menacing stalker watching her every move, there was no way out. She emptied the second bottle. Piper promised Cole she'd keep the kryptonite in check.

She glanced at the screen on her phone. One missed call from Justin and no messages. Cole's voice had stopped the onslaught of calls. She chuckled, remembering the voice male message: "Leave a message and I'll call you back. If you can't leave a message, that's rude so please take me off your list or don't call back. Ever."

Another round of karaoke started. A Dolly Parton imitator monopolized the mic for three songs. She wasn't bad, but she wasn't Dolly.

Piper visited the restroom, but on the way back a text from Cole distracted her. He was playing pool with Sawyer and Josiah at Hammered. According to Cole, Kelly turning Sawyer down for a date caused him to lose a game.

Piper walked through the bar, avoiding the dancers. A freckled-face cowboy grabbed her arm. He held her gently while his buddy pleaded, "Have a heart, miss, and help a guy out."

The dark-haired man held four bottles of beer, two in each hand palm up. He blushed and grinned sheepishly. With two guys on the left side and another on the right, he had plenty of help.

"Ask your friends," Piper said as she turned to leave, catching the eye of the observant military man. His brow dipped with concern.

"They want me to lose the bet and won't help, but you can. Please." The guy turned on a high wattage smile. "I can't put my arms down or I'll lose."

What a moron. She was intrigued even though she didn't approve of his poor judgment.

Cole

"Hey, Cole, where's your Russian bride?" Sawyer called across Hammered.

Cole ignored him. He ate the Fortuna fish special and kept reading. Sawyer laughed.

Cole would have liked to flip more than the page on his book, but Hammered was a family establishment. There were kids present, so he brooded quietly. He would like to confront that ornery old woman who had started the rumor. But would he strangle her or hug her? The jury was out on that.

Josiah and Sawyer were playing pool, and it was obvious Sawyer was in a foul mood. He tried to mask it with pseudo funny quips. It appeared that Josiah had the upper hand. Curiosity got the better of him and Cole finally moseyed over to the table. "What's going on?"

"Your wife, that's what," Sawyer spat. He stomped to the other side and jerked his stick up.

A smile crept to Cole's lips. Piper wasn't his wife, yet everyone liked to believe it. It made his heart trip a couple beats. "My wife, huh?"

Josiah chuckled. "I know. You don't have one, but it's her fault."

"What'd she do?"

Sawyer scratched sending the cue into a pocket. "She took Kelly out dancing."

The crime of the century. Cole's eyebrows lifted. "I don't think she's that type of girl."

"They're having a girls' night out," Josiah said. "Kelly broke up with him. Again."

"Oh."

"Yeah, oh." Sawyer rubbed his face. "She's hanging out with other single women."

"My wife?"

"Drinking and dancing with other men. Maybe singing karaoke, but having fun without me." He sat on the edge of the pool table, staring off into nowhere.

"Piper isn't dancing," Cole offered. He'd been in contact with her throughout the evening. Sawyer was right about Kelly. Piper reported Kelly having fun dancing, but Cole was more worried about Piper and the influence of kryptonite. He'd texted her about her intake.

"I don't blame Kelly for moving on," Josiah admitted in a low voice. Lifelong friends, Josiah knew Sawyer better than most, but even he felt sympathy for poor Kelly. "She wants to find love and settle down. She deserves to have her heart's desire. Kelly is a nice girl. Too nice for this bum."

"If he's so upset, he should go after her," Cole said.

"He's too stubborn."

"Until he reigns in that pride, he'll be a lonely man." Cole watched as Sawyer switched from sullen ex-boyfriend to flirting playboy as a group of women walked past. He tipped an imaginary hat, making them giggle.

The phone in Cole's pocket vibrated. He pulled it out and read "Just two, Dad," Piper added a winky face. He sighed with relief and replied. They had a short one-sentence texting volley, making him smile.

Josiah made his move, taking advantage of Sawyer's manic mood swings. The women returned from the jukebox and passed again. This time Sawyer ignored them while nursing his beer, but Cole offered a friendly smile. After they passed one said, "Did you see that smile on Cole's face?"

"I've never seen him like that."

"It must be his new wife." Together women sighed an "Aww."
Cole's face heated, but he was happier than he'd been in a while. Was it Piper or life in general? He reflected back to a few years before the hospital and chemo. The loneliness.

Cole glanced at his phone. Lost in thought, he'd missed a text from Piper. His face paled. "What the hell?"

Piper

Unaware of local Texas pranks, traditions or dares, Piper wondered about the nature of the bet. She and Fletcher had their share of dares growing up, each pushing to get away with things behind their parents' back. A favorite was running barefoot around the house outside in the snow. But these guys were like college hooligans trying to impress girls.

"What do you win?" Piper asked the man holding the bottles.

He closed his eyes and sighed. "Twenty from each."

"Sixty bucks. What do you have to do?" She glanced at the others. They grinned. Tweedledee and Tweedledum on the left wore plaid shirts, were skinny, and with baby faces, looked barely twenty-one. One elbowed the other.

"I have to hold these bottles up for the rest of the night," the poor sucker lamented.

"Looks like you can handle it." His defined arms might be sore the next day, but he'd live.

"I don't need help with the bottles. It's something else," he admitted. He blushed and glanced away.

"His barn door's open," Freckles said. The other two laughed.

Piper's gaze dropped to the bottle-boy's crotch. Sure enough, the zipper was down. A smile tweaked the corners of her lips. What a predicament. He couldn't fix the situation with bottles in his hands and his buddies had no intention of helping. He had two choices: go through the night with a breeze blowing in the barn door or ask a stranger for help.

"Some friends you have," she teased.

"Can you help?"

Why not? Piper chuckled, imagining what she'd tell Kelly. She got to play with a cute, but stupid, guy's zipper. She glanced over at the military man. He regarded the situation with a wary eye. Piper swallowed what nervousness she had. What could go wrong in a room full of people?

She shrugged. "Sure."

"You are awesome." He grinned and thrust his pelvis in her direction. Thank God the man wore khakis and not tight jeans. She tugged the zipper's slide. It wouldn't budge. She took a step closer and yanked again.

"It's stuck."

"Please, Miss, don't give up. You can do it." His friends continued to laugh at the dilemma. His brows dipped together. "Can you see what it's caught on?" His tone nearly begged.

She sighed and stepped back. She didn't want to get up close and personal with his junk. What if the zipper had snagged his boxers? Or worse? He'd probably be screaming. Standing, she couldn't tell what was wrong with the pants. She inspected the other patrons. No one besides the man at the bar paid them any mind. Fine, but this was the last time she stopped to help a guy surrounded by friends. She leaned to inspect the material. It revealed nothing. She'd have to get closer. She was in a dress so bending over was out of the question, but the guy at the bar probably wouldn't mind the view. Kneeling on the hardwood floor wasn't appealing either. She knelt on one knee. The man went commando. She glowered up at him. That was when she discovered his triumphant expression. Crap. She'd been played. Freckles put a palm on the back of her head and pressed her face into the bottle-boy's crotch. Nasty, and, oh, so wrong.

Pissed, Piper stood, and pushed against the jerk's chest, making him step backward and hit a table. The bottles wobbled but none fell. He cursed. The man at the bar stood, but she put up a hand to stop him. These punks picked the wrong girl to play. She poked the bottle-boy in the chest. She was tempted to knee him in the groin just to see where the bottles would land.

"Back off, honey," Tweedledum said.

"It was all a joke," Tweedledee said. Neither appeared apologetic.

"Sexual harassment is not a joke," Piper said. She whirled around, but Freckles grabbed her wrist. He yanked her back around to face them.

Big mistake.

The man at the bar grinned and leaned back to watch the show. He'd be backup if she needed it.

Piper jerked her hand out of the man's grasp but hit the bottle-boy's arm, sending two longnecks flying into the chest of Tweedledee and Tweedledum. The open bottles splashed down their fronts. Set off balance, the other bottles tipped, even though the bottle-boy tried holding onto them. The beer spilled on the freckled loser's boots. Cussing, he jumped at her. She laughed and hopped out of his reach.

Karma. Poetic justice. They'd all paid a price.

Piper meandered back to her seat and sat down with a clueless Kelly. Seconds later a waitress dropped off a drink for Piper. She hadn't ordered it. "It's from the guy over there," the waitress said, pointing to the bar.

The military man smiled and raised his bottle in salute. Grinning, she nodded and raised the hard cider. *Cheers.*

CHAPTER 8

Cole

"SO, PIPER?" COLE PROMPTED.

Kelly had insisted they meet to talk. Her eyes skittered around Stitts' while she sipped her iced tea. He smiled and reached to pat her hand. She drew back.

"Piper was awesome. She handled those drunken men like an expert. I think she would have kicked their hides if that man hadn't stepped in and sent them on their way," she said, brushing a stray auburn hair out of her face.

"Oh, yeah?" Cole casually asked. He focused on his coffee mug. His insides twisted in anxiety.

"Four men, Cole. She was ready to take on four men. God, it was crazy. It all happened so fast." Kelly shook her head and chuckled. She recited the story with great excitement.

When the cider had arrived, Piper reported the prank to Kelly, spilling all the details. They'd left after eleven. On the way to the car, the man who'd lost the bet pulled Piper aside. His cronies stood next to him. Piper didn't give him a moment. She jerked away yelling, "Get your hands off me, you perverted bastard."

The man mistakenly responded in anger. She kneed him in the groin, and while he was doubled over, she grabbed his hand, flipping him on his back. He landed on the blacktop with the wind knocked out of him. "His friends weren't happy, but Piper was as cool as a cucumber. A freckled guy moved to grab her, but another patron stopped him and offered to stop the

42

madness—Dakota Redd." Kelly sighed dreamily. "He has huge arm muscles and a spiky haircut. Piper swore he was military, and she was right. He used to be an Army Ranger but isn't active duty anymore." Kelly hinted that Piper's tough-girl attitude and her ability to stand up to trouble had impressed Dakota.

The Chicago native could take on four Texan bad-boys, yet trembled and was unable to answer the phone to tell off her ex in another state. *Interesting.*

"Next time she goes, let me know, will ya? Dakota might not always be available to watch her back." Cole smiled. Kelly agreed with a nod.

After Kelly left, he picked a new book from the shelf. Flipping the cover open, he checked the initials. Brad, Josiah, and Arlon had already read it. The retro cover and yellowed edges betrayed the age of the book. The novel sucked him in, causing him to lose track of time.

Piper

The March morning sky was an intoxicating shade of blue that an artist would have a hard time copying. Piper waited for the Barnes family on the front lawn of the church. She nodded, smiled, and chatted with people as they passed.

Ms. Hardmann approached her with a sweet smile. She looked the part of an innocent grandmother in her pale pink dress, white gloves, and hat with a pink bow. For all her orneriness, Ms. Hardmann was a classy lady. Her makeup was tasteful, unlike the chubby woman in the mint-green polyester skirt suit standing within earshot.

"Where's your husband?" Ms. Hardmann teased. The elderly bitty was a sly, old fox.

Piper sighed and barely kept from rolling her eyes. Coincidently, the Dart family pulled into the parking lot. "Parking the car," she said with a smile.

"Piper!" Beau screamed as he ran to her. The whole congregation turned and watched as she scooped up the running boy and spun him in a giggling hug.

"Don't you look handsome," she said.

The boy blushed, pulling on the collar of his blue polo shirt. "Thanks." He gazed at her with big blue eyes. "Your dress is pretty. I like sunflowers, but they stink. I wish they smelled good."

Flo and Cole walked toward them.

"I don't stink, do I?" she asked. Cole and Flo exchanged a look.

Beau laughed and shook his head. "No, silly-willy." He ran off and greeted a friend. Beau and the other boy ran around the sidewalks.

"What was that about?" Flo asked. The white pumps added a few inches to her height. Friends greeted her before Piper answered.

Cole's blue dress shirt brought out the color of his eyes, but the cowboy hat hid them in a shadow. A yellow tie with cobalt blue diamonds and khakis that fit as well as his jeans completed his ensemble.

"Hey, Piper," Beau yelled as he plowed into her legs. "Are you going to marry Cole?" His lips bowed into a frown.

"My Grandma says they're already married," said a blond boy who appeared next to Cole. He smiled at the astounded adults with a gap-toothed grin.

Beau frowned as he glanced between Piper and his uncle. She swallowed as a hush fell around them. Piper took a step closer to Cole and touched his arm.

"Did you cantaloupe?" Beau asked with a furrowed brow.

Cole and Piper exchanged a smile. He shifted and stuffed his hands into his pockets. "No, buddy, we didn't elope. We aren't married."

"But why not?" Beau pouted.

"Why do you want us married?" Piper asked. The kid harped on it every time she saw him at church or anywhere else. He must have heard more than one person mention it. The rumor wasn't funny if it would hurt Beau.

"I want an aunt," he said, staring at his brown shoes. "And I picked you."

"I think that's Cole's decision," his grandmother chided.

"I know, Nana." He glanced up, eyes filled with tears. "But I like Piper and Cole likes her too. *I know it.* He said so."

Cole turned bright red.

Piper sat so she was eye level with Beau. "Listen, Sweetie. I like you too. You're just the kind of boy I'd pick for my nephew."

"I am?" He wiped his face then smiled and hugged her neck. "Does that mean you're gonna marry Cole someday?"

Piper smiled sadly. A year ago, she'd planned a wedding and had a father to walk her down the aisle. Marriage wasn't in the future; at least, she didn't think it was. Her wounded heart skittered at the thought. "I don't know if I'll ever get married," she murmured softly. Flo gasped at the declaration.

"That's what Cole says too," Beau huffed, throwing his hands up. He stomped off.

Piper was never happier to see Jessie and Josiah Barnes. She waved and linked arms with Jessie as they strode into the sanctuary.

Sitting next to the Barnes, Piper felt at peace in the small church. The small white clapboard building could grace a Christmas card. The inside had blood red carpet, tan walls, and oak pews. A group of older women, widowed or single, including Ms. Hardmann, sat in the front row. Jessie leaned close and whispered, "Watch out for them." She covertly pointed to the women. "Ms. Deeds and Ms. Terchance are the worse for gossiping. They probably pray you're Russian."

"Aren't you gossiping about them?" Piper whispered back. She met Jessie's gaze, and they giggled. Josiah nudged his wife's knee. Piper had to train her eyes elsewhere to keep from laughing out loud.

Sawyer sat with another man, B.J. Johnson. Piper recognized him from dropping off books at Hammered. He was handsome with dark eyes and hair. Sawyer kept stealing glances at the Greene family, especially Kelly. She looked stunning in a lime colored skirt suit. The smile Kelly wore was authentic.

In church, Piper knew she should focus on getting her heart right with God, but she hoped he'd forgive her for trying to understand Cole's heart. He'd told his nephew he'd never marry enough times that the poor kid had become obsessed with reversing the notion. She had a reason to never marry, but what was Cole's? Is that why people easily believed he'd marry a foreigner instead of a local girl? It was possible. His father had left and his sister abandoned her child. Maybe he didn't trust any relationships.

He didn't want to get married. Neither did she. It was perfect, except she kept dreaming of his hands running over her body. She took a deep breath to calm her racing heart.

She turned slightly and glanced behind Sawyer to where Flo and Cole sat with heads bowed in prayer. Elbows on his knees, he'd removed the hat but still wore a bandanna. His eyes popped open as if he sensed her inspection. She froze and closed her eyes, praying he hadn't noticed.

After church, Piper stood with the Barnes talking. "Is there a good park for jogging?" she asked.

"I know a place," Cole said, butting in before Jessie could answer.

"Where?" Piper smiled when his cheeks turned pink.

"I could show you." He shrugged. "Would you mind some company?"

Piper crossed her arms, inspecting him. The red reached his ears. "You don't want to be bottled up in the car with a little boy bound and determined to marry you off?"

Josiah nudged Cole in the ribs. His lips lifted into a grin, and he nodded. "I'll take you to a park with a looping trail and you get me away from Beau's interrogation. It's a win-win. What do you say?"

She tapped her chin as she scanned him from head to toe. "Are you going to run with me?"

"Not in my good boots." Cole shifted from side to side.

"What are you going to do while I run?"

"Read."

"Really? You brought a book with you?"

"We can stop and get a bite to eat. Just about everyplace has books available—you know that. But I have one in the truck. I'll grab it and meet you at your car." He pivoted and met his mother at the vehicle. As Flo opened the door, Cole reached in. After a brief conversation he nodded. He met Piper at her car with a smile.

They found a picnic table under the shade of a large oak. Stanton Cove Park had a two-mile trail encircling a small lake. A decent breeze coupled with the shade made for a relaxing temperature. After lunch, she picked up the trash and returned to the car.

"Are you going to run in your church clothes?" Cole asked, following her.

She glanced at the dress, and then lifted a smile to him. "I came prepared." She opened the backdoor and reached in for white running shoes. One at a time, she exchanged her sandals for the athletic shoes and threw them into the car. Unzipping the dress, it fell to her feet. She tossed it in the back seat and closed the door. She stood in a sports bra and running shorts.

"Close your mouth, Cole. I told you, I came prepared." Heat crept from her gut to her face. She rolled her shoulders.

His face flared red, but he nodded.

"I'm going to run the loop. Are you sure you want to stay? I don't mind driving you somewhere first."

"I told you, I'll catch up on my reading." Cole waved her off. "Go on. I'll be here when you return."

She strapped her phone onto her arm, put in earbuds and played Shania Twain. Piper blamed Jessie for her newfound interest in country music. A quick glance back at Cole had her wishing she hadn't looked. He'd unbuttoned his dress shirt. The temperature of the spring day suddenly rose to summer. She fixed her eyes on the pavement, stretched and took off.

Finding a pace, she studied the park. The flat tree-lined trail followed the shore of an odd shaped lake. A few bridges spanned small bays. She waved at children and fishermen. Sweat trickled down her back. She tossed an empty water bottle into a recycling bin as she passed.

Even though she enjoyed running, she hadn't gone since Justin began stalking her. He knew the places and routes she liked to follow. She balled her fists, pumping her arms faster. Thank God he wasn't in Texas.

The yoga she got in three or four mornings a week, and the occasional horseback ride, weren't calorie burners like running. But she loved rising with the sun and stretching on the porch or lawn of the Big Deal's homestead cabin. Brad Davidson had offered to let her take a mare out on the trails and she took advantage of his generosity once a week.

Coming to the end of the circle, she spotted her car in the distance. Cole was stretched out on the hood, leaning back against the windshield with one arm bent under his head. He no longer wore his long-sleeve shirt, socks or shoes.

As she approached, it hit her again. The attraction to his long, firm body pulled her, like a magnet. The white T-shirt stretched tight across his broad, muscled chest. His hat shadowed his light eyes as they followed the words on the page.

It's a sin that a man could be this beautiful. She slowed to enjoy the view.

He moved his arm to turn a page and spotted her. Grinning, he reached to the side then offered her a water bottle as she approached.

"Thanks." Piper took the cool bottle and placed it against the skin on her chest and neck. The condensation helped the breeze cool her. She twisted off the cap and chugged. Her thirst quenched, she licked her lips.

Wide-eyed, he stared. One corner of his lips tipped in a grin. She glanced at the bottle. "Oh, was this yours?"

"No. It was for you."

"Thank you." Piper took a few breaths. Her legs and abs burned, but it felt good. "Would you mind if I make another loop?"

He grinned again. "That's perfect. I'm getting to the exciting part."

"Oh. The hero and heroine are hopping in the sack, huh?"

Cole sputtered, but she waved and turned toward the path. When she glanced back, she caught the man not interested in marriage watching her backside. Warmth spread through her, and she giggled.

CHAPTER 9

Cole

IT HAD TAKEN LITTLE TO convince Sawyer to join Cole on a spy mission to Under the Table. They'd been there an hour, and so far, Piper and Kelly were a no show. They may have gone to Hammered instead. Some might call the uncomfortable high wood backed booths cozy, but Cole felt enclosed and imprisoned, especially, with the karaoke singers torturing them. Waterboarding might be more pleasant than listening to the fat man serenade his date.

"He must really love her to make such a fool of himself," Sawyer said.

Sawyer chewed his bottom lip as he inspected the patrons of the bar. Disappointment showed in his eyes. Slouched over nursing a beer, he didn't resemble the usual confident playboy. They talked basketball, then rated the singer with a negative number for talent but double digits for bravery.

"He's going to get lucky tonight," Sawyer mused.

"Probably. If she had any doubt about her beau's love when she entered the building, it's now exorcised—along with my hearing," Cole said, chuckling.

Sawyer shifted and frowned, catching Cole's attention. Across the tavern, he witnessed Kelly laughing as she greeted a shorthaired man sitting at the bar. The tall, muscular man must be Dakota Redd. Kelly wore a denim skirt with a red bandanna ruffle around the bottom, a red tank top and shiny boots. A thick braid of auburn hair hung over her right shoulder. As she smiled, a blush crossed her cheeks. Dakota's hand held another that did not belong to Kelly. Cole recognized admiration in Dakota's eyes. Acid churned in his gut, knowing Dakota had been Piper's backup.

"You have competition," Sawyer said. He whistled long. "Damn, Piper cleans up well. I might have to—"

"No, you don't."

Sawyer snapped his head around, wearing an ornery grin. Cole fumed: he'd fallen for it. He turned back toward the girls just as Kelly shifted and another man moved, giving him a clear view of Piper. His breath caught. The tight jeans accentuated her long legs, leaving little to the imagination and her top... He swallowed and whistled low like Sawyer.

"I told you," Sawyer said with a grin. He folded his arms and leaned back wearing a smug smile.

In rippling shades of green, Piper's sleeveless shirt changed color as she moved. The rounded front dipped low, revealing more cleavage than he thought she had. He paused there, shocked. He yanked his gaze to her face and found makeup highlighting her features. Not that she needed it, but still, wow. Her straightened light hair hung loosely over her shoulders. Strappy sandals adorned her feet. She laughed at the other man, then leaned in to hug him. Dakota placed a quick kiss on Piper's cheek, and she glanced away, blushing.

A fire lit in Cole's stomach. It burned like acid. He needed to breathe but found it near impossible because he couldn't tear his gaze away.

Kelly pulled them away from the bar. She jerked to a halt when she spied Sawyer grinning as if she'd caught him doing something naughty. Piper bumped into Kelly's back.

Piper

Piper gasped and held on to Kelly's arm so she wouldn't fall. She took in the men's faces. Cole wore a sheepish grin. "Kelly," Piper whispered. "What are they doing here?"

"Um, I might've mentioned our plans," Kelly said, biting her lip.

Sawyer slid out of the booth and took Kelly's hands. "Hello, beautiful." He pecked her cheek and she blushed.

Piper slid in next to Cole. "Evenin'," he greeted.

Piper sighed. "What are you doing here?"

"Having a beer," Cole said.

Heat radiated off his body, but Dakota's cologne lingered. A smiling waitress lowered two hard ciders to the table. "For the ladies, from

Dakota." She tilted her head. Dakota sat at the bar again. He saluted Piper when she glanced at him.

Sawyer frowned but motioned for Kelly to sit, then he slid into the booth next to her. She waved at Dakota. The girls clinked the amber bottles together and took a long drink. "Look at that," Sawyer proclaimed. "They've only been here five minutes, and they get free drinks. It's hardly fair." He glanced at Cole.

"Come on, man. You know we're not as pretty," Cole reminded him.

"No. You're right." Sawyer's grin widened. "We're prettier." Kelly elbowed him.

Halfway through the cider a hand appeared in front of Piper's face. She twisted to see Dakota standing with a confident smile. "Care to dance?" he asked. His sandy hair glinted in the backlight.

Piper swallowed. "Like that?" She pointed to the crowded dance floor. The couples two-stepped around. She grimaced with intimidation. "I, um."

"You might as well learn," Kelly prompted, crossing her arms.

Fear balled in her gut as she glanced at Cole. "I can't dance," she whispered.

He gently pushed her out of the comfort of the seat. "I'll rescue you if you need rescuing." He grinned, but it didn't reach his eyes.

"You all right?" Piper asked. Cole nodded, failing to make a move toward her. Taking the hint, she inhaled a deep breath and grabbed Dakota's hand, allowing him to pull her up. Her poor heart. She wanted to learn to dance, but Cole had pushed her away and it hurt.

"Just so you know, I'm a virgin," she told Dakota, but the declaration was loud.

Kelly giggled, Cole gasped, and Sawyer could have given himself whiplash. Dakota grinned and stopped in his tracks. "Pardon?"

"I'm a two-step dancing virgin. Please be gentle," she pleaded.

Dakota's smile grew. "No way, darlin'," he said and tugged on her arm with determination. Piper's heart sped up, and she glanced back at her friends. Dakota took her right hand in his left then placed his right on her hip. She touched his shoulder with her left. "Take a deep breath. This is going to be fun."

"I'm not good at memorizing steps," she admitted.

"Relax. Soon it will be like breathing, you won't even realize you're dancing." He squeezed her hand. "Step up onto my boots. It won't hurt." It took a minute for Dakota to talk her into it. They circled the dance floor while she rode his feet. She learned the rhythm, then found the confidence to try. He kept it simple, and they danced and talked for a few songs.

She liked Dakota. Her gut told her Cole and Dakota would get along, but she'd hate to facilitate a blossoming relationship because she couldn't handle having two hot guys as besties.

"Tell me about your friends," Dakota said. He seemed interested in her relationship with Cole, but she talked more about Kelly and Sawyer's sporadic love life. She glanced over at the table. Cole had ventured to the bar, but every time she checked he was watching them. Kelly and Sawyer remained at the table, conversing.

A slow song played and Dakota pulled Piper closer. Her hands circled his neck. His hair was soft. Cole tapped Dakota, and he stepped back, but Piper quickly grabbed his wrist and whispered a favor. He nodded and walked away.

Cole stepped in and held her close. She breathed in his scent. Her heart raced as she smiled up at him.

Cole

Cole couldn't stand by any longer. He took a deep breath and stepped onto the dance floor. Piper's fingers reached around Dakota's neck, and she played with the man's hair. Cole tapped Dakota's shoulder. Dakota released her, but not before Piper whispered something in his ear to earn a smile. Dakota nodded and retreated. Jealousy nagged at him. He should have been the one to teach her to dance.

"Took you long enough," she mumbled.

Yeah. Cole had stewed, watching the other man touch Piper and make her smile. He'd tried to mask his feelings, but it hadn't fooled Kelly who asked, "Why didn't you dance with her, Cole?"

He'd shrugged and fingered the smooth glass of the beer bottle, pretending to be interested in the calories and ingredients. Cole hadn't danced since before the cancer. He hadn't wanted to appear the fool in front of everyone, especially Piper.

"I figure, I'd let him teach her then I'll take over. It will save my feet." He'd gestured to the couple on the dance floor. "I don't want to ruin my boots."

Kelly smiled sweetly at the scene. She'd propped an elbow on the table, her chin rested in her palm as she watched. A sigh caught her lips. "He likes her."

"Yeah, we can tell," Sawyer said, rolling his eyes behind her back.

"He's cute." Her gaze dropped to Dakota's backside. "I think he likes her strength."

"She's a girl," Sawyer said with disbelief.

"But she's strong." Kelly turned to them. "She can handle anything. You should have seen her. Four men were going to, I don't know, menace her, but she put them in their place. Dakota was there, but he didn't lift a finger. It was like he knew she didn't need help. It was strange the way those two communicated without words, like they had a connection."

Cole's teeth had clenched at the thought of Dakota standing idly by. Those goons might have hurt Piper.

"Piper didn't want help. She gave Dakota a look that made him freeze in his boots. Seriously, she was like a super hero. It was weird. I really didn't know Piper before that night."

"But now?" Cole asked.

Kelly grinned. "I'm learning."

Sawyer had wanted details. Kelly started in about the four punks and the prank.

Cole couldn't bear to hear the story again. He'd walked around trying to shrug off the angst. Circling the pool tables on the lookout for the jerks, he'd kept tabs on Piper, acknowledging Dakota could keep her safe.

The protective instinct for his family wasn't foreign, but its ferocity for Piper surprised him. It began when the ex-fiancé found her number and harassed her again. The horror on Piper's face when she realized Justin found her new number magnified Cole's desire to protect her. If he was honest with himself, the feeling had sprung to life when Ms. Hardmann announced his mail-order bride.

Piper deserved to live a long, happy life with someone who loved her. He couldn't be that someone, but thinking Dakota might have the opportunity made Cole mad.

He pulled Piper close to finish the song, closer than Dakota had held her. She snuggled into his chest with a sigh. He smiled like a fool and glanced around the room. Dakota talked to Kelly and Sawyer was as red as a ripe tomato. Kelly took Dakota's hand, and they returned to the dance floor.

Cole nudged Piper. "Kelly is dancing with Dakota," he spoke next to her ear, and she shivered. Piper's eyes remained closed, and she acknowledged him with a small nod.

After a few laps around the dance floor, Cole added spins and other moves. Nothing too fancy and nothing other couples weren't doing. Piper faced away from him. Her backside rubbed against his legs, so he spun her to put distance between their bodies. Piper's bright eyes gazed into his and he spun her again. Her eyes were harder to handle than having her rear rub against him. When he was about to explode, he turned her to face him once more. She smiled up at him.

"Do you like the view?" she teased. "I wish I could watch you wiggle." She winked.

A smile tugged at the corner of his mouth. Granting her wish, he twisted in her arms so his backside faced her. Her small hand on his hip seeped warmth through his shirt. He gave a wiggle for her pleasure and she fisted his shirt in response.

Did she like it or was it awkward to dance this way?

Cole glanced at the walls trying to find a mirrored beer sign. When he found one, it exposed her gaze, locked on his butt as if hypnotized. His heart jackhammered in his chest. He hadn't expected the way she affected him. Longing went straight to his groin. To hide the sudden tightness of his jeans, Cole turned around. She continued to stare, witnessing his arousal. She blushed, but didn't pull her gaze away. Dang, if he didn't want her more.

When she glanced up, he pulled her hard against him. She gasped, her face blazing red, grinned a tight-lipped smile, but didn't push him away. Her chest heaved rapidly as her body continued to rub against his.

The other dancers circled them. Sawyer passed with Kelly, and she giggled. Her skirt flared. Dakota had returned to the bar, surveying them with a pensive face. Dakota stiffened and frowned as his attention jumped to a young man with a passel of friends. Cole shifted to get a better look.

Cole needed to keep Piper away from those shysters. As if thoughts of pounding his face drew his attention, the man glanced over at the dancers, honing in on Piper. He leered and elbowed another man. They laughed, then glanced around, finding Dakota. They turned back to the flat screen.

Anger flared as lust dropped. Cole took a deep breath. It took all his control not to leave Piper.

"Don't worry, Cole. I'll protect you. Those guys are nothing." Piper nodded in the men's direction.

Stunned, he pulled her tighter. Leaning close, he sniffed in the fruity scent of her shampoo. "You smell good."

"So do you." She buried her nose in his shirt.

Cole raised an eyebrow; he'd been in the bar a good long time. "That's better than stinking," he laughed.

She laughed too. "You smell like soap, clean laundry and..." she paused.

"And?"

Piper sighed. "You."

"Me?"

"You know, manly," she whispered.

"Manly? Whew, that's good." He grinned when she slugged him in the arm. "Your scent is girly. Like..." Apples or strawberries and something else. "Your hair smells like summer. Like a meadow after the rain, or watching the sun set with the wind rolling over the field." He loved his job on the prairie. He enjoyed holding Piper in his arms, and her staring into his eyes.

"Do you notice anything different about me?" She gazed up expectedly.

A loaded question. He searched her face and looked at her jewelry. She'd put makeup on. His eyes dropped to her cleavage. "You have a new shirt?"

Her lips quirked into a half-smile. She shifted in his arms. "Well, kind of." Piper glanced around, then leaned close. "I'm wearing something Jessie made."

Cole's brows rose in surprise. Not that she wouldn't be privy to such things, working for an intimate apparel business and all, but the fact that she'd admit she wore the fancy undies... His gaze fell to her cleavage again.

"It's a demi-bra, you know, a push-up bra." Her gaze met his. "It works wonders."

Cole's mouth dropped open in defense of her body, but she hurried on.

"It feels awesome. Actually, it feels like I'm not wearing anything at all." Piper's eyes darted around again, then she tugged on the sleeve, exposing a delicate looking bra strap. "Feel it," she ordered.

He couldn't refuse, although he knew his blood pressure would rise. He touched it, expecting the emerald green lace to be stiff, but it was supple like her skin. "It's soft," he said, "and pretty."

"I'll show it to you later. The workmanship will amaze you. Jessie gave it to me as a thank you gift for modeling. God, I hated that, but it was worth it to get this matching set." She grinned. "I know she'll ask me all about it."

"You'll show me?" Cole's gaze raked her body and a smug grin eased onto his lips.

"Someday, when I'm not in it."

Cole pouted, making Piper giggle and playfully slap him on the arm.

CHAPTER 10

Piper

PIPER SAT ACROSS FROM KELLY and Sawyer. An awkward silence had formed between the couple. Kelly was ready to move on, but continued to harbor feelings for him. Sawyer's boisterous attempts at humor fell flat and Kelly kept checking her phone.

Next to Piper, Cole sat still. He didn't flirt or touch her. The intimacy experienced while dancing had evaporated into thin air. When Dakota's second bottle of hard cider hit the table, she saluted him across the bar. Piper smiled at the welcome break from the insecure thoughts about Cole.

The conversation, originally aimed at Sawyer, turned into why Piper ended up in Texas. "It was pure luck my mom stumbled across a boutique selling Double D Intimates while honeymooning in Dallas. So I didn't come to Fortuna to find love," she mumbled.

Kelly and Sawyer exchanged a look. Kelly rested both elbows on the table and placed her chin in her palms. Her gaze flitted between Cole and Piper.

Piper sat up. Oh, hell, no. "I didn't come to Texas to find love," she said with a frown. She glanced at Cole, but he shrugged. "I came for a job. My family says I ran away, and that might be true. I found a job and a new start, so I took a deep breath and jumped in with two feet. I wouldn't move anywhere for a man. Nope. So don't get any wrong ideas. I wasn't a mail-order bride, nor did I meet anyone on some Internet dating site. I doubt I'd know love if it hit me smack on the head, but," she stared at the wood grain on the lacquered table, "I learned what it isn't."

Piper pushed back against the wood seat and Cole's arm draped over her shoulder, his warm arm supporting her neck.

The aftermath of her and Justin's relationship had been the lowest point of her life. Time to start over and, maybe, that included finding love.

Dakota seemed interested in her. She could date him. And Matt Barnes asked her out every time he saw her. He was cute, but way too young. None of the other men she'd met got her blood pumping like Cole Dart. Strong and masculine, yet sweet and beautiful; Cole adored cheesy romance novels. The tough cowboy loved his family. Crunchy outside. Gooey inside.

Cole was protective to all those in his circle, including her. He glared at Dakota when he thought she wasn't looking.

She scooted closer to Cole. They fit together. He dropped his arm, trapping her, and she sighed.

Did she want another man in her life? Some day. Did Cole want a relationship? No, but sex was okay. Thinking of doing the horizontal tango with Cole sent a shiver down her spine. He must have felt it because he tilted his head and stared at her. Her heart galloped. "So, read any good books lately?" she tossed into the night.

Kelly danced a few more times, but Piper's feet hurt. She tried to hide a yawn, but Dakota spotted it from across the room and smiled. Piper needed to move. A trip to the women's room was in order. Staring into the mirror, she studied the blonde with lonely eyes.

Piper had what her mother considered a boyish figure, while her father had regarded her as athletic. Basically, her torso was long and thin and her boobs pretty much nonexistent. Although she'd gained cleavage enhancement thanks to Jessie's creative genius.

She smiled as she adjusted an exposed bra strap. Cole wanted to see it. Again, her heart raced and cheeks heated. What was it about the cowboy that got her blood pumping? She didn't even know the color of his hair. He'd always hid it under the hat and bandanna.

Piper weaved between the higher bar tables seeking Dakota. She spotted the bottle-boy and freckled-face man too late. When bottle-boy opened his mouth to say something, she held up a finger and said "no." She walked past them, giving them a wide berth. She glanced around for Tweedledee and Tweedledum, the other minions, but didn't find them. Dakota raised a hand. Glad he had her back again, she continued forward. She reached the handsome man, and then pivoted toward her nemesis. He was staring while the freckled man whispered into his ear. He sneered and winked at her. She feigned boredom and yawned.

"He won't bother you here," Dakota said with certainty.

"I figured. He doesn't want to be humiliated by a woman again. Dakota," Piper said, gaining his full attention, "thank you for dancing with me and for the drinks. It was fun..." Her train of thought wandered as she caught Kelly and Sawyer duck out the front door.

"I need to go. See you." Piper left him standing with his mouth open. She navigated the tables toward the door. Kelly was her ride; she wouldn't leave with Sawyer, would she?

Scents of warm asphalt, earth, fauna, and a hint of barbecue from the restaurant down the street hung in the cool night air. The parking area was lit by two streetlights that emitted a warm orange glow. Past the first row of cars, leaning against a truck, Sawyer and Kelly embraced, their lips locked in a battle to dominate. Piper halted; the door closed behind her. Newcomers wanted into the bar so she stepped aside. Gravel crunched behind her and she turned.

Great. Just great. Bottle-boy had rallied six minions. She crossed her arms.

"Hey, babe. It's great to see you again." He elbowed his closest friend.

"It's nice to see that you wised up and haven't taken any stupid bets tonight." A few onlookers snickered.

"I thought you might want a second look at the goods." He grinned.

"You think? Wow. I'm impressed."

Behind the lackeys, Cole stood frowning. Tall and brooding, shoulders back, and hat shadowing his eyes, he appeared menacing and ready to plow through the crowd.

"I knew you were impressed. The ladies usually are." He put his hands on his hips.

Piper rolled her eyes. The guy was dense. "It wasn't the goods that impressed me. In fact, the goods are lacking as much as your brains." More snickers.

He put up one finger, but stopped as her words registered. "Hey, that's not cool."

"Neither is smashing your genitals into a strangers face, cretin. What do you want?" she asked.

"Well, you, of course." He reached for Piper.

"Not going to happen," Cole proclaimed as he pushed through the group to her side. His laser beam gaze could have fried the men into piles of ash.

His muscles wound tight under his shirt and his hands clenched. It wouldn't take much for Cole to pounce.

"He's wearing his 'you don't want to mess with me' face. I think you better heed it," Piper said.

"Come on, Tom. Let's leave the girl alone," a short chubby blond man said. He was young and eyed Cole with wary eyes. At least one of them had some smarts.

"No, I got this," Tom reassured. His confident grin had returned.

Seven punks against two. No, make that three. Dakota appeared on the edge, flanking the goons. His gaze flicked over Tom's groupies as he sized them up. Tom took a step toward her. Heat radiated off Cole's body. She only needed him to stand there. Over her shoulder she said, "I'm fine."

Tom reached for her again. She grabbed his hand and yanked. She leaned in, and he fell over her shoulder, landing on the ground. The stunned man sprawled on his back. She held onto his hand, twisting his wrist at an odd angle. He cried out and tried to move, but she twisted it tighter. Tom stilled, grimacing. Piper grinned at Cole, but he wasn't smiling.

"Ah, ah," Dakota said as he moved to intercept one of the guys. They all froze.

"Listen, Tom, have you ever heard of assault or sexual harassment? Well, I could complain to the authorities, and I'd mention both." Piper smiled like the Cheshire Cat and tightened his hand, making him gasp.

Tom yelped then wheezed, "What are y'all waiting for? Help me out here."

"But you've assaulted him," the blond minion said nervously. His eyes focused on Dakota.

"Self-defense," Dakota snapped.

"And I've got it all on video," Kelly exclaimed, appearing next to Dakota. She shook her phone for everyone to notice. Sawyer stood on Kelly's other side.

With her shoe, Piper nudged Tom in the hip. "Here's what you'll do, Tommy. You're going to go back to whatever rock you slithered out of and crawl back under. And I'd like it very much if you never approach me or try to touch me again, or else Kelly might forget to delete that video."

"That's blackmail," Tom hissed through his teeth.

"I know," Piper said with a giggle. "This is fun."

"Piper," Cole growled in a low voice. Dakota smiled like she was providing the best entertainment he'd ever had.

"Fine. Don't poke the tiger with a stick," she whispered. She faced Tom's posse. "Well, are you going to remain on the dark side of the Force or are you coming back to the light?"

One man grinned, and the others glanced at each other.

"Come on, guys, it's not that hard. I'm right and Tom's in the wrong. My group is composed of strong, capable, and handsome men." With the thumb of her free hand she pointed to Cole. Her gaze momentarily met both Sawyer's and Dakota's.

Sawyer winked. "Don't forget sexy. Do what's right and go away." Sawyer pointed toward the bar. A couple took a few steps back when Dakota stepped forward. The blond man and another scuttled off toward the building.

"Did this ever happen in one of your novels?" Piper asked, turning toward Cole.

"No." He rocked back on his boots.

"Sometimes the heroine kicks ass," Sawyer said, "but not like this. The girl rescues puppies or the family business."

"Usually it's the alpha-hero who kicks the antagonist's butt," Kelly acknowledged, tilting her head.

"The man defends the woman, her honor, her family or something related to the love interest," Cole said.

"In the books I read the hero, or heroine, shoots first and asks questions later." Piper looked down at Tom with a dazed expression, then reached behind her back, fingering her waistline as if searching for a gun. Tom's eyes widened, and he squirmed.

"Piper," Dakota uttered.

She rolled her eyes. "You boys are no fun." She turned, shaking her bootie at him. "Geesh, I don't have it with me tonight. I was just playing." She eyed him, scanning his body from head to toe. "You've got yours, though?"

Dakota shrugged, an evasive gesture, but one that made the posse uneasy like a bunch of cattle before a storm. Two more left. The excitement had her smiling.

"So what happens now?" she asked.

"The hero and heroine take off together," Cole offered in a husky voice. The seductive timbre melted her insides.

"Yeah, and they have mind-blowing sex," Sawyer suggested as he wiggled his eyebrows.

"There are three heroes." From the ground, Tom laughed.

Piper opened her mouth, and then closed it tight. Cole, Dakota, and Sawyer had come to her aid. Her cheeks heated, and she refused to look at the men.

"Well, you can rule this one out," Kelly declared as she pulled Sawyer away from the ruckus. Soon they sauntered out of view.

"We have to take care of Tommy first," Piper said with an angry twist of the poor man's wrist.

Dakota came over and pried her hand off Tom's. "I can handle it from here."

Cole's hands gently squeezed her shoulders. He led her away toward the parking lot. Kelly and Sawyer's raised voices met their ears, and although she couldn't distinguish words, the tone was clear. They fought again. Piper watched as Dakota raised Tom to his feet, and then leaned in on the man. Again, words weren't heard but Tom cowered away from Dakota. The freckled man waited next to the bar's door.

Piper spotted Kelly leaning against her car sniffing, so she pulled away from Cole to go to her friend, but didn't make it five steps before turning back. Cole met her eyes, searching. A wash of gratitude hit her. This cowboy cared for her. He was a first responder to her safety.

She closed the distance between them and took his hand. The touch warmed her heart.

His blue eyes sparkled like gems. One side of his mouth rose in a tentative smile.

"Thanks for being there for me," she whispered.

"Always," he replied.

That did it. She lifted to her toes and caught his lips with hers. It startled them both, but his arms encircled her, crushing her against him. She sighed and tasted him. Her body became molten as his hands roamed her back. In that moment, she wished she could live out the heroine's happily ever after and take the cowboy home.

No. Kelly needed Piper. Her friend needed to know she wasn't the only turd in the toilet.

CHAPTER 11

Cole

THE MEMORY OF THE KISS haunted Cole. It had surprised him, but it'd been exciting. Cole looked for Piper at church, but she wasn't there. She wasn't home when he stopped by that Monday morning, Wednesday, or Thursday afternoon, either. It was like she was avoiding him.

Frustrated, he scrubbed his face with a hand and then picked up the guitar. He plucked out a country song, a rock ballad, then three classical pieces. Even when his fingers ached, he found it therapeutic. He needed to play more often, but he didn't want to because of the memories the instrument stirred. His father, Colson Dart. He clenched his eyes.

First, taunting thoughts of Piper, then his dad. His mind and heart warred. The guitar was the only property of his father he owned. His mother had given Colson Dart's clothes away years after the drunk had abandoned them. Dad's note apologized for his inadequacies and stated Florence, Cole, and Lynette would be better off without him. After emptying the meager bank account, he disappeared one night.

Colson had played guitar and Cole always idolized his father's talent, but after the man abandoned them, Cole decided he'd be a better man in all ways. That included the guitar. As he practiced, it was bittersweet. The Dart men could have shared the love of music. Instead, Cole harbored resentment, but it drove him to be a responsible family man. He wouldn't fail his nephew or mother.

Flo wiped off the already clean kitchen counter. She repeatedly glanced over. It was only a matter of time until the questions started.

After she'd put Beau to bed, she cleared her throat. "I talked with Lynette today." She paused and waited for his reaction.

His little sister was like their father. She left everyone she claimed to love. She'd birthed Beau and dumped the little guy after struggling to be a mother for a few months. Lynette constantly enrolled in school for a class or two but never completed a degree. She sweet-talked Beau when she called. The separation was always "temporary,", but something came up, usually money, a man or both. Lynette blew through men like shoes. Beau had his heart broken almost every time his mommy called, but the kid kept forgiving. Cole loved his sister, but had grown tired of the shenanigans.

"Did she want money?" he asked.

"No. She invited us down to visit her in June."

Cole turned to see if his mother had been teasing. "That's new."

Flo nodded, but a hint of a smile found her lips. "I didn't tell Beau."

"That's smart. I'd hate to see his hopes dashed again." Cole closed his eyes. Why couldn't his sister be mature enough to take Beau? She was missing his childhood. The kid would be a man before she got her act together. "She'll probably cancel the week before."

His mother sighed. "I know," she whispered. She walked over to the sofa, sat with her legs stretched out and wiped a stray tear. "Lynette asked about you."

He snorted out a laugh. Lynette never liked his working on the ranch. According to her, he was above such work. "Nothing new to report."

"Not true, son." Flo leaned back and closed her eyes. A peaceful look rested on her face.

Cole arched an eyebrow. "What now?"

"She heard through the grapevine you are married." Flo kept her eyes closed, but the dimple appeared with her smile.

"God," he breathed, "how in the world did she find out about that?"

His mother shrugged. "A friend, I guess. Here's the funny part. She assumed it's true, thinking you'd never have a planned wedding with all the bells and whistles." Her eyes shot open, and she giggled. "There's more. She wanted to know when your wife was due. She thought you were going to have a baby."

Cole frowned at this new rumor. First marriage, then a baby. What's next: divorce? "She actually believed it?"

"Oh yes, she was happily scandalized."

"What did you tell her?"

"Nothing, of course."

"Mom," he growled.

"I said it was your business. If she wanted any information about you and Piper, she'd have to ask you." She inspected Cole as he absently plucked a few strings. "You aren't nay-saying the rumor, which might mean you're sweet on the girl."

Cole froze, and then his neck thawed enough to swivel and face his mother. His voice barely audible, he said, "I can't have a long-term relationship with anyone. You know that."

"Why?"

"Because there's no guarantee it would *be* long-term." His volume rose with frustration.

"Honey, no one's guaranteed a tomorrow, but you shouldn't give up on love." His mom leaned forward and patted his arm.

Cole shook his head. "I can't do that to someone. I don't want to break her heart." He dipped his head and rested it in his hands.

"What if you live to be one hundred? You'd be alone for seventy years."

"What if I get married next year, and the cancer comes back? What then, Mom?" He sounded tortured.

She stared at him for a moment before saying, "Then you won't face that hardship alone."

Cole opened his mouth, but thought better. He put the guitar away and said goodnight. Sleep wouldn't find him anytime soon; it would be a long night of staring at the ceiling.

Piper

"Good morning, Curly," Piper said, strolling into the Big Deal's barn.

"Mornin', Piper." Curly tipped his hat. "Are you taking Lucy today?"

Piper took a deep breath, inhaling scents of horse, leather and sawdust. She loved visiting the barn. Lucy was strong spirited and fun to ride. Over the past few months, horse and rider had become acquainted. This past week she explored the prairies of the ranch and came up with the idea of commuting to work via horseback. How cool would that be? No rush hour traffic. Heck, no cars, period.

"Yes, I'm heading to the Double D." Piper found a saddle in the tack room. Curly helped ready Lucy.

"I hope you're fine with getting wet." Curly glanced over at Piper.

"I know it's supposed to rain on and off all day." She refrained from rolling her eyes.

"I didn't think you'd melt, but you'll get damp and potentially muddy."

"Jessie will let me use the washer and dryer if I need them." She walked Lucy outside.

Piper's jeans, red T-shirt and boots weren't the best rain gear but the light jacket would help repel the water. The wind whipped her hair, and she pulled it into a ponytail. The humidity hung heavy, and the air smelled earthy. She sucked in a deep satisfying breath. The saturated ground was littered with puddles. As she glanced at the sky, it started to sprinkle again.

Cole's truck pulled in next to Curly's. He walked to the barn. Piper tried not to watch his long legs. "Mornin'," he greeted.

"Good morning." She patted Lucy, grateful for something to do. Heat rose to her cheeks, remembering his lips on hers. She needed to make a quick getaway before her heart talked her into staying.

"Are you getting back from a ride?" he asked.

"No, I'm riding to the Double D this morning," she answered.

He glanced up at the dark gray sky and frowned. "I don't think so."

Instantly irritated, she snapped, "I do." She put a foot in the stirrup then swung her other leg up. She took the reins and clucked her tongue. Lucy responded.

"Don't be foolish!" Cole shouted. Piper ignored him, and turned Lucy toward the trail leading to the Double D. "Wait," he tried again in a more reasonable tone. She slowed Lucy but did not stop. "I'm sorry, Piper. Come here, a sec. I won't keep you."

The wind gusted, whipping her hair into her face. She expertly walked Lucy backward the few steps until she stopped next to Cole. He gaped. She'd told him about the lessons she took as a child, but he hadn't seen her level of skill. She could make a horse dance. Curly stood like a sentinel in the open barn door with his arms crossed and a knowing grin.

"What?" she asked. Lucy stomped a foot for emphasis.

"You're going to get wet."

"It's just rain, Cole," she said. This time she rolled her eyes.

"But it could storm." His brows dipped with concern.

"Lucy's rock solid. She won't bolt." Piper felt like a child being reprimanded.

"Thunder and lightning. Are you okay with that?" He placed a warm hand on her leg. Gazing into those fathomless blue eyes framed with worry warmed her body and made it hard to breathe. Tears pricked her eyes.

"I'll be fine. I won't be alone." She patted Lucy and smiled.

The hood blew back onto her shoulders. It wouldn't stay up but she'd live with a wet head.

"Wait a sec." Cole hurried to his truck and searched in the backseat. He returned and handed her a clear plastic poncho. "This should help keep you dry." Piper slipped the poncho over her head and stuck her arms through the holes.

"Here," Cole said, using the corral fence as a step-stool. He held up a tan cowboy hat.

She leaned toward him, and he put the hood up, then fit the cowboy hat over it. "There. Now you'll be able to see where you're going."

"Thanks." Piper couldn't help but smile. Her heart hammered a techno beat. "Where did you get this hat?"

"It's an old one of my dad's I keep around as a spare." A pained expression clouded his eyes then a tight-lipped smile appeared. "Get going before you're late. Be careful."

She gave a curt nod then nudged Lucy's sides, and the horse took off with a jump. Piper whooped with glee. She slowed Lucy once they turned onto the muddy trail. The steady rain dripped off the hat brim, keeping it out of her eyes. She'd have to thank Cole. Lucy's hooves kicked up muck as they traveled down toward the canyon.

The usually clear brook had transformed into a brown, rushing river. The wood bridge spanning the creek was solid and unmoving in all the tumult. She paused, studying the dirty water. The water level hit the support post midway. After several minutes without change, she deemed it safe to cross. The nervous horse was well-trained and responded to Piper's touch. She spoke soothing words to the anxious animal as they crossed the bridge.

Safely on the other side, Piper took a large gulp of air. The trail paralleled the creek for a mile along the canyon wall. She wanted to get out of the valley in case it flooded. Jessie Barnes told her a story of the canyon; two springs ago a flash flood washed away the herd, killing most of the calves. The churning water made Piper nervous. She glanced over her shoulder at the bridge. The water now hit the underside of the wooden platform. It rose fast. As she watched, it crested the bridge. Oh snap. Time to move.

She tried to ignore the creek turned river as it lapped the side of the trail. The bank beside her eroded away into the chaotic depths. She spurred Lucy harder. The muddy trail ascended but remained beside the river. Higher and higher they climbed, uphill and out of immediate danger. The trail plateaued as the canyon turned south. Solid ground was three feet above Lucy's head. Piper glanced down at the loud angry water and blew out a long breath.

Cole had been right; the rainy day wasn't good for riding. Glad he wasn't there, she glanced over at the opposing bank. A cowboy with a dark hat seated on a black horse watched her progress. Cole.

How long had he followed her? Anger churned like the water below.

The ground shook. Piper pulled the reins, stopping Lucy before she stepped into open air. The earth in front of them slid away in an avalanche of mud and gravel. Piper swallowed down panic. She couldn't continue forward or she'd plunge headfirst into the murky water, and moving backward was futile unless she wanted to be swallowed by the rising water.

Trapped. She blew out a shaky breath. She was the only turd in the toilet even though Cole watched from the other side.

The heavy rain hampered visibility. Instead of morning, it seemed as if night was falling. What could she do? Either direction of the trail was a dead-end, but safety was a few feet upward. The cliff face was slick with mud. She moved Lucy to the shortest area and tried to peer higher than the canyon wall.

A hand reached over, frightening her. She almost fell out of the saddle.

"Hey, little lady, need a hand?" An old man with a white beard and hair smiled at her. He wore a dripping floppy hat, denim shirt and pants. He smelled bad even from a distance. Lying on the ground, he reached forward, his arms saturated with mud and water.

"Yes, please." Relief washed over her like the rain. The old man looked familiar, but it wasn't the time to place him.

He grinned, exposing holes in his yellowed smile. "Stand on the saddle and reach for me." It was tricky to balance on a nervous horse. The dark leather was slippery. She squatted but finally pushed up, using the man's gnarled hand for balance. She gripped both of his arms and jumped when he pulled. Slithering up over the ledge, she held onto the reins. The poncho ripped and filth seeped to her skin. She sat up and shook off the muck.

"You need to leave the horse," he said sadly. He army-crawled away from the ledge.

"No." Piper knew Lucy had it in her to scale the cliff. She leaned over the edge and called to the scared animal. She gently yanked the reins up and the horse's head moved in her direction. "Come on, girl." It was up to the animal to overcome fear, but Piper had seen horses charge up steeper inclines.

Cole waited on the far bank. She waved to him. The roaring water would swallow a shout. He crossed his arms.

Thunder rumbled in the distance, a slow rolling sound. The mare's eyes widened, and she pawed up the slope. A flash of light was followed by a crack so loud she jumped. The horse surged up and pushed Piper with her chest. Piper fell on her stomach and, still holding the reins, was dragged a few feet. Mud caked her hair, body and clothes. She breathed hard as she picked up Cole's hat, then walked Lucy around, inspecting her legs.

The old man had disappeared. Piper mounted and streaked off towards the Double D.

CHAPTER 12

Cole

COLE WIPED THE WATER OUT of his eyes, but he kept his foot pressed to the gas. The glass steamed up and he fumbled to adjust the defrost switch. The rain came down in sheets, but he didn't slow down. Anger fueled his recklessness. He fishtailed into the driveway of the Double D ranch, lurching as the truck hit a pothole. He slammed his brakes and slid to the barn where the open door leaked warm light out into the dark storm.

Cole stalked into the barn following a voice. Piper's. He stopped to pinpoint the murmurings as she quieted the mare. Relief washed over him and he let out a long breath. A man laughed, and, just like that, the anger flared anew.

"You look like crap," Matt Barnes stated.

"You shouldn't talk that way to a lady. Isn't that right, Lucy?" Piper said, patting Lucy's shoulder.

Cole found the stall and studied the occupants. Piper had her back to him, brushing the mud off Lucy's coat. The wet horse looked two shades darker.

Coated in muck from head to toe, Piper still wore his tan hat. The torn red shirt, tainted brown, revealed scratches along her arms.

On the other side of Lucy, cocky Barnes stood wearing an engaging smile. His gray T-shirt and jeans were dry and clean. He spotted Cole and his grin faded. "Uh oh, your husband is here."

Piper spun and the smile slipped from her lips when she examined his face. The hat was covered by filth, like her, but damn if it didn't mark her as his. The possessive thought startled him and added to his fury.

"Cole," she whispered. Her eyes raked his soaked, clinging clothes. She swallowed and a blushed bloomed under mud-streaked cheeks. "Why are you here?" The irritated tone claimed she was okay.

His fists clenched, and he took a deep breath. "I came to see if you were still alive."

"I'm fine," she said in a clipped voice, and turned back to the saddleless horse. She rubbed Lucy on the neck. Piper must have made a face because the young Barnes tried to stymie a smile by ducking behind the animal.

"Dammit, Piper, you could have died," he shouted.

She whipped around. Her face was redder than before, but her voice was low and calm. "But I didn't, did I?"

"You could have been swept away by the flood or taken out by the landslide. The horse could have trampled you. You could have been crushed." He shook because of the foolish unnecessary risk.

"Go back to work, Cole," she said with a dismissive wave.

A tremble in her voice betrayed her calm. He wouldn't be so easily dissuaded from leaving. She'd had a terrible fright, hell, he'd had one too. The thought of losing her, of her dying that way, with him watching...

"You could have died," he said again. Didn't she get that?

Her nostrils flared slightly as her eyes narrowed. "I can take care of myself, but I'll give you it wasn't the best day for riding." She held her finger up when he tried to interrupt, "I didn't know how prone to flash-flooding the canyon is. If I'd known, I might have postponed my riding until another day."

"What?" Matt squawked. "The canyon flooded again?" His eyes morphed into large white balls. Throughout the conversation he'd watched and listened, but now the kid looked horrified. "We lost more than half the herd two years ago."

"I know," Piper snapped. "The water didn't rise until after I crossed the bridge. Lucy and I made it just fine."

"Then why are you all muddy?" he asked. He rounded Lucy and inspected Piper, taking in the disheveled filth and scratches.

"Landslide along the path," Cole answered. "It gave way in front of Piper, sliding all the way to the river," he paused remembering the impotent feeling. He could do nothing. Not even shout. "She climbed up the cliff wall."

Piper shrugged off Matt's look of awe. "I'm fine and so is Lucy." She seemed steady on her feet as she patted the horse again, but Cole noticed a discrepancy between her words and body. Her hand trembled. His heart twitched and softened. Part of his anger sloughed off.

"You're not fine," he whispered, placing his hand over hers.

Piper yanked back at his touch and stomped toward the house. The rain pelted the ground with the same ferocity of his blood hammering in his veins. He pivoted and growled, "Piper?"

She halted outside the barn door in the rain. Her shoulders stooped forward and hands clenched into small balls at her side. She took a deep breath, then took off his hat. Her hair was a complete matted mess. The rain could only improve her cleanliness. Her eyes narrowed and appeared feral. "Why are you here? I didn't ask you to check on me. Did Brad send you to see if Lucy was okay? No? Well, then go away."

Mud washed out of her hair, streaking her face with brown lines. Caked with filth inside and out, she held his hat with a death grip.

"I needed to check on you," he admitted with more vehemence than he'd wanted. It was that or the other emotions swirling around in his gooey interior would get the best of him. "You did something so foolhardy. I couldn't help you. God, Piper."

"I didn't need your help." She tossed her head to get the wet hair out of her eyes. "I can take care of myself."

"That's what I'm afraid of," he mumbled out loud, but she'd heard.

Piper squared her jaw, holding her tongue for a minute. She shifted her feet and looked as if she'd launch her body and pummel the hell out of him. Then she about-faced and stalked toward the back door of the house, ignoring him altogether. He tailed her to the back steps. She spun around so fast her hand hit his chest. She stepped back in surprise, then forward in anger with a finger jabbing him.

"You are not my keeper, Cole. I'm not your wife. We aren't dating. You don't have a say in anything I do. I can take care of myself. Get the hell out of here so I can get to work." She blew out a breath, turned and hopped up a step.

He snatched her wrist, stopping her. Words hung on his lips, but she started in on him again. He tried not to, but the corners of his mouth tipped upwards.

"What the hell, Cole? Go back to work. I'm sure Mr. Davidson is not paying you to gallivant all over the county. You can't get your jollies by rescuing a damsel in distress. She rescued herself, thank you very much, and now you're pissing her off. Go back to the Big Deal and leave me alone." The wild look hadn't left her eyes.

"Pipes, I just wanted to make sure you were safe..." Words stalled in his throat. He tucked a strand of hair behind her ear and slid his fingers to her chin, tipping it up. Her lips tempted him until her bottom lip trembled. He skimmed his thumb over the smooth skin.

She jerked away from his touch.

Dropping his hand, he hesitated like she had slapped him. The stabbing ache her reaction caused, surprised him.

"I'll need to buy you a new hat." She thrust it toward him, and then ran up the three stairs and into the house, slamming the door behind her.

Piper

Piper wanted to scream and cry, but that wasn't an option. Jessie and Josiah sat at the kitchen table when she'd entered the back door a muddy heap. The couple had glanced up from the conversation, their mouths the perfect shape of an O.

Piper didn't want to explain anything. "Sorry about the mess. I'll clean it up after I shower." She pulled off her boots, but left muddy footprints all the way to the bathroom anyway.

Covered head to toe in filth, she peeled off the damp clothes. The red shirt was beyond repair. When hot water stung her face, she smiled.

Opening the door a crack, Jessie called, "Piper? I'm going to throw your clothes into the wash. Okay?"

"Thanks." Piper pulled the curtain back and stuck her head out. "Can you bring me a towel and my basket of clean clothes?"

"Sure thing." Jessie closed the door with a soft click.

Piper first wiped the blobs off her arms, and then went to work on her hair. The hair was lumped and matted as if she'd used it as a mop. On the second attempt at washing it, the door opened. Jessie announced the basket of freshly laundered clothes and towel, but then there was shuffling.

"Throw your clothes out in the hall and I'll stick them in the dryer for you," Jessie said, talking to someone else.

Jessie had already taken Piper's dirty laundry. The only other drenched person was... Cole. Piper froze. She swallowed her anxiety. Briefly, the door opened and closed again. The light switched off. The curtain rustled behind her. Her eyes adjusted and could see plenty from the wide crack under the door. "Just turn the light on, Cole."

"No can do," he said touching her shoulder. She jumped and cursed under her breath, making him chuckle.

"I'm still mad at you." She faced into the spray and away from him.

"Maybe I can do something about that."

"I doubt it." He kneaded her shoulders. After a few minutes of working out the knots, his hands dropped to her lower back. A soft moan escaped her lips. She closed her eyes and stuck her head under the spray, sending water and suds down over his hands.

God, we're naked in the shower together and he has the better view.

"I need to wash my hair," she mumbled becoming self-conscious.

"Can I help?" he asked in a low, husky tone, sending a shiver down her spine.

"Actually, you can. I've washed it twice, but it still feels dirty. I need to condition it too but not until it's clean. Do you see any mud?"

"It's too dark."

"I told you to leave the light on," she said, reaching down for the shampoo. Her backside bumped into his front, and Cole moaned. She raised her hands playfully. "Don't shoot."

His low chuckle made her warm all over. Taking the shampoo out of her hand, he snapped open the cap. Both big hands massaged her scalp. The slow, rhythmic movement felt relaxing and erotic. Piper fought the urge to lean back against him. She wanted his hands washing her body.

"Rinse," he said. She leaned into the spray again, and he reached around her for the conditioner. He squeezed the bottle, and then his hands were on her again.

"You're great at this," she moaned. "I think I'll alert Desire Hardmann to your talents." She giggled at his groaning reply.

"Rinse."

As the water pelted her head, his fingers gently combed her hair. She squeezed the excess water out. "Now what?"

Soapy hands slid down her arms. His fingers laced hers. With a sigh, she leaned back against his hard body. He uttered a needy groan and hugged their arms across her belly, pulling them tighter together. He nipped her shoulder then licked the spot. Her body quivered with need.

"You smell good." His warm breath caressed her ear. She angled her neck, so he had better access. He nuzzled her with his nose.

"I hope so," she whispered. Her body warmed and hummed as he touched her. Her head rested on his shoulder. Her back pressed against his muscled front. She wanted to twist and loop her arms around his neck and lose herself in his kiss. "Are you still mad I lived today?" she asked.

His arms tightened around her. "God, Piper, is that what you thought?" His voice was pained.

"That's what your behavior said."

He rubbed his face against her neck, and then placed a string of nips and kisses from shoulder to chin. "I was afraid," he admitted. "The thought of losing you...All I could do was watch as you struggled. I couldn't do a damn thing, and it made me mad. I was powerless, and I hated that feeling. It took all my strength not to charge down the hill and ford the river." His hands slid over her smooth abdomen trying to possess her.

To comfort him, she spun in his arms. "You didn't lose me." Soft breasts met the hard muscled wall of his chest. Her arms encircled his waist. She couldn't look up at him for fear she'd let go. He shifted his hips and she squeaked as his hands cupped her backside. Her heart beat a rhythm to match his racing one. Leaning against his warm tanned flesh, she sighed.

"We can't do this," she mumbled in misery.

"I know," he tugged her closer.

"Cole." She took a deep breath, trying to get the raging lust under control, but it was hard to do with a hotter-than-Hades naked man sandwiched against her. "I work here. My boss is in the other room."

"She locked me in."

"Yes, it would seem Jessie is playing matchmaker." Not like they could shower elsewhere. Her place had the size and coziness of a port-o-john and his mother and nephew shared a bathroom with him. Nope. Not going to work.

A knock startled her. Jessie cracked the door, not saying anything about the light being off. "Sorry to cut you short, but...Justin Saine wants to talk to you. He's not going to back down."

Piper gasped like she'd been sucker punched.

"Sure, Piper will be out in a minute," Cole said.

"Okay," Jessie said. The door clicked shut.

Piper bit her lip to keep it from trembling. Cole's fingers tightened, and he tipped her chin so he gazed into her eyes. "You're one of the strongest women I know. You survived a flash flood and a landslide then climbed a cliff with a horse. Piper, you've got bigger balls than most men. You can take this loser."

Piper scrambled out of Cole's arms and the water. He stayed in the shower while she toweled off. She sucked in deep breaths, trying to calm her heart and wrap her mind around Justin being in Texas. How had he found her this time? Water dripped into her eyes. She glanced around the room for another towel, but the only one shrouded her torso.

"What the hell?" Piper muttered as she pulled the towel from her body and wrapped her wet head.

Piper glanced over her shoulder. Cole remained behind the shower curtain. She hugged herself and kicked the laundry basket. She'd washed three loads the prior afternoon, but the basket was practically empty. Green lace covered something denim. "Where are my clothes, Jessie?' she uttered. The room was too small to pace.

She stepped into the lacy, emerald green panties, and then fastened the bra she'd promised to show Cole. She recalled the way his eyes had shimmered when she had offered him a better look. Her heart raced as she reached for a pair of jeans. She stepped into them, but they clung to her damp legs.

The water turned off, then Cole pulled back the curtain and whistled.

Startled, she lost her balance and teetered. Grabbing the towel bar, she caught herself. She glanced over to find him studying her lacy bikinis. "Do you mind?" she asked, tugging her jeans up the rest of the way.

"Not at all," he replied with a smirk.

Her eyes narrowed, then dipped lower. Except for the ever-present bandanna, he was stark naked and not a damn bit ashamed. His masculine form was a work of art and perfectly proportioned—everywhere.

As she fastened the jeans, she swallowed but couldn't find her voice. Her blood boiled as her temperature rose. She tore the towel off her head and tossed it to him. On his abdomen, a long scar drew her gaze. She turned away and plucked up the only shirt in the basket, once again Jessie's meddling.

"Isn't that my shirt?" Cole asked.

"No." But it was. His gray shirt with the Hammered logo should have been retired as a cleaning rag. The back hem was torn and the left sleeve had three tiny holes. It hung to mid-thigh, but she knotted it in the back to make it fit. She'd acquired it from their sleepover and had intended to return it. The shirt had smelled like Cole.

"Piper." The concern in his tone made her turn and face him. "If he's on the phone; he can't hurt you. You won't let him. He's living in the past and you're living in the present. And a wise woman once told me 'I can take care of myself'."

Tension built in her gut. Her stomach growled its disapproval of the situation. She wished she could spew acid at Justin, but she heaved a big sigh. "I'm ready for this to end. I thought I was done with him." She paused in the doorway. "I just want him to leave me alone. Why can't he do that?" Her eyes filled, and she took a deep breath, then another. It wouldn't do to sound weak. She finger combed her damp hair, then left the nearly naked cowboy.

CHAPTER 13

Piper

THE HOUSE SEEMED QUIET, BUT when Piper tiptoed out to the kitchen Josiah was slicing lemons. A large green glass pitcher with a scoop of sugar sat next to him. He glanced up with a smile. "I've been given a chore."

"Yum. You make the best—that's why." Piper inspected the table, looking for the handset. "I have a phone call. Where should I take it?"

The tall cowboy tilted his head in confusion. "What phone call? You have a guest."

"He's here?" Piper whispered in disbelief, squeezed her eyes shut, then covered her face with quivering hands. "No freaking way." Dizziness hit her and she swayed. Josiah grabbed her elbow and sat her in a chair. He handed her a tall glass of water, which she guzzled like her life depended on it. She placed her elbows on the wood table, resting her chin in her hands. Justin had found her. She'd never be free of him. She needed to run, but where could she go?

Feet padded down the hallway from the bathroom, then a warm hand rested on her shoulder. Piper's tear-filled eyes glanced at Cole. "He's here," she croaked. A renegade tear broke free and ran down her cheek. He squeezed gently, but it did little to calm the angst. She felt a slight breeze as he passed her and peered into the living room. Jessie's laughter bubbled up. Justin was already charming her boss. Piper huffed and lowered her head to her hands again.

"Pipes, you got this," Cole said as he pulled out a chair next to her.

She scanned him. Cole wore one of Josiah's T-shirts and it fit tight over his chest. Under normal circumstances she might have paused and drooled

76

a little, but her gaze flicked over to Josiah. His face matched Cole's with brows pinched together in concern. "You're not alone," Josiah said.

She opened her mouth, but her voice didn't work. Clearing her throat, she tried again. "You don't understand this guy. He's a master manipulator. Justin can take anything you say and spin it to meet his needs and when you get angry, he stays calm. He's intelligent but a sicko. He wiped out my bank account; well, technically it was ours, but he did not add one cent. And those were his good traits."

"How much?" Cole asked through a clenched jaw.

"I'd saved over six hundred. It was a nest egg for our new life, but when I broke up with him he cleaned it out." She sighed wearily and rubbed her face. After the anger had passed, she acknowledged the theft as just another consequence from her mistake. It had been a cheap price to pay to be free of him.

"He's a thief," Cole growled with cold eyes. His body grew tense as if he'd jump up and beat Justin's face in.

Piper sat up straight and put a hand on his arm to stay him. "Listen, you will not make threats, even in teasing, and you definitely will not harm him." Both men stared at her. "He'll sue you. That's the kind of jerk he is. Josiah, if you throw him out, he'll run to the police station saying you threatened and manhandled him."

"Even if he's trespassing and overstayed his welcome?" Josiah asked.

"Yes. It happened to my brother, Fletcher, while I was living with him," she said sadly.

"God, Piper, what happened?" Cole asked. He leaned closer to her and covered her hand with his.

A shiver crawled down her spine, but she shook her head. "I don't want to go into it." She sucked in a deep breath. "Justin will use anything to get me to do what he wants."

Josiah and Cole shared a look. "Piper, you'll never be alone with him, because you're surrounded by friends. He's outnumbered and he's in unfamiliar territory," Josiah said in a reassuring voice. "We've got your back."

"Thanks, Josiah." She forced a pathetic smile. "It wouldn't matter to him. He'll only use it to humiliate me, anything to get his way. Guilt, humiliation, calling me names, oh it won't be blatant, but he'll do it, then Saint Justin will make it sound like my family sent him. I'll bet you twenty bucks he'll pull out the cost of airfare to get down here and use it to guilt me into going back with him."

"Really?" Josiah rocked back on his heels. "He claimed to love you when he introduced himself to us. He seemed nice enough." His head snapped sideways as Jessie laughed again, then his eyes narrowed.

The fact that he believed Piper, and didn't trust Justin with his wife, gave her hope. Maybe she could get through this with her friends' help. When she glanced at Cole, there was a mischievous twinkle in his eyes. Instantly thoughts of Justin disappeared, and the vision of Cole naked became prominent. She hadn't realized she stared at his lips until a slow grin manifested there. She swallowed.

"Twenty bucks? Okay, I'll take that bet." Cole crossed his arms and leaned back, exuding confidence.

"You're going to lose," Piper insisted.

"I'm in. I need to have some hope this guy won't give all men a bad rep." Josiah reached into his back pocket and pulled a twenty dollar bill from his wallet. He placed it on the table in front of Piper. Her fingertips touched the bill, but he pulled it back.

"You're going to lose." She grinned.

"I hope I do," Cole said with conviction.

"We aren't going anywhere, are we, Cole?" Josiah continued making lemonade and filled the pitcher with water.

Piper slowly stood. Cole pulled her against him. His body became a lifeline as her arms clasped behind him, anchoring them together. His fingers caressed her back, climbing up and down. "You've got this, Pipes," he whispered. "Just remember what you did to that weasel Tom, and picture Justin flat on his back looking up at you. You are strong, and all you have to do is convince him you aren't who you once were. You've got this."

Cole

Cole followed Piper out to face the devil. There was no way in hell he'd let her be alone with Justin Saine. They both walked into the large open room barefoot and freshly showered, but only Piper had the evidence of wet hair. He wouldn't mind if Justin thought he and Piper were together.

Justin sat in a brown leather chair with his legs crossed and a serene smile on his face. Sensing movement, the man turned his head and everything about his face exuded joy—except the fleeting moment when Cole made eye contact. The slight narrowing before a blink, let Cole know the game had begun. Cole kept his face a mask of indifference.

"Piper, sweetheart, you're looking well." Justin stepped toward her with arms outstretched, but Piper stopped, making Cole bump into her.

"Sorry, Pipes," Cole said, holding her arms. "You okay?" He didn't hurt her. He'd barely touched her, this was about the ex-fiancé. She nodded as he slipped past her to the chair opposite of Justin's.

"Justin," she acknowledged. She skirted him warily and sat on the sofa with Jessie.

Poor Jessie's face looked brittle from the false smile she held. Jessie scanned the group, taking in everything and when she locked eyes with Cole, she relaxed. He winked, earning a real grin. He'd known her since they were kids. Cole had graduated a year before her so they'd always been acquaintances. Even back then, he'd found her a trustworthy girl and now she was proving it again by helping Piper.

Justin settled back in his chair with a cool smile. His polo shirt wasn't wrinkled, and neither were his khaki pants. The man wore his brown hair short in a stylish cut. On his long nose perched an expensive brand of artsy glasses and his wrist was home to a Rolex. Cole knew it was a fake because Piper had told the story of how he'd obtained it. It was all about image with Justin, and outwardly the man looked like he had it together. Too bad Cole knew otherwise.

"How are you, Piper?" Justin asked in a suave tone.

"Why are you here, Justin?" Piper countered with a frown.

"Why? I came to see you, of course." He smiled and glanced at the others.

"Okay, you saw me, now you can go." She leaned forward and tipped her head to the door.

Justin laughed and Cole chuckled silently. God, he loved her gutsiness. "I can't leave yet. I just got here."

"You weren't invited," she said in a tone as speaking to a child. "This is where I work. Not only is this a place of business, the Barnes' live here. It's their home."

"I couldn't find you any other way," he said.

Piper stared at Justin as if he was stupid, and again Cole hid his smile. After a long awkward pause she said, "Well, if you don't have any business to conduct, I'll say goodbye, because I'm late to work." She glanced at Cole, and after a moment her cheeks turned pink. Yes, he liked making her late to work.

Justin wasn't ignorant to the unspoken exchange. "But I do have business to conduct," he offered.

"Oh, great," Jessie said, picking up a brochure. She switched to entrepreneur mode. "Are you interested in longhorns or lingerie?" Silenced by Jessie's question, Justin's mouth fell open, but nothing came out. She handed him a tri-folding paper.

The phone rang, and Piper jumped for the phone and headset. She slipped it on to greet the customer then patiently answered his questions while pacing back and forth. Cole was glad she continued to work, even with Justin present.

"Sure, Mr. Peters, I'll check on your order, but like I said, it already shipped." She stalked down the hallway, rolling her eyes at Jessie before disappearing from view.

Josiah entered, holding a tray of homemade lemonade. He poured one for everyone. His eyes met Cole's and he grinned.

Justin examined the brochure with interest. On the cover was the Double D Intimates logo, the Japanese caricature of a woman in a bikini. Inside spotlighted Jessie's newest line of sexy nightgowns, nine in total.

"My wife is a talented woman," Josiah said with pride. "She makes every piece by hand."

"I see," Justin said. "Business is good?" Justin failed to look up at Josiah and Jessie.

"So good she needed to hire help. The orders are doubling every six weeks." Josiah handed his wife a glass, then kissed her on the cheek. He tenderly brushed a stray auburn lock away from her forehead and tucked it behind her ear.

A horn honked outside, and the couple exchanged a look. Josiah went to the door and pulled it open. "It's the mailman."

The living room opened into the dining room. Brown paper packages and plastic tubs of novels were stacked on the long table. Cole itched to look through the books. Josiah picked up a stack of boxes and headed to the door.

"Wait," Piper called. She scurried into the dining room with a handful of papers and an electronic tablet. "I'm looking for the Peters' package." She scanned the boxes in Josiah's hand and matched addresses on the papers. "Mr. Peters? Your package is in the mail. I have resent the email with the tracking number. Yes, it will be updated; however, Double D Intimates has no control over the United States Postal Service." She twittered at something said on the other end of the line, and then Piper turned and stormed down the hall, all business once again. "Mrs. Barnes is not taking special orders at this time. There is a six-month waiting period..." her voice trailed off.

"Wow, six months." Cole smiled at Jessie. She shrugged, and a blush blossomed. Josiah returned for more packages, then left the house again. Cole twisted in the chair to watch out the picture window. It had stopped raining. Josiah and the mail carrier shook hands. The men talked beside a beat-up white Jeep. Cole figured package pick up was a common occurrence with the thriving business.

Piper returned to the room frowning. She sat on the overstuffed arm of Cole's chair. "That man is frustrating," she mumbled loudly.

"He likes you," Jessie teased.

"No, he likes you," Piper tossed at her with a grin. "He calls weekly to order your goodies."

"I'm not the newbie with the sexy phone voice or modeling slinky nighties," Jessie fired back, throwing another brochure toward them. It landed on Cole's knee. He opened it up and found it true. While the pictures didn't show the faces or feet of the models, Cole knew Piper by her legs. His fingers traced the lace neckline of a baby doll style gown. It was the same emerald and black as the bra and panties she wore. She'd earned them modeling. He grinned, figuring out her secret. "Nice."

Piper yanked the brochure from his fingers. Her face blazed red, but she stared at him with an arched brow. Suddenly his pants were too tight, and he shifted in the chair as the memory of her wet flesh pressed against him popped into his head. It was his turn to heat as a slow grin found her lips.

Justin jerked the paper out of Piper's hand and she cringed, almost sliding off the arm. Cole nearly bolted out of the seat after Justin, but instead glared while resting a stabilizing palm on Piper's back. He had all but forgotten the ex was there and had no desire to share Piper's modeling images with him.

"Why are you here, Justin?" Piper asked again, crossing her arms with a sigh.

"I came to bring you home," he said with a superior twinkle in his eye. He leaned forward, gearing up for an argument.

Piper jumped up, slapping her hands together. "Wow. That was easy. All right, come on." She walked to the door and opened it.

Justin stood but didn't move from the spot. His face was stone-like as his gaze slid around the group, trying to figure out an angle. From his vantage, Cole could see Justin was tall but thin and if need be he, Josiah, Matt or probably Beau could take this character down.

"You can leave now, Justin." She pointed outside and smiled sweetly.

"Why?"

"I'll go home as soon as I'm done for the day, so your reason for being here is moot. You can go. Now."

"You're willing to leave with me?" He hesitated, taking a step toward her.

"Oh no, I'll never get in another car with you ever again. Being kidnapped, twice, and held captive in a moving car for three hours was quite enough, thank you." Piper's stare could have singed Justin's eyebrows from his head.

"You were kidnapped?" Jessie gasped. She brought a hand to her pale face and eyed Justin with disdain.

"Of course she wasn't. Of all the silly, stupid things..." he pointedly turned to Jessie, trying to appeal to her. "We were engaged and had an argument. Everyone fights." With a sheepish grin, he shrugged like it was no big deal and sat back down.

Like a furry orange bolt of lightning, Tippy ran in the front door before Piper could close it.

"He wouldn't stop the car or let me out for three hours," Piper informed Jessie with hands on her hips. She narrowed cold eyes at Justin but kept a steady voice. She'd said he would subtly call her names and so far Justin used silly and stupid. Cole couldn't disagree more. Piper was nothing short of clever and smart.

"I wanted to work things out," Justin pleaded, sounding innocent.

Cole white knuckled the ends of the chair's arms, grateful Piper had enlightened him about Justin's unique talent to manipulate. He wanted to defend Piper then go on the offensive and put this loser in his place. He'd gladly pay the twenty to see Piper flip Justin on his back.

"Finally, he had to get gas. That's when I fled. It was miles from home, and I started walking." She glanced down at her hand and picked at a nail.

"I looked for you, but I didn't find you along the way," Justin said incredulously.

Piper snorted. "That's because I was walking home—to my home not yours. Why would I go back to you? It's the last time I made the mistake of getting in a car with you."

"So you're going home, but not with me?"

"I won't go anywhere with you. And, for your information, I am home." Her bright eyes seemed to dare him to test her resolve.

"Your family wants you home, and I decided to help them convince you to come back." His tone was gentle, but his brown eyes were hard and Cole watched as they narrowed in on Piper.

"My family asked you to come get me?" When he nodded and smiled, she pulled out her phone and pushed a button. A man's voice greeted her on speaker. She watched Justin react. "Hey, Fletch, sorry to bother you at work, but I need to ask you a question. Did you send Justin to Texas to retrieve me?"

The line was silent for a moment, then Piper's brother laughed. "Funny, Piper." He continued chuckling. "What's this really about?"

"I'm serious, Fletcher. When did you last speak to Justin?" Piper asked in a monotone voice. Her brother's voice raised an octave, and he rambled on in an agitated way, denying anything to do with Saine. He, his wife and kids wanted nothing to do with the man and Cole sighed with relief. "If it wasn't you that gave him my information then who was it? Mom?"

"Let's find out," Fletcher challenged, then hit a three-way option on his phone. There was a beep, a long ring, then a click as someone picked up.

"Hey, Mom," Fletcher greeted.

"Hi, Mom," Piper said.

"Both my babies, I'm dreaming." The woman's voice was gentle and melodic. Cole smiled, hearing affection.

"Mom, I need to ask you something," Piper said as she leaned closer to the phone.

"I'm all ears," she replied.

"Did you send Justin to retrieve me?"

All eyes turned to watch the stalker. His face was a mask of stone, with his nose stuck in the air. He appeared serene and calm as he sat with shoulders back and legs crossed, but Cole noticed a nervous tick in a jaw muscle. The man forced the cool exterior.

"What? Justin your ex-crazy-fiancé? Why in God's good name would I subjugate you to that asshole?"

Silence descended on the Barnes' living room. Justin's face and posture stayed the same, but his color changed three shades redder. Cole and Jessie shared a grin. Piper held a hand in front of her mouth holding in a laugh, but there was no such luck for her brother. A contagious belly laugh erupted coming from the tips of his toes. Soon the whole room laughed. It did Cole's heart good to see Piper smiling. She wiped a tear from the corner of her eye.

"I'm sorry, Mom, but you're on speaker phone," Piper admitted.

"Oh dear. Why? Who?" the older woman stammered. Fletcher laughed again, but muffled it somehow.

"I'm at work. Jessie is..."

"Jessie, dear, I apologize for my foul mouth. Normally I don't curse."

"Don't worry about it Mrs. Nutt. Everyone has an asshole." Jessie smiled at Justin as Fletcher burst out laughing again.

Cole waited for the laughter to subside. Soon both mother and brother knew Saine had traveled to Texas and was harassing Piper again. They adamantly denied any dealings with the ex. The conversation lasted only a few minutes. Mrs. Nutt gushed on about how proud she was of Piper finding her own way. Once her mother had hung up, Fletcher asked, "Where's Cole?"

"I'm here, Fletcher," Cole responded

"Good. You'll take care of her?" he asked.

With a half-smile, Cole glanced at the stalker and answered, "Always."

Piper

Piper's heart hammered and she balled her fists at her side. She tried taking deep breaths, but the fury didn't dissipate. An evil smile curled upon her lips as she realized she'd caught Justin in a lie, and she had witnesses. "You lied."

"I never said they sent me," Justin pointed out, "you did."

Piper heated as anger ignited. Exacerbated, she glanced down at Cole. He nodded, acknowledging her frustration. His jaw tightened and eyes narrowed as he swung his head back toward Justin.

She'd been subject to Justin's manipulation over and over again. It did her no good to argue when he twisted everything and threw it back at her. It had been easier to keep quiet and let him think he'd won. Most of the time, it had worked, but sometimes he'd push her over the boiling point and she'd explode. During those rare moments, he gave her the floor, but she'd be so angry she couldn't think straight. She wouldn't resolve anything. In fact, he'd turn it against her.

She closed her eyes and sighed. "For the record," she said through clenched teeth, "I don't want him here at work, or my home or in Texas period. It's just not big enough for the both of us." She sought Jessie's eyes; her boss had a right to know. The Barnes' were welcome to throw out the interloper.

"I don't want him here either, if you're uncomfortable," Jessie said. She glanced at her phone and sat up straighter. "Josiah took the liberty of contacting Ben." Jessie picked up a glass and sipped it.

"Oh?" Piper squeaked in surprise. Ben Moore, an officer for the Fortuna Police, was one of Josiah's friends. Was that code for Ben was coming to the rescue? Jessie winked at her. Piper grinned and met Cole's gaze. He'd told her to live in the present. She rubbed her chin, wondering how pissed off she could make Justin before Ben arrived.

She hitched her foot up and rested her heel on Cole's chair between his legs, the heat of his thighs warming her ankle. He curled his fingertips on her back and stretched them out again. She arched into his touch. She closed her eyes, angling her body, so he had better access. "That feels great," she said in a low sultry voice.

Cole chuckled, continuing to massage her back. "I like making you say that."

"Hm." Through slatted eyes, she inspected Justin. He glared, a vein throbbing on his tomato red face. His jaw slowly moved as if he was grinding something.

Cole slowed his rubbing. She glanced over her shoulder at him through fluttering lids. "Don't stop, Cole," she implored with a whisper. Her breath caught as he shifted and doubled his efforts, both hands sliding under her shirt to knead her skin. His hooded eyes gazed as if she stood in nothing but her lacy green underwear. An incredible urge to fall into his lap and claim his lips built.

Justin cleared his throat. "Piper, I didn't come all this way to watch you flirt with a farmer. It's time for this nonsense to stop."

"There's the door, Justin. Don't let it hit you on the way out." She gave Justin her most intimidating glare.

Justin laughed, although it sounded forced. "Charming as ever. Come on, let's go."

"Wow, he's persistent," Jessie noted with a frown.

"Do you see why I was looking into a restraining order?" Piper shrugged a shoulder.

Cole returned to the one-handed kneading of her lower back. She was grateful for his soothing presence but wished for a gun.

Justin exhaled loudly and rolled his eyes. "You're such a drama queen." He shifted forward, leaning his elbows on his knees. "Are you in a relationship? Is that why you don't want to leave?"

"Ugh, you egotistical jerk, I don't want to leave because I don't want to go anywhere with you." She jumped up with her hands on her hips. "I like my job and the people here. I like the town and the land. This is my home now. I love Texas. Why can't you get it through that thick skull of yours? I didn't want you in Illinois; what makes you think I'd reconsider in another state?" She glared at her ex, breathing hard. He never apologized for anything, but expected her to continue to bow to his wishes.

"I can change. It will be better than last time. Come on, sweetheart, I spent six hundred dollars on a plane ticket to come to you. It was a price I gladly paid."

Yeah, he paid with the money he'd stolen. She would not buy into the guilt because she'd never asked him to come. Piper glanced at Cole and giggled. Wide eyed, he gaped at Justin.

"I tried to warn you. Now I'm forty bucks richer."

"I can't believe it." Cole blinked and shook his head.

To Justin, Piper said, "I'm sorry you wasted your time. Actually, I'm not sorry at all. I have no reason to be. I've done nothing wrong." She grinned, feeling lighter, as if a weight had been lifted.

Justin stood and approached her. He acted sad, with his hands in his front pockets and chin against his chest. His calculating eyes gave him away. His fingers reached for her face. He stopped short because she backed away and Cole leaned forward as if to stand. "Didn't I mean anything to you?" Justin asked.

Piper rolled her eyes again. "Oh God, here we go," she muttered. She expected the verbal and psychological assault today but hadn't that night at her brother's house. It came as a terrifying shock. Justin had traumatized the children. Luckily, most of the venom he'd spouted had gone over her nephew's head, but her niece was old enough to understand the sexual references. Justin's outlandish words had tainted the intimacy they'd once shared, turning it sour. He'd embarrassed her to the point that she had fled inside to vomit. Somehow he thought she'd agree to come back to him if he stopped the taunting, but his actions had pushed her further away.

Justin squared his shoulders, with his arms bent at his side, he rudely gestured as a man thrusting into a woman. "Didn't it mean anything when you pulled me into you?"

CHAPTER 14

Piper

"THAT WENT WELL," PIPER MUTTERED sarcastically as she watched Justin's rental car pull onto the main road. With his hand on her shoulder, Cole stood behind her on the front porch.

Four people conversed near the hood of a white Fortuna police car. Piper was torn between going out to talk with Ben, the local lawman, and staying in the safety of Cole's encircling arms.

She hadn't wanted to deal with Matt Barnes either, not after he'd stormed into the house. A cowboy on a mission, he'd kissed her in front of Cole, Jessie and Justin. He'd stuck his tongue in her opened mouth. Gross. He wasn't a horrible kisser; in fact, he was better than Justin. When she pushed the nineteen-year-old away he'd given her a sad puppy dog face and left as quickly as he came with Jessie on his heels. Of course, Justin had ranted about bold cowboys.

Piper pulled away from Cole and joined the others. Josiah leaned against the car with his arms crossed and Jessie stood with her hand on his arm. Matt had the courtesy to blush when she closed in. "What the hell, Matt?" she demanded.

His mouth flopped open but Josiah answered, "Don't worry, Piper, I already ripped him a new one." He leaned forward and slugged his younger brother in the arm.

"Ow." Matt frowned, rubbing his arm.

"Just be glad it wasn't Piper," Cole added from behind her.

Piper nodded. If she hadn't been watching Justin intently, she might have punched Matt. She'd still like to knock him on his cute, egotistical butt, but she hadn't come out to the squad car to interrogate Matt Barnes.

"Hey, Ben, thanks for staging an intervention." Piper leaned in and kissed the officer on the cheek..

"It's no big deal. I was out in the area anyway," he said, staring at his boots. With his uniform and all the gear around his waist, he cast an imposing shadow, especially when he made the "don't mess with me" cop face.

"It's a big deal. You don't understand how hard it is to get rid of him." Piper drew in a deep breath. "Is your superior working today?"

With a quizzical glance to Josiah, he nodded.

"Good. Could you please call or radio him? I need to talk to him or her." She smiled while Ben tried to make contact. He sat in the driver's seat with the door open. An impatient voice called out. Ben answered then handed her the radio handset with a quick how to.

"This is Colin Copper, how can I help you?" A deep man's voice barked.

Piper introduced herself and gave a quick history. "Today my ex-fiancé showed up in Texas, and he wouldn't leave the Barnes' property when they asked him too. Luckily, Ben stopped over and got him to leave. I wanted to let you know I'm grateful to Ben. He was polite, but Justin wouldn't take a hint so Ben acted tough. I wanted you to know what happened here today because Justin will either be calling you or stopping by to make a complaint about Ben. There are others who witnessed the altercation." Piper listed those present to Colin. If he needed statements, he knew whom to talk to.

She leaned back against the seat and yawned. It wasn't even noon, and she wanted to go to bed and hibernate.

Jessie leaned and looked in the car. "Do you really think he'll run to the police station and rat on Ben?" She bit her lip.

"Count on it," Piper said. "I wanted to get the truth out there before Justin taints it with half-truths and false accusations." She exited the car and joined the huddle of humans.

Matt returned to his work in the barn and Piper needed to back to hers. She had emails and regular mail to sort through, files to file and orders to pull. The busy work would keep her mind from wondering back to Justin's perverted disclosure and her mounting embarrassment. The Barnes' probably wondered why she fell for such an idiot, but Justin could be charming when he chose.

Once upon a time, she had fallen for the sweet-talking man with lofty goals. She'd believed him with all her heart. He had wanted her to be the queen of his empire. Unbeknownst to her, the empire was pure fantasy. He wanted easy money and used her work ethic and labor to fund some trivial ideas for business startups. The man followed a submarine sandwich shop owner around, dropping the hint he'd eventually buy a franchise, but the owner caught on and that fell through. Next it was a pizza restaurant, but to buy a national franchise he needed money or an investor. No one bought Justin's line of making millions; of course, it didn't help that he never graduated college or stayed at a job for more than a few months. In the beginning Piper had supported and encouraged him. It soon became clear, he was intimidated by her employment and salary, but Piper worked her tail off at the company.

Looking back on the engagement, she could see numerous problems, like him not liking her church and insisting they have one of their own, but back then, love overcame all. The encounter today taught her he had never understood what love was and still didn't, but she'd learned what it wasn't. She'd hoped to be cherished, encouraged and wooed by her lover—not stalked, traumatized and forced into a relationship.

When Justin left, he'd told her she should worry about her reputation. Piper's face lit up in an angelic smile. In Fortuna, Texas her reputation was none other than Cole Dart's Russian mail-order bride and if Justin wanted to talk bad about her, he'd be dragging Cole into it. The locals frowned upon strangers bashing one of their own, and she belonged, thanks to Desire Hardmann and the crazy rumor.

The business line rang. Piper hurried inside.

Cole

Sitting on the front porch swing, Cole waited for Piper to be finished for the day. He made more phone calls that afternoon than he had in the past three months, but the result would be worth it. Piper's safety.

A balmy breeze blew. After all the rain, the Texas prairie grass would green up. Long dormant wild flower seeds would wake and bloom. The same might be happening to him. Thoughts of love had lain dead, but it only took Piper to show up in his life to make the longing blossom. He scrubbed his face. As much as he wanted Piper physically, he didn't know if he could give her what she really needed. He wanted to, and that surprised him, because after the cancer operation, he decided he'd never put a woman through what his mother had suffered.

There were two things he could do; he needed to choose one or the other, but they both involved his feet. He could run as far away from this woman as fast as possible or he could walk right into her arms and hold on tight. He looked down at the booted size twelve feet. They remained stationary on the wood floor. He sighed because he wasn't going anywhere. Piper needed him, but it was more than that—he needed her.

He needed her. He grinned. That would piss off her ex-fiancé.

Piper opened the door and shuffled over to him. Her body stiff, she remained quiet as she stared at the floor. He hated to see her cowed by Justin.

"Are you ready?" He watched as her gaze shifted to the property, and then the road. Justin wasn't near the Double D. No, that fool had gone to the police station, and then a local restaurant. He tried to get dirt on Piper, but everyone shut him down. When it came to Mrs. Dart, the town clammed up.

"I guess." Piper's voice remained whispery soft. "I hear you're on guard duty."

"Yes, ma'am." He stood and hugged her tight. Feeling her sigh against his chest made the moment worth the phone calls. Protectiveness flared, and he tightened his grip. There were safety measures in place. Tonight he planned to keep her at his home. She could sleep in his bed, and if Justin followed them home he'd think she lived in a house full of people. The Dart home would be a safety net, plus it'd support the crazy rumor they'd married. "You're staying at my house tonight."

She chuckled and tilted her head up. "How convenient."

Cole kissed the tip of her nose. "Now don't get excited, darlin', I won't be joining you."

Hooded eyes fluttered open wide. "Why not?" Her lips bowed downward.

He walked her to his truck, avoiding puddles, and opened the door.

"Don't worry. Nothing will happen." He had to work sometime. Cole had made a deal with Brad. He took the day off in trade for the night shift. Piper would be safe at his home. If Justin tried anything he'd be sorry. His mother knew how to shoot a shotgun and Ben promised a police presence in the driveway, on and off, throughout the night.

CHAPTER 15

Piper

PIPER STARED AT THE SEMI-DARK bedroom ceiling. She was uncomfortable despite the soft, warm blankets and pillows. Shoving them aside, she sat up. Her bare feet touched the floor. At the window, she pushed back the drape and gazed into the darkness. The slope of the drive, lined with trees, led to the road. At the end, a white police car sat. Her new reality. Why the hell did Justin think she'd want anything to do with her after the stunt he pulled at her brother's house in front of the kids, let alone what he'd done at the Barnes' home?

She flopped back on the bed and buried her face in Cole's pillow. It smelled like him. She longed for him, which was stupid. He now knew the intimate details of how she lost her virginity, thanks to Justin spouting the information. Why would Cole want someone like her, someone who'd fallen for a jerk like Justin? Sure, everyone made mistakes, but most weren't as colossal as hers. She was still paying for it and now Fortuna would too.

Piper groaned, remembering the embarrassing occurrence.

She'd chuckled at the priceless expression on Jessie's face when Justin had asked, "Didn't it mean anything when you pulled me into you?" It came as quite a shock to Jessie.

"Well, at least, there aren't any children around this time." Piper had said with hands on her hips.

"He said that around kids?" Jessie gasped.

"Wait, this is what—?" Cole started.

"Yes." Piper couldn't meet Cole's eyes, so she glanced at the coffee table.

"*I was your first, Piper. When you spread your legs and pulled me in, we bonded.*" *Justin's tone softened, but his gaze turned hard and cold. Jessie looked like she'd bitten into a lemon.*

"*No.*" *Piper's firm voice resounded.*

"*What?' Taken aback by her defiance, Justin grimaced.*

"*No. It doesn't mean anything to me—*"

"*But all those times you pulled me—*"

"*No! Whatever meaning there used to be has vanished. You make it sound like I did everything to lure you in, but if you remember, I didn't want you. I wanted my husband. I loved my husband.*"

"*Husband?*" *Jessie asked, confused. She'd glanced at Cole who'd shrugged.*

Piper had turned to Cole. Her eyes held his. "*I chose to wait to make love with my husband. It was supposed to be his gift.*"

"*It's an admirable yet old fashioned idea,*" *Justin said, waving a hand.* "*Besides, I was going to be her husband.*"

"*Yes, and look how that turned out,*" *Piper uttered. Epic fail.*

Every day for six months they had the same redundant argument. "*I'm saving myself for my husband,*" *she'd pleaded.*

He'd counter, "*But I'm going to be your husband—*"

"*But you're not—*"

"*I'm going to be—*"

"*But you're not—*"

"*I'm going to be.*"

Over and over, all day for months. Finally, she'd given in and the first time might have been slightly magical, but afterward it was boring. Standing in Jessie's living room, the realization had hit her—after they'd started having sex, she stopped reading any kind of romance books. She'd shelved them and picked up thrillers instead.

"*Justin is the reason I don't like romance novels,*" *Piper mused, crossing her arms.*

"*Why?*" *Jessie asked.*

Piper had tapped her foot and tilted her head, trying to put her thoughts into words. "*The hero satisfies his woman, varying ways, repeatedly.*"

"*Orgasms?*" *Cole asked.*

"*Magic mouths,*" *Jessie said. She'd blushed when she glanced out the window.*

"*Yes.*" *Piper sighed.* "*I didn't believe a man was capable of such talents.*" *A collective gasp circled the room.*

"*You never complained,*" *Justin said.*

He'd been a selfish lover and used her body to satisfy his needs without ever thinking of hers. To Piper sex was a bore, and she'd wanted it over as fast as possible. It became an obligatory act preformed with someone who claimed to care about her. With Justin, her body never had craved it or derived any pleasure from it. It wasn't until after Justin that she discovered the difference between a selfish lover and a generous one.

"The night he pulled the crap with my brother, I went out. Dancing and drinking." She'd acted out; partly the alcohol, but mostly her wounded spirit, was to blame. *"I had a one-night stand. I don't even know his name."* She'd giggled, but it rang hollow.

"All those things in the novels are true. You have to find a giving man. He did things to me, oh man, I can't even put words to..." The man had been a friend of a friend, and if she'd desired another hookup, she could have found him. But she hadn't wanted sex; she'd wanted to make love. She'd learned Justin's deplorable behavior, even in the bedroom, had been the state of his heart.

Piper rolled over, tears in her eyes. She had admitted to Cole, and everyone else, she'd slept with a stranger. How responsible was that? Especially after claiming to love her husband. She curled on her side and released a shuddering breath.

Cole

Cole sat near the campfire in the pre-dawn twilight. He poked the fire with a long stick. Earlier, dogs howling had caught Gimme's attention, and he rode off trying to find them. Arlon started coffee and soon the blue speckled pot would warm. The thick brown liquid would coat his throat and make him wonder what secret ingredients Arlon added. It always did.

"You leaving early?" Arlon asked.

"No, just tired of Gimme's talking," he admitted, then yawned, showing Arlon a few fillings.

"How are things between you and the girl?" The skinny old man sat next to Cole and stared up at the remaining stars.

Cole debated revealing everything. It was none of the ranch hand's business; however, years of life experience might shed light on the subject. "The woman is fine."

"That's good to hear. I like Piper. She's good for you, and I didn't want to hit you upside the head if you were muddling things up."

Cole grinned and twisted in his seat to face him. "I'm glad." He shook his head. "I don't know what to do with her."

"Hm?"

"Her ex-fiancé came waltzing into town and is trying to get her back."

"Does she fancy him?"

Cole chuckled. "Hell, no. She hates the guy."

"What's the problem?"

Cole stared into the fire, watching the colors change and flicker. He sighed again then scratched his head. "This guy will be trouble for her. He wouldn't leave her alone back home. He's dangerous. I'm afraid he won't leave town anytime soon."

"He won't let go, huh?" Arlon stood up and took the blue coffee pot, pouring Cole and himself a cup of the fresh brew.

Cole understood wanting to hold on to Piper, but Justin wanted to possess her—not cherish her. His actions were demented and cruel. Cole had loved it when Ben took his gun out and not so subtly released the safety. Justin shut-up real quick, then tried to spin it on Piper. Thank God, Ben didn't buy any bull.

The horizon continued to lighten. Cole relaxed and sipped the java. Once there'd been a time when he'd thought every morning would be his last. Then another morn would dawn. He never lost the wonder of it. A new day and a new lease on life. He'd shared those first few mornings home from the hospital with his mother as she nursed him back to health. Hard to believe he'd wasted away to a hundred pounds. The cancer had taken its toll on his body and the operation and chemo had weakened him further.

Yes, being near death's door made a man appreciate another sunrise. Even though he was healthy and cancer free at the moment, it could come back. *It could come back.* Cancer always hung over him like a cloud.

Color crept into the world as it woke, and Cole weighed the option of letting Piper into his heart. Could he put her in a position to hurt her?

"The boy won't like what the townsfolk say about Piper," Arlon said.

"Her ex-fiancé? No, he's not going to like hearing she's married; although it might protect her. He's quite the charmer. I can see him working on the women at the beauty shop, trying to needle the truth out of them. I hope no one falls for his wiles." Cole admired the pink hues lining the clouds.

Arlon refilled their cups and sat back down. He stroked his grizzled chin. "I think you're right. It will protect her." He turned to Cole and held his gaze. "You need to marry that girl to save her."

Cole's mouth fell open. He wondered if he should risk dating her, but marriage? A coherent string of words failed to form in his head, but his ears worked. A horse approached fast. Gimme jumped off the saddle and landed next to Cole. Arlon thrust a cup of coffee at Gimme. The winded man took the cup with a nod. He grimaced at the flavor.

"Ah hell, Arlon, is this motor oil? Are you trying to kill me?" He took another gulp of the hot drink, anyway. "I found the tracks, Cole." The man handed the empty tin cup back to Arlon. "Come on. You're never gonna guess what I've found."

Cole stood and stretched. He hoped Gimme wasn't excited about a caterpillar. "Hold your horses," he muttered as he climbed into the saddle.

"What'd ya find, boy?" Arlon asked.

"I found boot tracks. Someone is trying to trick us." Cole's head twisted in Gimme's direction, and when Gimme saw he held all eyes, he grinned. "Nobody has been up here in ages, and they're not Curly's, so don't ask. Oh yeah, they lead toward your girlfriend's cabin. Maybe she has a secret admirer."

"His wife," Arlon corrected with a smirk.

"Wife? You two're hitched? Wow, that was faster than green grass through a goose." Gimme laughed and turned away from the camp.

Cole thought it highly unlikely they belonged to Justin, but doubt nagged at him. During the flood, Piper had mentioned a bearded man who'd helped her. Could the prints belong to him? There was one way to find out. He kicked the side of the horse and raced after Gimme.

Piper

Piper had slept like a rock, despite the previous day's flash flood, the fight and shower with Cole, then Justin's dramatic arrival, disclosures and being kicked off the ranch property. Piper found a full basket of clean clothes, and not one Jessie had messed with, outside the door when she woke. Cole had planned everything. She missed him, but Beau did his best to entertain her. Florence arranged to drive her to the Double D ranch after dropping Beau at school. Seeing she didn't have her car there, Piper agreed.

Florence handed her a brown paper sack with a sandwich and cookies.

"Oh, Piper. Nana makes the best chocolate chip cookies. She gave you three 'cuz of me." Beau grinned while holding his own brown bag.

"Thanks, kiddo," she said as she tousled his hair.

As they reached the car, a truck turned into the driveway.

"Cole! Cole! Cole!" Beau shouted. Once the truck parked, the boy ran to his uncle. Cole lifted him and tossed him into the air. Piper might have worried if she hadn't seen it before. She inspected Cole. He was genuinely happy to see them, but after being awake for twenty-four hours, he looked exhausted.

Cole hugged his mother, then Florence called Beau to the car. Piper remained quiet, not knowing what to say to the man who'd rearranged his life to protect her.

"Morning," he said with a small grin. He tilted his head, surveying her. "Sleep all right?"

She glanced at his muddy boots. Guilty she'd kept him away from his own bed, she said, "I slept fine, but you should have been there."

"Wouldn't have slept at all then."

Her gaze snapped to his. Heat blossomed at her core. "How is that different from what actually happened?"

"Plenty different, and you know it."

Cole's blue eyes twinkled with mischief. She wanted to knock his hat and that stupid bandanna off his head and kiss him. The same animal magnetism she'd felt the first time she met him hadn't diminished one stinking bit, but she couldn't jump his bones with his mother and nephew watching. She sighed. "I'm going to be late to work."

"I like making you late for work." He chuckled low and husky as he focused with hooded eyes on Piper's lips..

"I'll bet," she said with a giggle. "I like it too."

He took a step toward her, but she hopped back, taking another toward the waiting car. "Cole?" She faced him again. Suddenly, his arms wrapped around her. He claimed her lips and she surrendered to him with a happy sigh. His grip tightened. He tasted of coffee, dawning day and passion, a delicious combination. His outdoorsy masculine scent tantalized her. When he released her, her legs wobbled. And she'd been the one who had a full night's sleep.

"Make me later for work," she whispered.

He chuckled and kissed the top of her head.

CHAPTER 16

Piper

ANOTHER DAY AT WORK. AS Piper shuffled the mail, she wondered if Cole dreamed of her. Jessie kept to the upstairs sewing room, working on a special gift for her sister-in-law Maggie's honeymoon. The couple would soon marry.

The business line rang. "Thank you for calling The Double D. How may I help you today?" Silence made her push the ear piece closer. "Hello?"

"Yes, how are you today, Piper?" Justin said in a confident tone. Since he'd called the business line she had to talk with him now, didn't she?

I was great until you called. "What can the Double D do for you?"

"Will you go out to dinner with me?"

"I'm sorry, sir, this is a business, not a dating service. If you have no business for the Double D, I will have to open the line for actual customers. Have a nice day." She ended the call. The phone rang before she stood up. Halfway up the stairs, she answered the line again. This time Justin asked about the contents in the brochure. "What about the gown in the middle?"

"What size would you like to order?"

"What sizes does it come in?"

Piper pressed her lips together, visualizing the brochure's information including sizes and colors. She pushed open the door, entering the sewing room. She paused, floored by the amount of paperback novels stacked against the walls.

Her voice rose an octave. "This is a serious business, sir. If you're interested in ordering, I can help you or you can visit the website." She rattled off the domain then ended the call. Immediately the phone rang again.

"It's him." Jessie surmised. "You weren't kidding. He's one persistent son-of-a-gun. Let it go to voice mail." She stood and stretched.

"That won't stop him." Piper removed the headset, sat it down and wrung her hands.

Jessie tapped the tablet on the table and woke the device. She maneuvered until she found the voicemail and changed it. It explained the Double D employees were taking lunch and the caller would have the option of leaving a voicemail. Justin would probably fill it.

"Jessie, it's beautiful." Piper examined the delicate lace bodice of the satin negligee. Small iridescent beads created a swirling pattern. "Maggie is going to love it. So will Guy." She giggled and Jessie joined in. Guy Manly, Maggie Barnes' fiancé, commissioned Jessie to make the gown for their wedding night.

"Thanks. Do me a favor and try it on." She took the peignoir off of a hanger and handed it to Piper.

The soft, white material resembled a lacy net. The floor-length robe had bunched material around the elbows and ribbons, bows, and beads. It was exquisite. Piper slipped it on and felt like a princess. She spun around.

"Tsk. Hold still, I don't want to poke you," Jessie said with a pin between her lips.

Piper stopped moving and let the intimate apparel queen do her thing.

Cole

All week Cole worked overnight at the Big Deal while Piper slept in his bed. They'd see each other in the mornings and evenings. He was firm about her not returning home unsupervised. They'd never found the owner of the boot prints near her cabin. The cowboys found a dead cow on the Big Deal property. It appeared to have been killed by animals, but someone had carved into the meat. It was unlikely the culprit had been Justin. It was more probable that the ranch had a squatter living off the land. The person knew how to remain hidden.

Cole had accompanied Piper to the homestead cabin twice. She'd picked up clothing and her laptop. He knelt near the ground and pointed to muddy prints outside the kitchen window. "Are these yours?"

Piper crossed her arms and glanced around the ground. "No." She shifted and met his gaze. "It's rained since we've been here last."

"You might have a Texas stalker."

"Don't say that," she said with a nervous laugh. They inspected her home and found a few things not right. Food stuffs were opened and sampled. From the bathroom she called, "All the toilet paper is missing."

"Are you sure you don't remember using it?" he asked. His body barely fit the frame of the doorway.

"I had a four pack. Look, here's the trash." She pointed to the small waste can with four cardboard rolls.

"Somebody has been using your bathroom?" Everything seemed in place in the small room. "Is anything missing?"

"No. Nothing. And he could have taken my laptop if he really wanted to. All my personal stuff and clothes are untouched." She sat on her bed, looking stumped.

Cole placed hands on his hips and shifted his weight, looking out the window. "I don't like that someone has been casing your home."

"You think I do?" She stood and dropped a bottle of lotion into her purse. "Somebody needed to use the restroom, and that's what they did. They broke in to poop. Could it have been one of Brad's men?"

"There will be hell to pay if it is," he growled.

Piper touched his arm. "Thanks for looking out for me." He opened his arms, and she slid in and sighed. They fit together. He kissed the top of her head, something he'd been doing a lot of lately, but he could not delve deeper right now. He needed to remain focused.

"You don't think it's Justin?" She shivered.

"Not likely." Cole blew out a deep breath. "Speaking of Justin, he's still in town. He's staying in a pay by the week apartment. You think he'll be leaving soon?"

"Not until I agree to either go home with him or marry him. He still wants to get married on our original date. That's in a few weeks. I hope he's not planning on hanging out here until then."

"Y'all would've had a long engagement."

She nodded. "Thank God I came to my senses. I can't imagine marrying that loser."

He chuckled, and she laughed too. "When was your wedding date?" She mumbled against his chest. "That's the weekend of the rodeo." Cole would make sure Piper remained supervised or the ex-fiancé might try to kidnap her.

"Kelly and I are going down to Nockerville this weekend, since I can't hang out in Fortuna without my husband." She sighed as she rolled her eyes.

"I'll go anywhere you want me to go." Cole smiled down at her.

"You, sir, need to go to work." Piper pushed gently against him, but he didn't let her go.

"How about making me late?"

Piper

Piper opened the door to the Tease Me & More salon and a little bell announced her presence. Heads swiveled in her direction. After a second of punctuated silence, the women all began chatting at once.

"The Russian girl is here," a loud woman with foil in her hair said. Someone shushed her, but that didn't stop her.

"That's Florence Dart's daughter-in-law?" asked a woman with a deep scratchy voice.

They kept throwing her glances and smiling. Piper nodded to the receptionist, Gloria Sass, who did nothing to hide her curiosity. Piper sat in the hard plastic chair and glanced around at the room straight out of the eighties. Pale walls with Wedgwood blue and mauve border and a country motif screamed "redecorate me." She picked up a styling magazine and thumbed through the photos looking for something she liked.

"Isn't she pretty?" Barbara Seville, Jessie's longtime stylist, said. Piper had been to get her hair cut one other time and Barbara knew Piper was single and American.

"Beautiful. She definitely looks foreign. I can see why Cole picked her," the loud-customer giggled.

"Do you think she's a commie?" the deep-voiced woman asked.

The room quieted and Piper could feel their stares. She flipped a page and glanced at Gloria, who still stared at her as if trying to work out an enigma. On the small counter behind the reception desk sat a Keurig, tempting Piper. She stood and pointed to the machine.

"Sure, help yourself," Gloria said before snapping her gum.

Piper made a cup of coffee, and while it brewed, the ladies continued to speculate about her.

"Doesn't she speak English?" the frog-voiced lady croaked. "I heard she doesn't know much. She hasn't been here long. Only a few months. I wonder how Cole gets on with a foreigner."

Piper watched as the short spunky owner, Desire Hardmann, emerged from the back office. "Don't you mean you wonder how Cole can get *it* on? I'll tell you. In the language of love, my friends, you don't need words." She made a crude gesture and waggled penciled brows at the women, earning giggles. Piper grew hot. She stirred sugar into her coffee and kept her head down.

"Do you see the way they look at each other at church?" A new lady jumped into the conversation, the stylist closest to Piper. The name of the certification plaque read Derry Yare. The heavyset woman sighed and fanned herself. "Such love and passion. I wished my man looked at me like that," Derry said followed by a round of collective sighs.

Barbara swept the hair up from under the chair while her client paid Gloria. The older patron with fluffy sheep-like hair nodded at Piper shyly, but on the way out she took her hand. Annunciating every word she spoke, loudly as if Piper was hard of hearing, "Welcome to America, suga'." The woman pumped Piper's arm like a hyperactive oil pump and grinned.

"Thanks." The word sounded thick, probably accented, coming out of her mouth.

"Come on, Ms. Piper," Barbara said with an ornery grin. "How are you today?" Of course, the others listened for her reply.

"Good." She blushed under the scrutiny.

First, Barbara placed a mauve smock on her and washed her hair, then she sat Piper in a chair. She combed out the tangles and asked Piper, "What are we doing today?"

"Just a trim, please."

The chair swung around fast, and Desire leaned toward her. "You got a hot date?" Even though Piper shook her head, her face blazed hot which meant she'd turned beet red. Guilty of starting the Russian rumor, Piper should call the old woman out. But she kept her mouth closed.

"Shoo, leave my client be," Barbara said as she waved a comb. Desire retreated with a wink. As Barbara clipped and clipped, Piper watched the world through the large front window and mirrors.

Cars drove past the building, oblivious to those inside. Piper learned that the stylist, Heddie Haire, was popular and had several appointments booked by grouchy Gloria. The young receptionist became all smiles when Desire came out of the office, but otherwise the girl wore a dower expression. She exchanged an over-chewed piece of gum for a new one. The deep-voiced woman spoke with Derry. Their conversation started low and hard to hear but grew louder. The women assumed Piper couldn't understand English. Barbara winked at her in the mirror.

"Who's this character investigating Mrs. Dart? He's a charming fellow. Do you think he's with the Russian secret service? What's that called again, the KFC?"

"He said he's from Chicago."

"Damn Yankee."

Barbara measured the length of Piper's hair by pulling the pieces straight on either side of her face. She snipped once then tried again. Perfection. She smiled then added styling goo. When the hairdryer turned on, the strange conversation about Justin dissolved into loud warmth.

Outside the building a battered red truck pulled into a slanted parking space. A wiry man climbed out of the truck and stretched. Piper tried to decipher which was older, the man or the truck. He tapped on the window and cupped his hands on the glass to look in. He waved and smiled, exposing chaw. Every woman, including Piper, lifted a hand in response. Arlon Topp entered the salon, gussied up in clean jeans and a plaid shirt. He wore good boots, not the work kind, and his belt buckle gleamed. Around his collar hung a bolo tie.

"Well, Miss Gloria, you sure are a sight of beauty for these old eyes. You have made my morning, little princess." He tipped his black hat as the girl giggled and blushed. Who knew the receptionist liked sweet talking old men? Piper chuckled, thinking Gloria was the perfect personality to be looking for a sugar daddy.

Desire appeared in the room, hesitated, then a grin broke out. "Well, bless my soul, if it isn't Arlon Topp. I didn't think you'd come back after that perm ran amok back in the seventies." Her hands landed on her slim hips.

"Ah Desire, you're just as feisty as ever, and you look good enough to eat," he said and leaned in, placing a kiss on her cheek. He looked like a seventeen-year-old boy about to ask a girl out.

Desire blushed, inspecting the floor. "You know it, but you haven't dropped by to get dessert."

Arlon coughed and glanced warily around at the women. He shifted his weight and moved his hand forward. Piper realized for the first time he'd hidden something in his hands. He offered them to her like he'd caught a butterfly and didn't what it to escape. "I've got a little something for you." He opened his hands exposing two small ceramic owls. One was orange and brown glazed and the other green.

"Oh, Arlon," Desire gasped in pleasure. "What a fine pair of hooters!"

He coughed again, embarrassed and pleased by her outburst. "I know you already have a nice set."

"Yes, that's true. Would you like to see them?" She grinned like a fisherman who'd hooked a big one and was about to reel him in. "Now my collection is complete."

"Some other time, little lady." He placed the small owls in her hand. When she pouted he said, "I'm meeting my sister for lunch."

"That's a pity. Maybe next time." Desire acquiesced defeat. "Tell Morgan hello."

"Will do." He kissed her cheek again then tipped his hat to the frog-woman and Derry. He took two steps toward Piper and Barbara. "Looking good, Piper."

"Thank you," Barbara said taking the credit.

"It's a mighty fine do," he tilted his head with a sly smile. "Piper, would you like to meet me for lunch across the street at the Pink Taco? I'd like to introduce you to my sister."

Piper nodded and Barbara grabbed her head, stopping the motion. "Yes sir, just give me a few minutes." He waved and strolled out with a wink.

Her long sentence confounded the others. She could actually talk and understand the English language? You betcha.

CHAPTER 17

Piper

THE LUNCH CROWD FILLED THE Pink Taco. When Piper entered, many heads bobbed up, eyes flashing as they recognized the newlywed of the town. The notoriety had been dying off, but then Justin had arrived in Fortuna, causing a fuss. She hoped to God the people would support Cole and not believe Justin's false accusations.

Her gaze roamed the restaurant searching for Justin. The pale pink stucco walls held pictures of Mexican heritage. A taco shaped piñata hung over the clerk who rang out guests at the cash register. She breathed a sigh of relief, finding the room safe and Justin-free.

A blonde woman joined Arlon at the table. She smiled when Arlon introduced her. "This is my sister, Morgan." Her body was rail-like, similar to Arlon's, but dressed in a pale gray business suit, she looked like nobility.

"So you're what the big deal is all about?" Morgan said, offering a hand.

Piper shrugged a shoulder. "I guess, but Ms. Hardmann started it."

"Yep, that woman stirs up a lot of dust in this town," Arlon agreed.

"I don't see you minding much," Morgan teased. "In fact, I remember a time or two when you were all for her schemes." She elbowed the red-faced man, who mumbled something that sounded like "ah shucks."

"She has a way with men, you make no never mind," Arlon said. He took a sip of iced tea.

Knowing Arlon was in his seventies, Piper couldn't believe Morgan and Arlon were close to the same age. She looked younger than Piper's mother.

"We're twins," Arlon said with a straight face. Piper's jaw dropped.

"Shut up. We are not." Morgan elbowed him again. "He's seventy-two and I'm not. We had the same daddy but not mamas. There are twenty years between us and probably lots of other brothers and sisters in between. Daddy liked women. He was married while he was out creating us."

"Yes, ma'am. I think it was four or five times he got hitched," Arlon added, rubbing his chin.

"He liked you, though." Morgan grinned at her brother.

"That's because I was the first offspring to have balls." He winked at his little sister. "And you were special because you're the youngest."

"With balls?" Piper asked with a giggle.

"That too," Arlon said. Morgan rolled her eyes.

The owner, Clint Torres, took their order. As people walked past, they greeted the Topps. It seemed Piper dined with local celebrities.

"I'm a social worker." Her clients were mainly in Fortuna, Nockerville and a small village called Bald Knob.

"How did you become interested in that?" Piper asked.

Morgan sighed. "I despise men like our father. Men who leave a trail of heartbreak wherever their penises have been."

Piper choked on her tea. She covered her mouth trying to hide a smile. "Go on," she squeaked out.

"I am just one person involved helping the children while the abandoned or abused women get their lives in order. Not all have a hardworking older brother who took on an orphaned half-sibling." Morgan leaned and patted Arlon's gnarled hand. The old man blushed under the praise.

"Good men are around," Piper said softly. "But sometimes it's hard for the head to tell the heart what it doesn't want to believe. We women want to believe what a man, who claims to love us, tells us. Faith gets many of us in trouble."

"Amen." Morgan agreed with a nod.

"Cole's a good man." Arlon slipped the juicy tidbit of obvious info in. He glanced out the front window to the parked cars lining the area of commerce. "Uh oh," he muttered. He pulled out his phone and sent a text.

Both women turned and followed his gaze. "Oh no," Piper groaned.

Justin Saine walked a circle around her small compact car then stopped and scanned the area. He checked his fake Rolex and moved toward a gift shop. It wouldn't take him long to figure out she wasn't shopping. The store was long and narrow and he'd be able to see the entire store from the entry. He returned to the street with a sneer and a determined crinkle in his brow. Three businesses later, he crossed to the Pink Taco's side of the street and she lost sight of him. The plate of food sat untouched before her. With Justin's appearance her appetite had fled. She wiped sweaty hands on the cloth napkin. Her feet itched to move, to run away.

"You've gone pale, girl. You need to eat something." Arlon nudged her plate.

Piper took a minuscule bite then drained her iced tea. Her stomach twisted in knots and grumbled in protest. The bell above the door jingled, and Piper slumped, trying to become invisible. Morgan shook her head. It wasn't Justin. Relieved, Piper let out a long breath. Both Topps raised a hand in greeting to the local who'd entered the building. Piper didn't turn around, but kept staring at the painted canyon scene at the back of the restaurant. She tried to steady her heart and regulate her breathing. Calming down took great effort.

Clint refilled their glasses and put more tortilla chips on the table. Piper smiled up at him. The bell rang again. One look at Arlon's face said everything she needed to know. Morgan and Arlon shared a look, and then they watched a figure walk toward them. Arlon squared his shoulders and leaned back in his seat. Morgan stuffed a chip in her mouth and chewed like it would save the world. A shadow fell over the table and Piper swallowed hard.

A hand clamped down on her shoulder, the fingertips biting into her flesh, making her gasp. "Hello, Piper." Those two words sent a shiver down her spine, and her heart went cold. Numb, her tongue stuck to the roof of her mouth. With wide eyes, she sent a pleading glance to Arlon and Morgan. The siblings opposed each other, Arlon holding a welcoming smile on his lips while Morgan glared and pursed her lips as if she might spit acid.

Justin ignored being ignored and squeezed her shoulder again, which pissed her off and helped firm her backbone. She tried to brush his hand away but ended up having to pry his fingers off. "Don't touch me," she said through clenched teeth.

"Fancy meeting you here." He chuckled and nodded at the curious folks who looked on.

"Stop following me," she hissed.

"I'm not. I was hungry. There's no crime against that, is there?" His eyes narrowed in on her then shifted to the empty chair.

"Go eat. Enjoy. Go away."

Justin placed a hand on the vacant ladder-back chair at their table as if he'd been invited to lunch. "Sorry, boy, this chair is reserved." Justin's snakelike eyes zeroed in on Arlon.

"You don't want to make a scene." Piper tried to reason with the man. Appearance was important.

"I'm not making a scene, you are." Justin raised the tone and volume of his voice. Another attempt to manipulate her.

Piper shrugged and popped a chip into her mouth. "These fresh ones are better than the first batch. They have more salt." The table started a lively discussion about chips and salsa. Arlon preferred extra hot like him. This earned giggles from the ladies. Justin shifted his weight from side to side standing there like the tool he was.

Cole

Cole's phone vibrated in his pocket. He'd kept vigilant, with the stranger haunting the Big Deal and Justin stalking Piper. She hadn't called much, but she would text him. That was the real reason he was a quick-draw when it came to his phone. He never knew when his boss, the police, his mother, the Barnes' or Piper would need him.

He glanced at the screen. Arlon had sent the text. That never happened. He scanned it, then ran out the door yelling, "Gotta go, Mom. Sorry to bail on you."

Ten minutes had passed when he parked next to Arlon's red pickup. He surveyed the street and witnessed Justin leave the small toy shop called the Tin Soldier. The stalker glanced down the sidewalk and over at Piper's car. A small sneer appeared, and then he pulled open the door of the Pink Taco. A petite elderly woman with a black cap of hair entered a minute before him. Cole smiled. If Ms. Hardmann was in there, Piper had another layer of protection. Arlon wouldn't let anything happen to her, and neither would Clint.

He took several deep breaths and closed his eyes. Justin brought out the beast in him. He'd never wanted to hurt, maim, or kill anyone in his life—until now. Cole walked to the door, but peered through the glass before entering. Piper tensed when the ex touched her, and she struggled to get him off her. It took control to stay still. Arlon saw him and winked.

Arlon smiled at the unwanted guest, but Cole recognized the old cowboy's "spider looking at a fly" grin. Morgan fingered her steak knife. Instantly, Cole liked her.

Piper exchanged words with Justin, but he didn't leave. The dumbass stood there trying to look important. Arlon, Morgan and Piper ignored him, carrying on a conversation. The other patrons lost interest and went back to their lunches.

Cole sucked in a deep breath. *Time to rescue Piper.* He yanked open the door and strode across the restaurant. His brow was set with determination. Flustered by the lack of attention, Justin hadn't seen Cole. His shadow fell over Piper's shoulder, and when he touched it she grabbed his hand and squeezed.

"I said don't touch—" It started as a growl but it ended with a mew. Cole bent to face level, and she touched his cheek with trembling fingers. "Cole," she whispered. She closed her eyes and muttered "thank God." Chewing her lip, she sighed.

Cole stood and tipped his hat at Morgan. "Ms, Topp, you're looking fine. Arlon, you old coot, how did you score a date with two of the loveliest ladies in Fortuna?"

The old man's face wrinkled in pleasure. "It's easy, son. It's my animal magnetism. I'm hot stuff and in rare commodity." Cole laughed long. "It's not that funny."

Cole kneaded Piper's tight shoulders trying to ease the tension. Her full plate spoke volumes. She feared Justin and his erratic behaviors. There was one solution. "Well, if you don't mind, I'm going to steal Piper away."

"I should get a box." She looked down at the now cold food and frowned.

"Piper—"

Clint interrupted Justin by sitting a brown paper bag down on the table. The top was folded and stapled with a receipt. "Here you are, Cole." Clint smiled and shook his hand. "Two beef chimichangas with a side of sour cream."

"Thank you, Clint." He pulled two twenties out of his wallet. "Thanks for putting it all together. Keep the change."

"It's always a pleasure. Say hello to your mother for me."

Cole smiled at that. Clint had asked his mother out several times, but Flo always politely declined. Clint turned and nearly ran into the stalker. "Right this way, sir. We'll find you a seat." Justin followed him but glared at Cole.

Piper glanced at Cole with owl eyes. He shrugged. He hadn't done a damn thing. It was Clint who led the bastard away. Cole took advantage of the moment and slipped into the empty seat. "Let's get out of here, Pipes." After reassuring her he'd paid for her meal, he took her elbow.

"Son," Arlon said, reaching out an arm to stop Cole. "You know how to make this end, don't you?"

Piper looked from one man to the other. She paled and shrunk against him, thinking of her own outcome. God, he hated the fear showcased in her eyes. Cole scanned the restaurant for Justin. A waiter took his order but his gaze remained fixated on his ex-fiancée. Cole placed a palm on her back and rubbed in a circle.

"We've already had this conversation, Arlon. You know I won't let anything bad happen to Piper."

Even as the old man grinned, Cole steered her outside. They made it to her car before her knees gave out. He caught and held her. Her fingers fisted the cotton of his T-shirt and even caught a few chest hairs. He tried to hide the wince. Once she found her feet, she pushed away from him and stood rock still. Her eyes glazed, like she'd gone on automatic processing mode. He leaned against her car, sat the bag down and stretched an arm across the roof and waited. He could see into the restaurant and the myriad of faces watching with open curiosity. She took a couple of steps then placed her forehead against his chest.

"What's going on in your head?" he asked.

"Why won't he leave me alone?" She tilted her head up with a pleading look. "Isn't it obvious I'm not into him?"

"His powers of observation are clearly lacking." Piper rewarded him with a slight chuckle. "I get why he won't let go. I'd never want to let you go either. Don't worry though; you're free to be you. If you want to take off and become a full time lingerie model, I won't stop you."

"You'd like that, wouldn't you?" Pushing back, she focused over his shoulder at the building behind him. "They're watching us."

"Yep." The girls in the beauty salon love a good romance. "Should we give them a show?"

Her eyes rounded in surprise. "No."

"It will piss off Justin."

"Okay." Piper's hands circled around his back as he pushed off the car. He caressed her face and she sighed. He loved that feeling. "You're my hero. You're there when I need you."

"Always." Tilting his head to accommodate his hat, their lips met in sweet surrender. He turned, exposing their profiles to both the restaurant and salon. He let one hand move to her stomach and caressed then patted it.

She glanced down. "What are you—Cole!" Piper gasped, grabbing his hand. She groaned, "People will think I'm pregnant."

CHAPTER 18

Cole

CLOUDS ROLLED IN AND THE overhead branches waved as Cole turned into the driveway. On the side of the road, the lights of a parked vehicle flicked on and it drove away in haste. He didn't think anything of it until he saw the small compact car near the front walk.

A week without incident, and Piper had returned to her cabin. He'd gone back to his normal schedule.

Earlier that day, his mother had reminded him she'd found a babysitter for Beau. His mother took a night once or twice a month to have dinner with her cronies. He'd usually watched his nephew. They'd make it a male-bonding night. Either watching sports, going to the Pink Taco or the movies. It never crossed his mind she would get Piper to sit for Beau, but it made sense. The boy loved her. Hell, the whole Dart clan did.

His heart raced as he shifted the truck into park. The only light came from the porch light and the interior's utter darkness frightened him. The people he held dearest to his heart might be kidnapped or worse: dead. His feet felt like lead blocks as he hastened to the door. Fumbling the keys, he finally unlocked it. A long creak punctuated the silence. Over the oven, a small light basked the kitchen in a dim glow. He breathed out a sigh of relief. The light lit two empty plates with crumbs and two small glasses.

With no evidence of foul play, he turned on the overhead light and took the stairs to the loft. He crept through the eerie quiet and peered into his room. Empty. He pushed the master bedroom door open a crack. The pale night-light washed the corner with yellow light. In bed, Beau had snuggled against Piper and they'd fallen asleep. Her hand had relaxed and a book had fallen open on her legs. Her face lay against his hair like she'd bent to kiss him.

He couldn't pull his gaze away from the tender scene. He took a step closer and the floor creaked. Piper's eyes shot open. She gazed around in a daze, then looked toward the door. The light from the landing outlined Cole's body, but his face remained shadowed. She sat up quickly but gingerly. He stepped back to let the light wash over him.

Piper smiled. "You scared me," she whispered. Then she breezed past him and skipped down the stairs.

Cole debated telling her about the car on the street.

"I'm late," she pointed to the clock. "I gotta run. I'm meeting the girls for a girls' night out. It's going to be fun." Piper grinned and kissed him on the cheek. The door closed in his face, and she'd left before he found his tongue.

Piper

Piper threw a hand up, waving to Kelly, Jessie and Maggie Barnes. The women wove through the tables of the tavern.

"I've never been to Under the Table before," Maggie asked as she perused the menu. "What's good?"

"The wings," Kelly blurted without thinking. "Try them with hot barbecue. Yum."

"Where's Josiah tonight?" Piper asked.

"Guys' night out, which really is guys' night in," Jessie said.

"Guy and my brothers planned to watch a movie and get pizza," Maggie added. "I want Guy to get to know my brothers before we get married."

When Jessie had learned about Kelly and Piper's girls' night she invited herself. Then Maggie joined Jessie.

A waitress set a hard cider before Piper and Kelly. She looked around for Dakota. It was his thing. She found him at the bar and toasted the bottle in his direction.

Jessie's eyes widened. "Who's that?"

"Don't you mean 'where's Cole?'" Kelly teased with a wink.

"Shut up." Piper bumped shoulders with her friend and they giggled.

"He's cute." Maggie's observation made the women turn to inspect the man. He'd turned away, showing off his perfectly shaped butt.

"That's Dakota," Kelly announced. "He likes Piper." Piper bumped her again.

"Does Cole know he has competition?" Jessie asked.

Embarrassed at the unwanted attention, Piper tried to divert the conversation away to something safer. "So how are the wedding plans coming?" she asked Maggie. It was the best topic she could pull out of her hat. Something that both Jessie and Maggie would gush about. But Piper hadn't counted on Kelly turning the tables.

"She needs pointers for her own wedding to Cole."

Piper slapped her hand to her face and groaned.

"I can give you plenty of tips." Maggie smiled. "I know where all the bargain places are in Nockerville, Fortuna and even Bald Knob has a cute little party planning shop."

"Of course, we know someone who can make super sexy honeymoon apparel. Maybe something of the crotchless variety?" Kelly elbowed Piper, and the others giggled.

"Do you have plans we don't know about?" Jessie asked.

"Hey, wait a minute. I thought you were already married," Maggie said.

"No, that was Desire Hardmann's doing," Jessie informed with a grin.

A grunt escaped Maggie's lips, and she made a face that read "say no more." The name Desire explained it all away. Jessie leaned close to fill her in. Maggie's eyes narrowed then widened; her head shook in disgust and then her mouth hung open in apparent shock.

"The rumor has been a good thing." Piper shifted and took a sip of her drink, as the girls waited for her to continue. "No one asked me out so I haven't had to turn anyone down. You know how men are. They have such delicate egos."

"When they're not trying to inflate them," Kelly snapped with a pout.

In agreement, they toasted men.

"Aren't we a complete set," Kelly said fingering her bottle. "The married woman, the soon-to-be-married woman, the pretend married woman and the never-wants-to-be-married woman."

"What?" Jessie gave Kelly a funny look. "You've always wanted to get married and have a family."

"Yeah, you'll be a great mom," Maggie said.

"I don't need any more kids. I've got twenty-two second graders. The situation is ideal because I send them home at the end of the day." Kelly smirked and leaned back.

"What about men?" Jessie tried.

"You mean, what about penises?" Maggie giggled.

"They're all right, I guess," Kelly said with a shrug. "The penis part—not the rest."

"But they're replaceable. I'll buy you a package of double As and you'll be set for a month." Piper elbowed her friend.

"Hello, ladies," Dakota said, nodding his head at the group. His light sandy hair caught the backlight giving him a blond halo.

"Well, speaking of penises, I mean men." Maggie giggled.

"Just one." Dakota stuck his pointer finger in the air. "Because one is all I need."

"God, see this is what I mean," Kelly grumbled. "An inflated ego to match the inflated penis."

"It's all poppycock," Dakota said and offered his hand to Piper. He led her to the dance floor, and they began to two-step.

"Thanks for rescuing me." Piper needed the mindless exercise. She stumbled a few times, trying to keep up with Dakota.

The girls continued eating appetizers, drinking, laughing and no doubt talking about men. Kelly's angry gestures probably meant she'd broken up with Sawyer again. Dancing with Dakota might benefit Kelly. It had helped Piper. Dakota was cute and smelled good. A double bonus. She leaned closer to take another whiff. The sleeveless sundress had been a good choice because Piper always worked up a sweat dancing. The dress kept her cool.

Dakota spun Piper around, making her dress flare. The smile slipped from her face when she spotted newcomers. The boys had invaded girls' night. Josiah and Matt Barnes pushed another table over to the girls'. Guy Manly sat next to Maggie, nuzzling the starry-eyed woman. Piper covertly surveyed the surrounding area. No Cole. A subtle pang stabbed at her heart.

Cole's absence meant the girls wouldn't heckle her anymore. Matt made things awkward enough without adding Cole to the mix. Even now Matt watched her sway with Dakota. She focused back on her partner, but Dakota's steps faltered as he looked over her shoulder. Someone wanted to dance with her, and Dakota offered her hand to... Cole.

As Piper's hand slid into his larger one, she reminded herself to breathe. Why did he have this effect on her? His eyes sparkled, locking unto hers without mercy. His blue shirt brought out their color; she could drown in their depths. One side of his lips toyed with a smile.

His one hand rested on her hip. Did he have a fire superpower? It was burning a hole in the dress. Her mouth went dry, and she longed for a drink. She caught a whiff of soap, as if he was fresh from the shower. She licked her lips, and his gaze fell and followed her tongue.

"You don't smell like a cow—"

"Cattle."

"Farm."

"Ranch," he corrected. "That's a good thing." She nodded, and he leaned forward and sniffed her neck. "Mmm. Berries, strawberries. You smell like summer."

She couldn't hide the smile, but tried to minimize it by looking away. "So why are you here? Are you trying to get the people of Nockerville to think we're going to have twins?" Her face flashed hot.

"There's an idea for church." He laughed when she stomped on his foot.

"There were rumors about Justin being at the Double D so I stopped in after Mom came home. False alarm. I should have known better. Just one of the ranch hands blowing smoke. Your ex hasn't shown up at the Double D or Big Deal. Anyway, while I was there the guys were trying to decide if they should crash the girls' night out. Josiah and Guy were feeling lovesick. They missed their ladies." He stopped dancing and walked her to the bar where he ordered a pitcher of beer.

"You and Matt are along for the ride, huh?"

"Well, there were four of you and four of us."

"No. There are four of them and four of us." He looked over at the table. "Four attached and four single," she clarified.

They joined the group at the table. Josiah told funny stories about Matt and Maggie then they did the same about him. Jessie kept a hand on her husband's knee. Guy's arm relaxed along the back of Maggie's chair. When she leaned back, he'd touch her shoulder or hair. The simple touches fascinated Piper. She longed for a relationship like that. Justin had only acted what he thought would make the best impression.

Piper pulled the pitcher of beer over and poured a glass. She might reach Kryptonite level, but Kelly was the designated driver tonight. She glanced at Kelly. She hadn't engaged in much conversation and looked constipated.

A shiver slid down Piper's spine as something trailed down the back of her bare arms. Cole's finger. He did it again. She bumped knees with him to make him stop. He leaned toward her and breathed on her neck. It wasn't obvious to the others; at least, she hoped not.

Dakota extended a hand to Kelly, and she smiled a real smile for the first time that evening. As the dance partners headed to the floor, Piper leaned back against Cole's shoulder. She watched Kelly blush. They moved smoothly together. Soon other couples were dancing, which left Matt, Cole and Piper to talk.

"Your ex-fiancé is a real piece of work," Matt muttered between songs.

Piper stiffened. "Tell us something we don't know," Cole said in an authoritative tone.

"I wish everyone would quit calling him mine. He isn't my anything." She took a long drink of beer.

Cole

Later Matt leaned toward Piper and said, "Justin was hanging out at Fu King Wok, drinking water. I'm sure they loved that. Every person who came in, he tried to pull into a conversation. He asked if they knew you and if they'd help reunite the two of you. Most ignored him or brushed him off. They were there to pick up dinner. They mostly assumed you two are a thing, but there was one that bought his sad story hook, line and sinker."

"Who was it, Matt?" Cole asked.

"Ms. Deeds." Matt surveyed the room like the woman would pop up and waggle a finger at him. Piper sucked in a breath.

"Ms. Hardmann will keep her in line." Cole spoke the thought out loud. Ms. Deeds was one of the spinsters of Fortuna. The older woman would probably eat up the charmer's attention. What news had Ms. Deeds delivered?

It was time to have a little chat with Justin. He wouldn't be hard to find.

Three different friends of his mother called to find out about Cole's wife. The corners of his mouth lifted. Having a wife was a definite perk. He slid his arm around her and tugged her close. Her stiff body complied, relaxing against him. Easing her worry warmed his heart. If only he could remove the worry for good. He traced a design on her bare arm. It must have tickled, because she grabbed his finger.

Matt Barnes cleared his throat. "Are you curious about the rodeo?"

Piper sat up straight, and a smile lit her face. Charged with excitement, she replied, "Yes, I can't wait. I've never been to one before."

"You know it's nearly a week long—"

"And they close the school. Kelly told me. I'm going to go every minute I can."

Cole leaned back. How could he protect her at the rodeo when he had to work? She shouldn't be alone, not on the wedding day picked from the foiled engagement.

Piper turned to him with bright eyes. "Are you going?"

"Most likely. Beau will bounce off the walls if he isn't allowed to eat cotton candy and ride the rides." He winked, causing her to blush. "You should join us."

"Make it a family outing," Matt teased. He barely ducked the fork Cole tossed at him. "Okay, fine. I'm going to see if my sister will dance with me." He pushed the chair back and left.

"I'm serious, Piper. It'd be my pleasure to escort you to the rodeo." If her smile could have gotten any bigger, he would have paid money to see it.

Cole leaned back in the chair, away from her. He had to, or else he'd pull her into his arms and make a scene in the restaurant. Cole didn't want to frighten her away, although he had a hunch he couldn't. He tipped his chair back, balancing it on two legs. They watched the dancers circle each other. He tried to think of a solution so Piper would be safe at the Rodeo without him.

Kelly smiled up at Dakota as they swirled back into the throng. A smirk tugged on Cole's lips: he might have an answer. He shifted his weight and fell back. He flailed his arms, trying to keep his balance. Piper's hand slapped down on his knee. The chair responded with a jaw-jerking stop. "Thanks," he said.

"I'm too young to be a widow," she said with a grin.

"Come on." He pulled her up to dance. They glided around the floor, working up a sweat. At one point, Maggie disappeared and Cole maneuvered Piper in to Guy's skinny arms. Guy took off with enthusiasm.

Cole found the man he was searching for and signaled with a tilt of his head. Dakota joined him, and they walked back to the table. He lifted a hand, catching the server's attention and placed an order. Piper might not like his conspiring without her, but she trusted Dakota, and if she did, he could swallow his pride and trust him too. Perched in Guy's arms, Piper spied them with suspicious eyes. Cole raised a glass of amber liquid to her and Dakota followed suit.

"To Piper," Cole said.

"To Piper," Dakota echoed. They clinked glasses and drank.

All business, Cole turned to Dakota. "I need your help."

CHAPTER 19

Piper

PIPER GROANED AS SHE SIPPED the coffee. Every sound echoed off the high ceiling of the A Hole in One donut shop.

"Is your coffee too hot?" Kelly asked.

They'd rolled out of bed with semi-tamed bed-head and no makeup. Wearing over-sized shirts with shorts, they'd decided to bum it. Piper's large shirt hid an embarrassing fact: she wore no bra. She couldn't fully blame the Kryptonite. Cole had the bra, and he hadn't earned it through an act of passion. No, she'd traded him for it. Stupid.

"No. I can't believe what I did. That's all." Piper grimaced.

"Honey, I might have done the same thing. You need more sugar and caffeine." Kelly pushed a bag of donut holes in her direction.

Piper nodded and obediently popped one in her mouth. The A-holes buzzed around them filling napkin holders, wiping tables and offering more coffee. Piper graciously smiled, her mouth full, to the teen who filled her cup.

"I can't get over the change in Cole." Kelly stared off like she was delving into the past.

"How so?"

"Well, he's hot. You know, fine. I don't remember him being so handsome. It's been so long since he's been social. I'd have classified him an agoraphobic, only leaving his home for work and church."

"Really?" Piper thought back to that infamous day at Stitts', the day Desire Hardmann announced she was Cole's wife. He'd admitted his insecurity about his looks. That flaw kept him home. Kelly had one thing right, Cole was drop-dead gorgeous. The feel of his smooth skin stretched over his contoured chest, and even the dark hair that ran down his belly got her blood pumping. Her thoughts dipped lower, and she choked on her coffee.

"You've brought the man out into the world again. *You.* He must think you're something special. I think you're good for him. Cole needs you, Piper. He needs to live again. He's been hiding away ever since the cancer. It's good to see the smile on his face."

Piper shrugged. Kelly didn't know the whole truth about Cole. According to his mother, the disease had changed him. He wasn't physically alienated, but keeps his heart hidden. He wanted no commitments. "Cole doesn't want a relationship."

"Bullshit." Kelly sat up straight and glared at Piper. "And I know bullshit because I'm from a ranching town. Don't you argue with me, Piper McCracken. He is head over heels in love with you or else he wouldn't care a flying flip about Justin Saine. Come on, the man upended his family to fit you into his home. He changed shifts at work to accommodate what's best for you, not him. Grab a clue out of the clue bag, girl. He's totally in love with you."

"He's afraid of commitment," she held up her hand, "because of the cancer. If it comes back, he doesn't want to leave a widow or girlfriend grieving."

"He told you?" Kelly leaned back, shocked.

"His mother. We've been talking." Piper held the mug with a death grip and stared into the dark liquid. "She thinks I've been good for him too. She likes me and I like his family. I could fall for him, Kelly. Fall hard. But I can't—" she breathed in deeply. "I can't give in to the hope he'll change his mind. Kelly, I won't make him change. I want a man to want me forever, not be afraid of losing what we have."

"Listen, he's got to be reevaluating. Especially after last night and the start of a new collection."

"God," Piper groaned. It echoed again. "Don't remind me."

"I can't help it. It was classic." Kelly's gaze shifted to Piper's T-shirt.

Piper closed her eyes and instantly remembered Cole's body pressed against hers as he backed her against Kelly's car. Poor Kelly had sequestered herself into the car so she wouldn't have to be a witness to the romantic interlude.

Cole's ego was hyper-inflated. She'd been tempted to touch him, but their bodies, pressed together, didn't allow any space. When Piper's sundress strap slid off her shoulder to reveal the black and emerald lace bra strap, he bent and kissed her shoulder. The heat shot straight to her sweet spot. She'd moaned, and he worked his way to her neck. Putty in his hands, she'd clutched his shirt.

The car window rolled down. "Piper doesn't have to go home with me, but if she is I'm leaving in five minutes," Kelly said, then the window rolled up.

Piper couldn't go home with Cole as much as she desired to. Going home to the Big Deal tonight was not an option either. Brad Davidson was on stakeout duty trying to capture the Big Deal stalker and/or Justin. She'd planned to stay with Kelly. "I parked my car in Kelly's garage."

"That's good," he said, pulling away winded.

Piper wrapped her arms around him and breathed in. Even if she couldn't have Cole, she wanted his scent all night long. "I want your shirt," she blurted.

"What?"

"Give me your shirt," she said, rubbing her nose on it and humming in delight.

"Well, I'll take your bra in trade."

"But I've been dancing, and it's sweaty." He'd liked the lacy thing, but seriously?

"Same." Cole pinched the fabric of his shirt.

She'd wasted a minute debating, then sighed. With a little shove on his chest, she'd met his hooded gaze. Again, she'd pushed but this time harder. Piper reached behind her, unlatching the hooks through the cloth. She'd shimmied out of one strap then the other and pulled the bra out of the dress. Cole's gaze never left her body. With the bra dangling on her fingertips, she presented it to him as an offering. He stretched his fingers to accept, but she said, "No, sir. Your turn."

He'd made a big deal of stripping off the shirt; slowly untucking it from his jeans and raising it inch by agonizing inch. She'd ached to touch his warm abdomen and lay her cheek against his chest.

She'd concluded it wasn't the shirt she'd wanted after all but the man.

Cole

Cole awoke to movement. He popped one lid open, loath to leave the dream where Piper wore nothing but the black and green lace bra and panties. A minute more and she would have mounted him like a wild bronco for the ride of her life. He let out a sigh and rolled over.

"Cole?" His mother spoke in that gentle voice that said 'I hate to bother you.' The tone had become familiar to him over the cancer ridden and chemo filled months. He threw the comforter aside and sat on the edge of the bed. Big mistake. It didn't faze his mother; she waited quietly. He found sweats and pulled them over his straining boxer briefs.

"Mornin'," he mumbled in a raspy voice.

"Good morning, son." She walked to the window and pulled open the shades while he lumbered to the bathroom. When he emerged, she hit him with the equivalent of a bucket of iced water. "It's Piper."

Instantly awake, no caffeine needed, he took two flying steps to his mother's side. Her face betrayed nothing. "What's going on?" For the first time he noted her opened palm holding a phone. He'd missed a call and texts.

"It's been making noise all morning. I didn't want to wake you, but I thought you'd want to know."

"Hell, yeah. Good call." Cole snatched the phone and read the texts. He ran a hand over his bandanna and sat down. He listened to her message on the voicemail. It wasn't an emergency. Thank God. His mom hesitated in the doorway like a mother bird. He gave her a thumbs up and she flitted out of sight.

He hit the recall button and waited, bumping his leg up and down. "Piper, you scared the hell out of me." He tried to sound tough.

"Why are you so grouchy?"

"You woke me."

"Oh, sorry." Her voice softened.

"What's going on?"

"Cole, the town prankster struck again. It might have been while Kelly and I were at A Hole in One. We had a nice long talk over breakfast. Suddenly an A-hole freaked out. She sounded like a squealing pig." Piper giggled.

"What happened?" he smiled at her giddiness.

"The prankster changed a sign."

"That's happened before."

"They have a soup of the day sign at the cafe across the street. It's a blackboard and the chalk can be wiped and rewritten. It read... Soup of the day: Beer."

Cole couldn't help but chuckle. He wondered how much business the restaurant would garner from that spotlight. When they ended the call, he took a relieved breath. She'd wanted to share with him and warmth tingled in his chest.

His eyes drifted shut and the vision of Piper in nothing but lacy underwear popped into his head. Cole savored the memory and rolled over, trying to find the token she'd given him. He stretched and relaxed back on the bed. The bra wasn't under his pillows. He stood and threw the blankets to the side. Nothing. The thing had gone missing. Just in case it'd become sandwiched between layers, he pulled everything off the bed piece by piece.

Cole scratched his head; he remembered bringing it in. As a last resort, he searched under the bed. He stepped out into the hall when he heard a telltale scream. His heart leaped into his throat. Swallowing, he peered over the wood balcony.

His mother glared up at him. "You have some explaining to do, young man." With her hands on her hips, her foot tapped an angry rhythm. Beau ran up the stairs with a frown. He froze when he saw Cole. His eyes wide, he shook his head in warning. He ran to the master suite and shut the door, leaving Cole to face the music alone.

"Come down here this second," his mother ordered.

Contrite, he walked the path to purgatory. He shuffled to his mother. She held Piper's bra by the strap. Her beet-red face and crinkled brow made her look like an overripe tomato.

"I can explain—" Cole said.

"Don't you talk to me."

"But Mom—"

"Not another word." She raised the lace to her face and examined the band. The tag held the emblem of the Double D. "Explain."

Explain. Not explain. Talk or not talk. "It's Piper's."

"I figured that much. It smells like her lotion. I want to know why a lacy bra was left on the counter where my grandson found it?" She snorted.

"I can't believe I left it there. I thought I took it upstairs. Sorry." Cole stuck out his hand, and she handed it over.

"It's one of Jessie's. It's a beautiful work of art."

His thumb caressed the black satiny cup.

His mother studied him with a level gaze. Cole did not want to have this conversation.

"Is it safe?" Beau asked from above. His round face peered between two slats.

"Yes, dear. You can come down."

Cole didn't have a pocket big enough to hide the bra from Beau's eyes so he stuffed it into his pants. He moved to pour a cup of coffee, and as soon as the material rubbed against him he was hard again. He hid his tent from the others by standing behind the kitchen island. The wire of the bra cups cradled his manhood. He found it hard to concentrate on his mother's words as memories, followed by desires, scrolled through his mind. There was a chance he'd be standing behind the island all morning.

"Cole, Nana got tickets to the rodeo." He pointed to the refrigerator as he bounded down the stairs. Several pieces of bright yellow paper hung from a Spider-Man magnet.

"That's awesome." Cole sipped the hot coffee, burning his tongue. *Pain, help erase the memory of the bra next to my balls, please.* He sighed, no such luck.

"Let's take Piper." Beau stared at his grandmother with big blue puppy dog eyes. "Nana?" He pulled on Florence's pants pocket. "Please."

Cole inspected his mother. She no longer resembled the angry beast from a moment before. She had morphed into doting grandmother. "Yeah, Nana, let's take Piper." Cole added and tugged on his mother's pants like Beau.

Her eyes narrowed but twinkled.

CHAPTER 20

Cole

AT CHURCH, COLE SAT WITH his mother while Piper joined the Barnes family. Desire and the first pew ladies kept glancing back at the crowd and then dipping their heads together to chat. One with a yellow hat pointed to the back corner. Something had caught the old bat's attention. Cole twisted in his seat and his heart jumped into his throat.

His phone vibrated in his pocket. Surreptitiously, he retrieved it. His mother frowned, but he shrugged, grinning sheepishly. He didn't have a choice. The derelict responsible for the cattle slaughter was still at large.

"He's here." Those words spoke volumes. He looked up to find Piper staring at him. Her skin had paled, and she sucked in her bottom lip. He longed to rush from his seat and hold her.

He tipped the phone to show his mother. Flo covered a gasp and gazed around. Cole pointed to a well-dressed man sitting prim and respectful, but looking as if he had a stick up his butt.

He quickly typed, "I'm coming to sit with you during the meet and greet." She glanced at her phone then met his eyes with a smile and a nod.

Pastor Drew Peacock encouraged his flock to shake a hand and greet each other. Catching his mother's eye as she greeted a friend, he pointed to Piper. She gave him a thumbs up. Cole meandered down the aisle to the row where Piper stood. He shook hands with the three Barnes brothers, the two sisters and parents that surrounded the row. He squeezed past Jessie while offering his hand. She gripped it firmly, and then let go as Piper hugged him. Tears filled her eyes.

"Piper?" A weight settled in his gut.

"They're happy tears." She whispered, "You make me happy." She squeezed his hand, and they sat down.

His heart raced, and it had nothing to do with the church having a new sinner. He'd brought her happiness, and he smiled. He caught Desire Hardmann's gaze, and she grinned and nodded. How in Hades did that woman know there was something between him and Piper way back when?

"Today's text is from the book of first Peter." Some of the congregation laughed. Cole covered his mouth to stifle a chuckle.

The prankster had struck the church announcement sign. "The Peter in You" it quoted. It wasn't the pastor's original text. However, the sign caught the eye of a record number of people, curious about the church nestled within the town.

After the service the Darts, Barnes, Greenes and a few other families migrated to the truck stop to eat. The bookshelf attracted as many people as the group. Cole and Matt both traded two books.

Forrest Greene entered the restaurant laughing hysterically. He wiped tears away from his eyes. After taking several deep breaths, the wiry man finally said, "Phew."

"What's going on?" Kelly asked her older brother.

"That prankster struck again while we were in church." A crowd gathered around Forrest. "It was another sign. Burger's Kraut Wagon has one of those sidewalk signs with the changeable letters."

"Oh no," Jessie groaned.

"Oh yes." Forrest continued, "The sign must've had letters removed. It read: Try our anus pounder."

After the laughter died, Kelly added, "I saw that sign yesterday. It said try our Angus Quarter Pounder."

Cole and his mother often guessed who the town troublemaker could be. They'd narrowed it from "pretty dang sure" to "I'm almost certain" but the theory had been shot to hell. He'd been worshiping with every single suspect in church that morning. He rubbed his chin. Maybe the town had more than one hooligan, or maybe they had an accomplice?

Piper

Piper slumped into her chair, wringing her hands. It'd happened again. The past was repeating itself. Justin showed up everywhere she went. It nibbled away at her nerves, sanity and peace of mind. She'd leave suspicious, then arrive somewhere else paranoid.

"Boo!" Beau popped up from the booth behind Piper.

She screamed, flinging her arms and knocking over two waters. Her hands trembled as she tried to blot the liquid with paper napkins. She apologized to Flo and Cole, who sat with her at the table. Flo received the worst of it but wasn't upset.

She gave Beau a stern look. "What do you say, Beau?"

"I'm sorry, Piper." Beau hung his head like a sad puppy.

Cole had noticed her trembling. He always noticed. She liked it, yet she didn't want to worry him. He took her hand and squeezed. He refused to relinquish it when she tugged. She smiled, grateful she wasn't alone.

Piper sat quietly in the booth and poked at the food on her plate with a fork. She moved it from place to place but had no appetite. To keep her mind busy, she watched families interact and the activity at the bookshelf. Two men had their noses in a book while shoveling in grub. The world kept living and moving around her, but she felt like a fragile observer.

"You all right?" Cole asked after Flo left to take Beau home.

"No."

"What can I do to help?"

"Besides killing me or Justin, I can't think of any other way to solve my problem." Piper stared at the mess of food on her plate.

"Death is not the answer."

If she glanced at him, Cole's lips would be set in a firm line and his forehead creased into a V. "I know." She sighed, closed her eyes and leaned back. "Can you think of another way?"

"I'm working on it."

Piper met his gaze with a lifted brow. What did it mean? Maybe he'd found a place to dump a body. Justin wouldn't technically have to be dead, the critters or environment would take care of that. But if Cole worked on it, she could count on it. He meant what he said and followed through. She trusted him. "Okay."

She didn't want to know. Plausible deniability.

They agreed she'd drive him home, but she passed him the keys. She wasn't in the mood to drive. Her thoughts couldn't stay focused. A pang of longing struck her. She missed her father. He would have known how to handle Justin.

Dressed in his uniform, Ben came in for a book and coffee. Cole excused himself and joined the officer. She doubted they'd be chummy if she wasn't in a predicament. Cole surveyed the room, and then he focused on Ben and leaned closer. It was a subtle shift. She tried to imagine his business-like voice, strained with care and frustration.

She closed her eyes and leaned back again.

"What a coincidence meeting you here, Piper." Those words from Justin settled in the pit of her stomach and acid churned. She didn't want to open her eyes and see his smug face. The obnoxious man had waited until she was alone. She shredded the paper napkin but kept her eyes closed and face relaxed. She was aiming for serene, but missed the mark with her eyebrow spasms.

"Coincidence? I know better. Don't lie." She opened her eyes and reached for an iced tea. "I'd only consider it a coincidence if I happened in on someplace where you were, somewhere you didn't know I'd be."

"Think what you will." His lips pouted.

"Oh, I will and I do." Piper sipped the soothing liquid. Before Texas, sweet tea wasn't a favorite, but now she loved it. Everything had changed. Her food tastes had matured and so had her idea about love.

"Did you enjoy the service?" Justin stalled.

Piper blinked twice. "Sure, what woman wouldn't enjoy a Peter inside her?" Scarlet red, Justin sputtered. She took pleasure in befuddling him.

"Now you're talking my language." Desire grinned as she slid into the booth across from Piper. "I could talk about Peters all day long."

Piper covered her mouth to stymie a giggle, but it didn't work.

"Why are you laughing so hard? I'm referencing the first and second Peter. Sometimes the second is better than the first," Desire said with a soft sigh. "Oh well, sometimes one isn't enough and you need them both at once. They fill many holes."

Piper's face heated. The ornery woman spouted innuendo like it was going out of style.

"I'm talking about the holes in your *heart*, dear." She winked.

Cole slid in next to Desire and gave the petite woman a kiss on her cheek. She blushed, as red as an innocent schoolgirl. "Good Lord Almighty, Cole, you are such a charmer. Your momma taught you right." She pinched his cheek. She faced Piper. "I told you about this one, didn't I?"

"You called him a hot tamale." Piper studied Cole's lips.

"Yes, dear. I call them like I see them," her hand disappeared under the table and Piper hoped the old lady only patted his knee.

"You called it right," Piper said. She didn't care if Justin witnessed. He was an unwelcome asshat.

"So Piper, how's Texas treating you?" Desire asked.

"I love Texas. It feels like home."

Desire elbowed Cole twice. He elbowed her back. She nudged him again. A small shuffle broke out with their elbows fighting for the same space. Finally, with a gesture of surrender, Cole gave up. "You win. Pipes, I'm coming over to your side." He pushed past an unmoving Justin then plopped next to her. His knee touched hers, and it sent a shiver down her spine. She took a sip of tea to counter the heat on her face.

"You know, Piper dear, everything is bigger in Texas." Desire wiggled her penciled brows and winked.

"I've heard that before." Justin said crossing his arms and glaring at Piper.

Her face heated. Cole stared at her with a guilty lopsided grin. He'd been there for the proclamation.

Cole

Cole recalled the day. They'd been sitting in the Barnes' living room with Piper's ex in one chair while she'd perched on the edge of Cole's. Waves of emotion had rolled off her. Piper feared Justin, not physically per se, but psychologically. Cole hated Piper being placed in that position. What real man manipulated people he claimed to love?

The ex tried his best to control his anger, but her lack of compliance pushed the limit. This new Texan Piper Justin didn't know how to handle.

Cole placed a hand on Piper's knee. It hadn't gone unnoticed. Cole smiled and traced a pattern with his thumb, Piper relaxing, just a little, at his touch.

"I don't get why you like Texas?" Justin had spat the words. It had been the wrong thing to ask because Jessie sprang up straight.

"What's wrong with Texas?" Jessie growled.

"Nothing, I mean, it's not her home." Justin tried to backtrack.

"Cowboys." All heads swung toward Piper. She stared out the window watching Josiah interact with the postman. "Cowboys are nice and cute."

"And sexy," Jessie added.

"All cowboys?" Justin scoffed.

"They're good men with strong work ethics and romance-loving hearts." Piper glanced at Cole.

"Crunchy gooey combo?" he'd asked her.

"Oh, yeah." She'd agreed with a wink. "There's plenty I like about Texas. The natural beauty is everywhere. The night sky is clearer, stars are brighter and the storms are louder. Juicer steaks and barbecue."

"The plains and blue bonnets," Jessie again added.

"What does Texas have that Illinois doesn't?" Justin had tilted his head, furrowing his brow.

Piper barely controlled the eye roll. After a prolonged blink, she'd said, "You don't live here. That's the greatest draw. And everything is bigger in Texas. Everything."

Cole's gaze had volleyed from Justin to Piper. He had caught her staring at his crotch.

"Everything?" Cole couldn't help himself. Her gaze had traveled upward until it met his, then she'd blinked and turned crimson. A slow grin formed, and she'd leaned back slightly and tilted her head. She had seen him, every bit except his scalp. She knew intimate details about his manhood. He'd shifted uncomfortably and caught Jessie's giggle. Bless that interloping woman. If not for her, maybe not everything in Texas would be bigger. He sat up straighter. Not that size mattered, but it did.

Justin looked like a pillar of carved marble. His face had frozen into a mask of contorted anger. He'd glared through squinched lids as shallow breaths blew through thin lips. He couldn't argue with Piper's opinion.

Then all hell broke loose. Tippy had raced under Cole's chair, around the back of Justin's and up over the sofa. One missing back leg hadn't slowed her down.

Matt Barnes entered the room, moseyed up to Piper, tipped her head and stuck his tongue in her mouth. She'd pushed him away and yelled at him. He cowered like a punished puppy then fled with Jessie storming outside in his wake.

Piper rubbed her forehead. "What the hell was that?" She'd looked as dumbfounded as Cole felt. He'd wanted to rip the kid to shreds, but hadn't reacted fast enough.

A nasally voice broke Cole out of his reverie. "Oh, young man," Ms. Deeds called from the entry. "Young man."

Desire's brows dipped, becoming one. Ms. Deeds wobbled next to Justin. He took her hand. "Hello Elberta, you look lovely today." She twittered at the praise. Piper thought she rivaled Barney the dinosaur in the fuchsia attire.

"Desire, I'm glad you're here. I need to talk to you about the church bazaar."

"Sounds like fun," Desire said with an overly toothy grin.

"Well, Ms. Deeds, why don't you and your young man take a seat here. We're just leaving." Cole helped Piper out and took Ms. Deeds elbow and eased her onto the seat. Piper stayed by his side as Cole paid for the meal. She was more than ready to leave Stitts'.

CHAPTER 21

Piper

UNFAMILIAR SCENERY SCROLLED BY AS Cole turned onto a primitive road, but Piper trusted his knowledge of Fortuna's back roads. The road curved and climbed a hill. Cole drove slow and avoided ruts. The further they were away from the familiar, the more she relaxed. There was little chance Justin would follow.

"I hated leaving Desire alone with Justin and Ms. Deeds," Cole lamented, gripping the wheel tighter.

"But we left Justin with Desire." Piper giggled, and Cole smirked. "I'm not worried about her. She'll be fine. Justin will be traumatized, though."

"Hopefully enough to leave town for good."

"I doubt it." She tried to lean on Cole's shoulder, but the road was too rough.

As music played, they speculated how Desire had grilled Justin. Forty-five minutes later, Cole stopped the car on a small plateau. Nothing but wildflowers for miles. Justin would have called them weeds. Piper pushed open the door and inhaled deeply. The occasional butterfly flitted around. A breeze fanned her face.

"Watch this." He reached into the car and honked the horn. Butterflies. Hundreds of monarch butterflies took flight.

Piper gasped, dazzled by the natural wonder. Tears threatened, and she touched Cole's arm. He pulled her back against him and held her. He whispered, "I hope you don't mind if we spend the afternoon with my friends."

"Not at all." She sighed back against him.

The aerial show lasted only a few minutes until the butterflies settled again, most hidden once more.

He broke their connection. "There's more." With a grin, he motioned for her to stay. He opened the back door and draped a blanket over his arm.

"Aren't you the sneaky one," she teased with hands on her hips. "How did you stealthily load my car?"

"If I told you my secrets, I'd have to kill you." Cole spread the blanket on the bank of the road. He tapped the blanket.

"You can't kill me if I guess." Lowering herself to the ground, she crossed her legs and glanced up at him.

Cole returned to her car and pulled out his guitar case. "S'pose, that's true. Take your best guess." He opened the case and handed her the guitar to tune.

"Hm." Piper strummed the instrument. "I've been so focused on Justin and avoiding him a twister could have delivered Dorothy Gale from Kansas and I wouldn't have noticed." She turned introspective while she tuned the guitar. When she handed it over she said, "I'm going to guess it was your mother."

"Right you are. We have a winner, ladies and gents." Cole clapped, sending the butterflies heavenward again.

Reclining, she put her hands behind her head. "It's a good thing you didn't bet twenty dollars. A girl could get rich winning bets off the cowboys of Fortuna." He nudged her with his boot and she giggled.

Cole plucked out a few simple songs then played a classical piece. The hectic invaded morning transformed into a soothing afternoon. Butterflies lazily flitting, clouds floating and a handsome man strumming beside her constituted a good day. As relaxed as a cat in a sunbeam, Piper's eyes fluttered closed. As a car passed, it honked, sending the butterflies sky borne again.

She stretched and reached for Cole, touching his leg. Her fingers lightly brushed his thigh, then stilled.

He hummed a few lines then abruptly stopped playing. She popped one eye open, inspecting him. His brows had dipped into a frown but his eyes frightened her. They glared past her car. Her heart worked overtime. A door slammed, and she bolted upright with a gasp.

Behind her car, a man opened a minivan's back door. Three small children stumbled out giggling and hushing each other. A woman joined hands with the man as the kids settled on the edge of the hill not far from Piper and Cole.

"God, you scared me. I thought Justin might have found us." She playfully hit him in the shoulder.

Cole glanced away from the family. "Sorry."

"A family makes you wary?" She lifted a brow. Could it have something to do with being self-conscious about his looks?

Cole shrugged and put the guitar in the case and walked it to the car. Piper pulled her knees to her chest. When Cole returned, he touched her shoulder as he sat. "I didn't want our time interrupted. I just wanted you to have an afternoon of peace and quiet."

Piper nodded. His thoughtfulness touched her heart. She refrained from pulling him into her arms and kissing him. "Thank you. It's fine. Look at the excitement on their little faces."

Identical twins about three and an older girl giggled and pointed to the field. The couple leaned against the van and the father reached in the open window. "Ready?"

"Go, Daddy."

The horn sounded, and the butterflies soared again.

"Butterflies!" the older girl chanted while clapping. The younger kids reached into the sky trying to catch them.

"Those two aren't much older than us," Piper said in a soft voice. "Can you imagine having three kids?"

"It depends. With you, yeah."

Piper sucked in a breath and whipped her head around. Cole studied the kids as they danced.

"Again, Daddy! Again, again."

The father reached in and honked the horn. Butterflies filled the sky once more. The mother captured the moment on her camera while the father picked up one twin and tossed him into the air. Cole often tossed Beau in a similar manner. Beau's joy coupled with her trust in Cole's strength always allayed Piper's worry.

The mother tickled the older child, and she squealed with glee.

The sweet scene and the effervescent sounds brought a smile to Cole's face. Piper reached to caress his cheek. He caught her hand and held it there. Everything else fell away. Mesmerized, she studied his fathomless blue eyes, ringed with sinfully long lashes and corners lined from laughter.

He skimmed the back of her hand. She shivered. The cowboy hat shadowed his face and the ever-present bandanna covered his head. One day she hoped to comb her fingers through his hair.

Cole pulled her next to him and held her tight. As he rubbed her back, she relaxed against his chest. His strong heart thundered, and every beat thrilled her. She couldn't imagine her world without him.

She was grateful Cole joined her in the toilet of life or she'd be circling the bowl alone.

Cole

Cole opened the passenger car door and nudged Piper. She'd fallen asleep on the ride to her cabin. He nudged her again, and she fell into his arms with a sigh. He carried her in and laid her on the bed. She snuggled into the pillow and rolled over.

He understood her exhausted state. She'd been hyperaware of her surroundings since Justin arrived. Her poor mind must be fraught with worry.

Cole examined the small cabin for signs of forced entry. The sink had a few dirty dishes, but the cup had lipstick stains. The bathroom toilet seat was down, and there were extra rolls. Outside, he walked the perimeter. The only footprints were from his boots.

He returned to the dining room table and inspected the small pile of books on it. There was the newest in the Loren Order series, one of her favorites. She's shared the first with him and he'd liked it. All the other books were romance novels. He flipped open the cardboard cover and saw the telltale initials: U.L.D. Undine Love Davidson: the woman who started it all. Undine was Jessie's grandma and an ex-stripper. The woman had a love story to rival any book.

With a deep sigh, he glanced at the long-legged woman on the bed. Big mistake. Her sundress had ridden up, exposing her creamy legs and showing a hint of lacy panties. He walked to the edge of the bed. His hand hesitated over the hem of the garment. Tug it down or pull it higher?

He clenched his eyes shut, hearing his mother's voice in his head, "Respect." He grabbed the throw on the end of the bed and spread it over her prone body. She turned slightly and smiled. He'd give anything to see into her dream. *Could it have to do with a shower?*

Cole swallowed and stepped back from the bed. If she opened her eyes, she'd know just how much he liked those panties. The color of the pillow caught his eye. He leaned to get a better look. Wow. The pillowcase was his T-shirt from the other night.

He untucked the white polo shirt he'd worn and pulled it over his head. The white tee tried to hitch a ride, but he caught it and tucked it back in. He gently sat the fabric near Piper's face and backed away. He found a pen by the phone and left a note on the back of a receipt. With one final inspection, he locked the door and pulled it closed.

He walked to the Big Deal office. By the time he'd reached the barn, his good boots hurt his feet. He'd only worn them to church and the occasional wedding or funeral. He pushed open the door to the bunkhouse. Gimme sat on the plaid sofa with a microwave bag of popcorn. He threw a handful in his mouth and chewed like a cow. A love story played on the TV. Titanic.

Cole shook his head and went into the back room, following Curly and Arlon's voices. The foreman sounded frazzled. Cole picked up his steps. He knocked on the door to announce his presence. "What's going on?" Cole asked.

"We found another longhorn butchered." Curly pointed to a map of the area. It was on the other side of the property. Far from the other carcass.

Arlon looked Cole up and down. "Church duds? You clean up pretty." He laughed and slapped a knee. Both men cracked a grin.

"Can one of you give me a lift?" Cole asked.

"What about yer lady?" Arlon asked.

"She's taking a nap."

"You wore her out," Gimme said from behind. Cole glared at him.

"Shut yer trap, Gimme. Haven't you learned yet about badmouthing women?" Arlon pointed to his eye with his fist.

Wide-eyed, Gimme disappeared down the hall.

"Sorry, Cole. Slim, Brad and I are heading out to ride the property's perimeter and examine the fence to look for evidence of wild dogs."

"I can take you, son." Arlon patted Cole's shoulder and moved past him into the hall. "Let me get my things."

"I took Piper to Chatwell Fields."

Curly's gaze rose from the map to Cole's face. He seemed to weigh the words. "That's a first for you."

"I've been there before. Every year."

"I mean, taking a woman with you." A smirk appeared on the corner of the foreman's mouth. "Send me a wedding invitation, a real one." His attention fell to the map once more.

Dumbfounded, Cole couldn't respond.

Instead, he followed Arlon through the hall to the kitchen. The old man plucked his keys off the counter and left the building. Arlon drove a rusty Jeep. Cole stepped up into the passenger side while he tossed a cowboy hat, a few cups and fast food bags into the backseat.

"Don't touch that." Arlon pointed to a cup where he spat his tobacco.

"No worries, I'm not thirsty."

"How are things with that Chicago riffraff?"

"He was at church today," Cole said. The image of Piper's terror-filled face flashed in his mind. He balled his fists and grit his teeth. Cole looked out the window and watched the prairie roll by.

"Church, huh? I heard they had a special message today." Arlon kept his gaze on the road.

The anger dissipated. "You heard about Peter?" Cole turned to Arlon.

"Was it about Peter Dunkin?" he asked with a smirk.

"That sounds like a friend of Desire's." They both laughed.

Arlon turned onto a wooded one-lane gravel road. It led to an area of homes on a plateau, with a few lanes veering off here and there. They exited the wood and climbed a gentle knoll. A trailer home, vintage nineteen eighties, sat close to another double-wide. Each had a yard barn. Arlon parked and offered "I need a beer" as the only reason for the pit stop to his home.

Bright colored lanterns hung from the awning over a picnic table on a cracked concrete pad. A grill, polished and decked out with a massive spatula and tongs, waited for use.

Hopping up the steps, Arlon entered the home. Cole sat at the cedar-stained table and glanced around. The neighbor had a small garden in the backyard filled with whimsical creatures like frogs holding toadstools and gnomes. A cellar built into a hillside offered storage and shelter.

The door opened with a creak, and Arlon stepped out holding two beers. He sat across from Cole. "Do you remember the last time you came up here?" The older man sipped the amber liquid and watched as Cole digested those words.

"Yes."

It'd been years now. Thinking back to that day left him breathless. He'd left the doctor's office with bad news, the kind of news that devastates a twenty-one-year-old man. Instead of driving home, he drove around town and further out, finally ending up at Arlon's door. Cole's swollen, red eyes and hiccupping breaths alerted Arlon something was wrong. He'd waited patiently until Cole could talk. He'd kept a steady hand on Cole's shoulder and even let a tear or two fall. Then the old man held him and let him weep in his arms. When Cole became too sick to continue working, Arlon had been one of the few people he'd let see him.

"You're a different man now, Cole. You've changed."

"Yes." He couldn't deny it.

"After the illness you retreated. You became a shell of the man you used to be. Why is that, son?"

Cole fingered the cool bottle. "I appreciated life, but I guess I stood back and watched it happen."

"That's the thing, you watched, you didn't take part. Well, you didn't until Miss Piper came to Texas. Something changed in you. She's a special lady, all right, if she woke the man in you."

Cole took a sip. Piper *definitely* woke the man in him every time he saw her.

The cancer could come back. What if he died? "I don't want to hurt her," Cole admitted.

"You don't want to take a chance, that's what you're saying." Arlon wiggled a finger at him. "You're afraid she'll say 'no' if you ask her out. You can't make the girl a widow if you haven't given the relationship a chance. Hell, you might only make it three months before you call it quits."

Cole folded his arms over his chest. "She's an all-or-nothing sort of woman."

"Son, the minute you met her and picked up your hand, you knew you were all in." He chuckled lightly. "You're in love with that girl. Come on. Admit it. You'd protect her with your life. You said 'she's all-or-nothing'. And there's *nothing* you wouldn't give to have *all* of her."

Cole couldn't help but smile at the old man. Arlon was nothing but a hopeless romantic. Crunchy on the outside and gooey on the inside, just like Cole. "Why don't you find a woman of your own so you stop pestering me?"

"Oh, did I hit a sore spot?"

"Are you evading my question?" They grinned at each other.

"I've had my share of women. If I feel a need, I don't usually have to blink and Ms. Desire is on me like flies on stink."

"Oh God," Cole groaned.

"Listen, she gives good hand-jobs."

Cole covered his ears. He didn't want to hear any more.

"Hey, sometimes a woman needs to feel useful and needed, especially a woman like Ms. Desire. She's alone and gets lonely for a man's touch. Even people my age and older want to be loved. So when she sees I'm lonely and looking down, I probably am. When she offers to aid in my recovery, I accept. I'm helping her feel womanly." He shrugged and looked away. "Sometimes you only get one shot at love, son. Mine happened a long time ago."

The sad expression in his eyes made Cole want to question the old man, but he bit his tongue.

"She's gone now, and she took my heart with her. I was afraid I'd smother her, but she loved me anyway. Me, a crusty cowboy. She was a peach. I wished you could have met my Annie."

"What happened?"

"Breast cancer, twenty years back."

Cole paled and extended a hand to the man. They squeezed hands, then clasped their bottles and Arlon raised his. "Here's to God for creating the woman and complicating men's lives."

"To God." Cole clanked Arlon's bottle. "Here's to authors and Undine Love Davidson for their romantic influence in Fortuna and my life."

Arlon raised his bottle. "To sex."

Cole nearly choked on the beer. Sex *was* something to cheer about.

CHAPTER 22

Piper

THE RODEO BUSTLED WITH MEN, women and animals. Piper stayed out of the way, holding a tablet, poised and ready for any notes Jessie dictated. Cowboys moved stock into pens. Cows and bulls awaited judging.

Piper stifled a yawn, out of the Double D intimates routine. Judges inspected a bunch. "How do you tell the difference between the cattle?" Piper asked Jessie.

"Besides the color of the coat and length of the horns?" Jessie said with a smirk.

Longhorns had some really *long* horns.

After delivering the cattle, Piper and Jessie took a seat in the arena and waited. Ceiling fans circulated the dust and heat. Jessie handed her a bottle of cold water and leaned close, pointing out the various ranch owners from around the area.

"There's one of the Nocker boys. The Nocker family founded Nockerville. Their ranch is huge. They breed horses and cattle." The muscular, tanned blond looked like an oil tycoon rather than a rancher. His cherubic face wore a grin but his eyes held a devilish glint. "Steer clear of that one. All three boys are drop-dead gorgeous, but they know it and use it."

Piper took Jessie's warning to heart, but her gaze had locked onto another cowboy. Cole.

"Look there's Daddy." Jessie stood and waved. Brad nodded then blew Jessie a kiss.

The sweet gesture made Piper smile wistfully. Bob McCracken would have yelled "Pipes," then flung both arms around her and add a dramatic cheek kiss. Her heart ached remembering him.

Glancing at her jeans and boots, Piper hoped she didn't seem like a greenhorn. With two dark smudges already, the short sleeve white cotton blouse had been a poor choice. When Cole peered up long enough to take notice, his gaze roamed her body, stopping at one smudge on her chest. She waved her hand to gain his attention. His face burned red, and a smirk manifested. She shook her head but grinned. He tipped his hat.

Later Jessie walked her through the grounds, and Piper signed up for the 5k to be held Wednesday morning. The scents of barbecue swirled around them. Jessie led her into a large hexagon-shaped barn filled with rows of animal cages. Chickens and rabbits of different breeds and colors. Ribbons adorned cages.

"Wow, they've already judged the animals. These people don't mess around," Piper mused.

Events lasted all day. Piper peeked in on the goat and horse shows, but she wanted to see the fun stuff, like bull riding and bronc busting.

"I'm bushed," Jessie mumbled, opening the truck's door.

Piper climbed into the backseat. She leaned forward and pointed to Josiah. "Is he making a deal?"

"He's talking to potential buyers. It's looking good."

"Yay. Job security." Piper said, making Jessie snort a giggle.

Early Wednesday morning, Piper pounded the pavement at the 5k. Men and women ran, but some brought kids and walked or jogged with a stroller. Piper pushed herself, knowing what she was capable of. A man passed, and she called out, "Dakota?"

He turned with a startled smile and slowed to match her pace. "How you feeling?"

"I'll live," she huffed. "Don't let me slow you down."

He nodded and took off toward the finish line. His neon yellow shirt clung to his body and his running shorts exposed enough leg to make Piper appreciate the view. Sweat trickled down her head, neck and back even though she only wore running shorts and a sports bra.

Dakota waited to congratulate her when she crossed the finish. Jessie and surprise guests Mrs. Dart and Beau were also there. Dakota gave her a quick hug and disappeared into the crowd.

"Who was that guy, Piper?" Beau asked.

"That was my friend, Dakota. He used to be in the Army." She sucked deep breaths.

"Dakota is cute." Mrs. Dart watched the man walk away. Piper shrugged.

After a refreshing shower and a few hours of downtime Piper slipped on a blue sundress and donned new brown boots. She sat on her front porch sipping sweet tea. If she'd have stayed with Justin it would be the week of her wedding. She shook her head, wanting to forget.

Piper returned to the bathroom to apply makeup then braided her light hair. She had a date, sort of. *Not really.* Dakota had asked her to the rodeo Thursday night. He'd wanted to hear a band play.

A car pulled up to her cabin. She glanced at the time. "Five-thirty. He's punctual," she said, grabbing her purse.

"Evenin' Piper," he said. Clean-shaven and smelling of soap, he bent to kiss her cheek.

"So what's this band you want to see?" Piper snapped her seatbelt. She picked a nail while inspecting the meticulously clean SUV. It was strange not hanging out with Cole.

"They're great. Not Over with Darryl B. Morticome. He's got a smooth voice." Dakota explained a previous performance. Piper relaxed, but a slight nagging guilt remained.

When they arrived, Dakota opened the car door and held her by the elbow. His bright eyes surveyed everywhere they went like he suspected trouble. She did the same but scanned for Justin or Cole, not wanting to bump into either.

I'm not on a date. Keep telling yourself and maybe you'll believe it. She shouldn't feel guilty; she and Cole had a pretend marriage. Except they had kissed and had a shower together.

She'd caught Dakota glancing at her and knew if she encouraged him they could start a relationship. He was a good man, cute and sweet, dependable and honest. The only thing he wasn't was Cole. Just thinking Cole's name got her hot and bothered. She sighed and scanned the crowd again.

"Let's get some food," Dakota suggested. Delectable scents wafted over her. They bought monster fries and a pulled pork sandwich. Later, he suggested deep fried cheesecake on a stick. After gorging, they played a few games, and he won her a small stuffed monkey. They perused the booths, and she bought a turquoise bracelet strung by Native Americans.

They meandered toward the confectioneries when she saw Cole. He didn't seem surprised, only tired. "Howdy," he greeted. Dakota dropped his hold of her elbow. The men shared a look, and Cole smiled.

"Oh no, this is about the other night. Dammit Cole, you did not pay Dakota to play babysitter, did you?" Cole swallowed. Piper swung her gaze to Dakota. He stared at his boots. She gripped Dakota's forearm and squeezed. "That night at Under the Table, Cole got to you."

"Listen, darlin'—" Cole started. The insolent grin burned her.

"No, you listen!" She jabbed him in the chest with a finger. "I don't need you instigating a panic on my behalf. Geez, Cole. The man's got a life."

"Dakota?" She faced Dakota.

"That night Cole confided in me, yes, but we didn't actually make concrete plans."

She crossed her arms over her chest with a huff, recognizing a diversionary tactic.

"He recruited me to watch your back when he couldn't be there. It happened to work out about tonight."

"Convenient." She inspected Cole again, taking in his dirt smeared clothes. Even his face bore proof he'd been busy. Her eyes narrowed. "You competed today, and you didn't want me to see you. Were you afraid I'd cheer too loud?"

"No, I didn't compete, I worked." Cole's arms out shot out. "I don't want you to get kidnapped. You wanted to experience the festival, and I wasn't available but Dakota was. We don't know what Justin is up to or how desperate he is." Cole put a hand on her shoulder and squeezed.

Piper pulled her arms tighter and leaned slightly. "This reminds me of the time when my dad paid the neighbor kid, Ty Coons, to go to the freshman dance with me. Dad told me he wanted me to feel special and not left out."

"Cole didn't pay me," Dakota mumbled.

"My dad would have killed Ty if he'd known Ty tried to get into my dress." She laughed bitterly. "Cole, do you see what you've done here? You're trying to keep me from the arms of one man by throwing me into the arms of another. Granted, Justin isn't much of a man especially when compared to Dakota. Dakota's got a cute face, nice hair and a hard body. Don't look at me like that, Cole. I just watched three women, various ages, walk past him and admire him like a piece of art, especially his backside." Piper reached out and jerked Dakota's arm, then pointed to his tight butt. "This is grade A male."

She chuckled at the stunned men. Red-faced, Cole's brows dipped in a frown while Dakota's mouth hung open. "He's hot, but he's also sweet, smart and trustworthy. It's nice to know you trust him with my body because he's my date tonight." Piper grinned, linking arms with Dakota. She tilted her head, placing it on his shoulder.

With both hands on his hips, Cole tapped a foot. Even dirty, the man's looks could turn her on. His gaze held hers captive as he weighed her words. Dakota shifted, placing a hand over hers.

The crowd continued to press past, except for one thin man with wire-rimmed glasses.

"Um, Cole." Piper bit her lip. Cole shifted his gaze to the unwanted character.

Justin inspected both men, then smiled at Piper. "You've got a new man, I see, or do they share you?"

Cole's hands fisted, and Dakota's gaze narrowed to the point it could set fire to Justin's forehead.

Piper giggled, which gradually turned into a belly laugh. "Share? Oh, wow. You think I get naked with these two hunks. Now there's an idea." Resting her head back on Dakota's shoulder, she hummed. "My dreams just became a lot better. Thanks, Justin."

Justin's conceited expression twisted into anger.

"Piper, Piper." A high pitch voice carried over the distance. Beau broke free from his nana's hand and ran toward her. Piper caught him and hugged his small body against her. "Are we still having a date tomorrow?" he asked, winded.

"How many men do you have, Piper?" Justin incredulously grumbled.

"Have you ridden the ferret wheel?" Beau asked with wide eyes. "Nana's scared of heights and won't go. Let's go ride it."

"Sure, let me get some money for tickets." Piper smiled and held her hand out to Cole. He pulled a twenty from his wallet and placed it in her hand. "You know where to find me," she called to Dakota over her shoulder. Leaving the three wary men, she walked away with a small hand clasped to hers in utter devotion.

Piper and Beau purchased tickets then joined the end of the Ferris wheel's line. The shadows grew long as the sun set. Beau grew more excited with every step nearer the front of the line.

The teenage ride operator was thin and tall. In a rumpled plaid shirt and jeans, it appeared he'd just rolled out of bed as a last-ditch replacement. A crooked smile under a peach-fuzz mustache did little to reassure Piper.

The ride's white baskets had blue lines and numbers. Each car slowed and people exited then reloaded. Beau pulled her forward when it was their turn. The operator secured the metal bar, and they lifted into the air. It lurched to a stop as the man unloaded and loaded the next car. Each time the car would swing Beau would say, "Whoa" then giggle.

Near the top the Ferris wheel began to move without stopping. Piper enjoyed the breeze. Rounding the top, she could see most of the grounds. The crowds moved like arteries. At the base of the ride, Piper spied Cole watching them. He spoke with his mother and Dakota. Clutching the bar, she scanned the area for Justin, but she couldn't find him. She blew out a sigh.

"I want to ride all the rides tomorrow," Beau said.

"Okay," she smiled at his determination. "Even the airplanes?"

"Yeah. All of them. I'm going to get a record and get a blue ribbon. Nana says if I ride that spinny ride I'll get sick. She means she thinks I might barf. Just so you know, I won't barf on you."

"Thanks, buddy. I appreciate not being barfed on." Piper chuckled. The ride jerked, catching her off guard. She yelped, scaring Beau. Piper inhaled sharply and glanced down at the ground. Cole looked as if he'd climb to rescue her. She waved him off.

The operator released riders car by car and the first stop had startled her.

After exiting they found Flo, Cole and Dakota.

"Nana, Piper is going to ride all the rides with me. We're going to pick her up early and get here right when it opens. I'm going to win a record." Beau grabbed her hand then grabbed Cole's. "Are you still not getting married?" Beau glanced up at his uncle with a tilted head.

"Not tonight," Flo said firmly.

"Aw. Okay." The grandmother pulled the boy away.

Cole threw Piper a look before he disappeared into the crowd, rewarding her with a smile. Her heart hammered, and she longed to run after him. She sighed when she could no longer see him. She and Dakota stood awkwardly together, staring into the area where the Darts had last been.

"So, the concert?" Dakota asked touching her elbow.

Piper nodded, inspecting Dakota. His long lashes were a sin. But his good looks did nothing to her innards like Cole's did.

"I understand," Dakota said softly. "Cole feels the same way about you as you feel about him."

Piper gasped, glancing away as tears pricked her eyes. "You're a good man, Dakota. I'm sorry you got messed up in the chaos of my life." Her voice warbled.

"That's what friends are for." He patted her arm.

They found a seat, and he bought them a beer. The band members could sing, but engaged the audience with humor.

"So we've traveled around this part of Texas while touring, and we never have experienced anything like Fortuna's town clown," Darryl B Morticome said into a mic. He turned to the bass player, Milo Strands. "Milo is from Nockerville and his family keeps him abreast of the antics."

"It's crazy, Darryl. Fortuna is a funky place." Milo laughed. "I'm glad we got to see the prankster's work with our own eyes. On a church sign, too."

"Would you like to hear it?" Darryl asked. The crowd responded with agreeable hoots and hollers. Milo snickered, and the drummer played a drum roll. "The sign read: With God, size never matters. Drew Peacock, Pastor."

Piper giggled. She hadn't seen the latest prank and surmised the pews would be filled on Sunday. Milo and Darryl mentioned a few other pranks before starting their second set, but she had a hard time staying focused. Every other minute she wondered about Cole.

CHAPTER 23

Cole

COLE LET BEAU HONK THE TRUCK'S horn. Piper hurried out of her cabin with a bag and hopped in the passenger side. The door creaked when she closed it.

"Piper!" Beau squealed. "Guess what? I'm gonna go to visit my mommy." He gave her a kiss on the cheek. She blushed and hugged the kid. He jabbered about the order he intended to ride the rides.

On the drive to Stitts' to meet his mother for breakfast, Cole considered his sister Lynette. Flo and Beau would leave the rodeo early to go visit her. So far, Lynette hadn't canceled the visit. The day was still young. Cole wouldn't hold out hope.

Cole, Piper and Beau filed into the dining room. He spotted his mother hunched over a menu. She glanced up then raised a hand. Beau ran forward and flung himself into her arms.

Piper nudged Cole and nodded toward three men who read romance novels. They slid into the booth and flipped the coffee mugs right side up.

The owner, Norma, filled their coffee cups and took their order.

"I've read two of those books," Cole said. His face heated under Piper's and his mother's scrutiny. He took a sudden interest in the steam rising from his coffee. "You would have liked one of them, Mom."

"Oh?" He glanced up and she asked, "What about it?"

He quirked an eyebrow. "It has kilts."

"Say no more." She leaned back against the booth and fanned herself.

"People gets kilt?" Beau asked, his forehead scrunched in thought. "That's not very nice."

Cole stymied a chuckle while his mother tried to explain. "No one gets hurt, honey. It's not killed, it's *kilt*. A kilt is a type of men's clothing from Scotland."

"Like a tie?" he asked tilting his head.

Cole stifled another laugh and threw Piper a look. Crinkled in mirth, her bright eyes looked into his and she covered her mouth to hide her grin. Warmth crept over his face again.

His mother sighed dreamily, then shifted her gaze around the restaurant until it settled on a man in the center. She quickly pointed to the man facing away from them. "See Gimme Malone there," she said in a soft voice.

Beau craned his neck around her then nodded.

"The pattern on his shirt is called a plaid. In Scotland, family clans used to pick a plaid with certain colors and stripes. People would know the family by their plaid. They would make clothes like cloaks and kilts with this plaid." Flo patted Beau's arm.

The server set their plates on the table.

"Oh." Beau nodded and grinned, pulling his chocolate chip hotcakes closer. "So a kilt is a type of coat? Does it make the man invisible?"

Cole couldn't hold back the laughter any longer, especially with his mother's deer-in-the-headlights expression.

"No, it's a man-skirt," Piper said, then giggled.

Beau gasped. Wide-eyed and open mouthed, he stared. Finally, he turned toward Cole, too stunned to talk.

"Piper's telling the truth," Cole said.

Beau gasped again then pressed his lips together, knitting his brows in a frown. "You can't make me wear a man-skirt."

Amongst the laughter, Norma returned to refill the coffee. Beau hummed in happiness as he tried his breakfast. Cole had to agree, the bacon melted in his mouth. He closed his eyes savoring the smoky flavor.

"How's the bathroom drain?" Piper asked Flo. Cole's eyes shot open.

"It's working perfect, thank you," Flo said.

"What's wrong with the drain?" Cole glanced from his mother to Piper.

"Nothing now, 'cause Piper fixed it," Beau said with a hint of awe. "She fixed it good. It had lots of hairs in it."

"I unclogged it. No big deal." She blushed and stabbed a pancake with her fork.

"Where was I?" Cole asked.

Around a mouthful of food, Beau said, "Working, but Piper wasn't. She fixed it good then asked Nana all about you while looking at pitchers."

"Beau," his grandmother said in a stern voice. The boy shrugged.

Cole eyed his mother. Her apologetic expression made his stomach churn. Piper must have inquired about his illness. His mother kept a photo album that inadvertently chronicled the progression of the cancer. She'd pull it out from time to time and counted her blessings. He'd been weak and pale. Devoid of hair, he'd seemed alien without eyebrows. Back then every movement had been painful, every breath labored. There'd been times he'd wanted to die, but he refused to leave his mother, so he fought. He wouldn't be like his dad.

Maybe his mother had only opened his baby pictures. He couldn't remember a time when his mother had pulled an album out for a girlfriend.

Girlfriend. His heart skipped a beat, then kicked into overdrive. He crossed his arms hugging himself, aware a goofy grin rested on his face.

Piper's golden head tilted as she listened to Beau discuss grits. She had the patience of a saint. For the time being, she was Beau's rodeo date, not his. Not yet. After Beau and his mother left the rodeo, Piper would be all his, and he had plans—the karaoke tent and meeting up with Kelly, for starters.

Piper tucked hair behind her ear, exposing the creamy, smooth skin of her neck. Hit with an urge to skim his finger over it, Cole jumped up, wiped his palms on his jeans and hurried toward the bookshelf. He pulled out a new book and flipped it open. Piper appeared next to him, reading the back cover. Her silver eyes scanned the lines of text. He could see down her pink V-neck T-shirt as she leaned close. Cole glanced away, again fighting the desire to touch her.

At the rodeo, his mother visited with friends at a quilting booth while he followed Beau and Piper around. Cole begged off the spinning rides and offered to take pictures and hold her purse while keeping a lookout for unwanted stalkers.

After lunch, they headed for the main arena so Beau could enter the mutton busting competition. Kids ages four to eight tried to earn the longest time. Piper and Flo waited anxiously for Beau to take his turn. When the gate opened, Cole held his breath for six long seconds. Beau held on to the woolly critter as it ran across the sawdust floor. He bumped and slid sideways until he fell off. A rodeo clown with neon socks and jeans cut off at the knee held up with rainbow suspenders helped him up then placed him on his shoulders. The clown trotted around like a horse bearing a king, making Beau laugh. He received a ribbon and cheers.

The barrel racing followed and Piper leaned forward to watch the women. Keeping her gaze on the rider, she tapped Cole on the arm and said, "How do I learn to do that?"

He smiled. "Jessie can teach you. She used to compete all the time."

Later, they snacked on cotton candy and snow cones while watching the steer wrestling.

"I've never seen anything like it before. I expected the cowboy to ride the cow, not chase it down," she said with eyes trained on the arena floor. The cowboy leaned off his horse onto the bull. Another horse ran parallel to keep the steer straight. Her hands flew to her mouth as she gasped when the cowboy hooked his arm around the horns and neck then used his weight and momentum to pull it down. It was crazy fast, like most rodeo sports, the participants earning times down to the hundredth of a second.

When his mother and Beau returned from a restroom break, Cole saw them talking to a clown. The same man who'd helped Beau during the mutton busting event. He had a white star outlined in blue painted on his cheek, the other side had a white circle. His mother nodded and blushed. Cole rubbed his face, the clown had earned another fan.

Beau's patience ended, and he wanted to ride more rides. Sun-kissed, Piper grinned as she took his little hand and stepped onto the Round-Up. Cole stepped back as the deathtrap whirled until the riders blurred. A hydraulic arm tilted it then lowered it again.

Beau and Piper wobbled off and Cole directed his nephew over to the kid's rides. Beau greeted a few of his buddies and joined them in line. Piper remained at his side. A phone rang and his mother dug in her large handbag. She checked the screen then walked off, talking on her phone.

"I hope my sister isn't canceling." Cole stuck his hands in his front pockets. "It will devastate Beau."

"If she does, we'll be here and make him forget." Piper sucked her bottom lip in and frowned.

At those kind words of support and compassion, Cole gave in to the longing he'd been resisting all day. He pulled her close and touched her face then dipped his head, meeting her lips in a sweet kiss.

"Are you going to get married now?" Beau asked, tugging on Cole's pant leg.

"Where d'you come from? I thought you were on a ride?" Cole asked, releasing Piper.

"It's done. Can I ride the motorcycle one? Please."

"How about the Ferris wheel?" Piper offered.

The three of them waited in line. When it was time to ride, Cole once again waited by the exit. Beau let Piper step on before sitting next to her. Beau's mouth moved so fast, Cole could envision him as an auctioneer. She covered her mouth to hide her smile and raised a brow.

When they were at the highest point Beau waved and Cole returned it, then blew a kiss.

Beau's hand shot out and snatched the kiss out of the air. With a look of triumph, he slapped the kiss to his cheek. Cole's head tipped back, and he almost lost his hat. He blew two kisses as the car passed again. Piper stuck out her hand but Beau moved fast stealing both invisible kisses. He smacked his cheeks in a one-two motion then laughed at the pout on Piper's lips.

Cole tossed a few more which Beau pretended to repel with karate chops. The kid worked fast, and Cole probably appeared to be dancing some new strange dance. The wheel slowed and as their car stopped, Cole handed the ride operator a bill then hopped on with Piper. Flo took the stunned but grinning Beau out of the way.

Trapped and blushing, Piper said, "Going to make sure the kisses find their mark?"

He took her small hand and held it. "Maybe," he said. One of her delicate brows lifted.

"I love the rodeo," he murmured. Laughter floated on the breeze. The smells of carnival fare hung in the air. He took a deep breath and leaned back. The car swayed and Piper grabbed the rail.

"Really? I thought you hated crowds." She studied him and he grew hot.

"Even in a crowd you can get lost in the background. The sounds and smells tingle the senses."

Piper placed a hand on his thigh, creating more tingles that ran straight to his groin. She rested her head on his shoulder. "I could watch the leather worker for hours."

"We'll have to go back."

She shivered. "No thanks. His assistant flirted with me too much. He said I smelled like berries. I don't know how anyone could smell my shampoo with all these other scents swirling around."

Cole leaned and inhaled. "I can smell it."

"Well, you're allowed, but some creepy carnival guy isn't."

He slung an arm behind her then pulled her close. She sighed against him and his heart jolted. He needed to get a grip. He rocked the car, and she squeaked, "Cole!"

"Kiss her, Uncle Cole!" Beau hollered through cupped hands. His mother covered her face.

"Great idea, kid." Cole gave him thumbs up. Piper tilted her cheek toward him, and he placed a chase kiss there for Beau's benefit. Higher, out of Beau's sight he tipped her chin and turned her head. He claimed her lips, and she opened for him.

Grabbing the back of his neck and nearly knocking off his hat, she held him firmly in place. He moaned and her hand strayed upwards. He caught it, not wanting to explode with desire. The rodeo sounds faded; all he heard was his heart galloping.

Cole led Piper to a table in the rear of a large tent. He pulled out a folding metal chair for her, but she pushed him down into it.

"I'm going to get napkins to wipe the table." Piper turned toward the condiment table that held a napkin dispenser.

Josiah Barnes entered the tent followed by Jessie. Matt trailed them with a pretty girl on his arm. Cole waved, catching their attention.

People flowed into the seating area with drinks and plates of food. A teenage girl took the stage. Holding the microphone away from her face like it might try to bite her, she sang a pitchy love song.

Piper returned with a few damp napkins. She started to rub the dried ketchup and beer and soda rings. Matt offered his date a seat then sat next to her.

Jessie slipped into a seat next to Piper. "Hey, how's the rodeo today? Any stalkers?"

Piper stiffened and frowned. "No, thank God."

Cole searched the crowd for Justin's weaselly face. A skinny man darted out of the tent and Cole jumped up. Never taking his eyes off the entrance, he nudged Josiah. "Should we get some beer?"

"Sounds like a plan," Josiah said rising. "I'm going to need it if I have to listen to these people sing."

Cole continued to scan the area as they returned with the beer.

"How are the sales?" Cole asked the Barnes. "Did that Montana business man find you?"

"Yeah, he wanted heifers," Matt said before Josiah could answer.

Josiah nodded and continued to talk cattle. Piper occasionally crinkled her brow, and Cole could tell she didn't understand the details of the longhorn business. Her polite smile hid her discomfort. Cole whispered in her ear, interpreting for her. "He wants breeding cows for his ranch."

"Thanks." She leaned against him. With his arm against the back of her chair, he tucked her against him.

Kelly and Mona spotted them. They wove through the tables and joined the group. Kelly's laughter rang over the droning of another karaoke singer as she extended her hand to show off a new turquoise bracelet. Piper gasped and leaned forward to admire it. After a moment, Kelly stopped talking, elbowed Piper and stared wide-eyed across the tent.

Sawyer Hickey and a posse of men gathered around a table near the front of the stage. The tabletop was littered with drained plastic cups. One of Sawyer's acquaintances moseyed onto the stage and picked a song to sing. The man gazed down at a small screen where the words scrolled. Behind him, a large screen displayed the lyrics for the audience.

He started to sing a sad love song. The skinny twig of a man sung bass. Then another man sang a Willie Nelson song.

"Can all Texan men sing?" Piper asked the group.

"No way, you should hear Josiah," Matt teased.

"You sound like a dying dog," Josiah retorted with a smirk.

"Look, Sawyer is getting up there." Piper pointed to the stage.

Cole knew he could hold a tune. He'd heard him in church and when swinging Kelly around the dance floor.

"Heaven help us," Kelly muttered, shaking her head.

Sawyer started to sing Garth Brooks' Friends in Low Places. He strutted around putting on a show. "He has a bloated idea of himself and needs knocked down a few notches." Kelly crossed her arms.

"Piper, you can out sing him and put him in his place," Jessie said.

Cole whipped his head toward Piper. Her mouth had fallen open.

"Come on, you know that Shania Twain song?" Jessie leaned closer. Piper giggled but shook her head.

"If you don't sing that song I'll kiss Cole to make Sawyer jealous," Kelly threatened with hands on her hips.

Piper placed a hand on Cole's chest. The possessive gesture made his heart lurch. She stood with a grim face, throwing Kelly the stink eye then stomped to the stage.

CHAPTER 24

Piper

PIPER PASSED SAWYER, MARCHED STRAIGHT to the man in charge and requested the Shania Twain song. She tapped her foot, waiting for Sawyer to finish belting out the final words of his song.

"Here you go, darlin'." Sawyer bowed and transferred the mic with flare.

Piper rolled her shoulders. Shucking Piper McCracken, she donned a dusty stage persona. She bent over slightly and when she righted, she wore a stage smile. The words started, and she sang softly at first, finding convergence in her knowledge of the song. Luckily, Jessie loved Shania Twain and played her music all the time. The songwriter liked men but had become frustrated with them and their pompous ways.

Piper strutted over to Sawyer, who hadn't left the stage, and made it look like she was pushing hard but barely touched his chest. "That don't impress me much." He ate the attention and played upon the words of the song. His indulgences brought a real smile to her face. She lost track of the number of times she pushed or waved him away throughout the song. The crowd cheered her when it ended.

"Sing a duet with me," Sawyer asked into the mic.

The crowd chanted her name, and she glanced against the lights toward her table of friends. Jessie gave her a thumbs up sign. She nodded, letting him pick something, praying she'd recognize it. She closed her eyes and breathed out a sigh when a familiar melody started. Sawyer sung the verses and through the chorus she harmonized. They faced each other smiling.

After the song, he picked another but with a faster tempo. She acted out the character and danced a few steps.

At the conclusion, Piper checked the table. Wearing a frown, Cole tipped his chair back with his arms crossed.

Kelly's arms stretched out and her fingers drummed the table. Pressed into a thin line, her lips had disappeared.

Piper thrust the microphone at Sawyer then hopped off the stage. She swiveled her hips to avoid hitting the tables and chairs. Kelly and Mona rose and exited the side opening. Piper hastened her steps.

"Good luck," Jessie whispered patting her arm. "We're going to grab a bite to eat." Josiah and Jessie stood, leaving Matt and his date with Cole.

Piper's gut twisted as she gazed into Cole's brooding eyes.

"Oh my God," Matt's date gushed, "your voice is amazing. You could so totally be a super star. Couldn't she?" She elbowed Matt. He nodded.

Piper took a vacant seat across from Cole and sipped her warm beer. She couldn't meet his eyes, but stared into the plastic cup. Awkward. She huffed out a loud breath.

A cold beer appeared in front of her.

"Here's to you, gorgeous. I wanted to repay you." Sawyer kissed her cheek. "Any time you want to be my partner you can." Walking to his friends, back slaps greeted him, then they threw him back on stage.

Piper preferred cold beer, she decided. Building up a Kryptonite tolerance would be easier than trying to get into Cole's head. She nursed the beer until it was almost empty.

She peered at her date. Cole glared at Sawyer's boisterous imitation of a Willie Nelson song. This wouldn't do. She had plans and they didn't include a grumpy man.

Piper reached under the table and picked up her bag. "I'll be back in a minute." She stood to go but added with a wink, "I have a surprise for you."

Cole's face seemed to unfreeze and his brows rose.

In the bathroom under the grandstand, she changed then examined herself. In the long mirror, her pale yellow sun dress showed off her tan. She smiled. Tonight she planned to get to the bottom of her and Cole's relationship.

As luck would have it Matt and his girlfriend had left to go dancing, leaving Cole alone in the corner. She walked to him and sat on his lap, straddling him.

"Hello, miss me?" She wiggled. He placed his hands on her waist.

His face softened. "Piper."

"I have plans for you tonight, and I don't want you to think bad thoughts."

"Plans?"

"Your shower is unclogged now." She caressed his cheek. His five o'clock shadow tickled her fingertips.

Cole's lips lifted in a small smile. Piper leaned close to his ear making sure her body intimately moved against his. "You remember what I told you about my singing in school? I was acting with Sawyer. It was a show. You know, right? I'd prefer you sing with me, but I'm pretty sure you wouldn't step foot on a stage."

"You're good. It was so real. And you're right. There isn't enough money in the world to get me up on a stage." He moaned when she took his earlobe into her mouth and suckled it.

"I have plans for you tonight."

"Hmm. I'm in."

"First, your surprise." She pushed back and gazed into his hooded blue eyes. Lacing their fingers, she covered his hands. "Do you feel that?" His fingers moved until they paused at the string of her thong.

Cole's eyes widened, and he swallowed. "Yes, ma'am."

"Those match the bra you have."

"Maybe I'll have the set by the end of the night." His brows rose, and she laughed softly.

"I guess I'll have to go au naturel." She pouted.

His gaze dropped to her chest. The material wasn't see-through, but it seemed he burned a hole with his stare. "That's enough. Too much attention and everyone will know," she whispered. She tipped his head and kissed him. Hard.

He raised his hand to cup her breast, and she leaned into his touch for a moment then said, "Not here. There are people pointing at us."

"Let's get out of here." Cole pulled her up and, with a hurried gait, led them to his truck.

He opened the door for her but spun her before she climbed in. Her heart raced as he pressed against her softness. His hands slipped behind her, feeling the edge of her thong and making her tremble. He devoured her neck, nibbling and licking. He had set her on fire. She needed him to quench her thirst.

They'd parked far from the activities but near a light pole. He rested his forehead against hers. "Pipes, reach in and get my bottle of water for me." His voice was rough.

She stepped up into the truck and leaned over the seat, reaching for the bottle stuck between the seats. He slid his hands under her skirt and up her hindquarters. She froze at his touch and let him explore. He flipped the dress skirt over her back, exposing her bare cheeks. Piper glanced through the windshield, watching for spectators.

"Turn around." The throaty tone of his voice sent a shiver of desire down her spine. As she shifted, he surveyed the new lace garment. Her breath hitched when his finger continued exploring the edge. The lace left little to the imagination. His hungry gaze ravished her. "I want you."

"Good." She caressed the side of his face. "I guess my seduction skills are excellent."

"You can add them to your resume." Cole pulled her to him in a rough kiss. While his tongue wrestled hers, his finger slipped beneath the lace. She inhaled with a gasp and a moan. He continued to work her until she was ready to explode.

Laughter echoed through the parking lot.

"Somebody's coming," she whispered.

"I want that somebody to be you."

She gasped again, this time granting his wish.

Cole

The voices carried over the sound of Cole's thundering heart. He broke the kiss but kept his fingers circling and rubbing. He should stop before he made love to her right there. She took quick breaths through wet swollen lips. Her eager gaze studied his face.

Possessiveness seized him. He wanted to keep her and make her his forever. Any other time a thought like that would've scared the hell out of him, but at the moment, it gave him a rush.

He knew one way he could stake a claim tonight.

A gust of wind pushed the door into him, knocking his elbow. The laughing voices, closer now, floated on the wind. He sighed and relinquished his hold on her and tucked her legs into the cab. "We aren't finished."

Cole closed the passenger door then got in and started the truck. With both hands clutching the wheel, he watched a couple walk by. They clung to each other, and it was a wonder they could walk. The man whispered into the woman's ear and she giggled. He put his hand on her butt and squeezed, making the girl squeal. Did he and Piper look like that? A smile crept onto his lips. God, he hoped so.

Piper relaxed her head against the headrest, her light hair cascading over the back. Her body molded to the seat like melted butter. Was he jealous of the seat? He shifted into drive.

"Next time I'm going to watch your face." He wasn't able to gage her reaction because of speeding through the parking lot.

"Then I'll check your plumbing."

Cole laughed so hard he had to slam on the brakes. A car honked. He waved it on. Finally, on the rural road he drove the speed limit plus.

"I've never been clogged before," Cole countered.

"I still want to give you a *thorough* work over. There are several tests I can run."

"Such as?"

"Taste test, for one." She licked her lips, making him squirm. He stomped the accelerator. He'd never complained about the speed of his truck before but now found it lacking. She reached across and fingered his zipper. A shock wave of heat rolled over him. He momentarily let off the pedal. Then he hit it again.

"Piper, don't. Just wait. I don't want to take you right here but you're making me crazy." He took several deep breaths and focused on the road when they rounded a curve. "I'll pull over," he threatened, but it had sounded like an invitation.

Her hand dipped lower, more aggressive. He wouldn't win the battle and decided not to fight, spreading his legs for her.

The drug store's lit sign loomed in the near distance. He hit the curb too fast and stomped the brakes. The jerk dislodged her hand. He took the opportunity to jump out.

"I'll hurry." He adjusted his manhood then slammed the door. He could feel her gaze so he shook his backside then turned and winked. Piper blew a kiss which he caught and placed on his crotch. Her eyes widened and she covered her mouth.

He reached the door and entered. Nodding to the young cashier, he strode straight to aisle ten. It had been years since he'd shopped from that row, but over the last month he'd visited it often. The other times he'd walked out hoping no one saw him. Tonight was different. Pleasing Piper was paramount, and he had it within his power. He picked up two things.

Remembering they'd run out, he also grabbed dishwashing liquid. He hoped this mundane item would make the other objects seem less obvious. The cashier swiped the barcodes and dropped them in a plastic bag. Cole shifted his weight and handed her cash, but she said nothing out of the ordinary. *Cowboys buying condoms must be a common occurrence.*

He grinned as he turned to leave, nearly running out the door. An elderly woman approached with an ancient man attached at the elbow. Cole nodded and greeted them, all the while watching the angel with a devilish grin in his truck.

Piper

Piper watched Cole check out. He'd glanced around, probably searching for acquaintances who'd report to his mother. Ironically, Flo had helped to arrange the night. Well, making sure she and Beau stayed away for the weekend, even if plans with Lynette fell through.

Cole snatched the plastic bag from the young woman like a cat grabs a mouse and stalked to the door. The polite cowboy held the door open for an elderly couple. Piper sighed, Cole was honorable even amid unquenchable lust. He tipped his hat then marched forward with a determined gleam in his eye.

With the bag on his lap, he started the truck. The small space was charged, and it'd only take a small spark to light an inferno.

"So, what did you buy?" she asked, knowing what he'd bought by the shape of the box showing through the bag. He rubbed the back of his neck and turned a deep shade of red. She snatched the bag and peered inside. Their eyes locked. She pulled out the box. Condoms. "Thirty-six size extra-large."

A cocky smirk found his lips.

"Sounds about right for what I've got planned."

His brows shot upward and he leaned toward her, but she fished in the bag again. "Lube." She didn't need it. Just being near him got her body wet. She pulled out the dish soap. "Squeaky clean?"

"It's for my mom."

"That's sweet. Here I thought you knew something kinky." She stuffed the bag into her purse. Cole's restraint ended and he pressed her against the seat. One hand plunged into her hair as he ravaged her mouth, and the other hand slid under her skirt again. Her eyes closed. He nipped and kissed her neck. She moaned, not caring if he left marks.

Oh, his hands.

Something rapped on the window. Piper's eyes shot open, and Cole twisted toward his door.

Officer Benjamin Moore smiled and waved. Cole tugged the dress to her knees then rolled down the window. "Can I help you, sir?"

"The question is: can I help you?" Ben wiggled his eyebrows.

"Ben, you can pay Cole twenty bucks to watch, but other than that, shoo." Piper motioned the intruder away.

Both men's eyebrows skyrocketed and their jaws dropped. They threw each other a glance then smirked.

"By the way, we aren't doing anything illegal, this is private property," Piper said, reaching around Cole and hitting the button to roll up the window. She gave a quick wave to Ben, who walked away shaking his head, laughing.

The wind blew trash like a tumbleweed across the parking lot. *A storm might be coming.* As if on cue, lightning flashed and the deep roll of thunder followed.

"Drive," she ordered.

"Yes, ma'am."

Piper untucked his shirt and played with the hair around his bellybutton. He moaned. Rain sprinkled the windshield. The pickup jolted to a halt in front of his house.

She opened the truck door, but the wind blew it shut again, nearly claiming her foot as a casualty. Dropping her purse, she used both hands to shove the door open and stumbled out against the wind.

Cole took her arm and led her toward the house. Feeling giddy, her heart galloped, and she inhaled deeply. He shifted his keyring, searching for the house key. Behind him, she ran her hands down his back, buttocks, and then around his waist. The soft faded denim strained with the hard object within. She caressed him and he dropped the keys.

"Shit." He pulled her in front of him and pressed her against the door, his forehead touching hers. His hands trailed downward until they rested on her hips. He took two giant gulps of air. "I need to get you inside." She latched a leg around his and tugged him closer.

"You said it wrong. You need to get inside *me.*"

He moaned and kissed her, grinding against her. Cole found the strength to pull away and grab the keys. His concentration lasted long enough to unlock the door and pull her in as the wind blew it closed behind them. Then her hands snaked under his shirt and his lips lavished her cleavage. "My purse is in the truck," she breathed.

"So," he muttered against her skin. She shivered.

"So... it has your purchases in it."

Cole yanked back, staring blankly at her. Then he jerked open the door and stalked into the rain. The door slammed against the wall, knocking pictures askew. Outlined by the lamplight, his silhouette filled the door frame. Grinning, he stepped into the room holding up her purse like a prize hunting trophy.

A siren wailed. She gasped. Fear ran her veins cold. "Cole," she whimpered.

"It's okay. Come on." He dropped the purse, took her hand and hurried into the rain. In the backyard, the storm cellar was built into the hill. Keys still in hand, he unlocked the door. Six or so steps illuminated when he turned on the light.

"Get down there and wait for me. I'll be right back." He didn't wait but headed back to the house.

"Yeah, right," she mumbled, rubbing her arms. She took a deep steadying breath and scurried into the darkness. "I don't want to wait alone. He must be getting something important."

Piper hurried back into the house, on a mission to rescue two things. The guitar Cole loved and hated, and his mother's picture albums. She picked up a pile of albums, one being the Cole recovery book and took the handle of the guitar case. Setting the case down, she slid the shoulder strap of her purse over her head then picked up the case again.

Down the hall, Cole muttered something. A radio sounded a warning. The tornado siren continued to scream "take cover." She lugged the stuff to the cave-like concrete room. Metal shelves lined two walls. Boxes, Christmas decorations, and pantry items resided on some shelves, but another held a battery charger and lanterns. Someone had stacked cots, blankets, and pillows in the back corner on top of a generator. Piper pulled the cots apart and sat the books on one. Then she moved the guitar under a cot to stow it out of the way. She dropped the purse on the floor. She wiped the books dry and set them aside. The chore had kept the panic in check, but since she'd finished, she had nothing to distract her.

Focus on something. Cole's body. His full lips. The color of his eyes and the ornery glint they got when he teased her.

Thunder cracked. She jumped.

The shower. Her bare rear backing into him, and how hard she'd made him. The angry red line across his abdomen. He'd almost died once but had survived.

Anything to make her forget Cole was out in the violent storm.

CHAPTER 25

Cole

COLE HURRIED THROUGH THE HOUSE holding the weather radio his mother called the "squawk box." His phone rang. "You got to get to safety, boy." Arlon's anxious voice urged. "This ain't no drill. People are fleeing the rodeo. You there?"

"No. Piper and I are home."

"Good. It's coming. I can hear it. Damn. It does sound like a freight train. Stay safe."

"Yes, sir. You too." The line died. He froze until thunder shook the house. "Arlon?" Cole's stomach turned into lead. He snapped out of it. He set his phone down to gather the birth certificates, important documents, and the laptop. He didn't bother locking the front door.

The night had grown eerily still. He made it to the shelter's steps. Over his shoulder, the trees bent near the ground. *Crazy.*

In the bunker, Piper's wide eyes seemed to glow with fear. She jumped up and ran to him. He set the items down and took her in his arms. Debris blew through the door and leaves swirled at his feet.

"I need to shut the door." He climbed the stairs and peered out into the angry night. Branches whipped back and forth. "The yard will be filled with limbs tomorrow, but tonight we'll keep safe." The door lay open outside, and he had to wrestle against the wind. One final gust nearly knocked him down the stairs. He latched the lock and stepped back. Something large crashed against the door.

Piper whimpered.

It had to be a tree, the one he'd seen bent in two. "It's just a tree." His voice belonged to someone else, sounding like a scared child. Her fingers curled around his.

"We're not the only turds in the toilets," she whispered. "Sorry. That's something my dad used to say."

Cole nodded. "We'll be fine."

"Will we?"

"Always."

The overhead light flickered off, and Piper's breath caught. "Here." She touched her phone screen. Pale light washed the room. He squeezed her hand then searched the shelf for a battery-powered lantern. The lights flickered again but stayed off.

Rocking onto the balls of her feet while hugging herself, Piper stared at the door like the bogey man might come calling.

He reached out and rubbed her shoulder. She glanced at him with wide eyes. An overwhelming sensation to protect filled Cole. Piper had been the only woman to draw it out of him. A distraction would help calm her. He kissed her.

She sighed into the gentle kiss as he embraced her. Instantly the flame, once extinguished by the storm, re-ignited.

Piper

Piper focused on Cole, his hands, lips, and heart racing in time with hers. She savored his taste and smell. Loving the warmth of his abdomen, he twitched at her contact. She slid her hands around to the back, fingering his muscles. She dipped lower, but not too low because the belt held his pants tight. That was a problem she needed to remedy. Her fingers worked his buckle, and he caught her hands.

"We can't," he groaned. "It's in the house."

She took his head and tilted it. He'd left his hat in the truck but the bandanna remained. She pointed to the open purse with the drugstore bag sticking out. "Is that...?"

"Yes, sir. I don't give up easy," she said.

Cole stared at her for a moment, placing his palms against the wall on either side of her shoulders. Piper recognized tenderness in his eyes. She'd seen it before when he'd read Beau a story and after he kissed his mother on the cheek. *Love.* Like a cozy blanket, warmth covered her.

She touched his chin; the rough hair tickled her fingertips. His soft, moist lips parted as she skimmed them. His dark eyebrows arched. "Kiss me, Cole." Her words seeped with longing.

He leaned forward. Only their lips touched, but that quickly changed to dueling tongues. She worked on the belt buckle again; this time she pulled it out of the loops. She slipped past the waist to his tight rear. He remained still as she explored his body. She raised his shirt and kissed his chest, flicking his nipple with her tongue. He moaned as if she tortured him. She scraped his skin with her teeth, tasting him. He pushed her back against the wall and felt the edges of her panties. He pushed them until they fell to the floor.

"Talented," she whispered.

"Just wait." He dropped to his knees and lifted her dress. She kicked the panties away. "Hey, those are mine."

"Only if I get yours."

"You've got yourself a deal." Cole's gaze locked on hers and he slid his hands up her legs to the spot they had previously plundered. Every square inch of her vibrated. She sucked in a breath when his fingers touched her most intimate place. He circled the area, teasing and making her squirm with want. Finally he looked down at her and moaned. "I'm going to taste you."

"Just like one of your novels." Piper grinned, then inhaled deeply when his tongue touched her. Her breath hitched when he spread her legs and plundered deeper. He sucked and licked, keeping his gaze on her face. He took one of her legs and lifted it over his shoulder. His hot breath against wet flesh burned.

"Cole, I'm ready." She rested her palms against the concrete. His fingers pumped her and threw her over the brink. Clutching his shoulders, she cried out his name.

"Oh hell, yes," she mewled, making him chuckle. "My legs are shaking, you've got to hold on to me."

"Always." He stood, holding her against the wall and kissed her neck softly.

After she caught her breath she ordered, "Your shirt is mine. Now."

"Yes, ma'am." In the dim light, he pulled it over his head and handed it to her sheepishly. She took the offered gift and brought it to her nose, breathing deeply while visually caressing his body. His shoulders dipped under her inspection.

"Cole, remember the first time you brought me to Stitts? You told me my opinion was important. I'm going to tell you what I think of you." His brow wrinkled and he bit his lip. He nodded and held her gaze. She took a few steps toward him. "You're special."

He tucked his head and took a deep breath. Her fingers skimmed tanned skin. "Your body, your mind, your character and your heart. All of you is alluring." Piper tipped his chin so she could see into those blue depths, but his tears obscured them. She hugged him. "I don't care what people say. You're perfect for me."

He kissed her neck then sucked gently. Her skin warmed with the steady heat of desire. "I have a confession to make."

Cole stopped and backed up. Now she glanced down at his boots. She walked to the cot and sat. "The first time we met, do you remember how I stared at you?"

He nodded and sat next to her, taking her hand. "You gave me a funny look because I asked if you liked romance."

"No. That wasn't it." Piper leaned forward. "The first time I saw you, I was drawn to you. The only way I can think to describe it is: if you would have picked me up, thrown me on the bed and ravished me completely I'd have been more than okay with it." She took a deep breath letting him digest the words. "I've never felt this way before."

Piper glanced up into his eyes and continued, "I've wanted you since I first met you, but then you kinda became my best friend. It didn't stop me from wanting you. I have to be honest, I envisioned you naked many, many nights, especially after the storm. I wished you'd hold and make love to me." She hoped her whispered fantasies and dreams would spring to life. "You're an extraordinary man, Cole."

He rose and started pulling the blankets out and arranging them on the floor. Her heart stalled when he didn't acknowledge her.

Cole

Piper's declarations sent Cole's heart into overdrive and his emotions threatened to overwhelm him. A lump clogged his throat, making it hard to breathe and impossible to talk. Cole felt like an idiot, turning his back to Piper after she'd opened her heart to him. He had to get his emotions under control. The mundane act of unfolding blankets and arranging pillows helped to center him.

Something screeched along the steel door. Most likely, a downed branch caused the eerie sound.

Cole chanced a glance at Piper. She'd wrapped her arms around her legs and tucked them against her chest, revealing her sweet spot to him. He swallowed.

"Piper," he started, pulling his gaze to her face. "I want you too. When Desire started the rumor, I thought she was crazy, but soon you had me wondering what it would be like to be with a woman. To be in a relationship."

Tilting her head, she surveyed his every move as a small smile spread.

Cole pulled off his boots. He slipped his jeans over his hips and kicked them to the side. The fabric strained against his boxer briefs. He'd had a continual hard-on all night.

He snapped the waistband. "Care to do the honors?"

In a cat-like manner, she stood and walked to him. Her hands slid around the band and pushed the boxers down. His erection sprang free.

The fruity scent of her shampoo swirled around him, making him long to plunge his fingers into her lush hair. The sundress brushed him as she tipped a grin up at him. He bit back the urge to pull it over her head. She stepped back and hummed the word "beautiful," then as if she'd read his mind, she shimmied out of the gown.

Bare before each other, she moved first, reaching to hug him with her soft warmth. Her breasts swayed when she moved, making heat pool between his legs.

"I love you," she whispered.

Cole sucked in a quick breath. Had any woman told him that before? No. His heart felt like it sprouted wings because it tried to launch from his chest.

"Cole," she purred. He glanced into her hooded eyes. With a smirk, she pointed to the bag. He chuckled and turned, but fingering his shaft, she stopped him. His breath caught as she explored. He fought not to lose control.

"Piper, please," he begged. He couldn't see straight. He wanted her to continue, but feared he wouldn't last long.

Piper dropped to her knees. She met his gaze as she swallowed him. He thrust his fingers into her hair and moaned her name. A couple flicks of her tongue brought release. She blinked, surprised.

"I couldn't help myself. You have that effect on me. Don't worry, we're not done." He was still rigid, still needy.

"We've got all weekend. We'll deplete that box."

"Damn. I better get busy." He retrieved the package.

Piper claimed a pillow and lay waiting. In the dim light, he studied the contours of her curves. She was the epitome of femininity. Soft in all the right places. He knelt and leaned to kiss her, starting at her chin. He sucked, nipped and licked his way down her neck to her breasts.

"Please, Cole," she said, wiggling. She gripped his shoulders and squeezed. "Now!"

The order went straight to his groin. Her boldness made his hands tremble. He tore the wrapper.

Cole nudged her legs apart. "Piper, aren't you waiting for someone?" he asked, remembering she'd attempted to save herself for her husband.

A slow, smile blossomed on her lips. She cupped his face. "I've been waiting for you, Cole."

He released a breath he hadn't known he'd been holding. "Good, because you're mine."

"Always."

He couldn't resist any longer and broke the barrier. She cried out as he moved. Her hands roamed, fascinating him. Cole moaned against her neck, making her shiver.

Piper sucked in a breath, and he pushed back. She sought his gaze. "I'm close."

It turned him on and he smirked. "I'll see what I can do."

"Do it faster."

"Yes ma'am."

Piper gasped and her eyes rolled back. She clenched and bucked, sending him over the edge with her.

He rolled to the side. Panting, he pulled her rag-doll like body into an embrace. He closed his eyes and relaxed, enjoying how full he felt.

Piper's head flopped back onto the pillow. She fingered his bicep. "Cole," she purred, "You're not naked."

Suddenly, the room closed in on him. He found her studying him. He swallowed and touched the bandanna on his head. A reminder of his cancer scare and the decision he'd made to never get involved with a woman. It was too late, he was in it for the long haul now. He couldn't keep to himself. He needed Piper.

"Take it off," he said.

"Really?" her dainty brows rose.

"I had you disrobe one head, why not the other?"

She giggled and touched his chest. Her eyes aligned with his as her hands traveled up his torso, his neck, to the bandanna. He sucked in a breath when she skimmed the edge. On either side of his head, near his ears, she pushed the material until it slid off onto the pillow. She rubbed his scalp, and he bit his lip, savoring her touch.

A few days prior, he'd shaved his head. The stubble tingled his scalp as she slid her fingers over it.

She leaned close and kissed him. He sighed. Yeah, I could get used to this. The slow passionate kiss made him hot and kept him hard.

He rolled to his back and she snuggled against him. They listened to the storm rage while she played with his chest hair.

The door rattled and the thing, tree, branch or whatever, clawed like it wanted in. "That doesn't sound good," he mumbled.

The wind shrieked. Cole's ears popped, and the door groaned like a giant vacuum sucked from outside. They scrambled upright.

"Cole," Piper whimpered. Her large eyes fixed on the door.

He tugged her into an embrace. "We'll be fine." He hoped to God he wasn't lying.

"It's a tornado, isn't it?" She yelled over the roar.

"Maybe, or it could be high winds." The doubt in his voice betrayed him.

With her chin on his chest she gazed at him incredulously. They huddled, listening to the creaking and screaming. He feared the earth would lift, and they'd be swept away.

Stretching, he kicked the guitar case. Tears welled as he reached to unlatch it. Piper's thoughtfulness astounded him.

He handed her the old man's guitar to tune. She tilted her head as she plucked the strings. Her hair shifted as she turned the tuners. Eyes closed, she hummed a cord.

"Beau's right. You do sound like an angel."

She grinned, passing it to him. He strummed it, grateful she had a good ear. One simple melody led to another. Piper added a line from the lyrics when she recalled them. Together they'd ride out the storm.

CHAPTER 26

Cole

COLE SAT ON THE OLIVE GREEN cot with a photo album open upon his lap. On the blankets nude, and stretched out asleep like a contented cat, lay Piper. His mother would appreciate the album Piper had saved. It held pictures of his parents before his dad left. A memory book, she'd called it. Cole had put his boxers back on before flipping pages because it didn't seem right to hold his parents on his lap while naked. Too intimate.

He looked down at the smiling face of his mother. She had been pretty when she was younger. He turned page after page, letting the sadness and anger come and go. His mother had made peace with his father; why couldn't he?

Cole was cursed with his father's looks. Luckily, Piper didn't mind. In one picture, a seven-year-old Cole sat on a horse with his father next to him, a reassuring palm on the boy's leg. Cole didn't recognize the smiling boy.

Something fell out when he turned a page. An envelope filled with letters and cards. He opened them and found them addressed to his mother from his father. She'd kept them hidden. Angry with how his father had treated his mother, Cole wouldn't have understood why she corresponded with the drunk. Although if his mom loved his dad like he loved Piper, it would be impossible to let go.

Looking at the dated postmarks, he deduced that his mother knew where his father lived and visited him regularly. Now he suspected that her monthly get-togethers with her friends was a tactic to see his father. Were they dating?

Cole straightened when he found a letter stating that his father was coming home to support his mother for Cole's cancer surgery. He'd stayed by Cole's side all night so Flo could get sleep. He remembered waking once to see a stranger, and the man gave him a drink of water. Cole had been hurting and too drugged to recognize his father. Huh. Strange happenings.

Was his father sober? Why didn't he return? Cole knew the answer to the last. Him. He sighed and closed the book.

A knock startled Piper awake. Cole made his way to the door.

A muffled almost frantic voice said, "Hello, hello! Cole? Mrs. Dart?"

"I'm here." Cole tapped the metal.

"Cole? Oh, thank God." The unmistakable voice of Ben Moore met their ears. "Hey, there's a tree covering the doorway. You okay in there?"

"Yeah, Piper and I are fine." He glanced toward her. She'd slipped his shirt over her head and searched for her undies. She'd never find them stuck in his jeans pocket. He grinned.

"Good. Listen, I've called for a chainsaw. A crew should be here any minute to help. I'll keep you updated. I'm glad you're safe."

Cole arched a brow at Piper. His erection strained his boxers. She glanced down and her mouth dropped open. With a wry grin, she plucked a package from the box and waved the wrapper. She opened her arms, and it was all the invitation he needed.

He planned to make love to her all day and all night. He'd take her to the shower and wash her from head to toe like he'd been dying to do since the shower incident. They linked fingers and her legs wrapped around his waist as the chainsaw drowned out their cries of pleasure.

Piper

Piper scoured the shelter, but she couldn't find her underwear. When Ben opened the door, she hoped to God a breeze wouldn't lift her skirt. Cole hopped up a couple steps but turned and pulled the edge of her thong out of his jeans pocket. *That little turd.* She lunged at him. He laughed and stumbled backwards up the remaining stairs.

Fully dressed, but wearing the look of a satisfied cat, sunlight hit Cole's face. He grimaced as his eyes adjusted. The dark shadow on his chin made her sigh. Highly skilled in the art of lovemaking, he belonged to her. She heated when his steamy gaze roamed her body.

Her fiery thoughts froze, as did her body, when she saw the destruction behind Cole. She must have looked horrified because Cole stepped toward her and clasped her arms.

"Piper, you-" Words choked in his throat as he surveyed the property behind her.

"Oh God, Cole." She uttered on a breath, and he pulled her close into a fierce hug. She clung to him as tears welled.

What used to be Cole's home was missing two-thirds. No kitchen, no living area, the stairs and the balcony and a half of each bedroom torn away. The rest of the building looked like a life-size dollhouse. Everything sucked out. Drywall hung down with studs exposed, wires and pipes ended in jagged pieces. Bits of insulation, wood and other debris scattered around the grounds in an apocalyptic mess.

She gasped. Cole's truck was on its side, wrapped around a tree trunk. The tornado ripped the trees from the ground on the right side of the drive like a giant lawn mower.

"We could have died," Piper mumbled.

Cole swallowed and made a strange gurgling noise. "What now?" he muttered.

Ringing pierced the air. They glanced at Ben, but he shook his head. His phone was at his ear already. The sound came from the cellar. Recognizing the ring tone, Piper flew down the steps. She caught the call on the last ring. Out of breath, she pushed talk.

"Hello?"

"Flo?"

"Oh, thank God. Piper, are you all right? I can't reach Cole and I'm worried sick."

Piper walked into the sunshine again. Cole and Ben discussed the storm damage. An SUV rolled up the drive and five burly men with dark clothes and florescent vests hopped out. They greeted Ben and Cole, then worked moving the limbs away from the shelter, barn and driveway, stacking the ones they could.

"The power is out," Piper told Flo, but she hesitated to break the bad news.

"Oh," the mother breathed a sigh. "His phone must be dead."

His phone? She couldn't remember the last time she'd seen it. It might be in a different county if he left it in the house, but there was a chance it survived in the truck.

"Cole wouldn't happen to be there, would he?" Flo giggled.

Piper swallowed and called, "Cole?" When his gaze shifted in her direction, she held the phone out. He took it.

"Hello, Mom. Yeah, we survived, but the house didn't." He paused with a sullen glance then strode toward the back of the house. "You and Beau should stay with Lynette for a while. It's an emergency. Surely Lynette will understand. Her son is homeless." He walked out of earshot.

The men started the chainsaw and cut the limbs. The tree blocking the shelter had a large root ball attached. It had slammed into the hillside, denting and blocking the door. If Ben wouldn't have happened along, they might have been stuck in there for days.

"Ben." She approached him. When he glanced up, he rubbed red eyes. "Have you been awake all night?" The disaster wasn't exclusive to Cole's home. Her heart jumped to her throat. "Is everybody all right?"

Ben shook his head then scrubbed his face. "The damage is terrible, but everyone we've found is safe. A few bumps and bruises. A few minor accidents and injuries pertaining to those. With the lines down and power off, getting hold of anyone is hard. Lots of calls for missing people, but like y'all, I suspect we will find them whole and smiling."

"Things can be purchased and homes rebuilt, people not so much." She patted his arm. "Thanks for getting us out."

"I should have left you guys until last."

Piper's face heated, and she couldn't help but glance at Cole. He knelt to pick up something from the debris. He pinched her lacy bra between his finger and thumb. His gaze locked on hers, and a lopsided grin appeared.

"Uh." Ben cleared his throat. "I mean, all those water bottles and such."

"Sure." Piper scratched the top of her head. She had tugged her hair into a ponytail, and it probably didn't look good. All she wanted was a hot shower. That wouldn't happen now. Or maybe she could at her place. Oh God. Her place. Her car. *How far did the destruction span?*

"Mom and Beau are going to take a vacation with my sister, whether or not Lynnette wants them to." Cole said, handing the phone back to Piper.

"I'll call Brad." She hit his name, and it rang. No answer. She tried the Double D and Josiah's frantic voice answered.

"Are you guys okay? How about the ranch?" Piper asked.

"The Big Deal and Double D are fine," Josiah replied. "We had a power outage, but that was it. No hurt animals or damaged buildings." Piper sighed with relief.

Ben touched her shoulder. "Ask if he's heard anything from Kelly Jo Greene. She's one of the missing. Her parents can't locate her."

Piper nearly dropped the phone but relayed the question.

"She's fine. Kelly, Desire and Brad have checked in with us, but I haven't heard from my parents yet. Oh, another call is coming through, gotta go." Josiah dropped the call and Piper relaxed.

She glanced at her boyfriend. "My place is fine, so you can stay with me if you'd like. I should get my car."

"I can take you," Ben offered. "Get in."

"Now?" she glanced toward Cole. She didn't want to leave him. "Okay. Would you like me to drive so you're able to take a power nap?"

The cop grinned. "I think the powers that be would frown on a civilian driving my squad car."

"What are you going to do, arrest me?" Piper cocked her head and placed hands on hips. "Well, how much sleep have you gotten since you played peeping Tom in the parking lot?"

Ben blushed and looked away. "I—"

"You just want to race the car with the lights on," Cole teased.

"Sh." Piper hushed. She stretched her arm palm up. "Hand me the key, Ben. Driving sleep deprived is almost as bad as driving under the influence. I know, I've seen reruns of MythBusters."

"Fine." Ben dug the fob out of his pocket. He barked orders to the crew and gave them the next address.

Piper couldn't believe she'd talked Ben into it. She smirked; she'd only known the man three months, and he'd handed her the key without protesting.

"He's crazy," Cole said, shaking his head.

"Jealous?" Piper asked.

"Only that he's driving off with you."

"I'll be back," she reassured. "And I'll bring breakfast."

"Don't forget the coffee, and lots of it.".

CHAPTER 27

Piper

PIPER RETURNED TO COLE'S ARMED with breakfast, one of his clean shirts, and friends. She parked near the road where there was less debris. Josiah pulled in behind her and Jessie handed items out of the truck to Josiah's brothers, Matt and Gabe. Near the barn, the brothers set up a table, then Piper brought out donuts, juice and coffee with the fixings. Jessie offered all the fruit she had.

Piper ran to Cole and hugged him. He'd been busy gathering remnants of his property. Filthy and sweaty, he'd made piles of metal and wood.

"What's all this?" Cole asked when he saw the Barnes family carrying a bunch of plastic containers.

"I wanted to buy totes to put your clothes in, but Jessie wouldn't let me. She already had these for the book stash and insisted we use them."

"No sense wasting time to go shopping." Jessie put the totes down. "Go ahead and use the Sharpie to mark these. You can buy me more later."

Piper marked three totes: Florence, Beau and Cole. They spent the morning organizing the blown away bits of the Dart residence. They stored the overflowing totes in the barn. Pots, pans, and other household items they stacked in the loft as the trash pile grew.

Matt and Gabe made a store run for more totes and lunch.

Ben returned to the Dart residence. Piper shielded her eyes against the sun and watched him walk up the driveway. The closer he came, the slower he moved.

"Looks like Ben needs another nap," Piper said. Earlier, she'd let the man sleep after she arrived at the cabin. She'd showered, dressed, made coffee and poured Ben a cup. She shook him awake and shoved it into his hands with a banana. The radio going ballistic helped to open his eyes. He drove off like a bat out of hell with a cloud of dust following.

Ben's stubble and red eyes with purple bags made him appear haggard. Not just tired, but drained. He found the table with now stale donuts and warm bottled water. He poured coffee into a paper cup. Ben grimaced as he drank but chugged the whole thing without taking a breath.

Cole shook his hand. He opened a cooler and offered Ben a beer, but he waved it off and picked up a water bottle instead.

Piper watched their interaction from the side of the house near what used to be the kitchen. She found cutlery stuck in a tree trunk and embedded in the ground. The plates were all broken, but she found a glass unscathed. There wasn't any rhyme or reason to the destruction. She moved closer to the foundation, looking at the concrete pad.

"Piper!" Ben yelled, startling her. "Get away from there. Those remaining walls could shift any time. I don't want you hurt or worse, dead. I can't deal with more of that today."

The pain in his tone made her hurry toward him. Cole opened one of the Barnes' lawn chairs and made Ben sit.

"Maybe you should go home, Ben." Piper glanced at Cole and he nodded.

"No," Ben stared at the plastic bottle in his hand, but didn't really see it. "Not yet. I want to keep my mind off of it."

"Oh no, Ben. It was the call that made you drive off like a wild man." Piper placed a hand on his shoulder.

He nodded. "Indigo found the bodies."

"That's horrible," Piper gasped.

"I'm sorry, Ben." Cole grasped his other shoulder with a short squeeze. He met Piper's gaze. *It could have been them.*

"I'm sorry too." Raw emotion cracked his voice, and when he looked at them his eyes filled with tears. He tried to blink them away.

Uh oh. Piper's gut twisted. In a small town, a death would touch the entire community.

Bodies. Plural. She shivered.

"Cole, I wanted to tell you myself before you heard," Ben shrugged. "You know, through the grapevine. Arlon's gone."

Cole's eyes widened and the color drained from his face. He stepped back, then again. His legs buckled with the weight of emotion, and he fell to his knees whispering the man's name. He covered his face and stilled. Piper rushed to his side and pulled him into her arms. The flood gates opened.

Jessie returned from the barn, followed by Josiah. Grasping the seriousness, seeing the two men with tears, she asked, "Who, Ben?"

"Arlon Topp."

Jessie sucked in a gasp and bit her hand. Josiah spun her into his arms and held her. She'd known the crusty cowboy her whole life. The ranch hand had mentored Josiah as well as Cole. Piper and Josiah's gaze met as they consoled their loved ones. Tears brimmed their eyes and spilled over, grieving for the lost soul and for the pain the others felt.

"Where?" Josiah asked with a scratchy voice.

"On the road near his house. Looks like he was trying to reach the shelter." Ben pulled out a handkerchief and blew his nose.

"Is Morgan...?" Piper asked. She'd only met Arlon's sister once, but she'd bonded with her.

"No. She's safe in town. The other couple was from Nockerville. Same road. They must have been coming home from the rodeo." Ben leaned back in the chair and breathed deeply, dabbing his eyes again.

Cole shook in her arms. She rubbed circles on his back. There weren't any words. Nothing took the sting of death away. He'd lost his house, truck, and everything in them, now Arlon. She reached out a hand to Josiah. He took it and they tightened the circle. Jessie pulled Ben in, and the friends collectively grieved a good man who'd left a mark on their hearts.

"Poor Morgan," Jessie whispered.

After a moment, Josiah opened the cooler and grabbed five beers. He twisted off the caps and passed them out. He raised his amber bottle and toasted Arlon's life. "To our good friend and a great man. May the good Lord keep a close eye on him or he'll try to wrangle the women."

Cheers and tears, they raised the bottles in memory.

Cole planned to stay on the property and Piper decided to join him.

"Unfortunately, there are bad folks who take advantage of disasters like this," Ben said with a frown. "They come and look for priceless items, credit cards. Anything they can sell or pawn to make a buck. Thieves will come for the copper or other scrap metal. Cole, I posted a no trespassing sign, but that doesn't mean they'll stay out."

"We'll be fine." He'd brought the generator out and had it ready to go when it got dark.

"They might go for the generator even with it chained. Bolt cutters are easy to use." Ben patted his side holster. "You should be armed."

"My guns were in the house, and we haven't found them yet," Cole said with his arms crossed.

"I'll lend you one of mine," Josiah offered. He fished in his pocket for keys.

"It's all good," Piper said with a smile. "I've got mine."

The men stared at her, and she swore she heard crickets chirping. "What? I have a real, live gun. You want to see it?" *Incredible.* "Cole, remember the package I asked my brother to send?"

She opened the hatchback and pulled out a crazy, big ass revolver and walked back to the group. "Her name is Sheila and if anyone says a derogatory word about her, I'll stomp on your foot or, maybe, your balls will disappear like Holden's."

Jessie giggled and high-fived her.

Piper smiled at the men's stunned faces. "Did you boys forget I had a stalker in Chicago?" Although if she would have waved it at Justin he would have gone to the police. "Girls like powerful engines and big guns to."

Jessie now elbowed her husband because, Piper was unfortunate to know, Josiah's gun hung on his body. It was an inside joke she'd easily worked out while working in the couple's home. Piper couldn't help but giggle too. "Isn't that right, Jess?"

"Oh, so right."

"Let me see Sheila," Ben asked holding out his hand. "Please."

Piper stroked the shaft before letting her baby go. The man inspected the gun, turning it over. "It's loaded."

"Thought we might need it." Piper shrugged.

"Safety is on."

Piper rolled her eyes. She took the gun and checked the ammo. "Can I shoot your house, Cole?"

"Uh, okay." Cole glanced from the other men to his house.

Piper clicked the safety off then targeted a light hanging haphazardly from the ceiling. She pulled the trigger and pop, pop. She stepped back into Cole. The second shot vaporized the glass bowl of the overhead light. She grinned, holding the gun now pointed at the ground.

"Satisfied?" Piper asked Ben. "I won't let anyone harm my man."

Josiah and Jessie exchanged a look, then Jessie squealed and hugged Piper and Cole around the necks, choking them. "I knew it. I'm so happy for you. You're so cute together." She sighed and Josiah pulled her back.

"Jess, you're hugging her man awfully hard. She might be your friend, but she's holding a gun." Josiah grinned, then shook Cole's hand.

With dusty clothes and a dirt smeared forehead, Cole returned the smile. Despite the devastation of his earthly belongings and the death of a friend, his relationship with Piper brought him joy. Piper's heart warmed. She hoped he felt lucky. Last night luck was on his side in more ways than one.

Piper kissed his cheek, making Cole blush while the others cooed. He needed his hat. She handed Sheila to him and started for the truck. Jessie followed Piper as she circled the mangled wreckage, inspecting it. After a day in the sun helping to sort through Cole's family's lives, Jessie looked tired. "What are you doing?" she asked.

On its side, Piper couldn't open the truck door unless she climbed on top. But she could squeeze in through the missing windshield. She examined jagged edges and then moved a tiny step at a time. The glove box gaped open. She gathered the papers then handed the pile out to Jessie. Searching the small squashed space for other items, she had an idea. Piper pulled out her phone and called Cole's number.

Cole

Cole turned the revolver over again in his hand. Piper never ceased to amaze him. The guys took turns examining it. Knowing his woman packed a piece like this *and could shoot it* made him proud. The reason she needed it in the first place made him irate.

"Hey," Matt called in a loud voice from the barn. "You're never gonna believe what I've found."

The men walked toward the door. Unscathed, except for a fork sticking straight off the side and a few missing shingles, the barn remained intact. All his tools, the tractor, Beau's bike, and even the tarpaulin-covered jalopy of his father's that his mother wouldn't let him get rid of had been untouched. How one side of his property remained unharmed while the other was utterly destroyed bewildered him.

In Matt's grimy hand sat Cole's smartphone. Miraculously, the phone's screen hadn't cracked, but the corner was dented with scratches the same color of the barn siding. He handed Sheila to Ben then picked up the phone. "Unbelievable. It still has a charge." He'd missed several calls. "Where d'you find it?" Cole asked.

"It started ringing. I found it in the loft."

"No kidding. Doesn't that beat all?" Cole sent a text to his mother, then pocketed the device.

"Cole." Piper's voice rang out from around the building. He hurried around the corner and nearly ran into her. The triumphant grin on her face caused his heart to hitch.

"Look what I found," she said, pointing to the top of her head where his black misshapen Stetson rested. He considered her smudged yellow tank top, dusty jeans, boots, and the crowning glory: his hat. A renewed possessiveness rolled over him.

"Thanks." He kissed her, and she set the hat on his head.

"I've got the paperwork out of your truck. I thought you might want the insurance info. I called your phone and thought I heard it ringing."

"Matt found it. Thanks, Pipes."

She tilted her head and scanned him. Did she see the shock and awe her thoughtfulness caused and love radiating from his heart?

CHAPTER 28

Cole

COLE LEANED AGAINST THE DOUBLE D ranch's porch post watching Piper talk in a business-like voice. She hadn't spied him yet. He waited in the shade, not wanting to interrupt. Today she wore a pale green sundress with a ruffled edge. It was short, and he enjoyed her toned legs. The red tips of her toes caught his attention. Why he noticed, he didn't understand, but he noticed things about Piper he'd never noted about other women.

After four days of exhaustion and emotional turmoil, his property's clean-up was coming along. Cole appreciated the townsfolk stopping to help gather things and Brad giving him time off. Since the storm, the Barnes had invited him and Piper to dinner each night.

The last few nights, he'd opted for Piper's warm bed and open arms over the concrete floor and cots. He'd drop her off at work then head out to his land. He'd return around dinner time.

Piper sat on the porch swing, in a calm voice repeating, "This is a work line. If you care to do business, I will place your order over the phone. Otherwise you can order online." While her voice remained steady and in control, it was apparent, by the color creeping to her face, frustration was shifting into anger.

"You already have that information. You asked for it three days ago. No. There's no need for me to repeat it. If you've misplaced it, you can find it on the website or in the little brochure you're so fond of quoting."

Snarkiness crept into her tone. Cole grinned because the potential client was about to get an earful.

"There's no need to make threats. This conversation is being recorded." Piper pulled the phone away from her ear and looked down at it like it reeked. "Why would you do that? It wouldn't be true, therefore, lying. Leaving a bad rating or making a false negative claim is slander." She paused and rubbed her temple.

"Listen, Justin, threatening to leave a bad review about the company I work for because I won't meet with you is blackmail. Following through with the inappropriate feedback is wrong. You haven't bought anything; therefore you don't know how the product is."

"*My* behavior?" She growled. "What's wrong with *my* behavior? I'm trying to get an order for the company. I don't meet special needs of clients. We're not that kind of business. I suggest you call someplace else if you're looking for someone to talk to."

Cole balled his fists and forced himself to remain still. It wouldn't do Double D Intimates any good if he charged over, yanked the phone from Piper, and yelled until Justin's ears bled. Although the visual made him sneer.

"*Now* you want to place an order. Uh, huh. What's your credit card number? You don't give that information over the phone?" Piper laughed. "Very well. I'll transfer you. Have a good day." She hit a button and sighed. She didn't, technically, hang up on him, she'd put him on hold.

Cole had heard the message. The web address and ordering information would repeat along with "all operators are busy at the moment." Jessie and Josiah gave voice to the recording.

Across the way, Jessie stood in the doorway, grinning at him. Focused on Piper, he'd failed to see her. Jessie winked then walked toward her employee. "You're lucky, he's only called three times today." Jessie sat next to Piper on the swing.

"The tornado knocked out lines, and the amount of people using their cell phones causing a system overload is the only good thing to come out of the storm. I'm lucky he hasn't gotten through as much." Piper leaned back and crossed her arms.

"Maybe you're lucky because you've got a man." Jessie elbowed her.

"Yeah I am, aren't I?" She sighed and stretched her legs.

Piper's words went straight to his heart. He pushed out of the shadows. "I tend to think so," he drawled with a smirk.

Piper squealed and ran into his open arms. He took a deep breath and drew in her scent. Her shampoo's smell and the silky texture of her hair reminded him of the unfinished shower. His arms tightened around her. It felt right to hold her. He buried his nose in her locks. "That jerk still bothering you?"

"Yes, Cole. He harasses Piper daily." Jessie looked down at the phone. "The asshole is still on hold waiting for an operator. I could dump him off the line, but he'd just call back."

"This way we know exactly where he is and what he's doing." Piper snuggled into Cole's shoulder.

"And we can waste his time as long as he has patience. Today it seems infinitely. I'll get rid of him." Jessie sighed and pushed a button. "Hello, sir, how can I help you today? No, she is servicing another customer."

Cole chuckled and Piper kissed him.

"I have another call on the line so if you're ready—what size garment? You don't know. Let's start with something you're sure to know. What's your name? Uh, huh. And the shipping address? Sorry, we do not offer a pickup service. Shipping address? I'm sorry, sir." Jessie argued with the man over and over for two minutes. "Like I said, I have another customer. A *paying* customer. Please do not call back until you learn your address and would like to place an order. Goodbye."

After dinner the Barnes, Piper and Cole sat outside in the cooling evening, sipping drinks and having pie. The Barnes' personal line rang.

"It's Desire," Jessie announced and hit speaker. "Hey, Ms. Desire. You're on speakerphone."

"Hello, dear. Is your handsome husband with you?"

"Yes, ma'am. Also, Mr. and Mrs. Dart are eating dessert." Jessie giggled.

Piper took Cole's hand and squeezed.

"Young people today. My goodness. I didn't know y'all were into that swinger stuff, but whatever floats your boat. Back in my day, I ate dessert in the bedroom, if you understand what I mean, and it was only one man at a time. I can see the benefits to more, mind you. Jessie dear, some of your grandma's books have opened my mind to new ideas."

The couples tried to stifle the laughter, but Josiah couldn't hold it in.

"Hi, Desire," Piper said. "Jessie makes a wicked-good peach pie. I'm sure she'll save you a piece."

"Oh Piper, dear, I'm watching my figure." Desire sighed. "It's dessert and not dessert. That's a shame."

"That comes later," Josiah teased. Cole felt heat creeping to his cheeks.

"I hope that's not the only thing," Desire added.

Piper sucked in a gasp. Cole laughed, but Jessie grinned. "Damn straight." Josiah smiled a promise at his young wife.

"I'm privy to some information. Young ladies, or old ones, only swear in the bedroom. It's acceptable. And," she whispered even though the men still listened, "it makes men horny when ladies ask for a good—you know, starts with an F and rhymes with luck."

"Yes, ma'am. I'll be sure to give it a try," Jessie said, swiping a tear away.

"Oh, I have some news. The town prankster struck again. This time it was the Alcoholic Anonymous meeting sign."

"That's not cool," Cole mumbled. People trying to get their lives together don't need someone fooling around with their choices. All the volunteers didn't need trivializing, either.

"The sign had switched letters?" Josiah asked.

"A completely new message," Desire said.

The couples glanced around the table waiting for Desire to drop the punch line.

"Do you want to hear it?" she asked, then snickered.

"Yes, please," Piper said. She turned to Cole and caught his eye. The signs had been funny, dirty or a mixture of both.

"It read: I was addicted to the hokey pokey," Desire paused, "then I turned myself around."

Josiah stared at his empty plate and repeated, "I was addicted to the hokey pokey then I turned myself around?"

"That's what it's all about," Desire said.

The women groaned and rolled their eyes. Cole laughed and shook his head. Dang, the prankster was a strange old coot.

"Good one." Josiah patted Jessie's arm.

"That's not the real reason I called, but the good news comes first." She cleared her throat. "I have the details for Arlon Topp's service. I thought y'all would want to know."

"Thank you," Cole said with a straight face. He'd kept his emotions hidden. He allowed his true feelings out a few times around Piper, but worried Arlon's death would remind her of her father's passing.

Piper had enough to handle with Justin's barrage of harassing shenanigans. Cole hadn't known the stalker continued to call the Double D. Hopefully Jessie reported it to the police.

How long would Justin stay in Texas and what would be his next step? Admit defeat and give up, or turn to drastic measures? Cole's gut twisted; he couldn't think.

Piper touched his knee, pulling him out of his thoughts. "Did you hear?"

Cole shook his head.

"Drew Peacock is having a service at the church. Visitation then a memorial and a graveside service. I've got the times."

"It seems weird to wait so long," Jessie mused as she stacked the dirty plates.

"Not anymore. A week or more is the norm," Piper said. "After my dad died, it took a week to get all the preparations made and for my family to arrive in town. One of my uncles was on business overseas." She sighed, offering Cole a sad smile. She picked up the pitcher of lemonade and followed Jessie into the house.

"So how are you doing?" Josiah asked him with a firm look. "The house, oh man, I don't want to even think about dealing with something like that."

Cole rubbed his hand over his face and took a deep breath. "My hands are tied. The property is in my father's name. I can fill out the paperwork and talk to the insurance people. I have all the papers, but I can't sign anything."

"How is that possible? Your dad left when you were a kid."

Cole put his elbows on his knees. "I don't even know if he's alive."

"Damn."

"Hopefully, my mom can get a hold of him. Right now, I'll clean up the mess, but eventually, we'll have to rebuild or move on." He leaned back against the chair.

"But wasn't your father's name Cole too?" Josiah asked.

"Colson. I'm just Cole."

"That had to have been confusing sometimes."

"Nah, not for me and Lynette. We called him Dad. Maybe for Mom."

"Did you have a stupid nickname like bubby? That was mine." Josiah lifted his glass and downed the rest of his lemonade.

Cole chuckled. "Lynette called me Lumpy, as in a lump of coal. Or B.B. for Big Brother." He shrugged, not wanting to talk about his sister or his father.

Around nine, the Barnes' phone rang. Spying the number, Josiah gave Cole a quick nod and answered the phone. He left the family room without looking back.

Jessie pulled Piper toward the stairs to inspect her latest creation. He watched Piper's legs as she climbed. At the top she stopped. His face heated as he met her eyes. She winked and disappeared from view.

Josiah returned from the kitchen. "Thanks, Ben. Cole's here." He handed Cole the phone.

"Ben."

"Cole." Ben cleared his throat, trying to talk over background noise. "Sorry about the commotion. The Pink Taco is offering a discount for the tornado victims. They're hanging out here before heading back to the church to put the kids to bed." The storm had affected thirty families. The church opened its basement as a shelter for the homeless or displaced.

"No worries. It's good of Pastor Peacock to open the church for them. I'm lucky to have a shelter and girlfriend willing to host my hide."

"It's what the church is meant to do, in my opinion." Ben mumbled something to the waiter. "I wanted to warn you. There have been looters."

"You've got to be kidding me. That's crazy. The shit's blown up. What could thieves want?"

"I know, I know. They're after scrap metal. Copper pipes. They're hitting debris piles, fields and going onto people's property. Especially at night with metal detectors. They scavenged the Fanning's house last night," Ben said.

"No way."

"Yeah. If you are staying at the house tonight, then I'd advise you bring your girlfriend's gun."

Cole chuckled and pictured Piper holding Sheila.

"I'm serious, Cole. If you camp out on your property—be careful. These criminals are armed. We've found a stash of stolen goods, not just metal, at the old Cummings warehouse by the railroad tracks. We're watching the warehouse now."

"Thanks for the head's up, Ben." Cole set the phone down and rubbed his chin. Should he stay at the property or should he go home with Piper? He didn't want to put her in harm's way, but he didn't want to leave her behind, either.

"I'll stay with you." Josiah's face wore an evil grin, and he carried a shotgun.

Cole smiled, probably looking malicious. "All right. What about the girls?"

Josiah and Cole returned to the living room. "Hey, Jess," Josiah called.

Jessie peered over the banister. She scanned her husband; her eyes widened as she spotted the gun. "Piper, come here." She waved her hand then pointed. Piper joined Jessie at the top of the steps. "What's up?" Jessie asked, hurrying down the stairs.

"Trouble." Josiah reasonably informed the women regarding Ben's warning and the decision to form a guard.

"Cole—" Piper started.

"I'll be fine." He locked gazes with her. "I promise."

She frowned, but nodded. Piper tilted her head, studying him.

Male company wouldn't necessarily be a bad thing. While he'd miss the hell out of Piper and her body snuggled against him, she was wearing him out. He rubbed his jaw, trying to stymie a smug smile. For the longest time, he hadn't had a woman to look after except for his mother; perhaps Josiah could offer some pointers.

What Cole needed was a shrink and a beer. Or maybe just a beer.

"I'll get the cooler and the beer," Josiah said.

Cole clasped him on the shoulder. "You've read my mind."

CHAPTER 29

Piper

PIPER STOOD IN THE BACK of the sanctuary, rubbing her hands and watching Morgan Topp. Arlon's sister wore a gray skirt with a white blouse and her long hair swept up in an elegant twist. Beside her eyes being puffy and red, she appeared to have stepped out of the office. Yet Morgan smiled as people shared memories with her.

In their Sunday best, Jessie and Josiah entered the room and greeted Piper. "You look nice," she said to Jessie.

She glanced at the hunter green dress that accented her slim waist and auburn hair. "Thanks."

Josiah scanned the area and raised his hand to his parents across the room. He fiddled with his striped tie. His light brown hair was devoid of the cowboy hat he usually wore, and he looked citified. "The community loved Arlon."

"He didn't discriminate with his friends," Jessie said, her voice catching. Josiah rubbed her arm and she dabbed her eyes.

Townspeople, country folk, ranchers, cowboys, and families waited in the long line to pay their last respects.

"Look," Jessie said nodding toward Morgan. "See the man she's hugging? That's Fortuna's mayor, Jasen Delay." She glanced around and leaned close. "I've heard rumors about Morgan and the mayor. There's almost twenty years between them."

"Was that before or after Cole's Russian mail-order bride?" Josiah asked with a grin.

"Before, of course." Jessie said, crossing her arms.

"Don't listen to her, Piper. You know firsthand how true Fortuna rumors are," Josiah said with a smirk.

"What about the books in city hall?" Jessie hissed quietly.

"What books?" Piper asked.

Again Jessie glanced around. "There's a whole bookcase full of naughty books."

Piper covered her mouth to staunch her laugh. "The whole town loves naughty books," she said.

Jessie blushed as she said, "If you like spankings—"

"Or whips and harnesses..." Josiah added.

"Oh." Piper rocked back on the heels of her shoes and glanced at the handsome, well-dressed mayor. She jerked her head back toward Jessie. "Wait a minute, how do you know about these books?"

Bright red, Jessie stammered, "Well, I, uh, saw them."

"Uh huh," Piper teased, "sure you did." Josiah opened his mouth, but Piper put up her hand. "I don't want to know."

Cole walked to her side and shook hands with Josiah. "I can't talk. I need to get Morgan a glass of water." He disappeared from sight and reappeared with a bottle of water. After Morgan had finished sipping, Cole set it aside. He had the box of tissues ready the next time she needed one.

Cole loved Arlon, in his own way, and he showed it by caring for Arlon's little sister. Piper's heart swelled with pride.

The Barnes joined Josiah's folks in line, and Piper took a seat in the back. She spotted Desire and a few of the church ladies toward the front. Desire took a few moments to reminisce then hugged Morgan. On her way up the aisle, Desire's reflective expression became hard as her brow furrowed.

Piper shrank into the pew when she spotted Ms. Deeds with Justin at her side. Dressed in a crisp black suit with a purple tie, he stood primly next to the elderly woman who bent his ear after each person passed. Even though his head didn't move, his gaze scanned the room. Justin found Cole and his polite, forced smile became a pressed line.

Desire stopped and greeted Ms. Deeds. Justin took Desire's hand and kissed it. She smiled and her cheeks blushed, but her painted brows dipped and her eyes hardened. He hadn't fooled Desire. Ms. Deeds introduced him to other church ladies and Desire slipped away.

Desire caught Piper's gaze and motioned for her to follow. She held her breath, waiting for a larger group of people to exit and ducked behind them. In the fellowship hall, Desire and Piper picked up a cookie and an iced tea and met Kelly and Jessie.

"I can't believe Ms. Deeds brought the stalker. What is up with that?" Kelly asked with hands on her hips and brows dipped in a frown.

"He's desperate," Desire said with a wave of her hand.

The girls burst out laughing. They hushed each other; it was a funeral, after all. Piper had a feeling Arlon wouldn't have minded. In fact, he'd be laughing along with them. He'd liked Desire's sense of humor.

"I could tell you stories," Piper said with an exaggerated dramatic eye roll.

"Actually, I've got one," Desire said with a shrug.

"It doesn't involve twenty dollars, does it?" Jessie asked with a wry grin.

"No. Forty."

Jessie snorted, and the girls giggled again. Kelly pulled them further out of the way and into a corner. "Spill."

"I visited Elberta, you know, Ms. Deeds. She had someone moving things out of her attic. My first glimpse of the shirtless man was walking up the stairs, and he had no butt, just one cheek, but it was a wallet. Elberta explained the boy needed money—he was quite desperate for it. I saw her watching that scrawny body, and I thought anyone would be better than that meatless fool."

The girls laughed again, and Desire smiled. "I wasn't talking about *that,* ladies. Honestly."

"Not yet," Jessie teased.

Desire giggled and waggled a finger. "Jessie dear, your grandmother would be proud of that deductive reasoning." She patted Jessie's hand and gave her a side hug. "So the young man goes up and down the stairs several times, moving things into the garage. He's working up a sweat. When he finished, we inspected the work. It wasn't bad, so Elberta wanted him to drop by the following day for some yard work. The charmer smiled and said he would if he could get another of the 'best chicken salad sandwich' he'd ever had."

"Yep, sounds like Justin," Piper mused. "She fell for it, didn't she?"

"Hook, line, and *stinker,*" Desire glanced around the room then leaned in. "I asked the young man if he wanted to make an easy twenty bucks and, of course, it intrigued him. But he seemed cautious."

"You asked him to drop his pants." Jessie smirked and crossed her arms.

"I'm old, not dead, honey." Desire leaned closer to the three listening women. "He refused. It seemed the family jewels were not worth seeing for twenty. So I upped it to forty and showed him the two twenty-dollar bills.

He wanted the money but still hesitated. So I said to him, 'listen honey, just drop your drawers and let us take a look at your goods for a few minutes. We're old women. We won't bite or grab, we just want a look-see. Besides, Elberta can't see real good. Do you want the money and to give two old ladies the thrill of their golden years?' I swear if that doesn't move them 'I've only got a few more weeks to live' does." She cackled like a witch.

"So did he do it?" Piper asked, searching the room for Justin. She'd have to duck behind Jessie if he showed up, or he'd make a beeline straight to her and they'd never get to hear the end of the story.

"Hold your horses." Desire smiled. "Elberta paled, but she didn't say a word. That woman wanted to see the boy naked in a bad way. Finally, he unsnapped the jeans and opened the fly. He wore tighty-whities. He insisted on the not touching. I guess he was smart enough not to trust me." She shrugged. "He pulled them down a little, and I told him 'take them to the floor or else.' He pushed them all the way down and then stood there like the embarrassed fool he was. Elberta and I took a gander at the bird and eggs in the nest then we glanced at each other. 'Is it dead?' she asked, and I began to wonder myself. I swear, it looked like a deflated balloon. We stepped closer and scrutinized the thing. It gave a little jerk and started to inflate. I guess it liked the attention." She hummed, then laughed.

"He mumbled something about crazy old ladies then fled. Elberta looked as if she was having a heart attack. It would have been a real shame to die over that sausage link. But then she smiled at me like I made her century. So I told her 'happy birthday'."

They laughed.

"It's so strange. Why is Justin staying in Texas?" Jessie mused.

Kelly shrugged. "If he ran out of money, he'd be stuck."

"Maybe his parents refused to help. They'd been suckered too many times." Piper frowned and glanced toward the entrance to the fellowship hall.

The speculative conversation about Justin faded as she focused on Cole entering the room. He swiveled his head, scouring the crowded space. The cobalt blue of his tie would normally highlight his eyes, but the whites were red. He rubbed his palms on his black dress pants. Pale faced, he fidgeted. Her heart ached to bear some of his sorrow, and she took a step toward him.

Cole

Cole froze when he saw Piper. The sweet smile that lit her face was a breath of fresh air in the stifling place. As he glanced around, curious stares followed him. He walked decidedly in her direction.

A serious expression replaced her smile. Her worry over him unnerved him. Her kindness and love could knock the wind out of him. Across the long hall, she hurried toward him, not quite running but not walking either, and when she met him, her arms stretched around his back. He lost himself in the scent of her hair and her soft embrace, and closed his eyes thinking of the other night when they'd stargazed. He ignored the pain in his heart.

Her fingers pulled in a straight line down his back. He sighed and tried to relax. Then he felt it. She tipped her head and saw what he didn't want to do in public.

"Come here," she cooed softly. The first sob bubbled up and caught him by surprise. She pulled his head to the crook of her neck and shoulder and held him. Raw loneliness hit, and he gritted his teeth. The grief he'd tried to sweep away and bury resurfaced. Why did it have to happen in a sea of people?

Another sob rolled up following the first and soon tears wet her neck. She did nothing but rub his back and stuff a hanky in his palm. He discretely wiped his eyes and blew his nose.

He was miserable, but he wasn't the only one. Brad and Curly Moe sat rigid with red-rimmed eyes. They were close to the old man and had worked alongside him for decades.

Arlon had been a kind man, rough around the edges and simple, but like a grandfather or father in many ways.

"I'm going to miss him," Cole said, not recognizing his voice. It sounded as if he'd swallowed sandpaper.

"I know. Me too," Piper said. "Whenever you miss him, you can tell me."

He nodded and buried his nose in her hair again. The sweet fruity smell worked to calm him.

"Morgan asked me to be a pallbearer." He sniffed and put a little distance between them. She squeezed his fingers. "Thanks for being here with me today."

"There's no place I'd rather be."

Brad signaled for him to come over. "I'm going to talk to Brad. Do you want to come with me or are you in the middle of a good Desire story?"

"It was a good story. I've already heard the one where you get a mail-order bride." Piper grinned at him. He placed a kiss on her cheek.

"It has a happy ending."

"Is that so?" She arched a brow. "Care to tell me the end?"

"I will later." He watched as she joined the ladies, then he shuffled to his employer.

"Cole," Curly greeted.

"Hey, I bumped into Warren Teed upstairs and he needs to speak with you. Also, what is up with that Saine character? He's acting like a paid escort to Ms. Deeds. When he's not on her arm, he's butting into everyone's business, especially yours and Piper's. He even asked about Jessie." Brad crossed his arms and leaned back in the chair. "I stood there listening to him and Parker Ford discuss food at the Pink Taco. Saine queried the man about the Double D, the intimate apparel lines, and if he knew the owner. Parker knew I was standing there and looked at me. I nodded and Parker told the truth but not the whole of it, if you follow me. Parker also said the Barnes are protective of those who work for them and their property."

"You think he got the hint?" Curly asked.

"I wouldn't count on it," Cole mumbled.

"I heard he's calling the Double D every day saying he has an order but never orders. What a time waster." Curly Moe rubbed his head. "The girls have been handling him."

"How do you know?" Brad asked.

"Josiah and Arlon," Curly said, then frowned. He stared down at his boots.

The fellowship hall filled and emptied almost like the building breathed mourners. Ms. Deeds and Justin stood at the cookie table. The old woman gushed and smiled eating up the attention like she shoveled down the cookies. Townsfolk murmured behind the backs of the odd couple.

In the corner, Piper elbowed Kelly, and they giggled. Cole narrowed his gaze to study Justin. A wave of relief rolled over Cole as Piper covered her mouth, hiding a laugh.

Justin encroached on Cole's territory. This was his hometown, his church, his friend's funeral, and his girlfriend. Emotionally worn, Cole wouldn't hesitate to finish anything Justin started.

"Cole." His name floated over the din. He twisted around. In uniform, Ben waded through the crowd. They shook hands. "I just stopped by to pay my respects. I can't stay long. You'll never guess who I saw on the way in: your mom."

"Thanks, man." Cole stood ready to search for Piper but found her next to him. "Mom's here."

"Good. May I join you? Someone just noticed me." Piper didn't look back. She took his elbow and pulled him out of the room.

In the entry, his mother wore a simple plum dress. She spotted them and turned on a full-watted smile. He took another step before Piper jerked him to a stop. Her wide eyes and dropped jaw alarmed him. Her gaze swung to him and she murmured, "It's so freaky how much he looks like you."

That doesn't make any sense. Piper started again and tugged Cole forward toward a tall man with a sheepish grin. *No way, not today.* "Hello, Colson."

CHAPTER 30

Piper

"LOVE LOOKS GOOD ON YOU," Florence said as she pulled Piper in for a bear hug. Flo squeezed her hand. "It looks good on him, too. Thank you for taking care of my boy." The soft words whispered near Piper's ear made tears well.

Cole moved in and pulled his mother into his arms, but his glare never left his father. Piper waited for Cole to introduce her, but the introduction never came. The older man remained resolute, holding his hat by the brim in front of him. He nodded at the people who entered. He wore a black suit and polished boots.

"Where's Beau?" Piper asked, glancing around.

"He stayed with Lynette," Florence replied.

Cole shifted his weight and looked as if he sucked marbles. Piper drew a deep breath. "Excuse me," she said, catching Colson's eye. "Would you be so kind as to step outside with me?"

Colson and Flo exchanged a glance and nod, and then he took Piper's arm and they walked toward the door. She glanced over her shoulder at Cole's beet-red face. "Don't worry, Sheila and I got this." His gaze softened as he gave a stiff nod.

Colson led her down the steps to the yard. Piper inspected the older man. What she knew of him wasn't very nice. He'd abandoned his family. Cole hated him to the point of being embarrassed he could play the guitar as well as his father.

Flo still cared for him. When she spoke Colson's name, her tone became wistful.

"Cole's a good man," Colson said. He watched the doorway of the church where Cole waved his arms in a heated conversation with his mother.

Ever the guardian, Cole had followed her outside to keep an eye on her. Piper's heart warmed. "Yes he is, so if you hurt him again I'll shoot you."

Colson laughed softly and slung his arm over her shoulders, pulling her into a side hug and squeezed. "I like you, little missy. I've heard all about you from Flo. She says you're bringing Cole back to life. I appreciate what you've done for my son."

Piper had threatened the man's life, and he hugged then praised her. She closed her mouth and took a step backward. Colson's skin had a healthy glow, the whites of his eyes weren't bloodshot, and his breath hadn't smelled like booze.

His lips twitched up into a grin as her suspicious gaze roamed his face. He would have had dark, almost black, thick hair, but the temples were gray and the top salt and pepper. The laugh lines at the corners of his eyes crinkled as he smiled.

A hunch settled in her gut. "Are you better?"

"If you mean am I sticking around, that I am. It might seem like bad timing, but I'm thinking the time is right." Colson studied his wife with a softened expression. "It's true, I wasn't there for my kids, but I was jacked up. I couldn't be a husband, let alone a dad. I left to get my life together. My father wanted nothing to do with me, and here I was doing the same to my kids. I deserve no better than the way he is treating me."

"He'll come around, Mr. Dart. Like you said, he's a good man." Piper winked at Cole.

Colson turned toward Piper once more. "It's the real deal, then."

"Yes sir." She nodded. *The real deal.*

The bells chimed a melancholy melody alerting everyone to the time. Piper took both of the older man's hands. "Give him space and time. He'll come around." She dropped his hands and met Cole at the door. His stoic gaze rested on his father.

"Are you all right?" Piper asked.

"Fine." His clipped answer spoke volumes.

Piper hooked his elbow, pulling him into the sanctuary. "Don't worry about him, Cole. I told him I'd shoot him if he hurt you again."

193

Away from his parents, he relaxed and his eyes twinkled with mirth. "Did you really? Of course, you did."

Her hands rested firmly on her hips. "I don't joke about shooting people."

Cole

Piper continually shocked him. Cole would have loved to have seen his father's reaction when she'd threatened to murder him.

Cole and Piper sat in the second row, listening to a summarization of Arlon's life. A few friends, including Brad, spoke, and Pastor Peacock recited the twenty-third Psalm.

Cole, along with the guys from the Big Deal, carried Arlon to the hearse then again at the cemetery, they hoisted him to the waiting platform. Morgan sat in a metal chair with her ankles crossed. Arlon would've said "she's just shy of being prettier than me." The bittersweet thought brought a quick smile. He and Piper stood behind Morgan, facing the horseshoe-shaped throng of people.

His mother dabbed her eyes with a tissue. Colson stood by her side with an arm around her waist. While Cole didn't like the man, he was glad his mother wasn't alone.

Arlon's antics peppered Drew Peacock's words of comfort. Laughter and tears filled the gathering. As they dismissed, Cole returned his hat to his head, glad the brim would shadow his swollen eyes. He wanted to grieve in private. Piper's fingers, threaded with his, anchored him.

Returning to the church, the deaconesses had spread food out buffet style. The crowd thinned. Cole and Piper sat, but didn't feel like eating and pushed food around on plates. He watched his mother make goo-goo eyes at his father. Colson had the good sense to blush.

Morgan made the rounds to thank everyone for supporting her and for the relationships forged with her brother. When she reached Cole, he stood and took her small hand. Morgan wouldn't have it. Grabbing him, she pulled him into a hug and started to cry. He didn't know what to do other than hold her.

Piper drove to his property and his mother and Colson followed in a Jeep. His mother stepped out of the car gasping at her first glimpse of their home's ruins. She covered her face and shook her head. Cole held her as she wept at the devastation. When she'd composed herself Piper said, "Come see what we've found." She led his mother toward the barn.

His father walked around staring at the damaged house. He whistled. "Where were you when the tornado hit?" he asked.

"In there." Cole pointed to the storm cellar. He loosened his tie.

"One of the best investments of my life," Colson said. "I'm glad you're all right, son."

Cole bristled at the word. "There's still a lot to do. I can't do a damn thing about the insurance—" he cut himself off and studied Colson Dart. *Was the drunk here for the insurance money?*

"If I can be of any help... I know you think I'm not much good, and I don't blame you, but put me to work. My back is strong and I'm willing." His father nudged a pine cone with the tip of his boot.

"That's great," Cole's tone dripped sarcasm. "I'm going to change. If you want to help, I'm still walking the property looking for Mom's stuff." He walked to the cellar, leaving the man with a surprised but happy face.

The shelter had become home base. The power restored to the cellar and barn made it bearable. A small fan and the fact the room was underground helped to keep it cool. He kept a few things on hangers but lived mostly from the baskets Piper brought him. One held clean clothes, the other dirty. He shucked off his dress duds and pulled on worn jeans and a T-shirt. He exchanged his good boots for work boots and laced them. Piper knocked and hurried down the steps. Her owl-like eyes stared at him like he was crazy.

"Your dad is going to help?" she asked.

"He offered." Cole shrugged. "There's a lot of acreage left to cover. He knows it and could help."

She nodded and turned. "Unzip me."

"Pipes, not now." He moved in and kissed her neck. As he unzipped the dress, he kissed down her spine feeling her shiver.

"Cole," she purred. She stepped out of the dress and held it up.

He hung it on a wall hook. The lacy white bra and undies made him swallow hard. "God, Piper look what you do to me." He pointed to his erection.

"It's the lace," she giggled.

He stepped up to her, trailing a finger down her cheek. He tipped her face and his lips softly brushed hers. "No, Pipes, you do this. Not some skimpy clothes. You." His hands slipped behind and under the lace, then he roughly pulled her against him. He moaned before kissing her hard. Her arms ringed his neck.

Taking a breath, she accused, "You like the skimpy clothes."

"True." Cole kissed her again. His hands slid to the front of her panties and she slapped them away.

"Your parents could walk in on us," she said, glancing toward the door.

"So? I need you," he replied before kissing her neck.

"Cole," she whispered. The temptation lingered in her touch. "Why does your kiss taste like pure sex?"

He growled and pushed her panties down. They fell to the floor. He reached for the hidden box of condoms, then staked her to the wall. It was hard and fast but they moved in unison and with need. Minutes later, both sweaty and sated, for the moment, they emerged.

His mother and Colson wore smiles, and both had changed into work clothes. Did his parents suspect he and Piper's love session or maybe they had their own rendezvous? They either changed in the barn or his dad's Jeep. He lifted an eyebrow and Piper shrugged.

"The front has been canvased pretty well. It's the back property past the hill that needs searching." Cole pointed past the barn to a ridge of broken trees.

"That's a lot of property left to scour." Colson said. "Do you want me to follow the creek bed?"

"Uh, sure. If you find anything you can start a pile. Clothes, trash, toys. Oh and be sure to look up. I've found crazy shit in trees." Cole handed trash bags to each person. He gave his father a pair of leather work gloves and slid on a pair of his own.

They separated but could see each other for a while. Cole's gaze swung side to side covering the ground, trees and people. A swatch of his mother's floral sheets was stuck in a low-lying bush. His father disappeared from view as the land dipped toward the creek. It wasn't much of one, barely a trickle from a spring.

Cole picked up yellow bits of insulation with his gloved hands. He stopped and dug in the dirt with the toe of his boot, revealing a small velvet-coated box, then picked it up and pocketed it. He shifted pieces of siding to look for treasure but found nothing except debris. Higher than he could climb, one of Beau's shirts hung from a jagged tree branch. Around two split tree trunks Cole found a photo frame intact and the remains of the living room bookcase. His mother would be happy about the frame. It held a picture of his maternal grandparents with Cole's parents, and him and Lynette. The smiling family looked ordinary. He vaguely remembered his grandparents. They died when he was young. He looked closer at the man who claimed to be his father. Piper was right. He couldn't deny his parentage. He resembled the younger version of Colson.

Cole hung his head. He didn't want to be his father. He kicked the bookcase and released a string of expletives. Colson was a complication Cole didn't want in his life.

Nothing green remained in his part of the woods, only monochromatic brown: dirt, bark and the tan meat of the decapitated tree trunks. Like a depressing scene from a dystopian novel, the sharp angles of the naked branches spiked heavenward.

He pushed the remains of the bookcase over and stepped back, startled to find a small patch of protected bluebonnets. He sunk to his knees and absorbed the flawless beauty.

"Cole!" By the inflection of excitement, Piper had found her own bluebonnets. She came running through the woods, clutching a priceless artifact to her chest and panting. "I found it." She grinned like a kid at Christmas in a toy store.

She unfolded her arms and there sat a treasured paperback novel. Not just any novel, the first in a series, signed by the author and a gift from her father, a Loren Order book. She'd let Cole borrow it. She hugged the book again. "My dad bought it for me." Cole matched her gleeful smile. "The author, I met him, you know, the week before I moved. I went to the book signing with my pile of Loren books. We talked guns. He seemed intrigued by my Sheila."

"I'll bet. Nothing sexier than a woman who likes guns."

"Shut up." Piper shoved his shoulder.

CHAPTER 31

Piper

AFTER VISITING THE WERTZ GROCERY store and buying a few of Cole's favorite things, Piper opened the trunk and began to unload the cart.

"Hello, Piper." A man's voice made her jump.

She turned toward him. "Justin." Even his face couldn't spoil her mood. She smiled and continued unloading the cart. "It's such a beautiful day, don't you think?"

"I guess so," he said, watching her with narrowed eyes.

"Don't you love Texas?"

"Not really." Justin crossed his arms.

"I love the wide open sky and the crazy amount of stars."

"That sounds romantic," Justin said.

"It's God's doing. He's a great artist."

From across the street, Cole hailed her. "Pipes." She rounded the car, leaving Justin by the trunk. Carrying a plastic bag from the drugstore, Cole hurried to her side. He caressed her cheek. "You all right?" He glanced toward Justin then back into her eyes.

"Yeah. Justin hasn't bothered me. He's just an annoying fly hovering around," she said softly.

"Would you like me to swat him?"

She giggled but shook her head. "Hopefully he'll get the idea and buzz off."

She studied the white bag. It resembled the one they'd picked up the night she seduced him. Against the side of the car, Cole pinned her.

198

Sandwiched between the warm metal of the vehicle and Cole's piping hot body, her temperature rose. Plumber's putty in his hands, she threw her arms around his neck. His tongue coaxed her lips open and ravaged it.

Justin cleared his throat and tapped his foot, but they continued kissing. "I love you," Cole whispered.

"What do you have there?" she asked, shaking his bag.

"Dessert."

"Hmm."

"But only if you're good."

She raised a brow and ran a finger down his chest to his belt buckle. "And what if I don't want to be good?"

"Ah, hell. I'll think of something." He grinned and rested his forehead against hers.

She pushed him back a step. "I have some things for you." She stepped around Justin. "Look here." Opening a grocery sack, she pulled out cold cuts and a few other items. She located a bag of toiletries and handed it to him. He peered in then smiled.

"Wow, you know me well." Cole said kissing her cheek. She blushed, and he hugged her.

A squad car slowed to a stop behind her car. Ben rolled down the window. He surveyed the ex and the lovers with hands on each other's bodies. A smirk appeared as he refocused on Cole. "Hey, man, no P.D.A."

Cole turned bright red and slid behind Piper, keeping his hands on her waist.

"It's a free country," Piper chided. "You're just jealous, Ben."

"That is so true, pretty lady," Ben said. He tipped his hat and winked. "Carry on."

"It's so weird how the whole town is freaked out by your friendly demeanor." Piper poked Cole in the chest. She returned to the task of loading her car but Justin had emptied the cart. He stood straight with his nose in the air, arms crossed and a superior sneer. "Uh, thanks for loading my trunk."

"Why, what's wrong with Cole?" Justin asked, his slatted eyes raking Cole.

"He's shy," Piper explained.

"Could have fooled me," Justin said.

"I know, right?" Piper laughed and hugged her boyfriend tight, glad he wasn't shy around her.

Cole had morphed into a statue with a pensive face. Reminding her cowboy of his past made him reflective. Piper turned him around to face her and grabbed his chin so his eyes had nowhere to stare but hers. "Listen to me Cole Dart, you will spend the afternoon thinking about dessert. I'm starving and all I want is dessert. When I see you later, I might eat dessert before dinner." She sucked in his bottom lip and bit it gently. Acting like a love-sick teenager—a horny—love-sick teenager, she was tempted to push him into the backseat of her car. He pulled her tight against him, and he rewarded her with a toe-curling kiss.

Cole

Cole headed straight toward the Big Deal office. Brad had an interview with a couple of men to pick up the slack with Arlon gone. The ranch owner needed more help—especially with a rogue squatter roaming the property.

Sawyer Hickey took Brad's hand and smiled. "Mr. Davidson—"

"Forget it, Brad, You can't hire this clown," Cole said from the doorway. He smiled and took Sawyer's hand. "On second thought, Lucy's stall needs attention."

"I'll do whatever y'all need." Sawyer's desperate declaration startled Cole.

Before the warehouse had closed, Sawyer worked for the Cummings shipping company. The creepy, abandoned building would make a great haunted house. Afterward, he'd worked for a landscaping company, but rumors indicated Sawyer and the owner fought.

Brad stood and circled the small office. Stroking his mustache, he paused in front of a wall of pictures from rodeos past. Some held the framed youthful face of his daughter, various longhorns, or ranch hand's performances. He stared at one picture of a man and frowned. "All right son, we'll give you a try. Do you need a place to stay or will you be living in town?"

"I'd like to stay here." Sawyer took his hat and stood. "Thank you, Mr. Davidson."

"It's Brad." He extended his hand. "Welcome to the Big Deal. Cole, take Sawyer to the bunkhouse and assign him a bed."

Cole swallowed. Arlon used to have that job. Cole hated stepping into those shoes, but someone had to do it. "Come on, Hickey." He led the recruit to the building. Cole pointed out Gimme's messy bed and Curly Moe's.

Sawyer picked the empty bed farthest away from Gimme. He sat down on the bed with his hands in his lap. His focus seemed bleary. He murmured something.

"What did you say?" Cole asked worry nagged at his gut.

Sawyer glanced at him. "I've lost her, Cole. This time, it's for good. I don't know what I'll do now. I'm hoping a fresh start will get her out of my head."

According to Piper, Cole knew Sawyer had commitment issues. It had been only a matter of time before Kelly dumped him.

Cole patted Sawyer's shoulder. "I'm sorry, man. Make yourself at home." He left Sawyer brooding and returned to Brad's office.

Another young man sat in the oak ladder-back chair, squirming at the questions being asked of him. "Cole, I'd like you to meet Chappy Pitts," Brad said.

Chappy jumped up, knocking over the chair. Bending to pick the chair up, he bumped his hindquarters on the desk, making a picture frame fall. "I'm sorry," he mumbled then repeated it.

When he finally stopped bumbling around and straightened, he was a good two inches taller than Cole. His mother would call Chappy "a tall drink of water." His hay colored hair stuck in all directions like a scarecrow. By his faded jeans and broke in boots, he appeared used to work.

Cole took the young man's hand. "Welcome to the Big Deal."

The slack jawed stare morphed into a grin. Turning to Brad, he asked, "Am I hired?"

"Cole's a good judge of character." Brad returned to reading his computer screen. With a wave of his hand, he said, "Show the boy around."

Cole led Chappy through the main barn, bunkhouse, and then to the outer building.

"I'm glad you showed up. New recruit?" Curly Moe smiled as he leaned against the wall with a cell phone at his ear. He ended the call then shook the shy boy's hand. Chappy stuttered out a greeting. "Slim needs a hammer for the water pump. Take Chappy with you and deliver that bag by the door."

Sawyer peered out from the tack room.

"I've got Sawyer organizing the tack and taking inventory." Curly pointed to a clipboard with a list and Sawyer added the item.

Cole and Chappy saddled horses and led them out of the barn. The spirited animals wanted to run. Cole tested the newbie's ability in the saddle. He relaxed and let Duke set the pace. Sundance and Pitts had no issue keeping up, and after a half hour of riding, the men neared the herd. The longhorns shifted uneasily. Cole waved to Slim then skirted the cattle. From a distance, Cole spied the windmill not spinning. Slim met them at the base of the windmill.

"Special delivery, with love from Curly." Cole threw the bag at the dusty sweaty man.

"I need a bubble bath," Slim said, wiping his brow with his denim shirtsleeve.

"Not with me." Cole grimaced then laughed.

"I don't blame you. I'm almost as pretty as your girl but not quite. So who's the greenhorn?" Slim dabbed his upper lip with a bandanna.

"This is Chappy Pitts," Cole said and Chappy nodded.

"Quit yanking my chain. What's his real name?" Slim asked.

"Chappy Pitts," Cole repeated.

"Get out. And I suppose his daddy is Harry Pitts?"

"No," Chappy said with a crinkled brow, "That's my brother."

Slim laughed, bending in half. "You're killing me." He snorted and laughed harder.

Cole shook his head, walking over to the pump. He climbed the ladder and inspected inside. The chain appeared rusted. "Throw me the spray lube," Cole hollered.

Gimme materialized below him. "That's not something you say to a guy, Cole."

"Help or shut up," Cole growled. He wiped his boots on the rung, sending grit onto Gimme's head. He bolted out from below.

"Fine." Gimme reached for the bag, but Chappy already had the container in hand. He tossed it to Cole.

"Nice shot, kid," Cole said.

Chappy blushed and relinquished the satchel to Slim. He rummaged in it and pulled out beef jerky. "God, I love Curly." He bit off a large chunk and closed his eyes savoring the flavor.

"Looks like we might need the lube after all," Gimme said, nodding his head. He winked at Chappy, who tried to tame a smirk.

CHAPTER 32

Cole

"YOU HAVE GOT TO BE kidding me," Cole growled as he pounded his fist on the steering wheel. He clenched his eyes shut listening to the beep-beep-beep of the semi-trailer backing into place. Stuck until it finished moving, he climbed out of his truck. "This sucks," he said, slamming the door.

The week had been going great until today—the one day he needed to leave work on time for an important appointment. His mother had asked Cole to be present when the insurance inspector came out to the property. He crossed his arms and leaned against the side of the truck, watching Brad and the semi driver talk.

Cole fumed; he'd had an extremely crappy day. First, Gimme couldn't work because he'd been sick. Even though Cole had appreciated the quiet due to Gimme's lack of yammering, no one cared for the extra work. While checking on Gimme in the bunkhouse, Cole barely missed being barfed on. Chappy had witnessed the projectile vomiting and started to dry heave. Chappy ran off, leaving Cole to clean up the sick. He'd mopped, then mopped again when Gimme missed the sauce pan. Cole laundered the bed coverings, all the while hoping he wouldn't catch the stomach bug and trying to ignore the sound of Gimme retching.

Cole paced the barn waiting for Brad and the driver to work out details. The semi was there to pick up sold cattle. The low rumble of the semi engine alerted Cole. Brad signaled for the truck to line up with the cattle chute. The semi moved, leaving Cole enough room to pass.

He just wanted to go home and play his guitar and relax with a cold beer. That wouldn't happen until after dealing with the insurance mess. He gritted his teeth, blasting the air in an attempt to cool-off before facing anyone.

Rolling his shoulders, he reached to hit the button for his favorite radio station but all he heard was static. He'd forgotten to change the presets in his new used pickup. He liked the extended cab because Beau's booster seat fit. It was more powerful compared to his old ride. The truck's color was nice too. The shade of blue had been an upgrade from rust.

He fishtailed out onto the paved, road exceeding the speed limit. As he passed the Double D Ranch, he tried not to think of Piper. They had argued; she'd mentioned the newspaper, but he hadn't cared about the latest local gossip. When he snapped at her, she'd given it back until she'd had enough. She'd hung up on him, which infuriated him. Cole couldn't decide who he was upset with more—himself or Piper. He'd apologize after the appointment when his blood pressure wasn't skyrocketing.

Cole's phone rang. He answered through his truck's Bluetooth.

"You're a real piece of work, you know that, right?" Josiah Barnes drawled in a low steady tone.

Cole clenched the steering wheel. "This isn't a good time, Josiah."

"I know you've been through hell but—"

"If this is about Piper, I'm fixin' to make things right."

Josiah remained quiet long enough for Cole to wonder if he'd hung up on him too. Finally, Josiah cleared his throat. "It's that Saine asshole..."

"What now?"

"Justin followed through with his threat and posted a negative review."

"Bastard." He closed his eyes and groaned. A gold Cadillac honked and Cole slammed on his brakes when a car ran a red light.

"I'm sick of this crap. He's messing with *my* wife and her business." Josiah's rapid breathing and tight words did nothing to calm Cole's blood pressure. "I'm calling an attorney. I wanted you to know."

"Thanks." Cole stomped on the accelerator. He hated Justin. But he and Piper wouldn't have developed a relationship if her ex had stayed in Chicago.

Cole flew up the driveway, stopping behind his mother's car. A man stood next to her holding a clipboard. They faced the house ruins. His mother wrung her hands and pursed her lips as if she held her tongue. His mother only wrung her hands when she was afraid or nervous.

"What kind of man upsets a woman who's lost her house and all her belongings?" He slammed the truck's door. Anger hanging over him like a cloud, he strode over to them. The man checked something on a list.

"This does constitute an act of God," Flo said an octave higher.

"Maybe," the man said, his mustache covered lip hardly moving. He clicked and unclicked his pen.

"Well, the tornado wasn't man-made." Her hands found her ample hips.

"Were you present when it happened?" he asked, glancing up.

"A tornado is a tornado whether or not it hit while I was here." Flo's eyes narrowed, and if Cole wasn't already in a bad mood, he'd have sat back and watched his mother duke it out.

"Actually, a tornado didn't destroy the house, can't you tell?" Cole stared at the dwellings remains. "A giant, rabid armadillo stomped on it."

The man's eyebrow dipped together looking like bird wings. "Ha. Not funny."

"You're right. Being homeless and having everything you own annihilated isn't funny at all. Neither is being intimidated by the people in our employ." He leaned over to his mother and gave her a hug. She sighed with relief. "Our home owner's insurance covered tornadoes. Damage to the home." He sighed. "Damage to other structures, loss and damage to the contents and, of course, loss of use in case the home is uninhabitable. Looks uninhabitable to me."

The man clicked and unclicked his pen again. "Are you the property owner?"

"I am, or I was, an inhabitant." Cole stood as tall as he could and stared down at the man. He struck an imposing figure which reminded himself of Colson, and it pissed him off more.

"I need to speak with the property owner." He ordered.

"No, you don't need to speak with the owner. He signed all the proper papers. According to the office, everything is in order." Cole took a step closer to the man. His face heated as anger took over. He flicked a glance to his mother then a small trailer. She nodded and headed toward his father. She knocked and when the door opened, she had a hasty conversation. Soon Colson's long-legged stride brought him to Cole's side. Inwardly, he groaned. He did not want to rely on his father.

"Can I see proof you're with the insurance company?" Colson stuck out his hand expectantly.

The man's mustache twitched as he fished in his shirt pocket for a business card.

"Mr. Jack Haas. Hmm." Colson read. "My name is on the deed and the policy, but you will deal with my son and I better not be disappointed or I will report you to your superiors. Do you understand, Mr. Haas?" Colson's piercing blue eyes bore into the man. Jack Haas nodded.

His father remained next to Cole while Jack Haas inspected the barn. The longer the insurance guy hung around, the angrier Cole became. He tried drawing peace from the endless, blue sky then a whiff of his dad's aftershave hit him.

His dad? When did he start thinking of him as a dad? Colson wouldn't be staying, he hoped. Or did he want him to stay? Dammit.

"You were lucky your barn survived the storm, Mr. Dart." Jack Haas aimed his comments and questions toward Colson.

Cole left the men and marched straight to the mini fridge. Pulling out an amber bottle, he twisted off the cap and sucked down half the bottle before he heard a soft sniffling. His mother sat on a cot, trying to hide she'd been crying.

"What's going on, Mom?"

"It's your sister." She dabbed her eyes and took a deep breath.

"Can I do anything?" He sat next to her and took her hand.

She signed and clamped her hands together on her lap. "I told Lynette about your father."

"Oh." Cole gritted his teeth. "I bet that was a shocker."

"She was angry. But Cole, that's not what I'm upset about." She took a shuddering breath. "It's Beau."

"What's going on?" He said briskly, startling her.

She blew her nose. "I'm worried. Lynette dropped Beau off with a friend so she could go to work. Beau needed to get stitches. He's afraid to go over to their place and won't talk about what happened. I'm afraid they have abused him. She took him back, and he stayed in the corner crying all day. Beau wanted me to come get him. He wants to come home. Lynette says I've spoiled and ruined him."

Cole jumped up, clenching his hands as he paced. He couldn't see straight, wanting to beat or kick something. "I'll go get him." He stuck his hand in his pocket and pulled out his key fob.

"No, you're not in any shape to drive." She leaned her head against the concrete wall and closed her eyes. "Calm down, Cole."

"I can't." He needed out of the stifling cellar. "I'm going for a walk." He took the entry stairs two at a time and disappeared into the woods.

Piper

"I'm sorry I've been neglecting you," Piper said. She picked up a fry and tossed it into her mouth.

"I understand. New boyfriend trumps hanging out with single friends." Kelly picked up her burger but turned and glanced over her shoulder when Sawyer Hickey laughed. She took a big bite and chewed like she ate sawdust.

"I wouldn't have eaten at Hammered if I would have known *he'd* be here." Piper cringed with Kelly when Mona Little's cackling laugh followed another of Sawyer's.

Kelly shrugged. "It's a small town, and I love Hammered. He won't chase me away."

"Good." Piper nodded and took a sip of tea. She stared down, wishing Cole was there to finish her food.

"Piper." Kelly waved a hand in front of her face. "Earth to Piper. What's going on?"

"Huh?"

Kelly pointed at her with a french fry and said, "You've been moping all evening. It's more than missing Cole, because every time I say his name your forehead crinkles as if you have bubble gut."

"I, uh..."

"Spill."

Piper sighed. "Cole and I argued, and I hung up on him."

Kelly blinked wide eyes. "Really? That sucks."

"Yeah. I let my anger get the best of me, but he was being so pigheaded. It pissed me off." She swirled the liquid in the red plastic cup. "I need to talk to him."

The loud clack of pool balls breaking made the women jump. Sawyer leaned over the table with the cue in hand. Mona responded with a slap to Sawyer's bum. He winked at Mona. Kelly retreated, focusing on her food. Piper noticed the bags under Sawyer's eyes. He acted normal but his eyes seemed dead.

"I thought she was my friend," Kelly said with a frown.

"Wasn't she dating Ben?" Piper asked.

"They'd gone on a few dates, but she didn't like him like that," Kelly said.

"Why not?" Piper asked.

"I know, right?" Kelly smirked. "Ben is totally cute, especially when he's in uniform." She hummed and glanced around the restaurant. She gasped. "Don't look."

Piper suddenly went cold. Her tongue stuck to the roof of her mouth.

"Justin just walked to the bar and took a seat." Kelly frowned as she assessed the situation. "He looked around but didn't see us. I can't believe he'd show his face in here."

"You drove," Piper sputtered, "he doesn't know I'm here."

Kelly's eyes widened, and she motioned for Piper to slide back further into the dim booth.

They paid Sharon and waited for the perfect time to exit. A man named B.J. Johnson scanned the spines of books on Hammered's shelf. He pulled one out, read the back cover then slid it back in. He plucked another then returned it. Another man joined him at the shelf. The older man pulled out a book and offered it to B.J. He took it with interest.

It never ceased to amaze Piper how the men of Fortuna liked romance novels. The *Fortuna Forum* reported a man locked out of his house in nothing but a red thong, devil horns, and tail. He'd been reenacting a story he and his wife read together. Like the hero, he planned to enter through the window but got caught when the cops shined the spotlight on his butt floss. The cops didn't arrest him, but the town found out when they reported his address. The wife appeared proud when everyone told her she was lucky to have a man act out her sinful pleasures.

"We're stuck here between the exes." Kelly crossed her arms.

Piper spied Sawyer smile at another woman. "One who won't commit—"

"And one who's over committed," Kelly said, perking up. "Quick. Justin's gone to the restroom. Now is our chance to get out of here."

Piper pulled a book from the shelf, opened the cover and didn't see Cole's initials. She took the book and hurried out of the restaurant. Once in the car Piper asked, "Can we swing by Cole's? I need to apologize."

Kelly reluctantly turned the wheel and zipped up the street. She pulled into the driveway and parked behind a big navy truck.

"Cole, Flo, and Colson's cars are here," Piper said.

Kelly pointed toward the house. "There he is. Looks like he's mad."

"I hope he still isn't angry at me." Piper swallowed, climbed out of the car and quietly approached. His free hand waved about wildly. Stiff and agitated, he paced in front of the house.

He used the deep tone that meant business and she hesitated, not wanting to interrupt. His pitch rose. "I don't know what to do. She's needy.

She thinks she can handle anything, but she can't handle squat. And she has the worst taste in men. When is she going to learn? I'm so tired of her shit." He stopped ranting to listen to the phone. He turned, heading away from her. Her heart stuck in her throat and it felt as if her feet had petrified.

Cole continued, "I tried to talk to her today and guess what? No. She hung up on me. That's right. Crazy bitch. Can you believe it? After all I've done for her. I can't believe she'd treat me like that."

Piper leaned against the truck, her heart racing. *Cole is beyond upset.* Tears pricked her eyes, but she forced them away. She hadn't thought she'd picked Mr. Wrong once more. She couldn't breathe. The book she was holding fell to the ground. *Lover's Quarrel* had looked like a romance Cole would like. She reached for it then set it on the hood of his truck. She wanted to flee, but he started ranting again.

"When I see her I'll give her a piece of my mind. I'm so done with it. She's so selfish—ugh. I want to hit something." He took a big breath. "I know. I've got enough crap in my life right now, the house situation, work, and Colson, I don't need any more crap." He growled the last part.

He stopped mid-stride, spying the idling car. His gaze shifted to Piper. His wide eyes and fishlike mouth almost made her laugh.

That's right, caught you. She stepped backward.

"Piper," he called.

She shook her head, stumbling another step away. The tears started, and she furiously swiped them. Lowering the phone from his ear, he shuffled forward.

Scanning Cole's masked face, Piper hugged herself. Her stomach churned as she realized their relationship was over. She pivoted and ran to the safety of Kelly's car.

"Drive." Piper slapped the dash. "Go now! Please, Kelly."

Kelly put the car in reverse and punched it. After they'd turned around, Piper glanced in the side-view mirror. Cole strode down the drive, his face twisted in anger. His lips moved like an auctioneer, and his hand flung wildly about.

Piper covered her face and sobbed.

Patting her arm, Kelly said, "Looks like you're staying with me tonight, and we're going to watch a funny non-romantic movie, drink wine and eat chocolate."

CHAPTER 33

Piper

PIPER GROANED WHEN THE DOUBLE D's phone rang again. Her stomach churned. Both Justin and Cole had called earlier. Luckily, Jessie took over the calls and put both men in their place. *God love Jessie.*

Jessie pushed her out the door to get lunch. "You need a break from here. Go get some good food and forget work for a while. Take your time. Don't hurry back."

On the drive through town, she happened upon the prankster's latest sign-switching gag. Piper didn't approve of messing with another person's property but she had needed a good laugh. Clint Torres, owner and latest victim, stood in front of the sign scratching his chin. It advertised "Jalapeño Poopers". Cars drove by and honked. The sign gained notoriety.

Piper parked and joined him on the sidewalk. "Leave it," she suggested.

Clint's dark eyes sparkled with mischief. "That's exactly what I was trying to decide. Thank you, Mrs. Dart." He grinned and nodded.

Mrs. Dart. Piper sucked in a deep breath and turned away, refusing to let her rocky emotions control her. In the restaurant, she waved to Morgan Topp. Morgan's smile was brittle and her eyes red-rimmed. *Misery loves company, right?* They hugged and Morgan asked Piper to join her. They sat in silence for a moment, scanning the menu. After ordering, they conversed about benign things like the weather and prankster shenanigans.

Toward the end of the meal, Morgan asked, "Is that man still bothering you?"

"Justin calls the Double D every day."

"I can't believe the Fortuna rag published that story about Jessie's business. It's a travesty. I wrote a letter of complaint." Morgan's brows bunched together and the wad of paper that used to be her napkin landed squarely on the table.

Piper's lip quivered, and she stared down at her plate. *Don't blink or the tears will fall.*

"Oh, honey, everybody knows it was that jerk. The hoity-toity boutiques in Austin and Dallas won't ever hear about it either." She reached out her hand and Piper grabbed it.

The horrible day the *Fortuna Forum* ran the front-page article, the newspaper accused "Jessie Davidson of Double D Intimates" of refusing to hire local. It down played any local involvement, including the several modeling gigs, and hometown rented venues. Ironically, the whole community recognized Double D Intimates as a fledgling company and understood Jessie did most of the work herself.

According to the reporter Nellie Neus, Piper, the out-of-town interloper, perpetrated lies to gain the trust of the community. She used "Her so-called mail-order bride farce" to get "cozy with the locals."

The reporter also quoted Justin, making him sound like a saint. "I love her, but after her father passed, she changed. I hoped to convince her to come home where she belongs." The reporter took Justin's innuendos and ran with them, making her sound half-crazy, delusional and ungrateful for a man like him.

If the article wasn't enough to make her stomach sour when she called Cole for solace, he'd yelled at her. It had stretched Piper's emotions thin; she couldn't bear being yelled at so she abruptly ended the call mid-sentence. Then later in the day when she'd overheard Cole, he'd wounded her like a knife to the heart.

Piper hadn't slept well since. She hadn't been brave enough to speak with Cole. Refusing to answer when he called, she sent him straight to his voice mail. Now Cole called the business line like Justin.

"Did you see today's paper?" Morgan asked. She reached into her large leather satchel and pulled out the newspaper. She handed it to Piper. "Look at the front-page."

"Holy moly!" Piper spread open the newspaper and started reading.

Ticked off in regards to the attack on Jessie's business, Desire Hardmann wrote a scathing letter. One small business owner coming to another's aid. She threatened to end her fifty-plus-year subscription and tell everyone else to do so also if an apology wasn't forthcoming.

"She skirted the reporter and went straight to the editor, who's a friend." Morgan said with a smile. "I love how she says that any reporter that is 'worth a lick of salt' would have asked the Double D employees and owners a question or two."

Desire blasted the paper for not asking the police if there had been any reports filed against harassment. All in all, it was a strong letter focused on the inadequacies of the reporter Nellie Neus and Justin, supposedly, trying to inform the community, who, ironically, came from out of state. Desire listed the numerous ways the Double D ranch and Double D Intimates impacted the community, from hiring a local web designer, buying all the fabric from stores within the county and hiring local people to help make the items.

"I love this part," Piper said, pointing to the paper. "Jessie Barnes is an artist inspired by her Grandmother Undine Love Davidson. Jessie, please do not share anymore of Undine's books with Fortuna until it gets its act together."

"That will ruffle people's feathers." Morgan grinned.

Piper glanced up with a smile. "Withholding the romance books might cause rioting."

Cole

"We love the Double D" embellished the A Hole in One's sign. Cole jerked his head, looking back. *Yes, that's what it said.* Other signs, the elementary school, library and fire station all had sayings of support for the ranch.

"What the heck?" Cole called Brad at the Big Deal because Piper wouldn't take his call. "Do you know why there are signs all over town about the Double D?" he asked Jessie's father.

"That S.O.B. boyfriend of Piper's had a bad interview with the paper."

"*Ex*," Cole corrected. "I'm her boyfriend."

"Right. Anyway, the interview was about a week ago. Desire Hardmann and a dozen other small business owners retaliated, calling for the town to support the ranch. I can't believe you haven't heard about it. I'm surprised Piper hasn't told you." Brad informed him of the claims and threats. A burning sensation formed in Cole's gut and continued to grow as Brad talked. "I have the newspaper in my office. You can read it."

A wave of guilt hit Cole. Piper had mentioned the newspaper and must have called him to talk about the article. He clenched a fist and blew out a breath. He wanted to apologize to Piper, but he hadn't been able to speak with her yet. At first, he'd been stubborn and refused to contact her. But after three days, longing threatened to consume him. He missed her. He ached to hear her voice, see her smile and know she was safe. His heart had a Piper shaped hole.

Matt Barnes let slip that Piper hung out at Kelly's watching action flicks most evenings. Cole caved, driving to Kelly's. He tentatively approached the door and knocked. Without unlatching the chain lock, Kelly opened the door a crack, exposing one eye. He took off his hat.

"What do you want, Cole?" she asked.

"To speak with Piper," he replied. He tried to implore her with puppy dog eyes.

The green eye stared, pondering him for a moment. "She doesn't want to talk to you. She wants nothing to do with you anymore."

"I don't understand." His voice cracked. The eyebrow shot up and her jaw dropped. "I love her, Kelly. Please." He needed Piper, dammit.

"Cole, now is—" Kelly started to answer, but the door slammed shut.

He pounded the door again. "Pipes, please. Hear me out."

"Go away, Cole. She's got Sheila, and she's not happy." Kelly's muffled voice warned.

Cole quit knocking, but sat elbows on knees and chin in hands, haunting the step outside the door. He'd wondered if she ever looked out the window. That'd been three days ago and nothing had changed.

He drove past the town square and the bronze statue of Buster Hymen. Buster wore a T-shirt with the outline of a bra reading "support your Double Ds." After he laughed, Cole sobered. Even the town prankster encouraged Fortuna to rally to Jessie's aid.

Cole parked and entered the law offices of Teed & Teed. He'd never heard a will read before except on TV. He shifted his weight as Laurel Ann Hardy, the receptionist, secretary and gift buyer for the families of Warren and Garren, welcomed him with a smile. She motioned for him to sit. He took a seat next to Morgan Topp on a small navy sofa. Desire Hardmann sat in a small burgundy arm chair. She winked at him and blew him a kiss. The old woman shouldn't make him blush, but she could without fail.

"Laurel Ann," Desire said, "how's that man of yours?"

"He's good." Laurel Ann pulled a thick folder together and then glanced up. She straightened the buttons on her mock turtle blouse.

"Is his back better?" Desire folded her hands on her lap.

"Mostly, but he still goes to the chiropractor." Laurel Ann's smile exposed all her teeth, her cheeks a deep shade of mauve.

"It's hell getting old, isn't it? Especially when you still want to play." Desire flashed a tigress grin.

Laurel Ann tilted her head to the side and nodded. "He keeps reading those novels. The next one he gets in his mind to act out might kill him."

"What a way to go, though." Both Desire and Laurel Ann giggled like eight-year-old boys discussing farts.

Cole and Morgan shared a look with raised eyebrows. Laurel Ann, like Desire, was well past her prime. Cole tried to ignore the conversation. He hadn't wanted to be privy to details of the old ladies' sex lives, but the fact they still had one impressed him.

"What was he trying to do this time, dear?" Desire asked. She leaned forward and steepled her fingers together like a shrink.

"Well, the police officer uniform had worked so well, he thought he'd try being a fireman. The uniform was hot," she giggled, "but the rescue attempt was not and I had to call the ambulance. Woo, those young men were gorgeous. Don't tell Hank I said so."

The lawyer, Warren Teed, fortuitously appeared and glanced around the room with a serious face. "Come on back." He held the door open and shook all their hands, then they sat in his small office. Desire and Morgan's skirts and blouses and Warren's suit made Cole feel out-of-place in jeans.

"Arlon left a little something for the three of you, that's why you're here." Warren opened the folder and read a lot of mumbo jumbo that didn't mean a hill of beans to Cole. A list of Arlon's belongings sandwiched between legal jargon. Cole wiped his palms on his jeans, wanting Warren to just hand him whatever knickknack Arlon had left him so he could return to work. Looking forward to reading about the slander of his girlfriend's job was a stretch but if it got him away from the stuffy office, he'd be grateful even to go do that.

"Desire." Warren leaned over and picked up a brown cardboard box the size of a toaster. "These are for you."

She took the box and opened the flap. She put a handkerchief to her eyes and sniffled. "God love him." A small wistful smile adorned her face. "He knew me so well. If only I were younger..." She sighed and sniffled again. Morgan reached a hand over and touched Desire's arm. The women gazed into each other's watery eyes.

Curiosity tugged at Cole, but he remained patient waiting for his own box.

"Cole, do you want to see my hooters?" Desire asked. She dabbed her eyes then stuck a hand in the box.

His mouth fell open, and he checked Warren to see if he'd heard the same. The lawyer's face remained solemn, but his eyes twinkled then one winked. Suddenly, a story Piper told Cole popped in his head. One about Arlon, Desire and owls. "Sure, Ms. Hardmann."

In one small hand sat a blue carnival glass owl about three inches tall. She put it back then pulled out a hand-painted ceramic owl. One by one, she carefully extricated and exhibited her new treasures. Fresh tears contradicted the smile on her lips. She hugged the box to her small body as she left.

Morgan and Cole waited for Warren to glance up from the paper he read. "Cole, this is for you. Open it and read it." He handed a duplicate yellow envelope to Morgan with the same order.

Cole took the large envelope. Opening the flap, he slid out the paper and read the title. His brow crinkled. "I don't think this is mine. It's a DNA test."

"It's right. I've got one, too." Morgan held up a paper.

"Why?" he scanned the words. "What the hell?" This couldn't be right, *could it?*

"Arlon took your DNA from something, a beer bottle, I think he said, and sent it off along with a few others. He was bound and determined to find all his kin. Looks like he hit the jackpot." Warren stroked his goatee.

"But I'm not a bastard. I know my folks. And I know my mother. Her heart has always been with Colson." Cole struggled to understand. He and Arlon were not brothers.

"My daddy was very prolific. We'll just say he had his iron in lots of women's fires." Morgan smiled empathetically. "Your daddy's daddy was my daddy."

"Wait, what?" Cole shook his head. "You are saying my grandfather was Arlon's father? Colson's dad?"

"Yes, son, that's what the DNA test shows," Warren said, "unless you think it's on your mother's side."

"My maternal grandparents didn't move here until after my mom was five. My grandma Dart was a single mother and Colson never knew his father." He leaned back in his chair and scratched his chin. Arlon was his uncle. Morgan stared at him with strange eyes. *His aunt.* His eyes started to water, and he tried to rub the sting away.

"It won't do any good," Morgan whispered. She moved next to Cole, pulled him in her arms, and together they wept.

"Why didn't he tell me?" he asked with a gravelly voice.

"He'd only just told me the week before the tornado. This had been his little project. He's found five siblings total. Three want nothing to do with the others. They've moved on and have lives of their own. I don't blame them for not wanting to complicate their lives." Morgan smiled sadly at the admittance.

"Does Colson know?" Cole asked.

"I don't know," Morgan replied, shaking her head.

"No," Warren said. "According to this, Arlon didn't know where your father was, if he was still addicted or even alive. He wanted this to be yours, not your father's."

"Wanted what to be mine?"

"His land." Warren gave Cole a chastising look.

Cole gasped and jumped up. "What about Morgan?" he stammered.

"I don't want that land, Arlon knew it. I have a house within the city limits. Don't worry about me, Cole. My brother left me a chunk of change and all his things inside the trailer. Except the twister destroyed the trailer, well, you know how it is." She waved a hand. "You get a clean slate. You can build whatever you want."

"Where?" Arlon's trailer sat next to a few others. He'd always assumed Arlon had rented.

"Here's a map of the acreage." Warren unrolled a large scroll of paper.

Cole leaned over the desk and followed the lines with his eyes. "This can't be right."

"Over twenty acres. He left you with some money for taxes, but the property itself is all paid for."

Cole blinked and rocked back on his boots. "*Holy shit.*"

CHAPTER 34

Piper

KRYPTONITE CALLED PIPER'S NAME.

She planned a carefree night of drinking with Kelly. At Under the Table, they'd listened and laughed at losers singing karaoke. Piper spent a paycheck on a new outfit, a majority of the money going to her first pair of cowgirl boots. Since all her pretty lingerie reminded her of Cole, she considered wearing the tank top braless. She decided against it, not willing to risk any unwanted attention. And *any* attention from men she'd consider unwanted.

Piper rubbed her temples, trying to work out the stress.

She'd taunted Justin and faced Cole earlier in the day. When Justin called, she'd said "Quit being an annoying prick. Man up and go home." Hopefully, her boldness would send him packing. He wanted a compliant, easy to control, Piper. That version no longer existed. She'd hung up on him.

Tears blurred her vision as she recalled Cole.

Nellie Neus, from the Fortuna Forum, dropped by the ranch to interview Jessie about the Double D Intimates line of her business. She appeared contrite about the prior article, stumbling over apology after apology.

Piper eyed Nellie warily and stuck to her job. She checked inventory, emails, packages to ship and answered the phone. She stayed in the office until the doorbell rang.

Not wanting to interrupt Jessie, Piper hurried to the front door. She pulled it open and gasped. "Cole." With the door open, she had atmosphere but still found it hard to breathe. It had taken everything to hold on to the doorknob and not launch herself into his arms.

217

His gray Hammered shirt pulled tight over his corded biceps, and his broad chest begged her to touch and explore. Her treacherous eyes continued a scandalous perusal of his body, dropping to a lone star flag belt buckle. Her fingers yearned to trace it, but more than that, the desire to unbuckle it rolled over her. A tiny smirk formed on his lips. Still unable to breathe and hot enough to spontaneous combust, she swallowed, trying to moisten her dry throat.

"Who is it?" Jessie called.

"It's Cole," she replied. As Piper leaned toward him, a hint of his cologne tantalized her. She whispered, "Now's not a good time."

Cole's smile fell, and he stared down at his boots. Piper swore she had seen moisture in his eyes. Causing him pain felt like a knife to the heart.

"Let him in," Jessie said.

Piper sucked in a sharp breath and opened the door wide. As he passed, she whispered, "The newspaper reporter is here." She quietly closed the door and prepared to retreat to the office.

"I'd like to ask you two a few questions," Nellie said, pointing at her and Cole. Piper trembled.

Cole stood in the room, facing Jessie and her guest. While Cole greeted them with handshakes, Piper studied his denim-clad butt. The time-worn material encapsulated it perfectly.

He took a seat in the same chair as when Justin had arrived. A sense of déjà vu stole over her, making her dizzy. As if sensing her unease, he patted the arm of the chair. She sat, inhaling a shaky breath. Her knee bobbed up and down.

Glancing at her note pad, Nellie said, "So a man, Justin Saine, claimed you and he are in love and he's going to take you back to Chicago. Is this true?" Her dark eyes measured Piper.

"If I was in love with a man in Chicago, don't you think I would have stayed in Chicago?" Piper crossed her arms and rolled her eyes. "Listen. Justin stalked me there and now he's come to stalk me here. There is a restraining order against him in Chicago. If you publish stuff about me being in love with him, which is as far from the truth as possible, I might never get rid of him."

Nellie furiously scribbled in her book. "What about Mr. Dart? When did you meet him?"

"I met Cole the first day here." Thinking back to that day and the three-cowboy welcome committee made Piper smile.

Nellie narrowed her eyes. Her blond curls bounced as she tilted her head. "Why are you smiling?"

"Cole asked me if I liked romance," Piper laughed softly. "You can imagine I was shocked, but then I found out about the romance novels. It's an interesting phenomenon

you have in Fortuna." Cole's hand rested in the small of her back. Lord, how she missed his touch. The tension seeped out.

"There are rumors swirling around town about you two. Are you married?"

"Not yet," Cole said.

Piper's head snapped toward Cole. A sly smile had formed. His face was as red as a Solo cup. Her heart stopped and cognitive thoughts failed her. The phone ringing jumped-started her heart again. She excused herself and, like a coward, had never returned.

Cole had left a card and a single red rose for her. Piper wanted to throw them away, but she couldn't. She hated feeling weak and refused to open the envelope. She wanted strength. So as she applied her lipstick, she thought strong whiskey might solve a few problems.

"You look pretty," Kelly said.

"Thanks. I just wanted to be me." She opened the visor and glanced into the mirror. "I didn't go overboard with the mascara, did I?"

"No. I can't believe how long your lashes are."

"They're light like my hair and brows." She flipped it closed. "I love that shirt you're wearing. It brings out the color of your eyes."

"Thanks. Who needs men when you've got girlfriends?" Kelly said, adding a giggle.

"Damn straight."

The Friday night air was balmy and warm. When the women settled into the booth at Under the Table, their stomachs growled. They ordered wings and drinks. They listened to various people undertake karaoke. Depending on the song, sometimes the dance floor filled. Piper had finished her second beer when a server delivered bottles of amber cider. *Dakota.*

Kelly and Piper turned to search for him as he slid into the booth next to Kelly. "Hey, Dakota," Kelly said with a grin. "Thanks for the cider."

Dakota nodded and relaxed back. The button-up Hawaiian shirt he wore toned down the military vibes, especially when paired with the smile. Noting Piper's frown he asked, "What's wrong?"

Fingering the bottle, Piper pulled the cider forward and took a drink. Kelly answered for her. "She's anti-men right now. And you, my friend, have a penis; therefore, you're a man."

"Oh." His gaze bounced from one woman to the other. "I can't help it. I was born this way. Is it all penises or just one in particular? What did Cole do?"

Piper couldn't meet his eyes. She read the ingredients three times while, once again, Kelly answered, filling him in about what Cole said regarding Piper. "It broke her heart," Kelly concluded.

Piper slapped her hand on the tabletop. "No it didn't. I don't break."

The woman currently singing karaoke chose a "Stand by Your Man" kind of song and it grated on Piper's nerves. She slouched and took another long pull of the cider.

"You overheard him speaking on the phone? Are you sure he was talking about you?" Dakota asked.

"One hundred percent. I hung up on him that day, and he told whoever that I'd hung up on him."

"Oh no." Dakota's mouth hung open a moment. "I called him. He was talking to me."

"You?" If that didn't beat all. She'd sensed Cole and Dakota had struck up a friendship, but hadn't expected they'd bond over the *crazy bitch*, or whatever Cole called her. She pushed out of the booth and headed to the karaoke stage. A minute later, with the microphone in hand, she belted out "Love Stinks" by the J. Geils Band. She watched Dakota and Kelly have an animated conversation, then Dakota stood with the phone at his ear.

The newly in-love lady started singing another happy song. Piper sat back down, wanting to pull her hair out. She clenched her eyes shut, refusing to cry. The girl wasn't even halfway through the song before Piper had her next song ready to go. Back and forth the two women sang, one lamenting heartache while the other kindled the flames of young love.

An hour later, the crowd had grown. After an hour and a half, the dining area was standing room only. Piper stepped up to the microphone, waited as the intro music played. Glancing over the crowd, she tapped her foot. Her gaze froze at the back of the room where Cole held a guitar case. The image vanished. Cole wouldn't play in public. She pushed the vision from her mind and sang.

Carrie Underwood's song was about how a woman wished she had the time back she invested in a man. She wanted to "undo" the relationship. Sounded good to Piper. She let the inner wounded woman soulfully express the hurt. When the music faded, the crowd applauded. Kelly wiped a tear away.

Piper smiled at the crowd and placed the mic on the stand. She waved to Kelly, but froze when she spotted Cole standing at the back. The black cowboy hat shadowed his eyes but his lips formed a thin line. He straightened his shoulders and stepped toward the right aisle.

Piper echoed his movements but took the left aisle. She couldn't breathe and found it hard to move. Lightheaded, she continued to step as Cole did. He, toward the front of the room, her to the back. When they had traded places and Piper thought she was home free, Dakota stopped her by holding her arm.

"You'll want to see this," he suggested with a nod.

She shook her head. "Air," she said, focusing on the door.

Suddenly, the euphonious tones of classical guitar swirled around her and the entire building hushed as if mesmerized. The melody ebbed and flowed. The pull of the musical eddy caught her, and she couldn't escape. She swallowed and glanced over her shoulder, watching his fingers weave tunes together. A musical magician, he teased her ears.

Dakota slowly nudged her down the aisle toward Cole. The cowboy's head tilted as if he listened critically, but his eyes honed in on Piper.

Someone had lowered the mic stand for Cole, and closing his eyes, he leaned in and began singing. Piper halted, and Dakota bumped into her.

Cole's passion combined with the melody caused an emotional vortex around Piper's heart.

He opened wistful eyes, and they bored into her. The song "Baby I'm Amazed by You" she'd heard before. The lyrics spoke of a man loving a woman and wanting to spend forever with her. Piper gasped at Cole's open declaration of love. He paused after the first chorus, but still strummed the guitar. Dakota prompted her forward again until she stood facing Cole. Her legs trembled and her heart ached. Tempted to both run away and run straight into his arms, her feet remained frozen in place.

"Pipes, I don't know what I said to anger you, but I apologize. I had a bad day, and then something came up with Beau. My anger got the best of me. I shouldn't have said those things about my sister either, but I was furious when she hung up on me." He paused, letting her digest the words. He stopped playing and reached for his hat and tossed it at her feet. The bandanna followed.

Remembering their conversation regarding his biggest flaw, Piper covered her mouth with her hands. Tears welled and her blood raced. The room faded and suddenly it was only Cole. His fathomless blue eyes projected the deep longing of his soul. She glanced at his dark hair, where a hat halo ringed his head. He'd conquered his anxiety over his physical appearance. For her, he'd played guitar, sang and apologized in front of a crowded restaurant regardless of what the others thought. *For her.*

"Piper, you're the yeast in my bread, the sugar in my cookies, the melody in my song. You keep me in tune, and without you my life is flat. I need you. I love you." He played the second verse then finished the song.

As the music faded and silence met her ears, she noticed Dakota behind Cole, holding out his hand. Cole handed him the guitar and then dropped to one knee. Piper gasped along with the audience. "I love you, Pipes, please become my wife and make me the happiest man in the world."

The ability to speak abandoned her. She touched his face, trailing a finger along his jawline. Staring into sparkling blue eyes so full of love, she nodded.

Cole

She said yes. Cole jumped and yelled, "She said yes!" The tavern erupted in cheers and applause. Cole picked her up and spun her around, kissing her senseless. Dizzy, he stopped and placed his forehead against hers, willing his heart to slow. The smile on his lips could be permanent. He had to be the happiest man alive.

"I love you," she murmured for his ears only.

His arms tightened around her. "I'm sorry for not finding you and explaining."

"I'm sorry too." She sighed against him.

"Oh, Piper, congratulations!"

Piper leaned back and her eyes widened. "Mom? Fletcher? What are you guys doing here?"

"Oh, you know, stopped by for your engagement party," Fletcher said with a grin. "This guy has been keeping us informed of his intentions and your stubborn ways." Her brother waggled a finger at her.

"You were awfully confident tonight." Piper said to Cole with hands on her hips.

"I've never wanted anything so much in my life." The seriousness of his voice, stalled her teasing. She touched his cheek, and the tender gesture brought a sigh from his lips.

They moved off the stage and over to a more open area where other well-wishers came to congratulate them. Flo and Colson, Brad Davidson, Jessie and Josiah Barnes and others from Fortuna had shown up. Most had witnessed her singing against love and him breaking down those walls.

"I almost forgot." He dug in his pocket. She gaped at the small blue velvet box. "It's not much."

"It's everything I ever wanted because it's from you."

A lump stuck in his throat, Piper was melting his gooey interior. He blinked back tears and focused on lifting the lid.

She hummed and took the box to get a closer look. "It's beautiful." Sliding the ring on her finger made it feel real. This sexy, clever, strong woman had agreed to be his wife. A cowboy's wife. He grinned like the happy fool he was.

"Show us the damn ring, already," Sawyer yelled over the noise. Piper lifted her arm and bent her wrist. The solitaire caught the light, bedazzling friends and family. They toasted and then danced.

Piper visited with her mother and brother while Cole returned his guitar to the truck. He held the pub's door open for a couple coming in and a teenage boy holding a single stem rose.

"Thanks, man." The teen hurried past, staring down at a piece of paper.

"No problem." Cole left the loud tavern and entered the dark of night. Cars sped by on the street, doors opened and shut with laughing patrons. Cole unlocked his truck and put the guitar on the back seat. He leaned against the cool metal and smiled. The extra-large cab would come in handy when he and Piper had kids. The thought shocked him. Love had changed him.

Knocking on the glass startled Cole. Ben Moore stood in civvies with a smug grin. "The show already over?"

"She said yes."

"Congratulations, man." Ben grabbed his hand and pumped it. "Let me buy you a beer."

"Sounds like a plan." He closed the door and hit a button on the fob. The doors locked with a clunk.

Somewhere in the parking lot, a vehicle's tires squealed. Ben shook his head and muttered, "Kids. Glad I'm off duty."

"Me too. I'm happy you can celebrate with us." Cole's phone vibrated in his pocket. He fished it out and looked at a text from Piper. "Oh, hell no. Piper!" He ran toward the bar.

CHAPTER 35

Piper

PIPER FUMED. ONE MINUTE A boy offered her a fragrant rose, the next she was bumping along in the back of a dark van. Justin did this.

The young man had lured her. "There are roses outside for you, ma'am." He'd glanced down at a photo of her and smiled. Now she recognized the photo as one of the engagement pictures she and Justin had taken and she had paid for, of course. He'd cropped himself out of it and given it to the kid.

Cole's engagement plan must have found its way to Justin's ears.

Her heart raced. How was she going to escape? Justin thought he'd knocked her out. When the kid brought her outside and around the building to a van with an open back door, she had hesitated. A vase held a dozen red roses. They were beautiful and drew her eye at first, then she noticed duct tape, a Swiss army knife and rope. She backed up into a man's body. He grabbed her and covered her face with a rag. It smelled like chemicals. She held her breath and fought him, but gave up and fell limp, playing the passed out victim. He'd tied her legs and wrists loosely.

Surprise would be her biggest weapon now. She loosened the ropes enough to slip a hand out. She pulled off the engagement ring in case Justin hadn't heard, and stuffed it down her front pocket. Justin, thank God, was an idiot and didn't take her phone. She trembled, hitting the wrong letters, but sent Cole a text, leaning over the device so Justin wouldn't see the light.

The van was light blue or gray, the color had been hard to discern in the dark with the orange glow of the parking lot light. The back of the minivan needed a good vacuum and smelled musty, like old lady perfume. The vase of roses tipped and water soaked her side.

Cole replied, but it wasn't useful. He asked questions she couldn't answer. With her phone set to silent, she dialed his number.

"Piper!"

"Sh," she whispered. The van's muffler needed replaced; she hoped to get away with a conversation. "I'm okay. Justin thinks I'm unconscious."

"Ben's here and we're getting the Nockerville and Fortuna police looking for the van. Can you tell us anything about where you are?"

"I can't see out."

"What can you see?" Steady and calm, Ben took over.

"The sky. It's black. There went a street light."

"Are you going straight or is it a curvy road?"

"Straight with street lights. The big tall gray kind with the orangey bulbs. He's slowing." She paused and waited. The vehicle came to a complete stop and started again at regular intervals. In fact, Justin cursed the lights. "There are a lot of traffic lights."

"Hang on, Piper, we're coming. That sounds like the parkway heading out of Nockerville to the interstate. Would he take her back to Chicago or to Fortuna?" Ben asked.

"You're in a car following me?" Piper closed her eyes, and a tear escaped.

"Everyone at the bar is. Your mom and Fletcher joined Nockerville residents so they could identify that bastard." Cole sucked in a breath. "Pipes, I'll find you. I swear it."

"I love you, Cole." She shifted and hit her head. "We're turning left and going uphill. I think he's trying to speed up, but the van won't go fast."

"The highway." The men said together. Ben relayed everything to someone else.

"Shit, shit, shit." Justin slowed, continuing to curse. "Stupid police." Soon she was bouncing around like a kernel of corn in hot oil.

"I think he saw the police and turned off the highway and onto a primitive road."

The van lurched to a stop, and the engine cut off. He opened the front door. Piper whispered, "Mute your phone so I can leave mine on."

She hid the phone and tried to look like an unconscious person who'd rolled around. Justin opened the door and touched her, checking her face and arms. "Sorry about putting you to sleep, love. I know you'll be mad, but it's the only way to get you to ride with me." He fingered her cheek a soft, almost tender, touch. "I can't wait until you see the place I have for you.

You'll love it, and me, too." His hand cupped her cheek, then her breasts. She wanted to kick his nuts and head-butt him, but her feet remained bound.

If she escaped now, he'd deny everything. He's say he'd only given her roses, and she'd been drinking. No, it would be best if Cole and Ben found her.

Justin started the vehicle again and continued down the bumpy road, her head jarring the side of the van several times. Finally, the road smoothed, but curved. Piper closed her eyes, trying not to get car sick.

"Hey look, baby, it's your work, the Double D." Justin kept talking about the brochure he liked to quote. "I hope you're wearing something special. I can't wait to check."

She shivered, nausea settling in her gut. "We just passed the Double D ranch. We're turning left. There aren't any street lights."

Justin turned on the radio. It was a religious talk station. He cursed and turned it to classic rock, then whistled along. The van slowed then hit two large humps. "Train tracks?"

How long could she fake being unconscious? Hopefully Justin was going on Hollywood's exaggerated timetable and not a scientific fact. Should she fake an allergic reaction?

The van rolled to a stop. Once he turned off the headlights, she was cocooned in darkness. She stuffed the phone in her boot. Justin placed her over his shoulder. His bony shoulder poked into her gut, adding to her queasiness.

He said nothing as he stumbled forward, and she took the opportunity to sneak a peek at her surroundings. A large building, abandoned by appearances, several stories tall loomed to the left. Broken windows, weeds and animal sounds—it wasn't exactly an erotic paradise. She lost control and shivered. He patted her bottom and she tried not to gag.

He entered the creepy space and his footfalls echoed. Anyone who stepped inside would make noise. The high-ceilinged room was empty except a few metal skeletons of defunct machines. He struggled up a long flight of stairs. She bit her tongue when he misstepped or lost his footing. He wheezed by the time he reached the top. After a short trip through a hall he opened a door, then dropped her. She landed on something soft and spongy, knocking the air out of her. Luckily the lights remained off, and he hadn't seen her panicked eyes when they opened.

Justin checked her ankle ropes then rolled her onto her back and inspected her wrists. Satisfied with his Boy Scout knots, he connected the wrist ropes to the wall. Her arms stretched above her head.

"Sleep now, princess. I'll check on you in a while." He exited, but not before he lit a candle. The aroma of Christmas, an ironic homey scent, filled the room. His footsteps faded, and she relaxed. She wiggled her hand free again and retrieved the phone.

"I'm in a bedroom in a big abandoned warehouse next to a train track. He tied me to the wall and lit a candle. Can you believe it? A candle." Piper pressed her lips together.

"We know where you are," Cole said.

"He'll see you coming. We're upstairs and there aren't any lights. He'll spot you miles away. Uh oh, I think he's coming back."

She thrust the phone under a pillow, shoved her hand back into the ropes, and pretended to sleep. She took deep even breaths.

Justin wouldn't really hurt her. Would he? He claimed to love her. Why didn't he understand kidnapping wasn't the ideal way to express love?

The door creaked, and a weight settled on the bed. Time passed, and he sat in the dark. When he turned on a light, he shook her shoulder, but her head lulled to the side. "Wake up, Piper." He slapped her face. He did it again, harder. She sucked in a breath and opened her eyes. Then closed them as if she had a hard time keeping them open.

"So... blue." Her gaze followed a dust mote.

"Piper?" Justin wanted her attention and rubbed her arm.

Her gaze slid to him, then past him to the door. The room had no windows but was furnished like a regular bedroom. Again, she watched a dust mote float through the air. "Do you see... it?" her lids became heavy. "I'm going to barf." She arched, so he was in her projectile path. She moved her arms and feet but her face contorted when she couldn't move. Her eyes glazed as she pretended to follow something unseen before closing.

"Weird." Justin said. "Sorry about the hallucinations. I didn't know that would happen; well, maybe I suspected it." He laughed maniacally. "Let me take a picture and send it to your boyfriend. I've got his number and when he sees this, your love will be tainted. He won't want a thing to do with you. You'll be mine again."

He tugged her shirt up, exposing her belly and bra. "Tsk, Piper, a plain white bra? Not exactly the thing I'd expect a girl who worked at a fancy lingerie shop to wear. Then again, the prices are outrageous." He continued to pull the shirt up her arms and over her face. Goose bumps arose on her flesh, summoned by the fear in her heart.

She waited, trying not to hyperventilate. The bed shook as he stood. She heard a zip then nothing. A faint noise caught her attention, and she held her breath. It sounded like... no. A fish hitting a palm. Then he moaned. Hot, wet goo landed on her abdomen. She bit her tongue so she wouldn't cry out or gag. He laughed and played with the mess on her stomach. "Say cheese." His phone clicked. "Got you. Cole won't want you now."

Cole

Cole's knee thumped up and down, matching the rhythm of his heart. Ben had driven his sports car, and they arrived, converging with others behind another smaller building up the tracks from the abandoned warehouse.

Colin Copper and Indigo Black as well as citizens who'd volunteer to help find Piper were all here. The Barnes brothers, Sawyer Hickey and even Pastor Peacock listened to Colin's orders. Cole's chest tightened at their generosity.

"Desire Hardmann was right about Ms. Deeds; she confirmed Saine is staying at the old Cummings warehouse. He told her that he was looking for capital to invest into the property. He was going to bring business to Fortuna." Ben informed his captain and the others.

"Ms. Deeds is probably getting read the riot act by Ms. Hardmann. That woman loves Piper. They're two peas in a pod." Josiah Barnes pondered the older woman's fate with an evil grin.

Cole's phone vibrated, alerting him. He woke the screen. The taunting message "I've marked her as mine" accompanied an image of Piper's bare abdomen and white bra. Cole breathed through his teeth and Ben pried the device from his fingers. In Ben's hands, the phone vibrated again.

"Let me see it," Cole demanded, holding out this hand.

"Not yet. You don't want to." Ben shook his head and passed the phone to Colin. Cole understood, but he hated anyone seeing Piper like that. It was no worse than the lingerie brochure, but it felt like a violation. Hell, it was. The bastard stole his fiancée.

"Cole, we'll find her," Ben said in a calm voice. Cole clenched his fists but nodded.

Colin sent the diversion. Two trucks filled with volunteer hooligans took off toward the front of the warehouse. Drew Peacock drove one truck. The diesel engine's rumbling reverberated off the buildings. He hit the track crossing like the Dukes of Hazzard. Through the radio, Sawyer hollered "Yeehaw!" Ben and Cole exchanged a look and a grin.

With Justin focused on the front, an extraction team could enter the back. The covert team would slip in and find her, removing her from harm's way. Men dressed in black gear assembled waiting for a signal.

"Sometimes there are perks to the job," Ben laughed. "Like four wheeling and acting like a redneck."

"I don't think Sawyer is acting," Cole replied, crossing his arms.

"You're probably right."

One truck stopped near the tracks and turned up the music. The other truck flew past and drove in screeching circles.

Ben turned at a commotion behind him. Dakota approached Colin. He had a long-range rifle slung over his shoulder with an arm casually wrapped around its stock. A large bag hung off the other shoulder.

Ben and Cole walked toward Colin as he deputized Dakota.

Ben reached his hand out and shook Dakota's. "Welcome. We appreciate your availability."

Cole and Dakota locked gazes. Then they gripped each other's hands. Ben led Dakota to the rear end of the vehicle with a map of the warehouses and property. Dakota spun the map, tapping Piper's suspected location. He spied the best vantage point for the sniper as the roof of the building next to him. Colin handed him a radio. "Keep in touch." Dakota nodded solemnly. A police officer joined him and they entered the building. Dakota would have eyes from above.

"He's a great resource." Ben slipped a tiny receiver in his ear. He inspected Cole with a frown. "He's only a safety precaution. A last resort."

"Let's hope." Cole wiped negative thoughts from his mind. Piper was tough, clever and resilient. Even if she couldn't get away, she'd sweet talk the asshole. A crooked smile appeared.

CHAPTER 36

Piper

RUMBLING ENGINES AND HORNS ECHOED off the abandoned walls. Twangy country music, laughter and shouts followed.

"What the—," Justin muttered, sprinting out of the room, leaving a trail of curse words.

Piper opened one eye. Justin had left the door open. Her heart raced as she listened for him, but she couldn't hear anything over the commotion outside. The racket ebbed and flowed.

God bless whoever lured him away.

She wriggled her hands out of the rope. Selecting a pillow, Piper hastily wiped Justin's semen, trying not to gag. She threw the pillow on the floor.

Piper kicked, struggling to loosen the ropes around her ankles. Her heart rate spiked when the cowgirl boots wouldn't shimmy free. *Come on.*

A fingernail broke as she worked the knot. "Crap." She stuck her throbbing finger into her mouth tasting the metallic tang of blood. Panic bubbled up, and she choked back tears. Flailing her legs in frustration, a boot loosened. She slid her foot out of the boot then pulled off the rope.

Free at last, she took a shaky breath and slipped her boot on then hopped off the bed. She paused at the door, glancing out into the dark hallway. Headlights streaked like a schizophrenic lighthouse, illuminating the vacant space. The passage was clear.

A mocking laugh reverberated through the warehouse. *It sounds like Sawyer Hickey's laugh. It can't be.* Freedom was within her reach, if she could reach whoever was making the ruckus. Pressing her lips together, she took a steadying breath. Pale amber light showed at the end of the tunnel-like hall. Barely visible in the other direction was the stair rail. She swallowed any desire to run to the exit. Any footfalls on the treads would alert Justin to her presence.

Who knew what he'd do to her if he caught her again? She shuddered, scratching at the dried crust on her stomach. A plan formulated. The hero, Loren Order, had been in worse situations. Granted, he was fictional, but he'd always triumphed. She balled her trembling hands.

The candle flickered, making the shadows dance. Piper jumped and spun around, her heart in her throat.

Something white caught her eye. Her phone! She snatched it and smiled. Hurrying to the doorway, she accidentally snuffed out the candle, throwing the room into darkness. The smoke might warn Justin. She closed the door, trying to hedge the odor.

"I'm free," she whispered, letting her eyes adjust.

"Pipes." Cole sounded distant. "Don't go out the front. It's a diversion."

"Okay. There has to be another way out." She glanced toward the end of the hallway. An obnoxious guffaw echoed. "Oh my God, it *is* Sawyer."

Cole chuckled then breathed deeply. "Ben and I are coming through the back. Try to get to the main level." She hummed agreement. "I can't hear you. The connection is bad." The signal lost, she stuffed it in the back pocket and tiptoed, following along on the mezzanine.

Hugging the wall, she peered into the large room. With his nose pressed to a window, Justin watched the distraction. Her breath caught.

A hand flew to her heart, and she stepped back. Out of Justin's line of sight, Piper studied the room, searching for an exit. One other door existed, but she'd need to dodge a torn sofa, soda bottles and piles of trash. The dank space smelled like body odor and garlic. With the concrete floor littered with debris, she wouldn't make it the length of the room without stepping on trash and Justin noticing her.

Piper squinted, noticing a neat stack of romance novels near the sofa. Had Justin caught the romance bug? A ghostly wisp twisted heavenward, causing her focus to shift to a pile of what looked like dirt. She covered her mouth and gasped, trying to make sense of the scene.

It would piss off the Fortuna citizens when they discovered Justin used romance books as a fuel source. *He must use them to cook food, what else could it be? It's hotter than blue blazes.* She peeked around the corner again.

Justin moved to the far side of the room. "When will these bumpkins get bored and go have incest?" he mumbled, scratching the back of his head.

The smoldering pile of ash released a tendril of smoke. Piper took a deep breath. She crept in, knelt behind the sofa and plucked the top book.

The Visitation. Tattered and worn, it was the town's all-time favorite. In fact, all the books appeared to be well-loved, with torn covers and yellowed edges. Justin chose books he probably thought no one would miss. Piper's eyes narrowed.

Cole

Cole shifted the night vision goggles to the left, but the view hadn't improved. Nothing but the backside of the decaying building. He shifted his gaze to Piper's phone. It remained mute, a lifeless block.

"Cole, it's a dead zone," Ben hesitated. "I mean, no cell service." He squatted next to Cole, analyzing the collective data. Colin had the place surrounded, but they hadn't located Piper yet.

"Dakota, can you see her?" Cole asked, hoping Dakota's unique line of sight would yield answers.

"Negative." He paused. "That idiot has a living room of sorts. It might be an old break room. The diversion is working, he's standing at the window watching the show."

"Can you shoot him?" asked Cole.

Dakota chuckled. "All day long."

"Do it," Cole replied, surprised by the malevolence in his tone. It sounded like a dare.

"Hold," Colin ordered.

"Yes, sir," Dakota replied.

"Let's cut the banter, boys. Stay focused."

After a period of silence, Ben gestured to Cole. They ran across the crumbling back lot to the loading dock. Hidden, they caught their breath.

Dakota came back on the com. "Target is moving. He's returning to the corridor."

"This is it," Colin said and barked orders to the team leaders.

Ben hopped up three feet into the cave-like docking bay. Cole followed. Every step they took, the deteriorating ground resounded. With his pistol drawn, Ben led and Cole attempted to tread as silent as the officer.

"Piper!" Justin shrieked.

Cole's heart hammered with rage. They needed to find Saine and eliminate the threat before he located Piper. Sensing the tiger ready to pounce, Ben placed a staying hand on Cole's arm and gripped firmly. He nodded and Ben dropped his arm.

Ben continued to lead into a narrow hallway. Cole had no option but to trust.

Piper

Piper crept down and swung under the corrugated steel stairs.

"Piper!"

Her blood ran cold. Justin stomped toward her, but her legs refused to move. Her right hand white-knuckle gripped part of the grimy metal banister. He'd spot her if he stepped onto the stairs. She swallowed, but her mouth had gone dry.

"I'll find you!" Justin growled.

From the other side of the warehouse, a noise crunched, like someone stepped on glass. Squinting her eyes revealed nothing in the shadow-filled realm of the abandoned warehouse. It unfroze her pseudo-paralysis, and she pushed away from the stairway as a beam of light cascaded over the second floor landing. The dim illumination granted her a glimpse of a doorway. It was the only place to hide. Running her fingers against the wall, she inched forward. Once past the entry, she continued along the wall. She passed several doors, some opened, some not. The wall hooked left. Another closed door, but she passed it. Her wounded finger jammed into the next door frame. She bit back a cry and shook her hand sucking in several deep breaths. A putrid smell hung in the air.

The room emitted a sewer stench. Muffling the light with her hand, she used the screen light to inspect the doorway. A little blue symbol designated it a bathroom. She pushed the door open a crack and ducked in. Feeling her way to the end of the counter, she dropped to the floor in the corner.

Piper checked her phone. No signal. She wrapped her arms around her folded legs and rocked.

The only turd in a toilet about to be flushed, she feared drowning in anxiety. The tears came. She clutched her legs tighter. Her bottom lip trembled. She was a frightened, injured woman against a demented man who was not only stronger, but knew his way around the godforsaken crap-hole.

Her finger ached. In the ambient phone light, she examined wounds. A drop of blood fell and landed between her legs. She butterflied her knees and risked brighter light and gasped.

Oh! I'm going to kill him.

Large gashes from the ropes marred the leather on both boots. Her new boots. Ruined.

Justin did this. He'd kidnapped her, tied her up and violated her. He'd stalked her, harassed her at work and on the phone. Alone and desperate, she cowered in a bathroom. He ruined her boots and her surprise engagement party. Piper shook with rage.

Cole. She closed her eyes, breath hissing through her lips. Justin hurt Cole by kidnapping her. That pissed her off even more. She turned off the phone and stuck it in her back pocket.

She hugged her legs again, this time training her ears outward. Outmatched with strength and weaponless, how could she defend herself? *What would Loren Order do?*

An evil smirk appeared. *Loren would want to kill that motherf—*

"Piper!" Justin's surly tone meant he'd finished being nice. She'd heard it before. Each time he'd kidnapped her and wouldn't stop the car and let her leave.

She needed to find something, anything, to defend herself.

The wood vanity had doors. She took the phone and lit the underbelly. The rotting wood and sewer odor hit her anew, corroding pipes sticking out of the wall. Attempting to pull a pipe free would be risky. Too much noise.

Someone had removed the stall dividers; only the vanity, commode and a slender object in the far corner remained. She doused the dim light and felt along the wall. The toe of her boot bumped into the squalid, cracked porcelain bowl. Once her hand met the corner, she bent and groped the darkness. Something poked her palm. She closed her fingers and lifted it.

A plunger. The large rubber cup on the end had weight. The wood shaft had to be close to two-feet long. She could use it to stun Justin. A hit could surprise him and keep him at bay. A strategic blow to the nose or balls would do the most damage and gain her time. Of course, the heel of her boot would hurt too. She took a deep breath. She wasn't completely defenseless.

The hooligans continued as a diversion. Sawyer's muffled laugh and another man's taunts reminded her she wasn't alone. Sighing, she blew out a long breath.

She started for the door but stopped mid-room. Piper grasped the plunger rod with both hands and swung it like a baseball bat. She stepped to the door and listened.

Justin growled her name. His footfalls thumped as he stepped on the steel stairs, drawing nearer.

Minutes before, she'd felt helpless. Amazingly, he no longer instilled fear. Never again would a man reduce her to a weak and nearly incapacitated state.

She closed her eyes and inhaled, calming her jangled nerves while straining to listen. Faint sounds echoed down the long corridor. Something crunched at the back end. Then silence. She hoped it wasn't rats, or something worse. Although she'd prefer rats over Justin.

Ben had mentioned a warehouse was the home base for looters. She hoped there weren't any other criminals in the building. Another crunch.

Piper bit her lip and jumped into the darkness, swinging the plunger. He caught the shaft and spun her, clamping a firm hand over her mouth. Hard things pressed into her back. She kicked and stomped. She wheezed as a man pulled her into the bathroom again.

"Piper," he said in a barely audible voice. "You're safe." She stopped wriggling and he released her.

"Cole?" It was hard to tell from the soft voice. He'd held her gently like Cole, but the cologne was different.

"No."

He touched her hand, pressing something against her palm. She examined it with both hands. Goggles? He lifted her arm toward her face. She put the strap around her head. The pitch room burst to life, illuminated in shades of dark green. Indigo Black, a Fortuna officer. His face bore a chiseled look of determination. He radioed, alerting the others he'd found her.

Quiet shuffling brought her attention to the hall. Leaning out of the bathroom, Piper waited. Justin rounded the corner. He felt his way along the wall. She tiptoed into his path to intercept. Indigo stuck his arm out, groping the dark, but didn't find her. He tilted his head listening, but she remained still. She squared her shoulders, threw a look toward Indigo then readied the plunger, hefting it like a bat.

"Piper," Justin growled. A truck honked its horn, and he paused, tilting his head. The green shades of the night vision goggles made it seem like a video game, but when his eyes reflected like a cat's she thought it more like hell. He took a step closer and paused again, as if sensing her. "I will catch you—"

One more step.

"And when I do, I'm going to spread your legs and—"

Piper swung the plunger and hit Justin in the gut. He cried out, doubling over. She stepped to his side and swung again, this time smacking him in the face. His glasses flew off in pieces. Justin staggered backward, holding his bleeding nose. She'd split his lip, too.

"You stupid bitch. You're going to pay," he screamed, swinging a fist.

She danced away as he lunged toward the wall. "Come here," he sputtered through blood.

Piper smiled. Not just a smirk, but a full-blown, cheek aching, gum drying smile manifested from her heart.

Justin jabbed at dead air again, stumbling away from the bathroom. "I sent your boyfriend pictures. He won't want a skanky ho like you." Piper bit her tongue, refusing to take the bait.

Indigo tilted his head. He'd edged closer, but Piper hadn't finished.

She crept behind Justin and raised the plunger over her head. With all her strength, she slammed Justin's back. He fell to his knees. She kicked him in the ribs, sending him into the wall, but he flailed and knocked her off balance.

The lights came on, blinding her. Justin jumped up and snagged her hair, pulling her toward him. He grabbed her wrist and pushed her in front of him. "Clever." He swiped off the goggles and they dropped to the floor.

Piper twisted to give Indigo an apologetic look, but he wasn't there. On either side of the hallway, spotlights shined. She hoped Cole was among them.

"Let her go, Saine!" Cole's angry voice vibrated from behind the light. Piper's heart soared.

"Never." Justin's grip tightened.

Piper sighed and stretched her arm out, hoping to convey calmness. She really didn't want her ex's brain matter on her new boots, even though they were ruined. "Never? You can't be serious."

"Very serious." Crazed eyes with constricted pupils inspected the line of men.

"Why?" Piper stared at Justin. "I don't want to be with you, Justin. I don't like you." She looked heavenward and mumbled, "I wish Sheila was here."

His incredulous glance flicked at her for a nanosecond, and he frowned. "You don't belong here. You aren't Texan."

Piper smiled. She belonged here, her heart told her so. "I don't belong with you."

"Yes, you do."

Laughter bubbled out, coming from deep down. Justin didn't like it and jerked her arm. She jerked back.

"They have the death penalty in Texas. As much as I wouldn't mind you getting that consequence for your criminal actions, I really don't want to be in the same state with you until they carry it out. So, I guess, it would be better if they shoot you." She tilted her head up, thinking. "Yes, then I wouldn't have to deal with you anymore."

Slack-jawed, Justin glared. His brows dipped into a V and his bloody lip dripped as he gritted his teeth. He growled, looking like a stray dog.

"You don't want to do anything," Piper soothed with a smirk. Justin ignored her warning. He tugged her closer, but she snapped her wrist free. Grabbing his hand, she bent and pulled him over her back, sending him to the floor. She twisted his wrist until he yelped.

"You're assaulting me," Justin yelled. "I'll sue you."

She giggled and twisted harder. Justin no longer held any power over her. A large weight lifted.

"Piper..." The voice offered a warning. Men approached from both sides.

She rolled her eyes and sighed. "You boys are no fun." Cole and Ben came from one direction and Dakota from the other. Indigo appeared from the shadows and took Justin's arm.

Piper stepped away, lighter than before. She glanced into Cole's loving eyes then fell into his strong arms. Home, she'd found it.

EPILOGUE

Cole

FRIENDS AND FAMILY STOOD AS the wedding march started. Everyone focused on the bride in an exquisite white dress—everyone except Cole. He studied the happy smile of another woman. Crowds still made him nervous, and he tugged on his suit jacket, grateful for the air conditioning. Beau's small hand clasped one of Cole's while Piper's fingers threaded the other. His heart was so full it was about to bust.

As Maggie Barnes pledged her love to Guy Manly, Piper sighed against him. "Are you sure you didn't want a fancy wedding, Mrs. Dart?" Cole kept his voice a whisper.

Piper shook her head, glancing up at him with hooded eyes. "Why? Then we'd have to wait for the honeymoon." He chuckled, sliding his arm behind her back, along her shoulder. He tugged her against him and kissed her forehead. Desire Hardmann watched them with a satisfied grin. He winked at the old woman.

At the reception, Beau placed the gift on the table then ran off to find his nana and papa. Staring at the abundance of gifts, Piper chewed her lip. "Do you think it's okay?" she asked Cole for the ump-teenth time.

"A toilet plunger might not be the average wedding gift but every house needs one, Pipes. And the card is cute." He squeezed her hand gently, caressing the back with his thumb.

"Congratulations on taking the plunge!" Desire said. She slapped Cole on the back, then walked off giggling. She appeared the perfect grandmother in her pink dress suit and hat.

239

Piper squeezed his hand and moved closer to his parents. Just two weeks ago he could have lost her. He watched the way her lips eased into a smile as she waved at Kelly.

The night of Piper's kidnapping had been the longest night of his life. Nothing mattered except holding Piper safe in his arms once more. Her disheveled hair and filthy clothes hadn't bothered her, but she wouldn't let go of the splintered wood shaft. She had clutched it with a firm fist.

That was when it happened, and it played out as if in slow motion.

Justin made a derogatory comment regarding cowboys liking the backend of cattle and Piper snapped. No one understood how close she had been to losing it. She'd jumped back toward Justin, twisting under Ben's reach, to elbow her ex in the chin. Fresh blood dribbled and his teeth were tinted blood red.

"Watch your mouth," she'd growled.

He spat at her, a misty bloody spray. Justin let fly expletives and Piper smirked. Surrounded by police, Justin had been smart enough to hold back.

"Here's a big prick to replace your tiny one." She jabbed the wood staff, stabbing him in the ribs. She punctured skin, but not deep because Indigo had intervened. The ambulance wailed. The EMTs escorted Piper to the waiting ambulance.

The doctors wanted to monitor Piper because Justin had exposed her to unknown chemicals. She hated staying in the hospital. "All I have is a hurt finger," she said. "I don't want to take a room from someone who needs it."

People kept visiting, her mother and brother, Desire and the Barnes. Kelly stopped in to chat after school let out. She jumped and hugged Ben when he dropped in to check on Piper. She had gushed about his part in the rescue, making Ben blush and glance at his shoes.

Nellie Neus, the Fortuna Forum reporter, knocked on the door. Piper lit up and curled her uninjured finger, beckoning her in. She pulled The Visitation out of her boot. She patted the bed and Nellie sat on the edge, taking notes. Not only was Justin a kidnapper, he was anti-romance and a book burning fool. Justin's mug made the front page news in a scandalous reveal-all article. Thanks to Nellie and the Forum, Justin had become public enemy number one and Piper became Fortuna's sweetheart.

They'd married the Wednesday after the hospital released Piper. With his parents, Beau, Lynette, and Morgan and Piper's mother and brother, they stood before Pastor Peacock in a simple ceremony. Friday night the Barnes hosted a barbecue at the Double D ranch in their honor, and the whole town showed up. They'd spent the next week at the motel and hadn't ventured out much. He liked that part: just he and his wife. *His wife.*

Piper handed him a beer and sampled her glass of blush wine. Guy's best man told a sappy good-natured story, which made the groom turn bright red. They toasted, then the matron of honor raised her glass and nervously read off a note card. A family member said a few words, and the crowd cheered and saluted the couple.

Desire Hardmann rose and walked to the front of the room. Cole heard a soft groan escape from Jessie's lips and those around giggled. "I'd like to toast the newlyweds, both sets. Cole and Piper, please stand." She paused as the crowd clapped.

Piper hesitated then stood, pulling him up with her. The guests hooted and hollered, clapping and whistling, bringing a blush to both their faces. He clasped hands with her as if it'd keep him breathing.

Desire raised her glass and everyone in the room followed suit. "To honor." She smiled and paused. A wicked grin sprang to her lips.

"Uh oh," Jessie sighed quietly.

"To honor," Desire repeated. "Get on her and stay on her."

"Amen!" Sawyer Hickey yelled from the back. The room exploded with noise as people laughed and cheered.

Piper hid her red face against Cole's chest. Cole glanced over at Guy, and they grinned at each other. Guy winked and tugged Maggie close in a passion filled, PDA-be-damned kiss that spurned more shouts.

"Sounds like a great plan," Cole said against Piper's ear. Her body shivered, and he wondered whether the tickle of his breath or the words made her react. He mimicked the other newlyweds and sought his bride's lips. The tender kiss turned deeper when she sucked his bottom lip in, making him groan. His hands slid to her backside and squeezed. Piper squeaked, and somewhere in the background noise Desire's distinctive laugh rang out. The old woman no doubt was proud of her accomplishment: the rumored Russian mail-order bride turned Texan wife.

He and Piper returned to their seats and let the couple at the head table become the center of the attention once again. Cole liked living in the background, but with Piper at his side, he could live anywhere and not care one bit. In fact, being Fortuna's book-saving sweetheart made her notoriety grow. In their neck of the woods, his wife was a superstar. He smiled down at her, catching her gaze.

"I have a gift for you later," he said. He glanced over the crowd and feigned disinterest.

Piper's hand shifted higher up his thigh. He cleared his throat and caught it. "Dessert?" she purred.

He chuckled and heat rolled over him. "You're always hungry for dessert."

"Always."

Damn. "I'm the luckiest man in the world." He moved her hand up, resting it on his tight pants. Her eyes widened and she blushed. "That's not what I was talking about. I have something for you to unwrap. Besides me. It came in the mail."

Her fingers moved along the zipper, and he had to bite back a groan. His eyes roamed the room, looking for a means of escape. Would it be rude to leave the wedding early? Definitely less rude then being found naked somewhere in the church. He shifted in the seat, and she shook her head and laughed.

"I can read you, Cole," she teased. "Choir room or your truck?"

His mouth fell open, but then he smiled. She'd been thinking along the same lines. "You've obviously put some thought into it, so you pick." The rewarding blush made his pants even tighter. He sighed happily.

The reception would last long into the night, but the wait would be worth it. They'd dance, eat cake and socialize then he'd take her home and let her open the gift. Yes, the hardback box set of Loren Order series would make her jump, shout, and run all around excited. He leaned back and crossed his arms. She'd hug him and kiss him hard, then they'd make love. He smiled and sighed again.

"Care to share, Mr. Dart?"

"I have plans for you." The phrase was code for: You and me, naked later.

"Oh?" she snuggled closer, nuzzling her nose against his neck.

"And I stopped at the drug store."

Piper pulled back and glanced at him. "Thirty-six extra-large?"

"Yes, ma'am."

"Well, it's a good thing Jessie gave me something new to test."

Cole jumped up, nearly knocking Piper to the floor. He leaned and said goodbye to his father, shaking hands. Cole pulled Piper to her feet and headed toward the exit.

"Cole?" Piper questioned, but the little smirk told him she knew.

He stopped outside the entrance. "My plans have changed," he said. She quirked an eyebrow. "Later has become now."

"I'm good with that." She took his hand and yanked him down the walk at a faster pace than he'd started. Piper grinned up when he yeehawed. "Let's flush this toilet!"

.

Love a book?

Please make sure you leave a review.

Reviews are like virtual hugs for authors!

SNEAK PEEK

Fortuna Fantasy
A Fortuna, Texas Novel
Book 3

Sex. It had been on her mind way too much lately, as evidenced by the screams of her passengers, the one-finger salute of the passing sedan and the flashing blue and red lights in the rear-view mirror.

"Holy crap, Kelly!" Piper yelled from the backseat. "You could've killed us." Then she laughed.

Kelly Jo Greene swallowed the bile in her throat, signaled, and turned into the parking lot of the Wertz grocery. She hated that feeling of seeing police lights behind her. She pulled into an end row as far from the store as possible and shifted into park. Pressing back into her seat, she closed her eyes hoping no one she knew would drive by. She drew in a deep breath.

"Uh oh," Jessie Barnes said.

Kelly's lids popped open in time to see her parents' wide-eyed, nosy neighbor Rose Bush driving past and slip into a handicap parking slot. Kelly grimaced. Her mother would know as soon as Ms. Bush got to a phone. Ugh. She'd get a lecture from her father about insurance costs. She groaned and Jessie patted her arm.

Sometimes living in a small town sucked. Nobody could get away with anything. Most times, it was a good thing, but she was a twenty-seven-year-old woman and a full-time teacher, and she could take care of herself. She loved educating second graders. A smile flitted across her lips but fell off again when she looked at the rear-view mirror.

The officer in mirrored sunglasses made her heart gallop. She glanced away, hoping it wasn't anyone she knew. But in Fortuna, Texas, that was impossible, seeing that her sister-in-law worked at the station and her father golfed with the chief, Colin Copper. And she had gone to school with most of the younger guys.

The side mirror revealed the squad car door opening. A man approached her car. She tried to meld with the seat but couldn't vanish. He paused next to her door, and she swallowed, lowering the window.

"Howdy, Ben," Piper said from the backseat. She stuck her hand out Kelly's window and waved. Ever since the officer had helped Cole, Piper's husband, rescue her from a kidnapping stalker, the couple considered him a close friend.

"Good afternoon, ladies." Ben tipped his head so Kelly could see his dark eyes over the mirrored lenses. "Kelly, do you know why I stopped you?"

No she didn't, well, not really. It appeared, daydreaming and driving don't mix. Kelly may have run a stop sign, almost hit someone, and nearly killed her friends. She opened her mouth to speak, but Piper answered for her. "Kelly's clueless. She's been thinking about sex."

"Again," Jessie mumbled.

Kelly jerked her head toward her friends. Her neck ached from whiplash. "What?" Her cheeks heated, and she knew her face was the same color as her cherry red car.

Ben pushed the glasses back and leaned forward. "Ladies?"

Jessie giggled, but Piper took command of the mystery. "She's had this brilliant smile for the last few days. It has to be a guy."

Kelly's face pulled tight into a high smile. She couldn't help it. She hadn't meant that night to happen, but it did. It had left its mark though.

"Yes, she's been smiling for days. It started Wednesday." Jessie looked to Piper to confirm.

"No, that smile was there Wednesday morning. It had to have been Tuesday night because Tuesday afternoon she wasn't in a good mood." Piper rolled down the back window letting in the warm humid morning air. "Whatever happened, happened Tuesday night. It just has to be a guy."

"Not Sawyer, either," Jessie chimed in.

Kelly clamped her fingers around the wheel and clenched her teeth at the mention of her ex-boyfriend's name.

"See. Look at that frown. It's definitely not him." Jessie pointed to Kelly's face as Piper stuck her head between the headrests to see it.

"I saw Kelly Tuesday night," Ben offered.

Kelly sucked in a quick breath and glanced at him with her peripheral vision. His eyes were hidden but one side of his lips quirked up in a smile.

Both of her friends leaned so they could better see Ben's face, their eyes wide in expectation. "Well, it was at Hammered. I suppose she was hungry because she sat down at the bar and ordered a burger. That was before she noticed Mona flirting with Sawyer."

He'd said Mona with a hint of hostility. They had gone on a couple of dates before Mona decided Ben wasn't her type. Kelly never understood why Mona wasn't attracted to Ben.

Jessie groaned. "Not those two."

Kelly crossed her arms and held tight. Mona used to be one of her best friends, but now that Mona had set her sights on Sawyer, Kelly felt betrayed. She couldn't stand to be around them when they hung on each other.

"Mona came over to talk to me." Ben looked back behind him, as if he'd find her there. "Kelly told her to take a hike. Thanks, for that." He nodded at Kelly and she shrugged.

"Mona retreated and must have boo-hooed to Sawyer because he came over next. He said some stupid things and made Kelly mad. She told him off, then got her food to go." Ben stopped talking and straightened.

"That's it?" Piper asked, blinking.

"I saw her leave the restaurant with her takeout." Ben shifted.

Kelly let out a long breath and relaxed her arms. Ben didn't say anything that her friends couldn't already have guessed. They didn't need to know what happened later. The smile returned.

"It's back," Jessie said, nudging Piper. Her brows crinkled as she inspected Kelly's face. "It happened later on Tuesday."

Kelly chanced a peek at the officer. His lips were pressed into a thin line but there were creases beside his eyes indicating his amusement. Ben looked good in his uniform, his shirt pulled tight over muscled biceps. He'd graduated a few years before Kelly and Jessie. She swallowed. Her face and body grew hot even though the air was on full blast.

"There's only so many single guys in Fortuna," Jessie hummed, rubbing her hands together.

"Kelly said she'd had the best sex ever," Piper prodded.

She'd said no such thing but that hadn't stopped her friend from trying to get her to admit something. Kelly clamped her lips shut and sent a pleading look to Ben.

That was a mistake. His smile, now full blown, shined like a beacon, even though his own face had turned beet red. She wished she could see his eyes.

"Are you going to give me a ticket?" She hoped the swift subject change would divert the conversation away from her sex life. She thrust her license toward him.

Ben chuckled and took it. As he stared at the information he asked, "So are you going to see him again?"

Both Jessie and Piper giggled and reiterated the question. Kelly closed her eyes, and the smile came back. She couldn't help it. Piper had been right—it had been the best sex ever. Kelly could have ignited remembering his body next to hers. She sighed as a wave of desire rolled over her.

"She has to," Jessie said.

"Call him, Kelly. Have him come over and make dinner for you naked," Piper giggled again. Kelly's eyes popped open, and she glanced again at Ben. His mouth hung open.

Kelly leaned in his direction and rested her arm on the edge of the open window. "This is what happens when both your best friends are newlyweds, all they ever talk about is sex. Do you have this problem?"

Ben stared at her then shook his head. She knew he lived the bachelor life with another officer, Indigo Black. The man was just as good looking as Ben, she didn't understand why neither of them weren't married. They were dependable men with smoking hot bodies and better catches than Sawyer Hickey that was for darn sure.

Ben cleared his throat. "You should call him."

Encouraged, her friends joined in. "Call him. Have him make dinner."

"Why should he make dinner?" Ben asked, leaning to view her passengers and echo her unaired question.

"It's every girl's fantasy to have a man cook for her," Jessie said in a whimsical voice.

"Naked is better," added Piper.

"Is this true?" Ben asked looking down at Kelly.

She smiled weakly and gave a one shoulder shrug. "It wouldn't be a bad thing." She wouldn't mind anyone cooking a meal for her, let alone a sexy naked man.

There were already people who'd done jail time for acting out scenes from one or two romance books but those had been in public places.

Indecent exposure, or almost, if not caught by the police in time. One incident had saved a marriage and made that couple the talk of the town. Soon, other men were trying to please their women in a similar manner.

Ben stood straight again and handed back her license. Tingles shot up her arm from where his fingers touched hers. He put his hand on the door frame and removed his glasses as he looked in. His brown eyes were framed with long dark lashes. He grinned at Kelly and her heart jumped into her throat. "I think you should call him."

Jessie gasped and Piper giggled. Kelly watched his snug fitting pants as he walked back to the car. "He didn't give me a ticket," she realized.

"I guess, he values the world's best sex," Piper teased.

Kelly rolled her eyes and put the car into drive. They needed to get to the new storefront Jessie had bought. A contractor was going to meet them there. Kelly zipped into the street, noticing Ben followed for a while. She parked and watched Ben slow as he passed. He gave her a salute and winked. The smile blossomed on her lips.

Fortuna Fantasy is coming 2019!

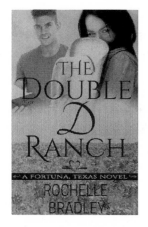

Also available by Rochelle Bradley: The Double D Ranch, A Fortuna, Texas Novel book one.

Josiah Barnes made a promise to Jessie Davidson's dying grandmother: keep Jessie safe. He aims to honor it, even if it means protecting Jessie from himself. Failing her in the past has him on high alert when her home, the Double D ranch, becomes ground zero for the arousal avalanche sweeping the town. As Foreman and a full-support, silent partner, Josiah will do anything to augment the Double D. But when Jessie starts selling handmade lingerie, keeping his hands to himself is easier said than done…

Visit RochelleBradley.com and sign up for Rochelle's newsletter. Never miss out on new releases, contests and giveaways.

ABOUT THE AUTHOR

Rochelle puts an artistic spin on everything she does but there are two things she fails at miserably:
1. Cooking (seriously, she can burn water)
2. Sewing (buttons immediately fall back off)

But she loves baking and makes a mean BTS (Better than Sex) cake. When in observation mode she is quiet, however, her mouth is usually open with an encouraging glass-is-half-full pun or, quite possibly, her foot.

She is a Bearcat, a Buckeye, an interior decorator, and fluent in sarcasm.

In 2008 she decided to get the stories out of her head. Midway through her first novel, hurricane Ike (yes, a hurricane in Ohio) rendered the laptop useless with a nine-day power outage. She didn't give up, but continued to pursue her dream.

Every November Rochelle takes on the challenge of National Novel Writing Month (NaNoWriMo.org) where she endeavors to write 50,000 words in thirty days. You can often hear her cheering the Dayton area Wrimos (those who join her in this crazy pursuit).

Rochelle shares her home with a big black cat, an itty-bitty orange tiger kitty, her daughter, her son, and her Prince.

She loves to connect with readers. You can find her on Facebook (search for Author Rochelle Bradley), Twitter, Pinterest, and Instagram.

Visit Rochelle's website to sign up for her newsletter to keep up to date about future novels and book signings (RochelleBradley.com).

Made in the USA
Middletown, DE
22 June 2019